THE
MESSAGE
WAS CLEAR

A NOVEL

EILEEN RODBERG

The Message Was Clear—A Novel
By: Eileen Rodberg

Editing by Faith Williams, The Atwater Group
Interior design and formatting by Champagne Book Design
Cover design by Rocking Book Covers

ISBN: 979-8-9862479-0-8
LCCN: 2022938058
United States of America

To my husband, Lee.
I could never have done this without his kindness and inspiration.

"Hold dear to your parents
for it is a scary and confusing world without them."
—Emily Dickinson

THE
MESSAGE
WAS CLEAR

PROLOGUE

October 6, 2016

P ROFESSOR ELIZABETH O'BRIEN SET THE GPS, PRESSED PLAY ON her cell phone, and listened to a student's music while she drove. The drive to Georgetown University was, mostly, uneventful. Although, there had been an occasional wrong turn or two when the music had taken her attention away from the road.

Before the dawn of GPS—when a woman's voice would order her to turn right or left—she could have ended up in Maryland or Florida. For Ellie, either was possible.

Today, the GPS guided her into an enchanting community. Once she'd realized her mistake, she wondered how far off the beaten path she'd driven, and followed the road deep inside a neighborhood filled with twists and turns. Ellie had lived in Alexandria, Virginia, for most of her adult life, and yet had never seen this charming neighborhood filled with old and restored homes.

The farther she drove down the tree-lined lane, the more elaborate the landscape. Each home had flowerbeds, with mounds of mulch and new fall plantings. She could envision the gardens in full bloom, even though the summer blooms had gone.

When the voice announced, "You have reached your destination," she stopped the car. The destination was the single blight on the entire street. Overgrown bushes and unkempt trees shrouded an old, run-down house from view. To call this a home in its present condition would be a stretch. After a quick head-shaking glance, she pressed her foot on the gas to find her way back to the university. The car rattled and shook. After a few feet, it sputtered and died in front of the neighborhood eyesore.

The gas tank was full, which was all Ellie knew about cars. Other than the occasional hot-wire during her troubled youth, a mechanic she was not. To get her bearings, she stepped out of the car and glanced around. Nothing was familiar. As her eyes roamed, they kept returning to the building, hidden from view. She walked up the driveway for just a quick peek. She couldn't help herself. How could anyone leave a lovely historic home in such disrepair in this neighborhood? She had to see more.

As a test, she placed one foot on the first rotted step. A loud cracking sound emerged. Most people would back away or consider the building too decayed to continue. That wasn't Ellie's way.

She checked each step to be certain it would hold her weight. When she stood on the large front porch, the house let out a deafening groan, as though it were in pain, begging for help. She peered through one window, and then another, until she made it around the entire house. With each exploration, she could feel her heart race in her chest. She closed her eyes and remembered the sound of giggles and small footsteps running through the living room and into the kitchen. *Her* footsteps and *her* giggles. It made her smile, then she trembled.

Ellie had no memory of laughing or even crying as a child. Abandoned as a toddler, her young life had been a complete unknown, which was why her reaction to this house was so intriguing. Something seemed familiar. That, she knew, was impossible.

With trepidation, she walked into the brush to unearth a For Sale sign buried in the weeds. This, too, was an unexpected path, but one which she felt compelled to follow. She picked up her cell and entered the real estate agent's number. She paused.

What am I doing? This is insane.

As she stared at the dilapidated house, the possibilities emerged. A white picket fence filled with pink climbing roses lined the edge of the property, while the smell of lavender followed a brick path to a deep Southern-style front porch. As a nod to her Southern roots, she would paint the house a crisp white with dark-blue shutters, with large blue hydrangeas along the front of the house. She'd even envisioned a swing hung from the one-hundred-year-old oak tree and couldn't help but smile.

What struck Ellie the most, and what disturbed her the most, was how much it already felt like her home. Any apprehension she had vanished. She pressed Send on her phone and planned to meet the listing agent the next morning.

Ellie grabbed the steering wheel and willed the car to start. This time, when she turned the key, the engine purred.

CHAPTER 1

May 8, 2017

AFTER SEVEN MONTHS OF ARCHITECTS AND CONTRACTORS, ELLIE had moved into her newly renovated home. Its decidedly Southern style was reminiscent of the historic district in Savannah, Georgia. The most recognizable feature being the deep Southern porch, with its haint blue ceiling to ward off evil spirits. Suspicions ran deep in Savannah, although not by Ellie. It was the folklore, passed down from one generation to the next, she found intriguing.

Every detail she'd envisioned for this old house had come to fruition. Not simply the wraparound porch, but also the kitchen, with its brick floors and tall white cabinets and marble counters. She placed antiques, gifted by her adoptive father, in every room around the house. Gardens she'd lovingly planted were about to bloom. The true mark of the official completion of the renovation was the swing hung from the centuries-old oak tree in the front yard. This was more than a house to Ellie. It was the first home she'd owned. And a home that triggered deep-seated memories she couldn't understand. She had every intention of finding out what they meant.

The first night Ellie laid her head on the pillow, she heard the squeak of a door opening, followed by footsteps walking down the hall, and the occasional giggle of a child. She wondered whether it was something her imagination had conjured, or memories of her past. How could she know? She sat straight up and listened for something familiar. It reminded her of the first day she saw the dilapidated house. *Maybe these were the echoes from another time?* A notion she summarily dismissed as one of those Southern suspicions rearing its ugly head.

By morning, every kitchen cabinet door was open. Baskets she'd placed on top of the cabinets now sat neatly in a pile on the floor. Random items had been moved from one drawer to another.

———

During the next three weeks, the incidents escalated. It wasn't a child's voice any longer, but an adult saying the same thing, night after night: "Find Bun." It wasn't loud, but a whisper in her ear, as though something stood or laid beside her. Each time the voice came, she left the comfort of her own home and ran.

Ellie resorted to sleeping with every lamp in the room switched on. The light calmed her, at least until it started again. She lay flat in bed with the covers held close to her chest while she scanned the room, searching for the unexplainable. Suddenly, the bedroom plunged into darkness—seconds later, the television switched on. The screen was black, but she could see the volume bar increase.

A garbled voice came through the speakers with the same message: "Find Bun." The sound was deafening. She tried to lower the volume, but the remote flew off the table and across the room. She placed her hands over her ears to block the sound. It was no help. All she could manage was to curl up into a ball under her great grandmother's quilt. *I don't believe in ghosts.*

It happened again. "Find Bun." This time, the windows vibrated.

A few minutes later, the lights turned back on. Ellie got out of bed and dressed for the day. She would once again retreat to safety in the middle of the night. And each time she ran away from her own home, her ire grew.

Ellie had faced challenges while living in Savannah for the first half of her thirty-three years. She grew up in foster care and spent time as a homeless teenager in New York City. During those years, she'd learned to take care of herself, to solve whatever problem had come her way without hesitation and, when necessary, without remorse. And often, with anger. She'd become a woman with unshakable grit and determination. Until now.

Now fear had her by the throat. Fear of what? Something supernatural? For Ellie, this was not only impossible, but irrational. A woman who had no belief in God would never believe in ghosts. After the last three weeks, the thought had crossed her mind. She wondered whether the superstitions she'd learned in her youth were true. There had to be another explanation.

Tonight, she glanced at the reflection in the mirror. She was thinner now, with dark circles under her eyes. That wasn't the problem. What she saw was weakness and fear. "You're such a coward." As she spoke, the mirror fogged up. She stepped back into the bedroom and watched through the doorway as the words "Find Bun" were traced on the glass, one letter at a time. No one was there.

In a fit of rage, she lifted a water bottle off the nightstand and hurled it into the mirror, screaming, "NO!" The mirror shattered into pieces and Ellie burst into a fit of hysterical laughter. Tears rolled down her face as she laughed—not tears of sadness or even panic, but of relief. The release was life-changing. "That felt great." She laughed again. "I should have done that a long time ago." She knew it was time to do whatever was necessary to stop the insanity.

The moment she controlled her fate, she looked to the heavens. "I'M DONE. YOU HEAR ME? THIS ROLLER COASTER ENDS NOW!" With each word she barked to the disembodied voice, her grit and determination returned. After she cleaned up the glass, she left her home, although, after tonight, she hoped to return with a plan.

———

Once a student and now a music professor, Georgetown University had become Ellie's second home. During these last three weeks, a bench near the Gothic structure of Healy Hall had become a makeshift bed. She used her backpack as a pillow and brought a small blanket to block the chill in the spring air. The sheer size of the clock tower dwarfed her fears, and being outside meant there would be no chance of a voice transmitting through the television.

When a spring breeze passed overhead, she closed her eyes and listened to the rhythmic sounds of the campus. The familiar rustle of the trees carrying chirping birds. The traffic in the distance, and the occasional footsteps of campus security, who, she knew, kept a watchful eye, and allowed her to sleep undisturbed. Each recognizable sound soothed the mind and lulled her into a deep sleep. At daybreak, the chatter of students returning to class crept into her consciousness.

"Good morning."

A voice that could wake up the dead sent ripples of sound into her sleeping mind. She leaped off the bench and placed her hand over her pounding heart. Ellie's adoptive father, Vincent O'Brien, a retired admiral in the US Navy, sat at the end of the bench. She pointed an angry finger. "Never do that again. What is the matter with you?"

He tilted his head, then stared at his daughter. "Do what?"

Still unnerved, Ellie leaned over and placed her hands on her knees to catch her breath. "You know damn well what. You shocked the hell out of me."

"Yes, I did. We need to talk." He was no longer playing innocent.

The last thing on Ellie's mind was talking. She sat down, then pointed that same finger to the parking lot. "You need to go away."

Her father stood his ground. She knew he would. He always stood his ground.

"The last time I found you sleeping alone outside, you were fifteen years old, covered in snow, and left for dead. Now I find you passed out on a bench in the middle of the campus. Exactly how long have you been out here?"

Ellie resented the comparison. She wasn't a fifteen-year-old homeless teenager any longer and was perfectly capable of taking care of herself. "I'm not telling you that. I'm not a kid anymore. Besides, I was SLEEPING." The word *sleeping* came out louder and more shrill than she'd intended.

"I've been trying to wake you for ten minutes. I nudged you—I called your name. Nothing worked. That's not just sleeping. Elizabeth Rose O'Brien, something's wrong with you."

"Why are you even here?" Neither expected Ellie's headstrong, indignant tone. When she saw the expression on her father's face, she recognized she'd crossed a line.

Vincent remained resolute. "We had a date for breakfast. When you didn't show up, I looked for you. I thought you might be in your office. I certainly didn't expect to find you out here."

It was then Ellie understood how much the lack of sleep had affected her memory. Having no recollection of their breakfast date was troubling. Her tone softened. "I forgot. Sorry."

She stood and paced, and as she walked, she rubbed her fingers together. It was a habit she'd developed sometime in her youth which revealed itself during times of great stress. It was her tell, and her family understood what it meant. She stopped the moment her father noticed.

"What's going on with you, Ellie? I'm not leaving until you tell me."

With his arms crossed over his chest, she assumed he was ready to argue until she conceded. After growing up in foster care, she preferred to handle things on her own. It was a habit she'd never been able to break, even after finding a permanent family.

"Nothing's wrong, Dad. Nothing I can explain, anyway."

"TRY!"

"Please, drop it. This is my problem."

"That will not happen."

"It will sound insane."

"That's for me to decide."

She groaned. Ellie had always had a caffeine addiction. During these last three weeks, she required caffeine to survive the day. The only way she'd ever make it to Saxbys for some much-needed coffee was to tell her father what had happened. She hesitated. "Seriously. You're like a dog with a frickin' bone. Why are you giving me such a hard time?"

"Two reasons. First, I FOUND YOU PASSED OUT ON A BENCH."

Students in the vicinity turned. Ellie noted the expression on their faces. They knew her father; he'd visited the campus often. But they'd never seen this side of him. They'd known him as a calm, fatherly figure. They appeared stunned to see anger on his face. Ellie nodded to reassure them everything was under control. Her father flicked his hand with a gesture and a glance that suggested they leave the area immediately. The students quickly complied.

Undeterred, he continued. "Second, when's the last time you looked in the mirror?"

That struck a nerve after shattering one that morning. Ellie didn't realize others had noticed the shadows under her eyes or the sallow complexion that stared back at her every morning. She paced again.

"You don't look healthy, darlin'."

Of that, she was aware. "You'll think I'm crazy."

"I won't."

Again, she hesitated. She didn't want to pull her father into this problem. There were other places to go. She could have asked her friend, Olivia Lombardi, for help. As a licensed psychiatrist, she was qualified. But the thought of being analyzed by her best friend made that impossible. She could have gone to Preston Bartlett. They met in New York City while Ellie was homeless. They bonded over stories of foster care. Preston protected her from other teenagers on the streets. And he understood her in ways no one else could, not even her adoptive father. She worried Preston would see her differently. He might even consider her unstable.

She relented and answered his questions. "I've been hearing voices." She looked at her father to gauge his reaction. There was none. "Well, a scratchy voice, to be specific."

Hearing those words coming out of her mouth sounded ridiculous, but her father wasn't laughing. He seemed concerned. "What did she say?"

"She?"

When Vincent ignored her question, Ellie continued. "Well, she says, 'Find Bun.' I don't know what it means. Don't you think I've lost my mind? Because I do."

"No. You're one of the most stable and courageous people I've ever known. You're not losing your mind. Put that aside."

Vincent's eyes showed such gentleness it touched Ellie's heart. She let out a breath in relief. "Thanks for that."

"Tell me, is the voice what's done this to you?" Vincent motioned with his hand.

"Yes, I suppose. It comes at different times during the night, through the static on the radio or television. Sometimes it whispers in my ear. I tried keeping the lights turned on, but last night she turned them off, then turned on the television and repeated the same words through the speakers. It keeps happening, Dad. It scares me. This morning, the bathroom mirror fogged up for no reason and she wrote the same message on the glass."

"Find Bun," he said.

"Yes. Each letter appeared as though someone was writing them. I swear, there was no one in the room. I'm too afraid to be in the house after she shows up, so I try to catch a nap where I can."

"That's why you've kept your distance the last few weeks? And why you were sleeping out here?"

Ellie nodded.

"Elizabeth, why didn't you come to me?"

She didn't respond for a full ten seconds, then shrugged. "I couldn't face the questions, and I hoped it would go away on its own. I don't understand what's going on." Her lips quivered, and when her frustration slipped out, so had a tear. She sat back down and cried. "What am I supposed to do?"

Vincent wrapped his arms around his daughter. "I can help, darlin'. Trust me."

Ellie eyed her father and realized he believed her. But why?

"I'm so sorry this happened to you."

She held back the rest of the tears that wanted to break loose. "Truth is, Dad, I haven't felt safe since I heard the voice. Not only at home, but everywhere, all the time. I can't explain it. It seems like something's watching me. I feel safer out in the open than I do at home. Is she trying to send me a message? If so, she needs to figure out a better way, because all she's doing is scaring me."

"Sweetheart, that's exactly what she's doing. She's probably tried to contact you in other ways, but you didn't understand."

Ellie frowned. "Why doesn't this surprise you? And how do you even know about this? And why do you keep calling it she?"

"I'll explain over a cup of coffee. You look like you could use a cup."

"Well, that's an understatement!"

———

As they walked to Saxbys in Georgetown, neither spoke. Once inside, they stepped up to the counter and placed their order. Ellie asked for a red-eye coffee with a double shot of espresso, while Vincent's order was hot and black. They sat at a small table by the window, deep in thought.

When the coffee arrived, Ellie smelled the aroma of the beans. She lifted her index finger in the air as though to tell the world to wait one second while she became human again. Her eyes were closed when she savored the first sip. "AHHH. I needed that. I swear, this is better than sex."

"Well, I have my own thoughts about that, but we'll leave that alone." Vincent shook his head, then smiled.

Ellie hadn't realized she'd spoken aloud. "Oops. Sorry about that."

They both laughed.

"Why aren't you concerned about me hearing voices?"

Vincent held his cup with both hands, blowing on the coffee to cool it down.

Ellie could see his mind working. She expected a discussion about her mental health or about losing weight. She was wrong.

"Your mother and I had always believed it was a miracle we found you during the blizzard. You were closer to death than you realize. We both assumed there was a divine intervention that guided us to you."

Ellie rolled her eyes. "Here we go."

Vincent let out a quiet laugh, then put his coffee down and placed both hands over hers. "I understand why you don't believe in God, darlin'. What do you think about spirits?"

A lecture about God wasn't what she had in mind this morning. Especially after such a long night. She'd often sworn it would take a miracle for her to believe. Lately, she wondered whether her miracle was sitting right in front of her, drinking his hot, black coffee. He might not be God, but a miracle nonetheless. "Spirits! Are you talking about ghosts?"

He grinned. "Yes. I was hoping the word 'spirit' would be less frightening."

She considered. Before today, the answer would have been a resounding no. Now she wasn't sure. "That's why you called it she. Because you think she's a female ghost."

"Yes."

"If there were ghosts, why wouldn't I have seen Mom after she died? Did you see Mom?"

"No, not that way. I dreamed about her a couple of times. We sat on the sofa together and talked, much like we're doing now. She let me know she was happy, but she also wanted to make sure I watched over you."

Ellie took a moment to imagine what that would have been like. To see her mother one last time, even if only in a dream. Would that have been as frightening as this ghost, or would it have been comforting? "That's nice. I had none of that. Why didn't you tell me about this before?"

"That's a good question. I'm afraid I don't have an answer. I guess I thought it might be too much for you to handle. None of this is part of your belief system."

"That's true." But Ellie didn't understand what to do with this information. In her mind, when you die, you die. "Why are we talking about this now?"

He paused for a moment to gather his thoughts. "If you recall, when you moved in with us, the gym was in the basement of the house. Soon after you moved in, when I went downstairs to work out, I found things moved around. I figured you were testing me, so I never pursued it and put the items back where they belonged. One morning, when I was lifting weights in front of the mirror, it fogged up for no reason. I stood, dumbfounded, while she wrote 'Train her' on the glass, one letter at a time. Sound familiar?"

"Yes. What did you do?"

"Your mother came downstairs and read the words aloud. She knew it wasn't my handwriting. I asked her what I should do. She said, I guess you should train her, then turned around and walked back upstairs. It scared me for a while. I took your mother's advice and trained you, and nothing ever happened again."

"That's when you taught me martial arts."

"Yes. We both sensed the ghost wanted you to know how to defend yourself. In case you ended up on your own. If you think about it, we didn't know if you would stay with us or run away. You were a handful at the beginning."

Ellie put her hands over her face, then let out a deep breath. The relief was palpable. For the first time in weeks, she wasn't alone in all of this. Other people had experienced this same ghost. "Thank God."

"That's an interesting phrase for someone who doesn't believe in Him." He glanced toward Ellie with a wide grin. "She won't leave until you do what she wants. Whatever that is. She's here for a reason, Ellie. You don't understand why yet, but you will."

Ellie closed her eyes, then shook her head.

"Come home after your classes and spend the night. It'll get you away from your house, and a good night's sleep will give you a fresh perspective. I'll make dinner and we can drink a bottle of wine while we discuss what to do next."

"She might show up at your house. After all, she's been there before."

"She might. Now you know what she is, and you won't be alone. She won't hurt you, I'm sure of it."

"Why do you think it's a she? You didn't hear a voice."

"Your mother believed it was a female ghost because of the message. Its purpose, in your mother's opinion, was to protect you."

"So, you're guessing?"

He smiled again. "Yes. But you heard a voice. Think back. Was it female?"

She took a moment to consider. "Yes. I guess it was." She stared out of the coffee shop window and thought about his suggestion. "Dinner's a good idea. Then I'll tell the ghost to piss off."

Vincent laughed.

CHAPTER 2

ELLIE'S ANGER HAD GROWN SINCE THEIR TALK AT SAXBYS. THE IDEA of being manipulated by a ghost, something she couldn't see or reason with, enraged her. The moment the wrought-iron gate opened to her father's farm, the tension eased.

She turned onto the long cobblestone road, where gas lanterns lit the way to the stone farmhouse. A red front door opened to a large foyer with ten-foot ceilings and wide-planked walnut floors held down by hand-forged nails. The stillness inside the thick stone walls quieted Ellie's mind and brought her back to the time she lived here.

Framed family photos dating back one-hundred-fifty-years hung on the walls, including that of Séamus O'Brien, the man who built this home, stone by stone. Ellie appreciated its history. Not knowing her own family roots had often overwhelmed her. She stroked the staircase railing, smooth and worn from the passage of time, then closed her eyes.

"Your expression reminds me of the first day we brought you here."

She grinned. "Sometimes I get nostalgic. I remember walking through that door for the very first time. I expected to be thrown out, but you treated me like a member of the family."

When Ellie stood in the foyer that first day, her mouth nearly hit the floor. Until that moment, she'd picked pockets to survive and, when cash was in short supply, had stolen food to eat. Suddenly, she stood in what she considered a mansion.

This house became her refuge, a place where no one could hurt her. But it was so much more. Her adoptive parents had healed her. They saved her from a life of misery.

"This home is in the middle of nowhere, yet I never felt alone. Yet, surrounded by thousands of people in the city, I felt completely isolated."

Vincent greeted his daughter with a warm hug, and she laid her head on his chest.

"I should've come home when I heard the voice."

"You're home now. That's what's important." With his hands placed on Ellie's shoulders, he looked her square in the eyes. "Elizabeth Rose, you are not alone in this world. You have friends and family who can help. It's important to believe that. Change into your workout gear. You need to blow off some steam."

———

They walked to the newly painted red barn, with its pristine white trim, where horses once lived. Soon after Ellie moved in, Vincent moved the gym from the basement of the house into the barn. It had everything imaginable. Treadmills, elliptical machines, and free weights sat along the edges of the large room. Workout mats used to train in martial arts and Krav Maga were placed in the center. A heavy bag hung from the ceiling in the corner. He'd even installed two showers to use after a hard workout.

When Ellie moved in with the O'Briens, Vincent taught her to use the heavy bag to work out her anger issues. Or in this case, frustration and fear. He selected a pair of bright-pink boxing gloves with rhinestones along the rim. They were a gift from Preston Bartlett, and each time Ellie put them on, she had a smile on her face.

Vincent insisted she follow her normal routine. She stretched her muscles and joints. Shadowboxed and jumped rope. Only then would he lace the gloves. She started on the heavy bag, slowly increasing intensity. Once her muscles warmed up, she kicked the bag with a force that sent it swinging.

"Now that feels good." As she fought, beads of sweat ran down her face and dripped off her long red curls. Her fierce, sea glass-colored eyes stayed fixed on her target.

"Who are you fighting?"

She didn't respond. Her muscular body punched and kicked until there was nothing left. The release reminded her of how she felt when she was a teenager. She stepped away from the bag and placed her hands on her knees to catch her breath.

"Tell me what's on your mind, Ellie."

She walked over and kicked the bag. "I was really scared." She kicked it again. "How can I defend myself from a ghost?" She punched it. "I don't believe in fucking ghosts." When she turned to her father, tears filled her eyes. He walked toward her, and she fell into his arms.

"I've never seen you cry before today. Even when your mother died. You've always been able to compartmentalize your emotions. To be honest, I was never sure if that was a good thing."

"I hate to cry. It makes me feel weak. I've done more crying in the last three weeks than I have my entire life. What am I supposed to do?" She stepped away from her father and paced.

"You need to understand the ghost won't hurt you. She sent you a message. She'll keep sending it until you listen. What you do with the information is up to you."

She turned to her father. "What does that mean, she'll stop haunting me? Haunting me. Good grief."

"It means no one can force you to do anything. Free will and all."

She scowled. "Seriously, I'm not in the mood for any religious gobbledygook."

He grinned and raised his hands in surrender. "I believe she'll go away once you understand her message. She did with me. You should listen, Ellie. For her to be so persistent, it must be important. Knowledge is power. You know who she is now, and the fear isn't gripping you. At least, I don't think it is, anyway."

"No, I'm much better, thanks to you."

"You decide what to do next. Not the ghost. Remember, she's here for a reason."

Her eyes widened. "Knowledge *is* power, isn't it? Well, I'm taking back my power." She turned around and gave the bag one last kick.

"Are you better now?"

"I'm getting there."

"Good, because you nearly put a hole in my bag."

They both laughed. Ellie picked up a towel and wiped the sweat from her face.

"Get cleaned up and I'll open a bottle of wine."

"Sounds great. Thanks, Dad."

"That's what I'm here for. Go on now, get showered for dinner." Before he left the barn, he leaned in and kissed his daughter on the cheek.

This time, she wasn't afraid to step into the shower. "Knowledge *is* power."

———

Inside the main house, Ellie sat at the table and reminisced about their life together while Vincent cooked all her favorites. With the best Irish brogue she could manage, she lifted a glass to toast her father. "Always remember to forget the troubles that passed away. But never forget to remember the blessings that come each day. Slàinte." She gave her father a nod and took the first sip.

The sound of the front door opening, then closing, made its way into the kitchen. Ellie frowned. For a moment, she wondered whether the ghost had followed her. She realized it wasn't a ghost at all and scowled at her father. "Who else is coming? I thought we would be alone."

Vincent cleared his throat and continued to cook when Preston Bartlett stepped into the kitchen.

"Hi there." He walked over and surrounded Ellie in a hug. "You look terrible." She punched him on the shoulder and a wide grin filled his face. He gave her a wink, poured wine into a glass for himself, then refilled Ellie's. "What happened?"

She drank her wine and told him everything, though that wasn't her original intention. She wanted to keep this between her and her father and not bring anyone else into her drama. Now she had no choice. Her father made that decision for her.

The man, her best friend, held her hand while he listened and never took his eyes off her. When she finished, he gently stroked her cheek. "How are you now?" There was no diatribe about not calling him for help. No anger or disappointment. He just held her hand.

"I'm getting better. I'm spending the night here."

"Good. So am I."

For once in her life, Ellie didn't argue.

———

She slept like a stone for twelve hours without a single dream and woke to the earthy aroma of Sumatra Mandheling coffee. When she opened her eyes, she found Preston sitting in a chair, his legs propped up on the bed, with a computer on his lap. "How long have you been there?" She stretched her arms over her head.

He shrugged.

"You slept in a chair all night?" Then she considered. "Wait, did you sleep at all?"

He shrugged once more and lifted the laptop. "I had lots of work to do."

"Yeah, right!" She crawled across the bed and kissed him on the cheek, then moved back to the pillows and covered up. "Thanks for being here. I'm not sure if I want to wake up yet. It's been so long since I've had a good night's sleep. How did I do?"

"You didn't budge, but you snore so loud I'm surprised Uncle Vince could sleep at all."

As Preston and Ellie's families grew closer, they'd each called their fathers uncle. Uncle Dave was Preston's father, and Uncle Vince, Ellie's.

Ellie threw a pillow at him. "I do not."

He guarded his computer and laughed. "Yeah, you keep telling yourself that. Better yet, I'll record it next time. When was the last time you had a good night's sleep?"

"As long as the ghost's been around. About three weeks."

He frowned, and Ellie understood it was a mistake to have shut him out. This was the most terrifying event that had happened since they met, and she'd kept the man who'd protected her for years out of the loop. *If that wasn't a betrayal, what was?* "I'm sorry, Preston. I should have come to you. Truth is, I thought I was losing my mind."

"You lost that a long time ago."

Ellie threw another pillow, and this time it made a direct hit to Preston's head.

"That coffee smells great," said Ellie.

He agreed, and they both sprinted out of the room.

———

Vincent handed each of them their favorite mug. Ellie's was much larger than Preston's. Her addiction to caffeine was legendary. An Irish breakfast with American bacon instead of ham, eggs with sausage, mushrooms and grilled tomatoes, along with hot fresh Irish soda bread slathered in butter, were on the morning menu. He skipped the black and white pudding and baked beans. Ellie would never eat them.

Vincent placed the large platter of food on the table in front of them. Ellie ate as if she hadn't eaten in weeks.

"When's the last time you had a healthy meal?"

She shrugged. "Everything normal in my life stopped when this thing started. Food, sleep, sex."

Vincent cleared his throat. Preston frowned, and Ellie laughed at them both.

Vincent grinned. "Thing? You mean the ghost?"

"Sex?" asked Preston. "With whom?"

Ellie knew Preston did not know if she was kidding or not.

"I'm still not sure I believe a ghost is haunting me. How do I deal with that? And why does she only say two words? If she wants me to do something specific, she needs to spit it out. Preston, did you know the ghost visited my father, years ago? She sent him a message when I first moved in."

"No."

"He didn't tell me either. But I bet he told your dad."

Preston laughed. "Of course he did."

Vincent repeated some of what he'd already said the night before. "I don't think she's haunting you. She's sending you a message, and you're resisting. And, for the record, Preston, yes, your father knows."

Preston's adoptive father, Admiral David Bartlett, had been friends with Vincent since their time at the Naval Academy. Ellie knew nothing happened in each of their lives without first informing the other. Much like her relationship with Preston—until now.

"Well, I don't like being afraid in my own home. She and I are going to talk, and that will be the end of it." Or so she'd hoped.

"I can come with you," said Vincent.

"So can I," said Preston.

"No. I can take care of this myself."

Vincent held up a finger in protest. "That wasn't a suggestion. We're both coming with you."

Once her father had made up his mind, she understood there was no use arguing. "You can't imagine how much you've helped me already. Knowing what's happening gives me the strength to take this on."

Vincent smiled. "This? You mean the ghost."

"YES! The ghost. There, I said it. Are you going to say that every time?"

Vincent leaned against the counter and took a sip of coffee, then grinned. "Maybe."

"I'm going to take a shower. If you hear screaming, you'll know the nonexistent ghost is back."

———

Vincent picked up the pot of coffee and refilled Preston's mug. "So, when are you going to tell her?"

"What do you mean?"

"I'm not blind, you know. Ellie might not see it yet, but it's written all over your face. You love her. I don't know when it happened, but it's obvious now."

Preston stared at the coffee. "I don't know when it happened. I can't tell her, and neither can you."

"Why?"

"Because it could ruin everything we have."

"Or it could make it better."

"Only if she feels the same way. I won't risk it."

"Preston, it's up to you to take the first step before she figures it out on her own. And for the record, you're making a mistake."

He nodded. "It's my mistake to make. Keep my secret."

"Fine."

———

They each drove in separate cars to Ellie's home. Vincent asked Ellie to wait for him, but she ran too fast. He tried to keep up, to no avail. "Wait for me."

Ellie was too focused to hear anything. She stormed up the stairs to the primary bedroom, taking two steps at a time. Preston and Vincent followed. Even Preston fell behind.

She spoke to the heavens. "I know you're here."

Vincent shook his head. "You won't get a response. At least, I didn't."

"I'm not afraid of you anymore, and I will not do what you want, so PISS OFF AND GET OUT OF MY HOUSE!"

Vincent grinned. "I see your resolve is returning." Then he looked in the bathroom. "What happened to your mirror?"

"Oh yeah. Can you help me hang a new one?"

"Elizabeth Rose, what did you do?"

"A bottle slipped out of my hands."

Preston let out a laugh.

CHAPTER 3

August 22, 2017

I**T WAS TWO IN THE MORNING BY THE TIME** P**RESTON** B**ARTLETT MADE** it to bed, although that wasn't unusual. Unlike Ellie, who'd enjoyed watching the sunrise, he'd prefer to sleep the entire day away. But not today.

This afternoon marked his semi-annual lunch with Ellie. Each semester, they would open her office and review class schedules, then go to lunch. In years past, they printed syllabuses and stapled piles of paper. Now everything was paperless, which meant less organizing and more time toasting new beginnings. It was a tradition they'd started after graduation, and it continued today.

Preston set Clocky, an alarm clock with wheels, for eight in the morning. He hated Clocky, but the gag gift was the one thing annoying enough to jolt him out of sleep. This time, he hoped he wouldn't stub his toe chasing it across the room. He'd only use it to be on time for his lunch date. Though, he reminded himself, it wasn't an actual date.

He dropped his clothes where he stood and flopped onto the middle of the bed. With his entire body stretched out, he resembled a large, naked *X*.

He slept, undisturbed, until five in the morning, when the voice of a woman whispered in his ear. "Save her."

Still asleep, he recoiled and put the pillow over his head.

"Save her."

The voice was somewhat clearer the second time, but still too garbled to understand through the pillow. And it was not yet loud enough to rouse him. Preston's subconscious dismissed the sound as someone outside.

"SAVE HER!"

The third time wasn't a whisper at all, but a high-pitched screech. And it wasn't outside but coming from the television in his room. Preston flew out of bed. He switched on a light and disconnected the television.

It happened again through the radio. "SAVE HER!"

"Who's here?" There was no response, and no other sounds in the room. Not a footstep or creak on the floor. Not even a drip from the bathroom faucet. He checked under the bed and opened the closet door. No one was in there. The door to the bedroom remained closed.

Based on Ellie's description months earlier, it didn't take long for Preston to surmise what had happened. The ghost was back, and now it was haunting him. His heart pounded in his chest. For the first time, he understood how terrified Ellie must have been.

"Are you the ghost?" Preston stood still, waiting for a sign. For a moment, there were none. He let out a breath.

"SAVE ELLIE!"

The voice was so loud, Preston covered his ears with his hands. Windows vibrated. Clocky soared past his head and smashed against the wall. His entire body trembled as he struggled to maintain control.

"Thanks. I hated that clock, anyway. But it was a gift from Ellie. She won't be happy with you." When he focused on what the ghost was repeating, he understood. She hadn't been haunting Ellie. She was warning her. Now she was warning him. "What's wrong with Ellie?"

"DANGER!" The voice turned into a growl.

Any concern Preston had for his own safety had all but disappeared. "SHIT!" He grabbed his cell phone to call Ellie. There was no answer. "It's five thirty. Ellie's on her way to the university. She won't answer the phone." He dressed, fumbling to put on his pants, then grabbed his knife in its sheath from the nightstand and slipped it onto his belt, and raced to the garage.

The ghost's now desperate voice followed him through the house. The radio and television on the lower level, and the speakers on his laptop computer, all screeched. "HURRY!"

Once in the garage, he picked up a helmet and jumped onto his motorcycle, then sped out the door. He weaved in and out of traffic, be-tween cars, up onto sidewalks. As he approached, traffic lights switched from red to green, clearing the way. Once on the highway, he hit the gas, grateful traffic was light this early in the morning.

"Go help Ellie!" he shouted, hoping the ghost could hear him. "I'll catch up." It was a wonder he hadn't crashed. He had one thing on his mind: to save Ellie.

From what was a mystery.

CHAPTER 4

ELLIE DISCOVERED, THANKS TO WEEKS OF BEING HAUNTED, SHE EN-
joyed rising with the sun. This morning was no exception. She
planned to meet Preston at the university at ten. The warmth of summer had always stirred her creative juices, which beckoned her to the university. It was impossible to resist. She planned to work on her music while
she waited for Preston to arrive.

The August heat had not yet set in, and she opened the car windows
to feel the morning breeze. Once she arrived, she pulled into the parking
lot by Lauinger Memorial Library, where a handful of cars sat, but none
she recognized.

Most days, students roamed the campus at all hours. Now, in-between
the summer and fall semesters, dorms were unoccupied and classes had
not yet begun. In this small, out of the way parking lot, she felt unsettled
by the void—by the emptiness. It was too barren for her liking. She'd attributed her unease to caffeine overload and dismissed it.

She locked the car door and hung a leather messenger bag over one
shoulder. With no one to keep her company, she pulled out her earbuds
to listen to music. This morning it was jazz.

As she headed toward the stairs, she checked email. She'd often cau-
tioned students about their phones, about being so engrossed in their
screens they'd forget to pay attention to their surroundings. *Do as I say,*
she thought, and noticed a call from Preston. There was no voice mail.
She'd call him back from her office.

It was then the sixth sense she'd honed during her troubled youth
screamed, *Watch out; something's wrong!* By then, it was too late. A man
grabbed her from behind, momentarily lifting her off her feet. Her bag

and cell phone fell to the ground as she thrashed back and forth, trying to free herself.

The attacker was male, with large, muscular arms that wrapped around her, with a pungent odor of sweat. A second, smaller man appeared out of nowhere and stood in front of her. He attempted to grab her legs, and she kicked him in the chest, pushing him to the ground.

The larger man tried to drag her away. Where he was taking her was unknown. A car, perhaps. Ellie couldn't allow that to happen. She needed to stay out in the open, where a passerby might see her.

The smaller man tried to grab her legs again. She kicked him in the teeth, breaking his jaw and knocking him to the ground. Blood streamed down his face, and he rolled around, moaning from the pain.

One down.

Ellie recalled a phrase her father had often repeated. *Remember your training.* At that moment, the memory felt like a call to action, to stay focused and summon the courage to fight these men. She took a deep breath and let out a primal scream, then flexed her muscles and pushed the man backward. He slammed against the building next to the sidewalk. The surprise move caught her captor off guard. He lost his balance and loosened his grip, but not enough. Before he could regain control, she pushed him against the wall, again and again. His grip weakened long enough to free one arm. She gritted her teeth and continually elbowed the side of his face until she hit the target. She struck his throat with such force, he released her and leaned over to gasp for air.

She ran for her life, up the stairs toward the center of the quad, still smelling the pungent odor of their filth lingering on her body. Their vulgar shouts told her they weren't far behind.

She reached the bushes surrounding the common area by Healy Hall and crawled through the brush to find the best place to hide. Her knees dug into sharp edges of the debris protruding from the dirt. Small branches scraped her arms, leaving behind droplets of blood. "I need something," she whispered, though she knew no one was there to help her. "A rock or a branch, anything—dammit." A tree limb dropped to the ground about five feet in front of her. There was no wind, no reason for something the size of a baseball bat to fall at just the right moment. She picked it up and judged the weight. "I can do some damage with this."

The two men were now in the clearing outside of Healy Hall, searching through the bushes and checking behind the trees. The smaller man found her. Before he could shout to his partner, she leaped toward him and swung the branch, striking his head. He lay unconscious on the ground. The larger man, searching the other side of the clearing, heard the commotion and saw his partner.

"One down," Ellie shouted. She paused long enough for it to sink into his thick skull. "I think he's dead. Too bad. Now, it's your turn."

Back in a fighting stance, holding the branch on each end, she swayed back and forth, then moved farther into the clearing to fight.

"I'm going to kill you!" He pulled a knife and charged.

Ellie used her makeshift bat to knock the knife out of his hand, then thrust the tree limb into his ribs. The blow had little effect. He took one step back and shook it off. She quickly picked up the knife and threw it out of reach, then paused again to gauge his reaction. To see where he might go next.

"I'll kill you with my bare hands."

A noise across the common area startled him. He turned to see whether someone was coming, and Ellie made her move. A double roundhouse kick, which would have taken most men down, had done nothing. He barely moved. It felt as though she was fighting Goliath himself. She changed her strategy. One kick square in the balls brought him to his knees. He screamed from the pain. It appeared his only weakness was between his legs. She swung the tree limb with all her might and struck him on the side of his face and jaw. He stared at her in disbelief, then closed his eyes and slowly dropped to the ground. When the unconscious behemoth landed, she half expected the earth to move.

Ellie turned around and found the smaller man on his knees, nearly unconscious, pointing a gun. He squinted to aim his weapon. Frantically, she searched for cover. The trees and bushes where she'd hidden before were too far away. With little time to spare, she had only one option. She sprinted to the one thing close enough and large enough to protect her. Three shots rang out as she lunged behind the behemoth laying on the ground. One shot wasn't even close. The other two hit his partner. One in his torso, and the other in his head. She heard him take his last breath.

One more shot sounded as a motorcycle raced up the sidewalk and onto the grass between Ellie and the gunman. The man pointed the gun at the driver, who placed his hand by his waist, then cast his arm toward the killer. A knife soared through the air and into the gunman's chest. He fell backward onto the ground, with his lifeless body still holding the gun. There was only one person Ellie knew who could handle a knife with such precision.

Preston Bartlett pulled over, threw off his helmet, and ran toward the gunman. He kicked the gun out of reach, then checked his pulse.

"Did they hurt you?"

"No, I'm good. But I think the big guy's dead."

He checked the larger man's pulse.

"What about him?" Ellie pointed to the gunman.

"He's dead." When he saw the scratches on her arms and gashes on her knees, he let out a gasp. "What did they do to you?"

When the vein pulsed in Preston's jaw, she knew, if it were possible, he'd wake them up and kill them again. "They didn't do this. I got scratched up crawling in the bushes."

"Thank God you're safe." He let out a breath in relief and gently wrapped his arms around her. "This was way too close."

Ellie agreed.

Preston guided her into a shaded area, away from the two dead men, and gently asked her to sit down on the grass. He cradled her cold, shaky hands in his to warm them. "Don't worry, it's the adrenaline. Your body will stabilize in a few minutes."

"I know. It's been awhile since I've been this scared." She took slow, deep breaths to settle her nerves.

Preston sat down and placed his arm around her, then pulled out his phone and dialed 911.

CHAPTER 5

PRESTON INFORMED THE OPERATOR TWO MEN ASSAULTED A COLlege professor at Georgetown University, and both attackers lay dead on the field in front of Healy Hall. The professor had minor injuries. The operator dispatched the Washington, DC Metropolitan Police, and an ambulance. With so many school shootings around the country, she promised a quick response.

This wasn't your typical school shooting. It was an attack on a woman. Two men, one victim. Preston noted the time on his watch. Since the danger had passed, he was curious how long it would take for the police to arrive.

With no armed men on campus, all they had to do was wait. They both needed this time to take a breath and calm down. And he needed a moment to thank the ghost who guided him there. For without the apparition, Ellie would surely be dead.

They waited under the trees, out of the August sun, which would soon heat up, and far enough away from the crime scene not to disturb the evidence. He noticed how desolate the campus was this time of year. With no classes or students in the dorms, it was eerily quiet. He expected to see a scatter of people, even this early in the morning. There was none.

"How are you doing?"

"As good as expected." She held out her trembling hands. "At least I'm not shaking as much. Thank goodness you came. But why are you here this early? Weren't we supposed to meet at ten?"

"Our friendly ghost paid me a visit this morning. She told me you were in danger."

"Told you?"

"Yes, with two words. Ellie danger."

She shook her head. "Still only two words. I wonder where she's been."

"I don't know. We can talk about it later. For now, if the police ask, tell them we were here to work in your office, then we were going to Saxbys for breakfast. It is true. Just earlier than we'd planned. I don't want to explain how I got here in time."

She shrugged. "That's understandable."

"Do you remember anything? Did they say anything?"

"Nothing other than 'I'm going to kill you.'" Then she considered. "In the parking lot, the smaller man appeared to be looking for someone. He might have mumbled something, but he could have been checking for witnesses. It seemed a little odd, that's all."

"Parking lot?"

"Yes. They attacked me by my car, as I was about to climb the stairs. I fought them off and ran up here. They followed."

"Tell the police. They'll extend the crime scene to include that area. What do you mean…were they looking for someone specific?"

"I don't know, but I can't rule it out. Also, something up here distracted the behemoth when we fought."

Preston smiled at the description. Based on his size and shape, it was on point. "Any idea what it was?"

"A noise, maybe? I can't be sure of anything. It's all a blur. I ended up having to kick him in the balls to take him down." When Preston winced, Ellie smiled. "It was like fighting a one-hundred-year-old live oak tree."

He rubbed her back to relieve the tension, and she closed her eyes. "It'll be okay, don't worry. For now, try to relax."

She took his advice and sat in the field with her blood-speckled legs stretched out. Her hands rested on the grass, and she repeatedly breathed in, then out.

Each time, Preston could see her tension ease.

From the corner of his eye, he saw a man peeking around a building. *Who are you? A student or a threat?* It was impossible to know. For a moment, he questioned his original assessment. *What if there were more men? What if he was one of them?* His only weapon was in the dead man's chest. He stood, placing his body in front of Ellie's, ready to defend her, even if it meant using his bare hands.

The stranger nodded, then waved a hand and pointed toward the men lying in the field. Preston shook his head and signaled they were dead. He now understood this man was no threat. When the stranger crouched down and left the safety of the building, it took Preston by surprise. He wondered why he would expose himself unnecessarily.

The stranger walked the edges of the crime scene, methodically checking behind bushes and trees and any hidden crevices. The way he moved caught Preston's attention. *He's well trained, probably military.* Preston imagined an infantry rifle in his hands while he completed a house-to-house search, looking for the enemy. But he was missing his team—his backup should someone leap out of the shadows. Preston didn't want to leave Ellie's side. Neither did he want this man to risk his life. Not alone. But what of Ellie?

"You need to help him," insisted Ellie. "You know I can take care of myself."

Preston reluctantly agreed and joined him. The two men worked quickly, searching every corner of the quad. Neither carried a weapon. Once they completed their inspection, Preston returned to Ellie, and the stranger moved toward the men in the field.

Preston worried he might inadvertently destroy evidence, but he appeared to know what he was doing. He checked their vitals without disturbing the scene. Other than verifying their deaths, he touched nothing. As he made his way back to Ellie and Preston, his eyes moved from building to rooftop.

"I'm Preston Bartlett. This is Professor Elizabeth O'Brien."

"I'm James Dawson." He reached out and shook Preston's hand, then kneeled in front of Ellie to check her wounds. "How are you feeling, Professor? Any injuries, other than the cuts and bruises?"

"No. Are you a doctor?"

"Not yet. I'm in medical school. But I'm trained in first aid."

That explained why he checked on the men in the field. And Preston guessed he knew much more than your average first aid responder.

James looked into Ellie's pupils and examined the cuts on her arms and knees, then took her pulse. "Your pulse is only a little elevated, which is surprising. Are you always this cool under pressure?"

She grinned. "You wouldn't have said that a few minutes ago."

"Have you called campus security yet?"

"No," said Preston. "I called 911."

James picked up his phone and contacted campus security. He told them about the attack, where they were located, and that 911 had already been called. Then he asked for a medical kit.

"You're lucky they didn't kill you. Who are these people?" he asked Preston.

"We don't know."

Preston noticed how gentle he was with Ellie. When he spoke, there was a calmness in his voice that put her at ease. His face was unshaven, and he appeared half asleep, as though he'd been up all night. "Why are you here so early? Classes aren't in session yet."

"I was studying in that building." He pointed to the Lauinger Memorial Library. "There are areas that are open all night. I was on my way home when I heard the shots and ran outside. That's when I saw your motorcycle enter the quad."

"Are you in the military?" asked Preston.

James grinned. "I was about to ask you the same thing after seeing you handle a knife."

"No, not me."

"I was a Marine until about a year ago."

This was another moment of clarity for Preston. Even after being out for a year, the Marine's instincts to protect kicked in.

"Why would you run outside?" Ellie was almost scolding him. "You should have called campus security and sheltered in place once you heard the shots. Suppose there were other men. They could have killed you."

"I came out to neutralize the threat, and to help the injured."

"And because he's a Marine," Preston insisted.

"Oorah." James smiled, then rechecked Ellie's vitals.

———

Two campus security guards ran toward them, carrying a bag with the words *First Aid* written on the side. One guard was quite a bit older than the other.

"We're okay," Ellie shouted.

Knowing they were safe, the guards moved toward the field to check on the men. They verified their deaths and looked at their wounds, as James had done. The older guard also examined the crime scene and followed the motorcycle tracks on the damp morning grass. He saw the knife and the bullet holes, then appeared to reenact what had happened in his mind while his eyes moved from one area to the next. This man was an investigator, and Preston wondered whether he was a retired cop.

Just then, a shelter in place alert sounded on James's phone.

Preston was so deep in thought, the sound made him jump. "Jesus."

Ellie smiled. "The older security guard is Ted Rodriguez. He's a good man, Preston. We can trust him. I don't know the other guard."

After growing up in foster care and living on the streets, trusting a cop was difficult for them both. If she trusted this guard, so would he. At least until he gave him a reason not to.

Preston became keenly aware of the mounting number of sirens racing toward the university.

So did James. "Sounds like the entire police department is coming."

Preston agreed, then glanced at his watch—eight minutes since he called 911. It was all happening too fast for his liking. Soon he'd have to face the police and give an official statement. The thought made his stomach turn.

After Rodriguez completed his tour of the crime scene, he and his partner came to Ellie and Preston.

"I'm Preston Bartlett. This is Professor Elizabeth O'Brien and James Dawson." When Preston stood to greet them, he noticed his knees were a bit wobbly, as was his voice. Nerves were getting the best of him.

"Mr. Bartlett, I've seen you around campus many times. I know you and the professor are friends." He turned to James. "Dawson? You're the man who called campus security."

"Yes."

Rodriguez kneeled next to James and placed the medical kit on the ground between them. "How are you, Professor?"

"I'm okay."

"Thank God. Are there any other threats in the area?"

Preston shook his head. "We haven't seen anyone else."

"Can you tell me what happened, Professor?" Rodriguez asked.

"Those men attacked me by my car at Lauinger Memorial Library, down there." She pointed to the stairs leading to the parking lot. "I dropped my bag and phone during the attack. Can I get them back?"

"I'll take care of it."

"After I got away, they followed me up here and I fought them off. I'd probably be dead if it weren't for Preston. He saved my life."

"The knife is mine," Preston admitted.

"Yours?" Rodriguez held out a hand to stop Preston from speaking. "I advise you not to say another word."

Preston nodded. He was both grateful and confused. *Was this man a cop, or a lawyer? Or, as Ellie mentioned, a good man?*

Rodriguez turned his attention to James. "After your call, we sent out a shelter in place alert. Why are you out here?"

"I saw that man shooting at the professor and Preston. I wanted to help."

"To help! They could have killed you. You witnessed the attack while it was happening?"

"Yes. Part of it."

"Which part?"

"The part where the knife went into that man's heart. It was self-defense."

Rodriguez shook his head. "I should separate all of you."

"You can try." Preston had an edge to his voice now. "I'm not leaving her."

Rodriguez turned around and saw the police drive through the front entrance. "Let me tell you what will happen in the next few minutes. The Metropolitan Police will secure the scene and take statements from each of you. Including you," he said to James. "You may be the only witness." Rodriguez asked his partner to escort Dawson to the officer in charge.

"No! I'm not leaving my patient until the paramedics arrive." He opened the medical kit and cleaned the cuts on Ellie's arms, ignoring Rodriguez's order.

"We're required to separate anyone who witnessed the attack until the police take their statement. It's procedure."

This, Preston knew, was true. It was a way to prevent people from creating and coordinating their own stories about what had happened. That would be collusion. But Preston believed it made little sense in this situation. They could have created an alternative narrative before the cops had even arrived.

"The police are here now," said Rodriguez. "You'll have to explain all of this to them. Don't leave this spot. Be prepared—they may separate all three of you."

Preston nodded.

Rodriguez asked his partner to stay with them until the police took over while he updated the officer in charge.

"I need to call Professor O'Brien's father and let him know what happened," said Preston.

Rodriguez considered, then nodded.

———

Preston walked a few steps away, picked up his phone, and called Vincent. He started by reassuring him his daughter was unharmed, then told him the horrendous news. "Two men attacked Ellie in front of Healy Hall. I don't have the details. She needs time to calm down. I swear, she's not hurt. She's scratched a little. I called 911."

"What's the situation now?"

Before he responded, he turned and checked on Ellie. She seemed perfectly fine. At least on the surface. But as much as he tried to remain calm as he spoke to Vincent, his voice betrayed him. "I'm not sure where to start."

"Then start from the beginning."

He struggled with how much to say over the phone. Should he tell him his daughter hid behind an unconscious man to avoid being shot? Should he tell him the man was now dead from bullets meant for her? And should he tell him he'd threw his knife into a man's heart? He took a breath. "It's hard to explain."

"Take your time."

"I came to meet Ellie to help her organize her office. We do it every year."

"Yes."

"When I arrived, two men had attacked her. One man was lying on the ground unconscious, and the other was shooting a gun."

"SHOOTING!"

"He didn't shoot Ellie," he said quickly, to reassure her father. "But I didn't see much. When I drove my motorcycle into the quad, the gunman turned his weapon on me."

"YOU! Are you hurt?"

"No, I'm fine." He lied. He held his free hand out in front of him—it was still shaking. "We need to sit down with her to get a complete picture of what happened."

"And the gunman?"

"I had my knife and…" He hesitated and thought of what might have happened. Of Ellie lying on the ground with a bullet to the head, in a pool of her own blood. And of the gun being pointed at him. The next time he spoke, there was an edge in his tone. Not fear or remorse, but unadulterated anger. "I didn't miss. He's also dead. It was him or me. Or worse, Ellie. I couldn't let that happen."

The phone fell silent while Preston processed what he'd done. He and Ellie had trained with Vincent and his father for their entire adult lives. They knew how to protect themselves. Although knowing how to kill and actually killing were two different things.

"Preston."

"I'm here."

"You did the right thing. Don't worry."

"Thanks for that." For the first time since he threw the knife, the trembling in his hands was subsiding. "Right now, I'm more concerned about Ellie."

"Well, I'm concerned about both of you. I'll call your father. We'll both be there as soon as possible. Everything will work out, I promise."

Vincent's reaction reminded him of his teenage years. If he was in trouble, Vincent's voice had always remained measured. He never showed anger, though sometimes it boiled below the surface. Preston heard Vincent's car through the phone, followed by screeching tires. He hoped he wouldn't run up a tree, trying to get to his daughter.

"Can I speak to Ellie?"

"Your dad wants to speak to you."

Ellie nodded, then took the phone.

"Hi, Dad." When Ellie spoke, there was a slight tremble in her voice. She couldn't control it.

"Sweetheart, Preston told me everything. Are you okay?"

She gritted her teeth until the tears beneath the surface had waned. "I'm not hurt. There are gashes on my knees from crawling around in the bushes. That's where I hid until I figured out what to do. Those thugs really scared me, Dad."

With those last few words, a single tear ran down Ellie's face. "I keep imagining what might have happened if you hadn't trained me. If you hadn't trained both of us." Her voice was little more than a whisper, which was Ellie's way of maintaining control. Any louder and she'd fall apart. Then she recalled the words written by the ghost: "Train her." She realized the message given to Vincent eighteen years earlier had saved her life today.

"I'm so sorry this happened, Ellie. Have you ever seen these men around campus?"

"No. I doubt they're students. They didn't dress like students. I feel so stupid, Dad. When I pulled into the parking lot, it felt more isolated than normal. But that was because classes haven't started yet. I should have listened to my instincts and parked somewhere else, and I should have checked for a weapon after I took out the little guy. I really screwed up."

When her voice sped up as she spoke, her father stopped her. "Ellie, slow down. You don't need to talk about this over the phone. Try to relax."

"What about Uncle Dave?"

"I'll call him, and we'll both be there."

With each passing minute, there were more sirens and flashing lights. "The area will be inundated with police. They're everywhere. I doubt the cops will let you on campus."

"Don't worry about that. We'll be there. Hopefully sooner than later."

Her father's demeanor helped Ellie calm down. As she spoke, and she thought about what might have happened, her voice had also changed. It became stronger, cold even. Much like Preston, her emotions had shifted from fear to anger. "Trust me, this will never happen again.

The next time someone comes after me, I'll make sure they're dead. Preston could have died."

"He didn't, Ellie. Don't allow yourself to go there. It's not helpful. Besides, some men have harder heads than others."

She let out a tiny laugh. "True."

"You did what you needed to do. You both did. I'm on my way. We'll be there as soon as we can. Love you."

"Love you, too. I'm good—really. Don't worry."

———

While the paramedics checked the dead, an officer at the scene introduced himself to Preston and Ellie, then asked what happened. After giving a brief description, once again, they were told witnesses could not interact.

They searched Preston for other weapons, sat him on the grass, and assigned a cop to stay with him. Preston was thankful they didn't place him in handcuffs. The paramedics brought Ellie to the ambulance, and another police officer escorted James from the scene to take his statement. Preston could keep Ellie in his sights, so he didn't protest. Although, he realized, it wouldn't have mattered if he had. And when he heard Ellie refuse to go to the hospital, he knew she would be okay.

It was time to shift his attention elsewhere. He wanted to go through the dead men's pockets, to get their names. As a skilled hacker who worked for the FBI, he could find out plenty with a little information. But it was too late. The police had already cordoned off the area. He'd get their names soon enough.

Instead, he spent his time combing the area, trying to remember the details, and discreetly taking photos with his phone each time the cop guarding him looked away. Ellie might question her memory about what had happened, but he did not. If something had gotten her attention, it had also gotten his. He'd review his photos later.

Georgetown security guards managed the growing crowd while the Metropolitan Police secured the scene. They kept spectators far enough away to observe without interfering with the investigation and without seeing the gruesome details. Stunned faces watched as yellow police tape marked the circle where violence had invaded their peaceful campus.

Preston concentrated on the people. Some were locals coming to see the spectacle or, most likely, the splatter of blood. Others were administration personnel. A handful were students who lived locally and studied in the libraries in-between semesters. He questioned why they left the safety of the building. They should have received a shelter in place alert. He was missing something.

"How badly is the professor hurt?" a woman asked the security guard in front of the crowd.

She knew Ellie was a professor, Preston thought. Which meant she wasn't a random person from the neighborhood. He took her photo.

"Did she kill those men?" asked an unshaven older man with a cup of coffee in his hand, wearing disheveled pajamas and slippers.

Preston grinned. *Must be a neighbor.* As the crowd grew, Preston covertly took as many photos as possible. He worried whether there was a third man, that he might be watching. *But who? And why would someone want to hurt Ellie, or worse?*

Preston was so focused on the people, he was startled by the sound of the notification on his phone. He glanced toward the cop next to him and asked permission to check his messages. "Would you mind? It's Twitter." Before the officer could respond, there was another tweet. Then another, and another. The phone kept beeping.

"You should check." The officer then read the messages over Preston's shoulder.

Each tweet asked about Ellie, wanting to know if she was badly hurt. Some asked what happened and whether she needed help. Most were in shock. Preston wondered how they knew about the attack so quickly. Then he saw something he hadn't expected. "Is that what I think it is?"

The cop moved closer to the screen. "Looks like someone attached a video."

Preston saw Ellie and the large man on the small video embedded in the tweet, along with a one-word message from Johanna Bowers: HELP! All he had to do was hit play. Preston's finger hovered over the button. Did he really want to see those men attack Ellie, or his knife fly into the man's chest?

Rodriguez returned with Ellie's bag and noticed the expression on Preston's face. "What's wrong?"

"I think there's a video of the attack."

"You think?"

"I'm afraid to watch it."

Rodriguez took the phone and stepped away from Preston to watch the video, then returned. "This is important evidence. I'll have to give this to the officer in charge. They're going to want to talk to Johanna Bowers."

"I'm going to need my phone back."

Rodriguez nodded. "I'll take care of it."

CHAPTER 6

RODRIGUEZ AND HIS PARTNER STOOD IN FRONT OF THE CROWD and shouted, "Can I have your attention?" A sea of cell phones shifted toward him. "This is an open investigation. If you witnessed anything, please come forward now. Everyone else stay back or, better yet, go home. Do not interfere with the investigation."

A young African American woman stepped forward and identified herself as Johanna Bowers. She was so tiny, one strong wind would have blown her away, and when she spoke, her voice was little more than a squeak. Preston could barely hear her from where he sat, but it was clear she was quite shaken.

Rodriguez and Johanna stepped away from the crowd and moved close enough for Preston to eavesdrop, and far enough away not to raise suspicion from the cop guarding him. Rodriguez glanced at him with an expression that told him to listen without interfering. This, Preston knew, was not procedure. Rodriguez was doing him a favor.

The cop assigned to keep him away from Ellie didn't ask him to move. Another favor, perhaps. Or maybe he thought it impossible to hear their conversation and moving was unnecessary. Johanna spoke so softly Preston had to strain to make out each word.

"Can you tell me what happened?" Rodriguez asked Johanna.

"Yes, sir. Those men attacked Professor O'Brien. That man started shooting at her." She pointed to the smaller man lying dead in the field with a knife in his chest. "Then the motorcycle came into the quad and the shooter turned his gun on him. That's when the driver threw the knife. He saved the professor." As she spoke, her voice sounded more frantic.

"Please start from the beginning. Where were you when this happened?"

"I hid over there." She pointed to the massive stone entrance into Healy Hall. "I'll show you." She pulled out a tablet and cell phone from her backpack. "When I saw what was happening, I quickly pressed record on my tablet and placed it on one of the stone pillars. Then I crouched down and dialed 911 with my phone, then sent out a tweet in case any of my friends were here. That was before the gunfire."

"I'm sorry. You did what?"

She displayed the message on her phone.

Men are attacking Professor O'Brien by Healy Hall. NEED HELP! Rodriguez read the message aloud. Preston assumed that was for his benefit.

"A few people replied to my tweet, but they weren't on campus. Most students aren't moving in until this weekend. Thank God for the motorcycle driver."

"Did you say you recorded it?"

"Yes. I recorded it so the police could identify the two men if they took off."

"What did you do with the recording?"

"I tweeted it out."

And there it was, Preston thought. The missing piece of information, and the reason people believed it was safe to come outside. Anyone who viewed the video knew the attackers were dead and would have thought the crisis was over.

"Why send out the tweet?"

"Those men are dead!" she shouted.

Preston had no trouble hearing her now; her tiny voice grew stronger and louder than he thought possible. Neither did the cop guarding him, who frowned.

She continued to raise her voice enough for all to hear. "I've seen too many people go to prison because no one believed them. I tweeted the video to make sure the world knew he was defending himself from those men." She pointed to the two yellow tarps on the ground.

To Preston, her reaction almost seemed intentional. As though she were notifying the media that he had no choice. Even though he understood her reasoning, he wished she would have given the video to campus security or the police instead of uploading it.

It wouldn't be long before the media would broadcast the recording, and it would go viral. Millions of cable news viewers would watch Ellie fight for her life and see him throw a knife into a man's heart.

"Did you do anything else?" asked Rodriguez.

"There wasn't much I could do. I mean, look at me."

Preston hid a small grin. She was right. If someone her size tried to help, they would have killed her with one blow. Ellie survived because of her training.

"No one showed up to help. When the professor started fighting that gigantic man, I threw a couple of rocks into the trees over there to distract him." She pointed to an area in the opposite direction of her location. "I was hoping he would think someone was coming and leave her alone, or the distraction would give the professor time to run. It didn't work the way I expected. He looked toward the trees, and she moved in to fight. That is one brave woman."

"Yes, she is."

"That happened before the other man started shooting. When he pulled a gun, honestly, I didn't know what else to do. I stooped down in the corner in case there were stray bullets."

"I'll need to give the police your tablet to show them the video. They'll return it."

She agreed.

Smooth, Preston thought. *The cops will receive the video from the person who uploaded it and he'd get his phone back.*

"Your hands are shaking," said Rodriguez. "I'm going to have the paramedics on-site check you out, then the police will want to speak to you. They may take you to the precinct for an official statement."

Preston waved for Rodriguez to come over and speak to him. "When you take her to the paramedics, introduce her to Ellie. It will help, and Ellie will want to know what she did."

He agreed.

Preston remained seated in the grass and watched Rodriguez explain what Johanna had done. When Johanna burst into tears, Ellie wrapped her in a warm hug until the tears had waned, then signaled to the paramedics to take over.

Rodriguez walked to Preston and returned his phone.

"Ellie said you were a good man. She was right. Thanks."

He nodded, then walked to the officer in charge and handed him Johanna's tablet.

———

Another vehicle drove through the entrance, but this car was unmarked. Preston suspected it was someone with more authority. Maybe the police detective assigned to the case. He'd be the only person allowed to park so close to the crime scene.

A man stepped out of the car with a badge in full view. He arrived sooner than Preston had expected. Then he saw the name Saxbys written on the side of his coffee cup, which explained his quick arrival. Saxbys was just around the corner. After tossing the empty cup into the trash, he made his way to the officer in charge. The two men shook hands. The detective pulled out a pad from his pocket and took copious notes as they discussed the case.

Preston's stomach ached, and the nausea returned. "And so, it begins."

This detective resembled many men his age. About forty-five years old, with wrinkles in both his face and his clothing, and a small, middle-aged gut that hung over his belt. There was an air about this man, in the way he swaggered when he walked. The way he spoke to his men. His approach seemed all too familiar. The detective's demeanor brought Preston back to New York City—to a time when cops bullied him.

As an adult, he understood there were only a handful of corrupt cops who targeted unsupervised teenagers. The cops who aimed their wrath at him left behind an indelible mark. Preston wasn't a teenager any longer, and he'd done nothing wrong. Yet, he now felt as though he was a sixteen-year-old all over again. He kept a close eye on the detective, but he didn't take notes on his cell, which was his usual way to track information. Instead, he followed Johanna's lead—he pulled out his cell phone and pressed record. If there were questions later, he'd have his own evidence.

The detective, along with the officer in charge, inspected the scene. But they ignored the victim.

"Typical," Preston whispered.

They wore plastic gloves and removed the wallets from the bodies. The same wallets he clamored to get his own hands on. Doing so would have disturbed the crime scene. After they checked their identification, they removed a wad of cash, counted it, and marked it as evidence. The detective used his pen to lift the shirt around the knife enough to see the entrance wound. Preston zoomed in to record the detective stooping down to read the inscription on the handle. He then wrote something in his notepad.

After he inspected the scene, the detective watched the video, then gestured to see it again and again. And each time, he pinched the screen to zoom in and get a clearer view. Without a word, he lifted his eyes toward Preston. Both he and Ellie had lost faith in cops at an early age. Preston's attitude had changed when he left the streets. The moment the detective shifted his attention to him, those old feelings returned with a vengeance.

CHAPTER 7

As the detective moved toward him, Preston broke out in a sweat. He imagined being carted off in handcuffs. *And what then? Prison for manslaughter?* He knew there was nothing else he could have done in this situation. Those men would have killed them both. He'd have to take his chances with this detective. He stood to greet the man who could arrest him on the spot.

"I'm Detective Josh Ferris. I'm in charge of this case. Come with me, please."

Preston followed him to the ambulance, where he was asked to have a seat next to Ellie. *So much for separating witnesses.*

Rodriguez joined them.

"You're Professor O'Brien." Ferris then turned to Preston. "And you're Preston Bartlett. The man on the motorcycle."

Preston opened his mouth to speak but had momentarily lost his voice. He nodded, warily.

"Are you a student here?"

He shook his head.

"A professor?"

He cleared his throat and willed himself to speak. As he spoke, his voice cracked. "No."

Ferris wrote something in his pad. "I'd like to ask you a few questions, Professor. Are you up to it?"

"Yes."

"Can you tell me what happened?"

"Those men attacked me by my car, down there." Again, she pointed to a set of stairs next to the library. "When I got away from them, I ran up here. They followed, and I fought them until both men were unconscious. Or at least I thought they were. I turned around and found the smaller man on his knees, pointing a gun."

"You hid behind his partner," said Ferris.

"Yes. When I saw the gun, I dove behind him because the trees were too far away. He shot anyway. I didn't expect him to shoot his friend. Why are you asking these questions? Didn't you watch the video multiple times?"

Now Ferris cleared his throat. "Yes. It's been my experience victims often remember something new when they talk about what happened."

"Sounds reasonable, I guess."

"Have you ever seen these men before?"

"No."

"Have either of you seen the video?"

"No," said Ellie.

"No," said Preston.

"That reminds me. You returned my bag with my computer and keys, but my phone is missing," Ellie said to Rodriguez.

Rodriguez frowned. "The police secured the scene. There was no phone, Professor."

"I had it in my hands when they attacked."

Preston placed his own cell on speaker and dialed Ellie's number. Voice mail immediately picked up. "Did you turn your phone off?"

"No. I was reading email. I dropped it when they grabbed me from behind."

Ferris ordered another officer to recheck the area, then continued to ask questions. "So, most of this happened before Mr. Bartlett showed up."

"Yes!" argued Ellie. "Let me restate the obvious. I hid behind that behemoth because his partner started shooting a gun at me. Preston showed up while the shots were being fired and he then turned his weapon on Preston."

"And then Mr. Bartlett killed him," said Ferris.

"In self-defense." Her face now reddened.

"I'm not the enemy, Professor."

"Then try not to act like it."

Ellie was on edge from the attack, and Ferris was making it worse. Preston knew if he pushed her too far, she would push right back. It was clear she was losing patience with this cop.

Ferris shifted his attention to Preston. "I have multiple questions for you, Mr. Bartlett."

"Please, call me Preston." He wiped his sweaty hands on his jeans.

"Preston it is. You're not a student or a teacher. Why are you here?"

"I was helping Ellie open her office for the new semester. Afterward, we were going to Saxbys for breakfast. Are you familiar with the place?" He knew the answer after seeing the detective throw his Saxbys coffee cup in the trash minutes earlier.

"What kind of knife is that?"

"It's called the Kidlat." He reached to remove the sheath from his belt, but the detective stopped him.

"I don't need to see the sheath. It looks custom."

"It was a gift from my father. Will I get it back?"

"Yes, in time. Why carry that kind of knife?"

"Why not? I don't carry it to cause anyone harm."

"And yet two men are dead. One by your hand. I have all the information I need for the moment. My partner will drive you to the precinct to get your official statements. I'll meet you there. Thank you."

"Am I under arrest?" Preston's tone was belligerent. He knew better. Ferris's questions weren't unreasonable. He had, in fact, killed a man. But he couldn't help himself. This felt like an interrogation.

"That's not up to me." He then turned to leave.

"What did you expect me to do in this situation, Detective?" The word *detective* rolled off his tongue with disdain.

Ferris turned to face him. "Exactly what you did."

"I'm sorry, what did you say?" Preston was both shocked and relieved. Then angry. His face felt red with rage and his jaw twitched as he clenched his teeth.

"I'm not accusing you of anything, Preston. As the professor mentioned, I watched the recording multiple times. Though I must tell you, this conversation might have been more difficult without it."

Preston placed his hands over his face and let out a deep breath. "Thank God."

"The people you should thank are James Dawson and the woman who recorded the video. Between their statements and the recording, I have what I need."

Ellie stepped into Ferris's personal space. Close enough to smell his cologne. "What is the matter with you? You scared the crap out of him. For what?"

This was an aggressive move, and as she spoke, her tone became confrontational. Preston knew it was not helpful.

Ferris stepped back. "I apologize. I needed a complete understanding about what happened here. And if you must know, Preston, I wondered who you were."

"I don't understand."

"Why would an average guy handle a knife with such skill and precision? The knife went between that man's ribs. And I suspect the coroner will report it punctured his heart. All while you were driving on a motorcycle, taking fire. That takes serious skill."

"Believe me, it was a lucky shot."

"Yeah, I doubt it was. You didn't flinch when you drove toward a man shooting a gun, and the knife flew out of your hand and into his heart with ease. It was a practiced move. Not to mention you showed no signs of fear. Until now. Why is that?"

"Ellie is my best friend, Detective." He emphasized each syllable of the word *detective*. "They could have killed her. Saving her life was the only thing on my mind. As for the knife, it's added protection when I ride my bike into DC. Nothing more."

"Based on your reaction, you and the professor don't seem to care for cops. I suspect there's a good reason. You need to understand, I'm on your side. It may be hard to believe, but you can trust me. As I mentioned before, it was a heck of a throw. Who do you work for?"

"The FBI."

"In what capacity?"

"You don't have the proper clearance." It was true, to a degree. He could've told the man he worked in the cyber division and couldn't talk about his work. He chose not to. "Our fathers are on their way. Will you let them through the crowd?"

"Tell him to meet you both at the precinct." Ferris then handed Preston a card with the address.

"What about my motorcycle?"

"It's part of the crime scene. You can come back and get it after the CSI team leaves the area."

From the back of a police car, Preston sent a text with the address of the precinct to both of their fathers. "At least I'm not in handcuffs. This cop might not be as bad as I thought. Maybe we can trust him."

Ellie huffed. "Yeah, well, we'll see."

CHAPTER 8

PRESTON PACED AROUND THE TABLE, WIPING HIS SWEATY HANDS on his jeans, waiting for Ferris and his partner to arrive. This was not an interrogation room, which gave him some hope Ferris wouldn't charge him with a crime. And the people at the precinct weren't treating him like a criminal—at least not yet. That could change after Ferris completed his investigation.

When their fathers walked through the door, Preston was more than relieved. His stress immediately waned. He let out a breath.

"Thank God you're both safe." Vincent wrapped his arms around his daughter.

David walked over and hugged his son.

What Preston saw in his father's eyes was both fear and relief. He'd never seen that side of him. His father was a man of few words, with great compassion. Today, even those few words had temporarily escaped him.

David sat at the conference room table and looked around. "I can't believe we're in a police station. We brought you into our homes so you would never experience something like this. I'm so sorry this happened."

"I'm okay, Dad. Really."

He placed his hand over Preston's and squeezed. "Well, we're not. I want to know who these men are and why this happened. They're talking about another school shooting in America on the news."

"On television?" asked Preston.

"I don't know," said David. "We were in the car."

"This was a shooting on the grounds of a major university," said Preston. "It's a big story. Ferris did us a favor by bringing us here. But there is something you should know; there's a video of the attack. I'm guessing that's all over cable news by now. Neither of us have seen it yet."

Preston could see it on his phone, and it was already on Twitter. He wasn't quite ready to watch it.

"Who would record something like that?" asked David.

"A concerned student. She also called 911. It was all she could do to help. You should have seen her; she was so tiny. If she tried to help us, they would have killed her. Without her video, I might be behind bars. I may send her some flowers or a bottle of wine."

"I'd wait until after this is all cleared up."

Preston agreed with his father, but he still planned to get her address. "The media may classify this as another school shooting, but I'm not so sure."

"What do you mean?" asked David.

"It's a gut feeling, I guess. This isn't the time of year to have a school shooting. The campus is empty, and it was really early in the morning."

"You think it was a random attack?"

"I can't be sure. All I'm saying is it doesn't add up."

"If it's on the news, we need to call Olivia," said Ellie. "I don't want her to hear about this on the radio or get a news alert from Google."

"I already called her," said Vincent. "I told her to meet us at the farm."

———

Not five minutes after Vincent spoke those words, Olivia opened the conference room door.

"I thought we were meeting at the farm," said Vincent.

"This is a traumatic event. I belong here."

Ellie didn't want or need a therapist. She wanted her friend, and Preston wondered which version had walked through the door: Olivia or Dr. Lombardi.

"I came as fast as I could. Oh, my God, I can't believe this happened."

Preston grinned. *Friend.* She seemed frantic, which caught him off guard. Olivia had always been the person in complete control of any situation. But not today.

"How are you?" She didn't wait for Ellie to answer. She immediately checked her injuries. Her tone had momentarily switched to that of a doctor, making sure they treated her patient properly, then quickly reverted to a distraught friend.

"I'm tired, that's all."

Olivia embraced Ellie so tightly she could barely catch her breath.

"Breathe. Olivia, I can't breathe."

"Sorry."

After she released her grip, Preston noticed a change in her demeanor. It was anger, but much more. He'd never seen rage on Olivia's face before, not in the eighteen years they'd known each other.

Olivia moved to the front of the conference room and stood with her hands on her hips. "What happened? Who are these animals?"

"The police are looking into it," said Preston.

"'Looking into it'? They'd better be doing more than that."

No one could answer her questions. At least, not yet. He realized they'd all had time to calm down and come to grips with what had happened. Olivia needed time to catch up. His immediate concern was whether Ferris would charge him with a crime.

An hour later, Detective Ferris entered the conference room.

David stood. "I'm Admiral David Bartlett. Preston's my son. This is Ellie's father, Admiral Vincent O'Brien."

Ferris nodded and shook each of their hands. "How much do you know, Admiral?" He frowned. "Admirals."

"We know two men attacked Ellie, and my son protected her."

"Have you seen the video?"

"No!" said Vincent. "I'd like to see it now, please."

Ferris nodded. "It's probably all over YouTube, so there's no harm."

"I don't want to watch it. Or hear it," said Preston. "Not yet anyway."

Ferris placed his computer on the table and muted the sound before he hit play.

Preston watched their fathers' faces as they viewed the attack. They were both stunned.

"Thank God you're all right," said David. "They could have killed you both."

"Dad, the detective asked about my knife."

"It was a gift from me. Is there a problem?"

Ferris shook his head. "It's not the knife I wondered about. It was the skill it took to throw it into the man's heart. What job would require that level of expertise, and why is it that both Preston and Ellie are so calm? Preston seemed more concerned about me than killing a man."

"Vincent and I are former Navy SEALs, Detective. We trained them both on how to use a knife, among other things. When Preston was a teenager, he and Ellie competed at a local club. Ellie's as accurate with a knife as Preston."

Ferris seemed perplexed. "You trained them?"

"Yes," said David. "We also taught them to trust their training, which turned out to be a good thing, wouldn't you agree?"

"No question."

"It's also why they didn't fall apart."

"Training," Ferris repeated.

"Yes," said David.

"Preston, it sounds like your skills had nothing to do with your job at the FBI."

"I didn't say it had."

"Watch yourself. I'm getting a clearer picture of what happened here, but you're beginning to piss me off. All you had to do was tell me the truth."

David stopped him. "Detective, what do you know about them?"

"Not much. We've done a background check on each of them. They're both highly educated, in different fields, and clearly well trained. Neither has a record, not even a parking ticket. There was no need to dive any deeper. Why?"

"They were both foster kids. When Vincent met Ellie, she was homeless. We adopted them when they were teenagers. They took care of each other when they were alone. It's what they're doing now. Their reaction toward you isn't personal, it's instinct."

"I suspected as much." Ferris glanced toward Ellie and Preston. "But you're both adults now. You'll have to get over it at some point."

They each nodded in agreement.

"We taught them self-defense, but they're also responsible adults. Are you charging my son? If you are, I'll advise him not to speak."

"No. I spoke to my boss and the assistant district attorney, and we're all in agreement. Your son was defending himself and protecting the professor.

I'll speak to the witnesses, and we'll need your official statements, then you can go home. It may take awhile."

"Why give him such a hard time?" asked David.

"I don't believe I was. Admiral, two men are dead and it's my job to understand what happened. They were both defensive the moment I walked onto the scene."

Preston glared at Ferris, then reconsidered. "It's true, Dad. I couldn't help myself. It felt like I was being interrogated, and it brought me back to a different time."

"Don't worry about it. What did you find out, Detective?"

"Not much yet. We're just starting our investigation. Both men had $5,000 in $50 bills in their wallets, which is curious."

Preston struggled with whether to tell the detective about Ellie's instincts. He wanted to investigate the third person on his own and he didn't want to confuse the situation. When Ferris turned to leave, he stopped him. "Detective, Ellie thought someone else was there. Tell him, Ellie. Someone tried to kill you."

"He's right; you should tell us everything. It's the best way to find answers."

Ellie frowned. "I'm not keeping anything from you. There really isn't much to tell. It was my sixth sense kicking in, nothing more."

"Trust me to make those decisions."

Ellie relented. "The little guy might have mumbled something about another person when we were in the parking lot, or maybe something about a car. I can't even be sure of the words or the context. He could have been looking for his own car. It's all a blur."

"If your instincts are correct, it gives me cause for concern. They had an unusually high amount of cash in their wallets. Someone could have hired them to kill or abduct you. I'll investigate these men to see if I can find a link to the money. Preston, be thankful there was a video. My partner, Detective Logan, will take your statement. Meanwhile, we'll check out these men."

"Thanks." Preston stood and shook Ferris's hand.

Ferris walked toward the door, then turned around. "Watch your back, Professor."

After he left the room, Preston caught a glimpse of Vincent's expression.

It had changed. No longer did he see worry, or even anger. It was the cold, hard face of a Navy SEAL. A chill ran down Preston's spine.

"It's unbelievable that anyone would kidnap my daughter or worse," said Vincent. "I intend to find out who is responsible."

"I don't want to think about what they might have done," said Preston.

"Neither do I," said David. "The problem is, Vincent, we don't know what we don't know."

"Well, the detective can do his investigation, while we do our own."

"Care to share?" asked David.

"No. I need time to think first."

If they investigated, Preston wanted to be part of it. Until now, he hadn't appreciated what it meant when Navy SEALs defended their own family. "I'm in. I need to find out who's responsible for me killing a man."

David walked over and wrapped his arms around his son as though he were holding on for dear life. "I never wanted this for you. If I could have taken your place, I would have."

"You don't need to worry about me."

David patted his cheek. "It comes with the job. Vincent, these people are dangerous. I'd like to understand what you have in mind before the kids get involved."

"Give me until we get home, then we'll decide together. Everything will be within the law, Preston. Understand?"

"Yeah, yeah."

"Why not let the police handle it for now?" asked David. "We can get involved if we're not satisfied."

"I want to explore what happened from a different angle. It may be a dead end, in which case, I don't want to lead Ferris down the wrong path. We won't interfere."

"Wrong path?" asked Preston.

"Let's assume Ellie is correct and there was someone else there. She has spent her entire adult life on this campus, surrounded by a small group of close friends. Can you give me one good reason anyone would abduct my daughter? Or worse, kill her. Who was this third man?"

"If there was one," said Preston.

"He's right," said Ellie. "I can't be sure."

"Preston, do you trust Ellie's instincts?" asked Vincent.

"With my life."

"Me too. We start with the premise that there was a third man. Let Ferris do his own investigation. Hopefully, our paths will cross, and we can work together."

There were no answers to any of these questions, Preston knew. But he understood Ellie's father and his own. They wouldn't stop until they found the person responsible. Ellie once described her father as a dog with a bone when he committed himself to something. *Now*, Preston thought, *he's a Navy SEAL on a mission to save his daughter. God help the people responsible.*

———

After giving their statements, Olivia drove to the farm while David drove Preston, Vincent, and Ellie back to the university. The crush of cars and reporters had gone, but the yellow tape and CSI team remained, which meant Preston and Ellie still had no access to their vehicles. David and Preston walked the edges of the crime scene together while Ellie and Vincent waited in his car.

"I took photos of the crowd while I was here." Preston showed David a picture of the people holding their cell phones over their heads, taking photos or videos of the area. "I'll have to see what they uploaded once I get home."

"Good. Send them to me. We can both look for anomalies."

David separated from Preston to examine the crime scene on his own, though how far he could go was still restricted by the CSI team. Preston watched as his father analyzed the field where the bodies once laid. He moved to the bushes where Ellie hid, and the stairs where she ran for her life, then walked down to her car.

He completed his first pass and then started again, reliving the entire battle in his mind. To burn every detail into his memory. Preston wasn't sure how he felt about his father reconstructing the moment he threw a knife into a man's heart.

After David spoke to the CSI team, they released Preston's motorcycle and Ellie's car and they all drove to the farm.

CHAPTER 9

Olivia guided Ellie into Vincent's office, where she laid on the deep leather sofa, weathered from years of use. Her head sank into a large feather-down pillow while she wrapped her arms around another. With her eyes closed, she inhaled the scent—citrus and rosemary, with a hint of musk.

"These always remind me of my parents. Even Mom. It feels like she's still alive, working in the kitchen."

Olivia held a third pillow to her face. "You're right. The musk reminds me of your dad."

Vincent entered the room, carrying a vintage quilt made by his great-grandmother, Catherine O'Brien. The Celtic weave quilt had been hand-stitched in the now faded colors of Ireland, softened from a century of use. It was Ellie's favorite, especially when she slept in the old part of the house, lit by the fireplace. She could imagine Catherine in the room with her. He gently laid the quilt over Ellie, then patted her head. "I love you."

"I love you too, Dad."

"Do you have any herbal tea in the kitchen?" Olivia asked.

"Sure, I'll put the kettle on. One or two?"

"One for Ellie. Thanks."

Olivia closed the office door and sat on a chair next to Ellie, then reached over to take her pulse.

"I don't need a doctor, Olivia. There's nothing wrong with me. I'm a little tired, that's all."

"That's expected. You've been through a lot."

"Are you sure you're not the one who needs the tea?"

She grinned. "Maybe. I couldn't help imagining what they were going to do to you. Who were those people? Why would they want to hurt you?"

Ellie shrugged. "I guess we'll find out soon enough. Are you going to sit in here while I sleep?"

"Yes."

"As a friend or doctor?"

"Both. I'll watch for signs of stress from the attack. I doubt you'll have a problem. You're the bravest woman I've ever known."

"Thanks. That's sweet."

"I expect you'll take a quick nap, eat as much as Preston, and be back to normal."

Ellie shook her head. "Whatever normal is."

"I'm most concerned about what happens next. What if they send others in their place?"

"We don't know if there are any other people involved. It could have been a random act, and they're dead."

"Not with $5,000 in their pockets. Someone hired them. How are you, really? Between us girls."

"I'm confused. Angry. And grateful Preston showed up when he did."

"How are the men?"

Ellie's eyes widened. "You should have seen my dad's face when he first came into the conference room. He's out for blood. I think he's planning something."

"They'll never let this go. Not if there's someone else involved. And not until they're behind bars."

Ellie agreed. "None of them will."

Vincent returned with two cups of tea. "I brought one for each of you. Drink up. It'll help."

"What is it?" asked Ellie.

The scent reached Olivia as Vincent handed Ellie the mug. "Excellent choice. It's chamomile. It'll help us relax."

After she drank the tea, Ellie wrapped herself in her great-great-grandmother's quilt and fell into a deep sleep.

When David and Preston returned to the farm, Vincent heard Preston's stomach growl from across the room. He realized no one had eaten all day. The thirty-three-year-old man who still ate like a growing teenager had missed both breakfast and lunch. It was well past the time to feed the beast. He needed to make a quick meal for Preston, then work on lunch for everyone else. If he waited too long, Preston would rummage through the pantry, eating anything he could get his hands on. Just as he'd done when he was fifteen.

Preston made his way into the kitchen. "I smell bacon." He hovered over the stove, and pounced each time a piece of bacon hit the plate.

Vincent glared at him. "No more."

"What?" he said innocently, with his mouth full, licking his fingers as he waited for more.

"Go away. Now!"

Preston sulked and moved back into the family room.

When Vincent reached for a cabinet door to retrieve a plate, the glass front fogged up. He stepped back and watched as the letters *GA* were traced onto the glass. He quickly pulled out his phone and took a photo. Seconds later, the letters disappeared. "Well, well." After three months without an appearance, the ghost had returned with a message for him.

"*GA*. What does that mean?" he whispered. "Does this have anything to do with what happened today?" There was no response, although, based on his past experience, he hadn't expected one. As he filled Preston's plate, the answer came to him.

Preston entered the kitchen. "You okay, Uncle Vince? You're frowning."

"Yes, I'm fine. It's time to eat."

He wasn't fine, but at least he had somewhere to start. All he had to do was convince Ellie.

Vincent placed a three-egg omelet with sliced brie on the table in front of Preston. More bacon with a toasted English muffin slathered in butter soon followed. He understood, after years of experience, this meal was merely an hors d'oeuvre.

"Oh man, look at that. Thanks." Preston whiffed the plate, then devoured his meal. "Can I live here?"

"You always ask me that when you're hungry. The answer will

never change. NO!" He placed a large mug of coffee on the table next to Preston's plate, then stood in the kitchen to watch the man eat. "I can't afford to feed you. Besides, you're a better cook than I'll ever be."

"Thanks again. I'm starving."

"Believe me, it's the least I could do for the man who saved my daughter's life."

Preston nodded. "We're even. You saved mine."

Preston and Ellie had always been mindful of their next meal. Their reaction to food, Vincent realized early on, was primal, which he attributed to living in foster care or on the streets. Or, in Ellie's case, having to steal food to eat. He discovered neither were picky eaters. It was the food they gravitated toward, not the preparation.

Preston became an accomplished chef, with an organic garden in his backyard. He'd even put up food in case of an unforeseen disaster, and his pantry was always fully stocked. Vincent half expected to find a chicken coop next to the garden. Ellie's culinary skills were basic at best. Of the two, she remained the most cognizant of the moment he placed food on the table.

Ellie woke from her nap, relaxed but hungry, and as usual, she entered the kitchen as lunch was being served. They often sat together for their family meal, but for Vincent, this meal felt more important. He asked everyone to hold hands to create a circle of protection, then bowed his head to say grace. He wasn't giving thanks for the food, but for moving the bullets away from Ellie and Preston, and, God forbid, for guiding the knife into the gunman's heart.

After grace, David opened a bottle of wine while Vincent served his famous grilled cheese sandwiches. Some had prosciutto with American cheese, while others contained sliced apples with melted brie. Each was served with a bowl of hot chicken soup.

"Son."

Preston grinned. "Dad."

"Why were you at the university so early in the morning?"

Preston stopped mid-slurp, then peered over his soup spoon at his father. He wasn't ready to tell them what had happened. Not in front of

Olivia. She was the one person at the table who knew nothing about the ghost. He worried this news might blow her mind and couldn't imagine her taking the leap to believe.

"Preston, why were you at the campus so early?" David asked again. His voice was an octave lower. A sign he was losing patience. "Don't tell me it was to meet Ellie for breakfast. We all know better."

Everyone at the table nodded their heads in agreement, followed by mumbling about the likelihood of Preston being out of bed at dawn.

"Why was he on campus so early, Ellie?" asked David.

She shrugged. "We haven't talked yet. He said he'd explain later."

"Later is now!"

Preston stood to top off his mug, then gestured to ask whether anyone would like a refill. No one did. They each sat around the table with their eyes glued to Preston, waiting for his response as he continued to stall. "You won't believe me. I'm having a hard time believing it myself."

Ellie placed her elbows on the table with her head in her hands. "You don't need to tell me the details. I don't want to know."

"Well, you need to tell me!" His father's patience was growing thin.

Preston held his gaze, then took a deep breath to prepare them for what was to come. Or to delay the inevitable shock on Olivia's face.

His father was not amused. "Pull off the Band-Aid, son."

"Fine." As Preston crossed his arms over his chest, he noticed his own movements had unintentionally mimicked his father's. He shook his head. His eyes moved around the table from one person to the next, then stopped at Ellie. "Around five fifteen this morning, I heard a woman's voice. It woke me from a deep sleep. At first, I thought it was someone outside, so I put a pillow over my head and went back to sleep."

Everyone sat a little taller, waiting for the rest of the story. Their reaction reminded him of telling ghost stories around a campfire. When Preston continued, his voice became melodramatic. He couldn't help himself. After all, the subject was a genuine ghost.

"It happened a couple more times before I realized the voice was too clear to be outside." Preston stood and paced around the table. "It was in my room, coming from the television. I swear I turned the TV off when I went to sleep, and the room was empty. By then I was awake enough to understand what it was saying."

Olivia seemed perplexed, but Vincent appeared the most interested in his story. His father continued to glare.

"It?" asked Vincent.

"The ghost. She kept saying, 'Save her.' The last time, she shouted, 'Save Ellie,' and Clocky flew across the room and smashed against the wall. Sorry, Ellie, it's in pieces, but she got my attention. I damn near pissed my pants."

It had also gotten everyone else's attention.

"When I asked what she meant, she shouted, 'Danger.' That's when I got on my bike. To save you."

Ellie met Preston's eyes and placed her hands over her heart. "Thanks. I don't know what I would have done if you hadn't shown up."

"Seriously," said Vincent. "You wait until now to mention the ghost? Why? Is there more?"

"No more, I swear. Everything else is on the video. I didn't mention it because I hadn't told Ellie yet. I wanted to wait until she had some time to recover. To be honest, after bullets whizzed by my head, the ghost didn't seem as important." Preston saw a distressed look on his father's face and regretted his description. He knew it wasn't the ghost that brought the pained expression; it was seeing someone try to kill his own son on the video.

"The ghost wasn't there to haunt me, or you, Ellie. She was trying to warn you when she first appeared. Today, she wanted me to protect you."

"Crap," said Ellie. "Warn me? What's going on?"

He shook his head. "I wish I knew. Don't worry, we'll find out together."

Olivia's eyes widened. "I'm sorry, did you say ghost? What are you people talking about?"

Preston couldn't hold back a grin.

Olivia scowled at Vincent. "Why aren't you at least a little freaked out? Preston's talking to a ghost! Why is it no one seems astounded by the mere mention of a ghost? What else haven't you told me? I need the details to help Ellie."

She seemed, Preston thought, more irritated with them than concerned about a supernatural event. Which meant she believed nothing.

To clear the air, Ellie told Olivia everything. About the words "Find

Bun" being repeated night after night, which scared her half to death. About the weeks without sleep, about telling the ghost to piss off and the real reason she'd replaced the bathroom mirror. "I don't know where she went. I was just glad she wasn't here."

"'Find Bun'? What does it mean?" With each sentence, her voice grew louder. "Why didn't anyone tell me about this? Don't you trust me?"

Preston understood it was the deception, not the video, that caused the anguish on her face. It was like a knife to her heart. He doubted Ellie realized what they'd done.

"Stop!" Ellie shouted at Olivia. "I don't know what 'Find Bun' means." She used her fingers as air quotes, then stood and paced. "I heard a disembodied voice, Olivia. And if you want to know the truth, the idea of a psychiatrist analyzing me scared me more than the ghost."

"Why? What were you afraid of? After all these years of friendship."

"That I've lost my frickin' mind."

Even though Ellie's voice sounded angry, Preston detected something else altogether. *Fear.* He'd never seen fear in her eyes. Not like this. He believed her reaction had nothing to do with the ghost or even fighting the two men. It was the missing third man that had her on edge.

Vincent stepped in before the conversation turned down a path from which they'd never return as friends. "Calm down. Both of you." Olivia retreated to her chair, while Ellie, whose attitude was unapologetic, continued to pace. He blocked her. "STOP! Listen to what I have to say. And be warned, you won't like it."

Ellie had no choice but to comply. Each time she tried to move around him, he stepped in front of her. "WHAT!" She clenched her jaw.

"Sit down."

Preston remembered the tone, although it had been over a decade. Vincent hadn't raised his voice. He spoke succinctly, with a pause between each word. *Sit! Down!* It meant this wasn't a game, and they were to do as they were told. Even as adults, they felt compelled to obey, which had always perplexed him. They both knew Vincent wouldn't do anything. But he knew Ellie wasn't ready to listen to anyone, not even her own father. Her mind was still processing the day's events. She skirted around him.

"You both need to calm down and stay focused. Once Ferris gives us an update on his investigation, we can decide on our next steps."

Ellie nodded, then sat down. "Ghost! I hoped she had gone for good."

"Don't worry," said Vincent. "I told you before, the ghost is on your side. I'm sure of it."

CHAPTER 10

AS THE CONVERSATION TURNED TO FERRIS, THE DOORBELL rang. Vincent answered. There stood the man they'd been discussing. Ferris peeked inside, beyond Vincent. Without uttering a single word, he walked through the foyer and into the living room. Vincent allowed him to pass but was now unimpressed by this detective's manners.

"We need to talk," said Ferris.

He watched this stranger wander around uninvited, soaking in every detail about the victim. About him. To see how they lived. To discover what was important to them. He understood a detective's curiosity was the nature of the beast, but he questioned his motives.

"You like antiques?" asked Vincent.

"Sorry. I often find myself enamored with the past, imagining what it was like to live here back then." He strolled over to the large stone walk-in fireplace with an iron pot hanging on a swing arm, and utensils on their hooks. "A family lived in this exact room. They cooked meals in that pot." He moved toward the old family photos hung on the wall. "Was this their house? What, a hundred years ago?"

"Closer to a hundred sixty. Séamus O'Brien, built the house in 1860. He was a stonemason from Ireland. There have been additions with each generation."

"Incredible. I noticed a message carved in the lintel over the door. What does it mean?"

"*Baile Mo Chroí* is Gaelic. Its translation is *Home of My Heart*."

Vincent called everyone into the living room. Preston, the note taker, was the first to appear, followed by Olivia. She would not only listen to Ferris, but analyze every word. Ellie, who didn't want to be there in the first place, walked in with David. He was Vincent's backup should things go awry. Ferris knew everyone in the room except Olivia. Vincent introduced them, then offered him a seat. The others scattered around the room.

"Good afternoon, Professor." He handed Ellie her cell phone. "Angel Clayton found it in the bushes close to your car and turned it in to campus security."

"I know Angel. You can trust her. And please, call me Ellie."

He nodded.

"Didn't the police check that area multiple times?" asked Preston.

"They did. Angel received a tweet requesting volunteers to help search for your phone. I believe the tweet came from you, Preston. After the crime scene was clear, the students who live in the area went out in force to search. Angel found it when she kicked the mulch around."

"I sent out a tweet to a couple of students I know. They must have passed it along. I guess your professional investigators missed it."

Preston's attitude toward the police remained front and center. Ferris appeared unfazed.

"It happens sometimes. Although, someone could have found it earlier. When you sent the tweet, they could have decided it was too hot to keep and placed it where a student would find it."

Preston relented. "That's possible."

"How are you feeling, Ellie?" Ferris asked.

"I'm good, thanks."

"I have information about the men who attacked you."

The room fell silent, waiting for the additional information. Before Ferris spoke, Preston placed his cell phone on the table and pressed record. "Do you mind?"

"No. That's fine. Their names were Manuel Nunez and Duane Young." Ferris flipped through the pages from the small pad he kept in his shirt pocket. "They each had long records, but mostly petty crimes, and they both had ties to a gang when they were juveniles. What troubles me is why these men would move from petty crimes to murder for hire. That's a big jump."

"I agree," said Olivia.

He frowned at Olivia, as though he wanted to ask a question, but shook his head.

"I've done some profiling in my past," said Olivia.

"Good to know." He stared at her a little longer than was appropriate.

Ferris's focus appeared to be split, which often happened when Olivia entered a room. She was beautiful and brilliant and caught people's attention.

Vincent redirected the conversation to him. "What did you find?"

"I spoke to the families. They told me the two men hadn't worked in a while and were desperate for money. Based on their statements, I don't think they were killers." He paused, then turned to Ellie. "This means your instincts were correct. I believe a third man paid them to abduct you. It's a guess. Our investigation is in the beginning stages."

Preston grimaced.

"Preston, I'm not at all suggesting you shouldn't have killed the man. People make their own choices in life. They tried to abduct Ellie, armed with a gun. When he shot the gun, he intended to kill you both. You had no choice. Don't worry, we'll find out what happened."

"Thanks. I appreciate it," said Preston. "Who were they?"

"They were day laborers. The family gave me the address where they waited for work. I just returned from there. A tall, thin, white man, about six feet, with gray hair picked up the two men in a dark-blue BMW X5 twin power turbo V8."

Ferris grinned. "They couldn't give me a more accurate description of the man, but they knew their cars. They gave me every detail, even the make of the tires, and the color of the pinstripe. Unfortunately, not the number on the license plate." He delayed for a moment before he continued. "Ellie, would you mind if we speak privately?"

"Sure."

"Not without me," said Vincent.

"Of course."

Vincent guided Ferris down the hallway, where wide plank floors with hand-forged nails flowed into the kitchen addition. A second large walk-in fireplace caught Ferris's attention.

"Look at these floors." Ferris stood in front of the fireplace. "How did you manage this? Who does this kind of work these days? Check out the craftsmanship."

Vincent thought it best to humor the man, to stay in his good graces, and to get information for his own investigation. His patience, however, was wearing thin. "We're related to stonemasons in Ireland who wanted to visit America. This way, Detective." Vincent directed him into his office through massive wooden double doors.

"Nice." Again, Ferris strolled around. He stopped at a photo of Ellie and Preston in a flying kick with both Vincent and David in the background. "You really did train them."

"Yes."

There were photos of Vincent, his late wife Evelyn, and Ellie. There were also photos of David with his late wife and Preston scattered among the shelves. And, of course, Olivia with her family.

"You've been close for years."

"We have," said Ellie.

Vincent noticed Ellie now had the same tone toward this man as Preston. She was losing patience with him.

"Can we get on with it? You can have a tour later, after we find out who's trying to kill me. Why did you want to meet alone?"

Vincent understood Ellie's suspicions. Ferris was essentially inspecting their home without a search warrant. "Have a seat, Detective." He indicated a chair in the corner.

Ferris sat in a wing-back chair while Vincent sat next to Ellie on the sofa. He placed two manila folders from his briefcase on his lap. "Sorry. I love old houses, but I also wanted to understand the relationships in your life."

"There's nothing to see here," Vincent insisted.

"I agree. Everyone is more protective than defensive. Even Preston. Those two men tried to kill you, Ellie, and I don't believe this was a random act. Because of that, I needed to delve into your entire life."

Ellie frowned. "My life!"

"It's standard procedure. I needed to find out if someone from your past could be responsible. You are the target."

"Target?" said Vincent. "I hadn't thought about it in those terms."

"I've already spoken to a few students, and I met with professors in your department."

"Why?" asked Ellie.

"To see if anyone had a grudge against you. Not one person thought it was even possible. Your students love you. Then I remembered your father said he adopted you."

Ellie interrupted his train of thought. "So what if I am adopted? What does that have to do with anything?"

"Bear with me, please. I'll explain."

Ellie nodded.

"I found out you grew up in Savannah. Because of that, I took a leap and expanded my search into Georgia."

Ellie's nails dug into Vincent's arm.

It was all he could do to pull away and place her hand in his. He glanced down and checked for blood.

"Why Savannah?" she asked. "Couldn't this be random?"

"Not if someone hired them. You have a good life here, Ellie. My search is preliminary, but I could find no reason for anyone to hurt you. I needed to rule out your past."

"I haven't been there since I was nearly fifteen. Why would you even consider Savannah?"

"I can't explain it—call it a hunch. I found two items of interest." Ferris placed one file on the coffee table in front of him, though he didn't open it.

"No one cares about me down there. They never have."

Ferris continued, despite Ellie's objections. "I found out your foster father attacked you when you were fourteen."

"WHAT!" Vincent glared at Ellie. "Why wouldn't you tell me that?"

Ellie rolled her eyes. "This is old news."

"Don't worry, Vincent; she wasn't hurt. It seems your daughter could defend herself even before you trained her."

"Your point?" Ellie asked, angrily.

"According to the report, you got away from your attacker long enough to grab a bat and beat the hell out of him. You broke his jaw, an arm, and multiple ribs." Ferris smiled.

When he met Ellie's eyes, Vincent saw compassion. Admiration, even.

"I bet he didn't expect that. He deserved what he got. He tried to rape a child. The report states your testimony put him behind bars for ten years. Not long enough. They should have thrown away the key."

Ellie agreed.

"You were a brave kid. But I couldn't find anything about you after the trial. They sealed your juvenile records."

"I moved to New York. That's where I found my dad."

"Found him? I assume there's more to that story, but it's not related to this investigation. You were very fortunate."

"Yes, I was—I am."

"I checked into your attacker to see if he could be responsible for what happened today. I don't see this guy as a threat. He's old now, bald, and only about five feet six. Not six feet with gray hair. He doesn't fit the description."

Ferris lifted the second file. "This is the one that concerns me." When Ferris placed it on the table, he slid it toward Vincent, not Ellie, then opened it. There were two photos stapled on the left side of the folder. Police and medical reports were stapled to the right. The first photo was of a child, around three or four years old, lying in a hospital bed with intravenous bags attached to every part of her tiny body. She lay unconscious, intubated, and close to death.

"Mother of God," said Vincent.

"Someone poisoned you," said Ferris. "Do you know what happened?"

Ellie remained silent.

The second photo was after Ellie had woken up. She sat curled up in the middle of the bed, staring into the camera. She looked, Vincent thought, so terrified he could almost feel her tremble. He closed his eyes in disbelief.

"This is still an open case."

"Are you telling me someone got away with this?" shouted Vincent. That someone could hurt a child and not be in prison astounded him.

"Unfortunately, yes. What do you remember, Ellie?"

"Nothing. That time of my life is a complete blank."

"Well, that makes sense. A child would block out a traumatic event to survive."

Vincent placed his arm around Ellie.

"What happened to your birth parents?" asked Ferris. "Do you remember their names? Or can you describe them?"

"No, to both questions."

Vincent found out more about his daughter in this one interview than he had over the past eighteen years. He listened as Ellie answered Ferris's questions. As he read the medical and police reports, his anger grew.

"Ellie," said Ferris. "The only part of your life that raises any flags is in this file."

"I'm sorry, I don't remember. And I never wanted to know."

"I understand, but I'm afraid you have no choice now. Someone tried to kill you, twice. Why? Who would do this to a small child? And what happened to your parents? That's why the case is still open, and why I believe this is the key to what happened today. At the very least, I'll make some calls."

"May I make a copy of your files?" asked Vincent. "After Ellie has had time to absorb what's happened, she may decide to read them."

"It's not procedure, but since they're Ellie's records, I have no problem with it."

Vincent pulled the two manila folders from behind his desk and walked to the copier. Once he created his own files, he handed the originals back to Ferris.

"I'll let you know what I find out."

After Vincent walked Ferris out, he returned to the kitchen and placed the manila folders in the center of the table. Preston took the one on top. David opened the other. And Olivia stood behind Preston to read over his shoulder.

"Ellie has not read them yet."

They all glanced up to acknowledge they heard what he'd said, then returned to the page.

He removed a bottle of Jameson Whiskey and two glasses from a kitchen cabinet, then opened the door to his office. Inside, he found Ellie on the sofa in the fetal position. He poured a shot of whiskey for each of them. "Ellie, sit up and drink this. It'll help."

He knew she preferred beer or wine, but she didn't protest. After drinking it down, she choked. "How can people drink this stuff?"

He smiled. "It's an acquired taste."

"Are the cases linked, Dad? How is that even possible?"

"I don't know. But I agree with Ferris. We need to check into it."

A few minutes later, she placed the glass on the table and stood. "Let's get this over with."

"Are you sure you're ready? You should take a little time to grasp all of this."

"Of course I'm not ready. All I know is the sooner I find these people, the sooner I get my life back." When she held her hands out in front of her, they trembled. "This needs to stop."

She walked out of the office, sat at the kitchen table, and saw the photo of the small child hooked up to machines. She closed her eyes, then placed her hand over her mouth and ran into the bathroom. When she returned, she sat next to Preston. "I can't read these."

Preston rubbed her back, and she placed her head on his shoulder. "It's okay. You don't have to. That's why we're here."

"What happens now?" she asked.

"We go to Savannah," said Vincent.

"Savannah?" asked Preston. "You think who ever attacked Ellie in Georgetown is connected to what happened in Savannah decades ago? Why?"

"They tried to kill a child. If someone could do that, what makes you think they wouldn't follow her here? I don't think this will end until we find out the truth."

"The truth about what? There's not much to go on."

"About Ellie," said Olivia. "About what happened before that photo."

"Why would anyone from Georgia come after me now? I haven't been there or spoken to anyone from there since I was a teenager."

Vincent agreed with Ellie. On the surface, it made little sense. But he knew something the others didn't. "It started there."

Ellie frowned. "And you think it ends there?"

"I do."

"Crap."

Vincent snickered at his daughter. "Is that all you have to say?"

"YES! Do I have a choice in any of this?"

"No!"

She glared at her father. "You do realize it's the middle of August."

"I do."

"Bless your heart," she said with a strong Southern drawl.

"Watch yourself, darlin'. I know what that means."

Ellie grinned, though everyone else appeared puzzled.

"What does it mean?" asked Olivia.

"Let's just say it's not a compliment," said Vincent.

Preston pulled out his phone to research the temperatures in Savannah. "It's in the 90s. It's like that here some days."

"Yes," said Ellie. "Now check the humidity."

Preston searched again. "Humidity is in the 80s. Well, that's not good."

"People who live in Savannah don't want to be there in August. Be prepared to melt into a puddle on the sidewalk."

Preston searched the words "bless your heart" on his phone and found multiple definitions. Some were what you'd expect, but one made his eyes widen. "You actually said that to your father? You are a brave woman."

She smiled. "Or incredibly stupid."

"What does it mean?" asked Olivia.

"It could be a term of fondness or sympathy."

"What's wrong with that?"

"Or it could be the sweetest 'fuck you' you've ever heard."

Olivia laughed. "I go with stupid."

"I won't ask which one you had in mind," said Vincent. "We should go to Savannah tomorrow."

"Tomorrow!" said Ellie.

"Someone is trying to kill you. This is not a vacation."

"We're going hunting," said Preston.

"For what?" asked Ellie.

"For clues about who wants you dead," said Preston.

"How do you propose we do that? Shouldn't we have a plan? Or are we going to drive around Savannah to see what happens? Or better yet, wait until a ghost tells us where to go."

Preston grinned. "I go with the ghost."

Ellie laughed. "You would."

"We start with Social Services," said Olivia. "I don't think they'll help us over the phone. But you'll be asking about yourself, not someone else. Take your identification, your passport and driver's license. Even your birth certificate and adoption papers."

"Why?" asked Ellie.

"You'll have more success if you look them in the eyes and have documents to prove who you are. People have a harder time denying a request in person. When they realize you're from out of town, they'll be more accommodating. It is the South. I've always been told everyone's so much nicer down there."

Ellie snorted. "It's Social Services, Olivia. Have you seen how many cases they deal with every day? Clearly you've never dealt with them."

"Well, the drive might trigger memories. Either way, it's an important trip. Do you recall the name of your social worker?"

"Yes. That's a name you never forget. Her name is Maria Garcia. She drove me from one home to the next."

"How many homes?" Olivia asked.

"I'm not sure. And before you ask, I'm not dodging your question. A large part of my life is a complete blank. It was true when I said I didn't remember."

"Well, we have a name," said Vincent. "It's a place to start. We'll leave tomorrow morning. I suggest everyone go home and pack, then spend the night here. That way we'll get an early start."

"I'll stay behind," said David. "I can keep in touch with Ferris while you're gone."

CHAPTER 11

EVERYONE RETURNED TO THE FARM, READY TO LEAVE IN THE MORNing. Once they settled in, they moved into the larger, more comfortable family room to discuss their strategies. As usual, Vincent had taken charge while Preston took notes. "I'll update Ferris after we're finished here."

"And tell him what?" asked Ellie.

"I'll let him know where we're going, and why. He can investigate the case from this end, and David will be available if he needs any local help. Frankly, I imagine he'll be happy to get us out of his hair."

Ellie grinned. "By us, you mean you."

He smiled. "True. I don't believe Ferris will find anything. Do you? I'm going on the premise that someone hired those men to abduct you. There's nothing in their criminal record to suggest they're rapists or murderers. And let's not forget, they were desperate for money. We should focus on your life in Savannah to see if the two paths cross. I suspect they will."

"You're connecting my thirty-year-old case with this one. Why? I'm having a hard time following the logic."

"It's a gut feeling."

"A gut feeling?" said David. "What exactly is that gut telling you?"

Vincent knew, after so many years of friendship, he could never fool David. He tried to ignore his question without success.

"Everything should be on the table, Vincent. Especially if the kids are putting themselves at risk."

Vincent glared at his friend, but he understood. He pulled out his phone and displayed the message the ghost had written on the cabinet door. "This happened when I was making Preston's eggs." They each leaned in to see the letters *GA* written on the foggy glass.

Ellie was the first to understand its meaning. "You think the *GA* means Georgia."

"I do."

"So, we're driving to Georgia because of the f—" She hesitated, as though to curb her language. "Ghost."

She sounded belligerent, but Vincent shared her concerns. "That's part of it. It's the only thing that makes sense. We should at least investigate to rule it out."

After learning about a small piece of his daughter's history, he believed every fear Ellie'd had, every heartache she'd felt, happened in Savannah. He intended to find the underlying cause, with or without her. But he worried about her emotional state. Would facing her past give her a sense of clarity, or would it cause more harm than good? He didn't know. Either way, they had no choice.

"Which hotel would you recommend, Ellie?" asked Vincent. "I realize it's been a long time, but any ideas?"

"Well, it depends. Do you want luxurious or average?"

Vincent considered for a moment. He wanted Ellie to have a unique experience. To create a few good memories to counter the bad. Yet, he recognized that was a lot to expect from one hotel. "Luxurious."

"Well—we should stay at the Marshall House Hotel. It seems appropriate on so many levels."

"Why there?"

"It's one of the oldest hotels in Savannah. And there are rumors it's haunted by ghosts." She laughed. "Sounds ideal for us."

Vincent rolled his eyes.

"When I was a teenager, I peeked in the windows. It's beautiful."

Preston Googled the Marshall House Hotel and found an article about Ghost City Tours. "Listen to this." He read from the website. "Savannah's most haunted hotel, the Marshall House, is well known to any fans of ghosts and hauntings in Savannah. Once a Civil War hospital, this hotel always seems to have more than its fair share of ghostly activity and paranormal happenings. Stay here for a haunted Savannah experience!"

"Seriously?" said Olivia.

Ellie laughed.

Hearing laughter in the room, especially coming from Ellie, eased the tension. That she was talking about a ghost and not throwing bottles into mirrors was an improvement.

"Preston, don't you think one ghost in our lives is enough?" asked Vincent.

"Our ghost might find a friend and leave us alone."

"We can hope," said Ellie.

"Do you want me to read more?" When Olivia glared at him with daggers in her eyes, he stopped reading.

"You'd like the area, Olivia," said Ellie. "It's in the historic district."

Vincent volunteered to make reservations for four rooms. "We'll see how haunted this place really is. Next question—do you want to fly or drive?"

"Drive," said Preston. "I can keep tighter controls on my equipment. And we won't have to worry about getting our weapons through security."

"Weapons?" said Olivia. "I never even gave that a thought. Are you sure we shouldn't let the police handle this?"

Both Preston and Ellie said, "No!" and Vincent reassured Olivia he would involve the police. Ferris would investigate locally, and, if necessary, he'd contact the police in Savannah.

She shook her head. "If necessary?"

Preston dismissed her concerns. "I have my dad's knife and my gun. We might want to check the armory for more ammunition. At least a couple more clips."

The armory was in the basement of the original house. A thick wooden door opened into a large windowless room with stone walls and rough, hand-hewn wooden floors. It had been the family root cellar for generations, until Prohibition, when it became the ideal cool, dry place to store, hide, and even distill barrels of Irish whiskey.

After Vincent had taken over the family home, he removed the old empty barrels. The massive wooden door now disguised another made of heavy steel with a combination lock. The cellar, which still held the slight aroma of Irish whiskey, became a walk-in safe, which Ellie and Preston had aptly named the armory. Over the years, the name caught on, though Vincent wasn't a fan. It brought attention to a space he'd rather keep secret.

"I'm bringing my lock picks," said Ellie.

"I have mine, too," said Preston. "It's a good idea to have duplicates."

Olivia placed her hands over her eyes as though she were about to explode. "What is the matter with you people? You're acting like you're going to a frickin' war."

Whenever Olivia used anything that remotely resembled a swear, it got everyone's attention. It meant they needed to listen. And it meant there would be a verbal rant. The entire room stopped what they were doing to hear her concerns.

"Why do you need any of this? I can see a gun for protection, but how much ammunition do you need? And what are you going to be hacking into with all that computer equipment?" she said to Preston, then stood and paced around the room before she shifted her attention to Ellie. "What locks are you going to be picking? Aren't you going overboard?"

"No, we're being prepared," said Preston. "Maybe you should stay home."

His face held the tiniest grin, though it was clear to Vincent, he wasn't joking. After years of experience with Olivia, he knew she was just getting started.

"I'm going to Savannah. You're asking Ellie to walk through places she's blocked for decades. I need to be there, as her doctor, but also as her friend. This is nonnegotiable."

Though Vincent had never considered asking Olivia to stay home, he now wondered how she would handle this trip.

"Olivia, what's the worst thing that could happen? The hope is we'll be lugging all this stuff around for no reason," said Preston.

"No, you could get arrested for killing someone."

"Olivia," Vincent said, sternly. "Be careful." He knew the torment Preston felt about killing a man, and he doubted Olivia thought that statement through. She was more upset than he'd realized.

She frowned, then reconsidered. "Sorry, Preston. That was a stupid thing to say."

Preston brushed it off. "It's okay. If something happens, we'll have you there to bail us out." Only this time, when he looked directly at Olivia, his smile covered his entire face.

"What if you're shot?"

That same smile disappeared. "Don't even go there."

"Well, someone has to. Especially after what happened today. This is not a game, Preston. These men are serious. They could've killed you both."

"Which is why we need our weapons," insisted Preston.

"Which is why the police should handle this," Olivia insisted, then stormed out of the room and returned with a beer in her hand.

David followed her lead and brought drinks for everyone. "We could all use one of these. Son, you and Ellie should go to the armory to collect what you'll need after we're finished here."

Ellie sat in a large chair with her legs pulled up to her chest, drinking her beer. She appeared nervous, and Vincent understood. This was uncharted territory. Someone wanted her dead. That was bad enough. Now she was going to the one place she'd blocked from her memory. A place she ran away from, hoping to never return.

———

Vincent was the first to rise in the morning. David soon joined him. The sun had barely risen, but both men often woke before dawn. After a lifetime in the Navy, it had become engrained in their DNA.

First, he made coffee for the lot of them, then spent the early morning hours preparing food for the trip. David added drinks to a cooler while Vincent made sure there was food for everyone, including Olivia, who ate like a bird. A vegetarian, gluten-free bird.

Everything was ready, except for his three passengers, who had yet to make their way downstairs.

"You look worried," said David.

"I am. We don't know what we're walking into, and we both know how that can turn out. I'm most worried about Olivia."

"Why?"

"Because Preston and Ellie have deep-seated survival instincts. Olivia does not. She learned to fight in a gym—there's a difference. She'll be there to help Ellie, and I understand she can take care of herself—"

"But?"

Vincent threw ice in the cooler with a little more force than he'd intended. "I guess this whole thing pisses me off. Someone wants my daughter dead, and we don't even know why!" He slammed down the lid. "Did you see Ellie's expression last night?"

"I did. It reminded me of when she first moved here. She didn't trust anyone back then. God, I remember those eyes. She'd sit in the corner and her eyes moved around the room, checking everything. I wasn't sure how it would work out for you guys."

"We weren't sure either, but Evelyn and I agreed she wasn't going back on the streets."

"And now she's a professor at Georgetown. Who would have guessed?"

Vincent nodded. "Yeah, well, look at her now. She's preparing herself. She'll have to sharpen those survival instincts."

"And she will."

"I hope so. It's been a long time since she lived on the streets."

"She's a powerful woman, Vincent. And she's more prepared now than she was when she was fifteen. I'm not worried about her. I am a little worried about you."

Vincent raised his brow. "Me? I'll be fine. All I need is for Ellie to walk away from this alive and well. I can't guarantee what will happen to the person responsible."

"I'm with you there. Olivia's right, you know. You should give the police time to do their job."

"Olivia's right about a lot of things, and I'll deny it if you tell her I said that. My instincts are telling me to go. I have to trust them."

"Okay then."

It was seven o'clock when Olivia entered the kitchen, perfectly dressed, down to the makeup. Vincent realized he'd never seen her without makeup or designer clothes. Even the T-shirt she wore had a label plastered across the front.

Ellie was next to make it downstairs with damp, curly hair, wearing shorts and a Georgetown T-shirt with fresh butterfly bandages on her knees. Without makeup, her freckles were more pronounced. She resembled an image of the girl next door. *The girl next door with the skills of a ninja*, Vincent thought, then hid a grin.

"I'm going to drag my son's ass out of bed." David left the room with a large mug of coffee.

Thirty minutes later, they sat down for breakfast, though it was quieter than normal. Everyone seemed eager to get started, but they also appeared a little anxious. Vincent believed this trip would change all of them, though how was unknown. They were going hunting for an animal, but this animal was human. He considered the instinct to survive absolute, and Ellie had fine-tuned those instincts during the first half of her life. Now she'd have to summon those senses again. He wondered whether that was even possible.

Olivia, he noticed, kept a close eye on her friends. As a former profiler, she would check for kinks in their self-made armor. Preston would be the one to collect the data, and Olivia would analyze it from a human standpoint. This was an impressive team, but were they prepared to take on this task and live with the consequences? He hoped so.

After breakfast, Vincent and David finished the dishes while the others packed. They stacked the luggage by the front door and filled to-go cups of coffee for the first leg of their trip. Preston filled two. Vincent questioned how many stops they would make along the way. The man had the tiniest bladder, but only when stuck in a car. It had always been his excuse to stretch his legs.

"I'm loading the car," Vincent shouted as a warning. "We'll be leaving in a few minutes. Start hitting the bathroom." He looked directly at Preston, as he had when he was a teenager.

"Shotgun," Preston called out.

Ellie slapped him on the back of the head, then ran to the car.

"A few minutes ago, they were checking their weapons. Now they're calling shotgun," he said to David. "What's wrong with this picture?"

David smiled. "You know my son. It's his way of cutting tension."

"True."

Vincent climbed behind the driver's seat of the SUV to begin their ten-hour road trip to Savannah.

CHAPTER 12

August 23, 2017

THE DRIVE TO SAVANNAH WAS UNEVENTFUL. PRESTON SAT IN THE front seat for the first half of the trip. Both Preston and Olivia had their noses in their phones, while Ellie stared out the window. She seemed, Vincent thought, to be in her own world. And with each mile they drove away from the city, the more withdrawn she became. What he would give to know what she was thinking.

Vincent used the car's GPS to direct them around any traffic backups, and Preston used Google Maps on his phone. Each device announced where to go in a distinct voice, with a slight delay between messages. Vincent would hear the woman in his car's speakers, and a few seconds later, another female voice from Preston's cell would order him to turn right or left. He laughed every single time. "There's an echo in this car. At least the two women agree."

He glanced in the rearview mirror and saw Ellie asleep, with her head on Preston's shoulder and with their fingers intertwined. They weren't a couple, at least not yet. But they were adults in their thirties. It was time for them to decide whether they had a future together. He suspected this trip would be the catalyst to help them move forward, one way or the other.

They drove straight through, with bathroom breaks along the way and the obligatory stop for ice cream at South of the Border. They all wanted to keep going, to see where Ellie had lived, and to find out what this was all about.

Hours later, Vincent's GPS announced, "You have reached your destination," and after a slight delay, Preston's had done the same. Something was wrong. This was not their hotel. They'd stopped on a small neighborhood road somewhere in Savannah. At least he'd hoped it was Savannah. At that moment, he didn't know where he was, although he could guess who was responsible for this misdirection.

Everyone else in the car was sound asleep. "Guys," said Vincent, loud enough to wake them. "We have a problem."

———

Ellie was the first to get out of the car. She walked in a complete circle, taking in the neighborhood. She smelled lavender and roses. "I remember this place. Or at least the smells."

Lavender grew in front of a picket fence to mark the edge of the property, with a thick bouquet of pink climbing roses. It was a wonder it hadn't collapsed under the weight. Beyond the fence, on each side of the driveway, were one-hundred-year-old live oak trees dripping with Spanish moss, creating a tunnel-like canopy.

Preston squinted. "Do I see water? Is that a boat pier?"

When Ellie looked beyond the trees, she saw something else. Something familiar. The colors of summer surrounded the entire front yard. A flower-lined brick path meandered its way to the sizeable home with crisp white paint and dark-blue shutters. Enormous blue hydrangeas spanned across the front of the house. Baskets of impatiens hung on the deep Southern-style front porch with a haint blue ceiling. "Check out the house."

"Oh my God," said Vincent. "It's exactly like your house, down to the landscaping. All that's missing is the swing hanging from the tree."

"Why?" It was the only word Ellie could manage. She felt overwhelmed by the smells, by the house.

"Why what?" asked Preston. "Why are we standing in front of your house on steroids? Or why are we on this street in the first place? I can answer both questions with one word."

Ellie snarled. "The fucking ghost."

"Okay, technically that's three words, but you get the idea." He gave Ellie a wink, and when she shoved him, he laughed.

"Why don't we go back to the car to talk about this?" said Olivia. "We can look at an old-fashioned map to see where we are."

Ellie ignored her friend. Without saying a word, she raced toward the house, leaving everyone behind. She appeared to be in a trance, unaware of everyone and everything.

"Where are you going?" asked Vincent.

When there was no response, they followed. By the time they'd caught up, she stood on the front porch, gazing out at a rainbow of colors scattered throughout the extensive property. No one spoke. They each gave Ellie the time to digest what was happening. Vincent was the first to walk onto the porch.

"Olivia and I will stay here." Preston stood at the bottom of the stairs. "We'll wait here until the police arrest us for trespassing."

Ellie ignored him.

"What's going on?" asked Vincent. "Do you remember something?"

"Yes, everything. Or at least everything about the property. The roses on the fence. The smell of the lavender. I planted annuals by that brick path, though it was more like digging in the dirt. But I have no memory of people. When I was here, the hydrangea along the front of the house and the roses on the fence were much, much smaller."

"So, you've been here before?" asked Olivia. "That may be an important memory."

"It's more than that. I think I lived here. I can't tell you when or with whom or even for how long, but I must have been little."

"Why?" Olivia asked.

"I don't know. It's a feeling, that's all. This is frustrating."

While Ellie stood on the porch, the front door opened. It startled everyone. A man, about her age, stood at the entrance. A woman in her fifties stood in the hallway behind him. Ellie stared at him without knowing what to say. She looked him square in the eye to see whether something, anything, seemed familiar. But he was a stranger.

"I'm Vincent O'Brien. This is my daughter, Ellie. Behind me are Preston Bartlett and Olivia Lombardi."

"I'm Alexander Mathews. This is my mother, Charlotte. What can I do for you?"

"Well, it's hard to explain. Do you have a minute?"

There was no minute to explain. After Vincent had introduced everyone, Ellie peeked inside. Without asking permission, she moved past Alexander and walked into the house.

"Hey, what are you doing?" Alexander followed her.

"Ellie," said Vincent. "Come back here." He also followed.

Ellie walked past Charlotte.

"What are you doing?" Alexander asked again as he trailed behind Ellie. The sound of his voice changed from friendly to angry.

Ellie ignored him. She didn't run. First, she strolled into the kitchen and breakfast room, then moved through the dining room and family room. Then into the office. She checked every detail and touched nothing.

"Are you crazy?" Alexander called out.

She stopped for a moment and turned. "A few months ago, I would have been able to answer that question."

She then turned around and moved toward the front door but stopped when something caught her eye. There was a pink bunny sitting on the fireplace mantel in the formal living room. It seemed an odd place for a child's toy. After a closer look, she gasped.

The bunny was hers.

A tangible piece of her past, one she could hold in her hand, sat right in front of her. If only she could move her arms to reach for it, or her hands to lift it, or any other muscle in her body. She stood frozen in place, afraid to touch the bunny for fear she might relive a memory she'd blocked for a lifetime. Memories of why she lived in this house and with whom.

Charlotte moved past Alexander, toward the fireplace. She picked up the bunny and placed it in Ellie's hands. "I believe this belongs to you?"

Ellie nodded, then closed her eyes and pressed the stuffed animal against her heart and let out a deep sigh. When she looked at her father, a tear ran down her face.

Preston and Olivia moved into the room to help, but Vincent placed an arm out to block them. "Wait," he whispered.

"What's her name?" Charlotte picked up a box of tissues and handed one to Ellie.

She wiped her face and managed a small grin. "Bun Bun."

"Well, Bun Bun's been sitting on that mantel, waiting for you. She seemed to know you were coming."

Ellie frowned. "I don't understand."

Alexander appeared perplexed by the whole situation. "Neither do I."

"It's a little hard to explain. I'll tell you about it over a cup of tea." Charlotte hooked her arm into Ellie's and led her into the kitchen.

"Come on," she said to everyone else. "Tea is for everyone."

———

Ellie stood by the French doors, studying the grounds at the back of the house. The deep Southern-style porch wrapped around the entire house, with wide stairs descending onto a patio. Live oak trees, strategically placed over one hundred years ago, brought pockets of shade from the hot Georgia sun. A swing hung from a tree with a perfect view of Wilmington River.

"Would you mind if I walk out back?" Ellie asked Charlotte. "It'll only take a few minutes."

"Go ahead. Come in when you're ready."

Ellie and Olivia walked the grounds together. Deep, lush flowerbeds traveled from the waterfront and beyond. As she stood in the middle of the yard, a summer breeze passed through the garden, creating ripples of color and bringing the garden to life. Waves of color moved with the wind around the entire property, mimicking the water as it drifted to shore. *Brilliant*, Ellie thought. "Whoever created this garden had great vision."

As Ellie studied the grounds, she thought about what it meant to be at this house, and wondered why it held such a powerful memory. It couldn't be about retrieving her beloved stuffed animal. There had to be more to it. "I remember running around back here."

"Anything specific?" Olivia asked.

"I sat with someone under these trees, drinking lemonade. The firepit's a recent addition. Other than that, no, nothing specific. It's frustrating to realize part of my life was here and not recall any of it. I have so many questions, Olivia. Did my parents own this home at some point? Could it be that simple? And why can I remember the view but not the people?"

"If your birth parents owned this house, where are they now? And why were you in foster care? We've only just arrived, Ellie. You need to give it time."

"Time is something we don't have. And to tell you the truth, remembering scares me."

"That's understandable. Don't worry, we'll work through it together."

"We should go inside."

When they opened the door, Vincent was in the kitchen making tea, while Alexander and Charlotte prepared the food. Alex placed an enormous charcuterie board garnished with fresh rosemary and thyme in the center of the table with enough small plates to serve each of their unexpected guests. It held brie and smoked gouda, next to a block of cream cheese topped with spicy jelly and crackers. Bowls of raspberries and cherries, with an assortment of olives and nuts, were randomly placed on the board between slices of pepperoni and salami.

"So, this is what's meant by Southern hospitality," said Vincent. "This is beautiful. Are you the cook in the family, Alexander?"

"Please, call me Alex. I do like to cook. But this isn't cooking."

"It is to me," said Ellie.

Vincent laughed. "She's telling you the truth. Boiling water is a feat for Ellie."

"I'd like to argue the point, but I can't. Tell me, Alex, how long have you lived here?"

"I've owned the house for three months. I moved in two weeks ago."

"Three months," Ellie repeated. "When did you find Bun Bun?"

"We found the bunny the day I settled on the house."

Ellie tried to recall something that might have happened decades earlier. "In a bedroom closet, maybe? I'm guessing."

Alex smiled. "Yes. Did you live here?"

"It's possible. Or at least I visited."

It had been three months since the ghost last haunted Ellie. Now she suspected this was where the ghost wanted her to go all along. To Find Bun. This was the message she didn't understand. She glanced toward the counter where the bunny sat. *Why are you so important? And what does any of this have to do with the two dead men?*

"I updated the kitchen and baths before I moved in. We tried to keep the Southern charm of the old house."

"It's beautiful," said Ellie.

"How did you know the bunny belonged to Ellie?" Vincent asked Charlotte.

"My mother thought there were, let's say, mysterious circumstances behind my finding this house," said Alex.

"Let's say?" Vincent repeated. "You'll need to explain."

"For a moment, we wondered if there was a ghost."

Preston nearly spit his tea across the table.

"But we were wrong," he insisted.

Charlotte shook her head and picked up the bunny. "There are no co-incidences in this life, my dear. I told Alex from the beginning there was a reason we found this cute little thing. I knew you were the reason the moment you wandered into the house."

"Me?" asked Ellie. "Why? Did something happen?"

"No!" Alex insisted, though Charlotte's expression implied something else altogether. "How did you end up here?"

"You mean, why did I burst into your home unannounced and uninvited?"

He grinned. "That's one way of putting it."

Ellie let out a quiet laugh. "How much detail do you need or want?"

"Everything," insisted Charlotte. "I'm interested in anything involving this house. Who lived here, with whom, and for how long. It's part of its history."

Before Ellie began, the front door opened. A tall, thin man, about her age, walked into the kitchen. When she saw his face and noted his demeanor, she abruptly stood, as did Preston.

"You called the cops," said Ellie. "Not that I blame you, but really?"

"No!" Alex also stood.

Ellie's eyes widened. She felt the same fear she had when she was a teenager living in Savannah so many years ago. Other than walking into a stranger's house uninvited, she knew she'd done nothing wrong. Her reaction was a reflex. A muscle memory from her youth. *Cops*, she thought. *That's all I need.*

When Charlotte's eyes met Ellie's, she quickly intervened. "This is Jonathan Hadley. He's been a friend of Alex's since they were children."

Ellie glared at her father. "A cop and a lawyer? What's going on? Why are we here?"

Jonathan appeared confused. "Okay, what did I miss?"

Charlotte introduced everyone at the table. "Jonathan, this is Ellie O'Brien. She owns the bunny."

He seemed surprised. "You came here looking for a stuffed rabbit?"

"No." She paused. "Yes." She paused again, then shook her head. "It's hard to explain."

"For the record, I'm a detective."

Ellie snorted. "There's a difference?"

"Actually, yes."

"Would you like some tea?" Alex asked Jonathan, then smiled and tilted his head.

"Bite me," Jonathan mumbled under his breath on his way to the fridge, where he pulled out a beer.

Ellie snorted again. She appeared to be the only person to catch Jonathan's comment.

"And who are you?" he asked Olivia, then smiled and sat in the chair next to her.

"I'm Dr. Olivia Lombardi."

"Doctor?"

"Psychiatrist."

"Shrink! You're a shrink?"

"You realize the word shrink is insulting, right?"

"Alex rarely has such beautiful women visiting."

"Now that's more like it."

"Seriously! Does that really work for you?" Ellie asked Jonathan.

"It works for me," Olivia insisted, then met his eyes.

He looked at Ellie with a wide smile, then scooted his chair a little closer to Olivia.

Ellie rolled her eyes.

"Ellie, how did you know Jonathan's a cop and my son's a lawyer?" Charlotte asked.

"Look at him. He screams cop. The way he walks. The way he stands." Ellie caught her mistake. "Sorry. I should have said detective. No offense."

"None taken."

"As for Alex? I don't know how to explain it; I just know. Maybe it's the designer clothes and the $6,000 watch."

"That's so true." Jonathan laughed. "He even irons his jeans."

"Now that's funny," said Ellie. "How in the world did you two become friends?"

"There was an incident on the playground when we were four years old. We've been friends ever since."

"Even after he became a lawyer?"

"Yeah, well, by then it was too late."

"May I remind you, you're sitting in my house, drinking my beer," said Alex.

Vincent also reminded Ellie about her relationship with Olivia. "Olivia's wealthy and a psychiatrist. Both things you loathe."

Ellie laughed. "True."

"Be nice," said Olivia. "You may need me on this trip."

"Please don't tell me you paid $6,000 for a watch," Charlotte said in a huff.

Alex winced, then glared at Ellie.

"Sorry about that."

The banter back and forth continued, which helped Ellie feel more at ease among these strangers. Even the cop. She wondered whether there was a reason they were all brought together. It seemed too convenient that a cop walked into the house.

"You grew up in the system, didn't you?" asked Jonathan. "That's how you knew I was a detective."

"No, that's how I knew you're a cop." Again, the word *cop* came out with some disdain, even though she tried to stop it.

"I'm sorry you had to go through that. It couldn't have been easy."

Ellie wasn't used to sympathetic cops, especially in the South. Everything about this situation was beyond her grasp. "Thanks."

"What do you mean by growing up in the system?" Charlotte asked Jonathan.

"It means she grew up in foster care."

"Oh, my. I'm so sorry, sweetheart."

"Aren't you her dad?" Alex asked Vincent.

"Yes. My wife and I adopted Ellie. She came into our lives when she was a teenager."

The level of understanding this family had about her young life moved Ellie. And Charlotte reminded her a little of her own adoptive mother, whom she sorely missed during this time.

"When someone grows up in the system, they develop certain

instincts," said Jonathan. "Like a sixth sense. One of which is being able to pick a cop out of a crowd. Those instincts help keep them safe and hopefully out of trouble. Preston, do you have the same background?"

"Yes, but not as long as Ellie."

"I can see why you became a detective," said Ellie. "I put those instincts aside years ago. That is, until recently, when something happened that brought them to the surface. I don't mean to offend anyone."

"Is that why you're here? Because of what happened? Something dangerous, I presume."

Ellie nodded. "You seem to have your own instincts."

CHAPTER 13

"I'll explain." Vincent asked Alex for a beer before he started. He wanted to give them a complete understanding of his daughter, in hopes this would spurn a discussion that might be helpful. *Should he start with Ellie's young life?* he wondered. *Or tell them about the danger she was in today and why they were in Savannah?* The beginning, he decided.

"Ellie lived in Savannah until she was nearly fifteen, when she ran away to New York City. That's where my wife, Evelyn, and I found her. We took her in and later adopted her."

He pulled out his cell phone to show them a photo his wife had taken during a blizzard. In it, Ellie sat on the stairs of a building, propped up against a pillar covered in snow.

"You look like a statue," said Alex.

Jonathan shook his head. "She looks dead."

Charlotte gasped. "Jonathan."

"It's okay," said Vincent. "She was close to death. We took the photo before we noticed it was a living person. I ran over to get her out of the cold when my wife took this one."

The second photo showed Vincent carrying Ellie across the street. She was unconscious, with her arms and head dangling. She had no winter gear, not a coat or hat or gloves. Not even a pair of shoes. Her face was impossibly white.

Jonathan stared at the second photo longer than the others. "You look like a statue in the first photo, but the second …" He appeared unable to finish his sentence. The thought of the young girl so close to death upset him greatly. "This image will stay with me forever."

"I'm sorry. I should have warned you. We took Ellie in when we found out she was homeless."

"A homeless teenager in New York City." He closed his eyes and shook his head.

Vincent could see the depth of understanding on his face. He knew the danger Ellie had faced every single day from the weather, from hunger, and from the predators on the streets. She could never close her eyes without wondering whether this would be the night someone found her—attacked or killed her.

"Where were your clothes?" he asked.

"Stolen by two teenage boys."

Vincent watched as Jonathan's eyes met Ellie's. This man, this cop, had taken him by surprise. He suspected Jonathan had seen far too many young deaths in his chosen profession.

"You were lucky. Most don't find families. I'm curious. How did having a stable home change your life?"

"I became a music professor at Georgetown University."

When his mouth nearly hit the floor, Ellie let out a laugh.

"I should have guessed with the Georgetown T-shirt, but a professor? That I didn't expect."

"I couldn't have done it without my parents. They saved me in more ways than I can count."

"Talent had more to do with it," insisted Vincent. "Ellie's a musical prodigy."

"Really! Were your birth parents musical?"

"I have no memory of them."

"I'm sorry." But he wouldn't take his eyes off her.

"Why do you keep staring at me?"

"Because you're so familiar. I feel like I've seen you before and can't put my finger on it. It's driving me crazy."

"I thought you never forget a face," said Alex with more than a little sarcasm. "Where are those cop instincts now?"

Jonathan gave Alex the finger.

Ellie laughed.

"It'll come to me. Just give me a minute." He drank his beer and stared at Ellie.

"You're creeping me out."

Jonathan wouldn't turn away. "That's it!" He slammed his beer on the table. "I should have known the moment I read your T-shirt. I Googled your name to see what happened to you, but there were no updates. Now I know why. You're here."

"What?" Charlotte asked in frustration.

"She's Professor Elizabeth O'Brien. Yesterday, Ellie was all over the news. You probably didn't watch it, Alex, because you were in meetings. It was everywhere."

"I saw that," said Charlotte. "Lord have mercy."

"You're the guy on the motorcycle," said Jonathan. "Wow. You guys were awesome. I can't believe you both made it out of there alive. Jesus, that throw. How did you manage that?"

"Guys," said Alex. "What are you talking about? Someone tell me what I missed."

"Yesterday, two men attacked Ellie on campus," said Vincent.

"WHAT! How can you be so calm?"

Ellie shrugged.

"They took them both out," said Jonathan. "It's all over YouTube."

"Took them out? What does that mean?"

"Exactly what you think it means." Jonathan pulled out his phone to show Alex what had happened. "Would you mind?" he asked Ellie.

"It's okay. That's why we're here."

When Ellie closed her eyes, Vincent noticed how much it overwhelmed her to know the worst day of her life was being viewed by millions of people. But there was nothing he could do about it. She'd have to wait until the media moved on to someone else's tragedy.

Alex watched Ellie fight off her attackers. Then the motorcycle came into view, and the knife soared through the air into the gunman's heart. "Oh my God." He looked up at Preston, wide-eyed, shocked by what he'd seen. "Are you in the military or special forces?"

"No. Our dads were Navy SEALs. They trained both of us."

"Unbelievable. You're lucky to be alive."

"You said that's why you're here," said Jonathan. "What's up?"

"I'd like to start from the beginning, if you don't mind," said Vincent. "It won't take long."

"Start wherever you like."

"When Ellie was three, someone abandoned her on McQueen's Island Trail. More than abandoned—someone poisoned her and left her for dead. The only reason she survived was because a jogger found her in time. The police never found her birth parents or the person responsible."

Charlotte and Alex were both horrified. This was, Vincent knew, beyond Alex's imagination. A man who could afford a house on the water and a $6,000 watch could never comprehend being so hungry you'd steal to eat.

Jonathan became more focused on the case. "That's why you were in foster care. And you think there's a connection between what happened in Georgetown and what happened here, what, thirty years ago?"

"It seems plausible," said Vincent.

Jonathan scoffed at that idea. "How is that plausible?"

"Ha," said Ellie. "Good question."

"I'm guessing you don't agree with your dad."

She shook her head. "No, I do not."

"We don't know if they're related," admitted Vincent. "How likely is it for someone to be targeted twice in her lifetime?"

"Targeted? You think it was a targeted attack in Georgetown, not random?"

"That question remains. Ellie believed the two men were looking around for someone during the attack."

"You thought there was a third man?" Jonathan asked Ellie.

"They never spoke about a third man."

"That's what your instincts told you?"

"Yes, I guess."

"You've been around people like Ellie for your entire career," said Vincent. "Would a woman in the middle of a battle be aware enough to suspect there was a partner? Is that possible? Would you believe her?"

"I would always take it into consideration. You can't discount anything. Someone like Ellie, with her experience…" He thought for a moment. "I would trust her instincts any day."

"Me too."

"Even if those instincts are rusty?" asked Ellie.

"They're never that rusty. So, you're here to find a link between the two cases?"

"Yes," said Vincent. "If there is one."

"Jonathan will help," said Charlotte.

He glared at Charlotte, then considered her suggestion. "It's a cold case. I'd have to get permission from my captain. But, sure, I'll help."

Ellie resisted. "This isn't your fight."

"I'll check into it. It's the least I can do. What do you have so far?"

"Detective Ferris, of the Metropolitan Police Department in Washington, DC, is investigating the attack," said Vincent. "He went through the attackers' clothing and found $5,000 in cash in each of their wallets. The two men were day laborers and in need of money. A witness told him a tall, thin, gray-haired man driving a BMW picked them up. Ferris felt $5,000 wasn't enough money for a hit, but it might be enough to deliver her to someone else. They each have a record, in petty crimes, but nothing like this."

"That depends on how desperate they were for money," said Jonathan. "I've seen people kill for a lot less."

"So far, Ferris has found no reason someone would want to abduct or kill her. I understand there could be no reason at all. They could have seen her on the street and…"

Jonathan finished his sentence. "And wanted her for themselves."

"Yes. The only part of her life that raised questions in Ferris's mind was when she lived here."

"Why would he even worry about Savannah if she left when she was a teenager?"

Ellie pointed a finger at her father. "See! I asked the same question."

"No reason. Ferris wanted to cover all bases, that's all. When he couldn't find a hint of anything at home, he expanded his search, which brought us to Georgia."

Vincent handed Jonathan the two files he'd gotten from Ferris.

Jonathan went outside to read the files in private. Fifteen minutes later, he returned to the kitchen. "I'm in. I agree with Ferris. We should at least check into what had happened. There might not be a connection, but we have to rule it out."

"We?" asked Ellie.

"Me and my partner, Dominick Briggs."

"Crap." Ellie walked to the refrigerator and pulled out her own beer. "I hate the idea of digging into my past. I put all that behind me."

"That's understandable. I'm afraid you have no choice. Help me understand something, Vincent. Instead of allowing Ferris to do his job, you came down here to investigate on your own?"

"Yes, that pretty much covers it," said Olivia.

Jonathan opened the file and looked at the photo of Ellie curled up in the hospital bed. "Look at her. No one could stop me from working on this case."

"Ellie, you never explained how you ended up at my house," said Alex.

"I remembered this place when we were driving around." She lied. "I had to stop to see if I was correct."

"And the bunny?"

"I didn't remember the bunny until I saw it on the mantel."

That part, Vincent now understood, was true. He pulled out his phone and showed them a photo of Ellie's house. They were all stunned. The house was identical to Alex's, right down to the landscaping.

"Except mine is not a mansion," said Ellie.

Alex smiled. "What does this mean? Other than Ellie remembering being here."

"It means she has a deep connection to this house," said Olivia. "That's how we found it." She also lied. "It means she not only remembered this house, but probably lived in it."

"Come to the precinct tomorrow at eight a.m. I'll have more information by then. If you can convince my captain it's a worthwhile investigation, we'll begin."

———

After dinner, they drove to their hotel. Vincent hoped the GPS worked. A building known for being haunted didn't give him confidence that all would be well. When both Preston's phone and his GPS directed them to the front of their hotel, he let out a breath. "Let's hope there are no more surprises tonight. I could use some sleep."

CHAPTER 14

August 24, 2017

BEFORE THEY LEFT THE HOTEL TO MEET JONATHAN, ELLIE PLACED Bun Bun in the front pocket of Preston's backpack for safekeeping. Jonathan met them in the precinct's lobby and directed them to an upstairs conference room. When they arrived, there were strangers sitting around the table with a line of files running down the center.

Vincent stopped at the door. "Pardon me. We didn't mean to interrupt."

"You're not," said Jonathan. "They're with us."

Each person stood the moment they entered. When Ellie saw Maria Garcia, the social worker assigned to her case, she backed out the door.

Vincent stopped her. "What's going on?"

"That's my social worker. I'm out of here."

"No! Keep walking."

Ellie reluctantly followed her father.

Jonathan worked his way around the room, introducing each person. He started with his captain, Lynn Crawford, and his partner, Dominick Briggs. Then Maria Garcia, Rose Hurley, and Mr. Christopher Hubbard.

The captain, who appeared to be about seven or eight months pregnant, began the meeting. "Jonathan called me last night about this investigation. I have to say, I'm not inclined to pursue such old cold cases. Especially one like yours."

"Like mine?"

"Yes. The time you'd spent in Savannah may have been difficult, but with the help of your adoptive parents, you seemed to have moved on with your life. You've become a productive member of society."

Ellie agreed.

"Then I was told you were the woman on the news, and I read the file again. I changed my mind." She opened the manila folder with the two photos of Ellie in the hospital and pointed to the toddler intubated, struggling to survive. "There may not be a connection between what happened here and the attack in Georgetown, but if I can find who did this, I'm all for it. We're moving forward."

There were thirteen files running down the center of the large conference room table, and Ellie suspected what each one represented. Two of the files were most likely the police reports she received from Detective Ferris. One from the day they found her on McQueen's Island Trail, and one containing a police report from the day her foster father tried to rape her.

That left eleven separate files splayed across the table. Considering Maria Garcia was sitting in the room, Ellie suspected the other files were for each of her foster homes. *Eleven,* she thought. *Is that even possible? Why can't I remember?* She looked down the table at her life on paper and frowned. "Why do you need all of this?"

"Because we're starting from the beginning," said Captain Crawford. "Did you read this file?" She pointed to the first.

"No!" She took a deep breath.

"I read it," said Olivia. "We haven't talked about it yet, Ellie. But this stands out more than the rest." She pulled over the file to show Ellie the photo with the equipment and the IVs attached to her tiny body.

Ellie grimaced, then shook her head. "This is not a photo of someone else. It's me. And it makes me feel sick to look at it."

"I'm sorry. I think you'll need to help us with this. Which means, you'll need to look at the photos and read the files."

Ellie hesitated, then nodded.

"See the machine in the corner? That's used for dialysis. On rare occasions, they'd use dialysis to get poisons out of a patient's system, but only if there is no other solution. It was a long shot. They took a chance because you were so close to death. They even had to intubate you." She pointed to the doctor in the corner of the photo. "The doctor is on his knees, praying. God, Himself, is the reason you're alive today."

Ellie pushed the folder out of visual range, but Olivia continued. "The other reason you're alive is because someone found you in time."

"That was Liz McNeil," said Maria.

"Liz McNeil?" asked Alex. "I bought my house from Nicole McNeil. That's how you're connected to the house."

There was a knock on the conference room door. It was Charlotte Mathews. "I know I'm not supposed to be here, but I need to give this to Alex." She handed him a shopping bag. "I forgot all about this."

He looked inside. "Ah, me too."

Jonathan invited her in. "You're involved in this case as much as the rest of us."

Charlotte didn't argue. She sat in the corner of the room, away from the others, and listened.

"Liz was running on McQueen's Island Trail when she saw vultures flying overhead," said Maria. "She checked to see what they were waiting for and found you lying on a bench by the water. She picked you up and rushed you to the hospital."

Ellie knew if vultures were flying around, they were waiting for something to die. For her to die. "Where's Liz now?"

"I'm afraid she passed away."

Charlotte made a hissing sound to get Alex's attention, then pointed to the bag.

He placed it on the table. "I bought Liz's house from her daughter Nicole three months ago. She left behind several antique pieces. My mother found this inside a drawer." He pulled out a quilt wrapped around a photo album. "We both forgot all about it until you left to go to the hotel. I should have remembered when we found out the bunny was yours. I'm sorry. But that was months ago, and I placed it back in the drawer and forgot about it."

Alex placed the album in front of Ellie. When she saw what it was, her hands trembled. Inside were photos of her smiling, playing in the grass, and planting flowers in the dirt. She seemed normal, even happy. And in each photo, she carried the pink bunny. On the last page, she was in the arms of a young woman. "Who is that?"

"That's Liz," said Maria. "You won't find her in any of the files because she wasn't an official foster mother. You stayed with her while the police searched for your parents. Liz and Rose didn't want to put you through any more than was necessary. It was against the rules, but they were insistent.

I'm afraid the police never found your family. Not a trace of them. Once they gave up the search, we placed you in your first foster home."

"At three," said Preston, angrily.

"It happens. I'm not the bad guy, Preston."

He shook his head. "I understand that, but it pisses me off."

"What doesn't happen is someone trying to kill a three-year-old," said Jonathan. "That's what pisses me off."

"Are you suggesting my parents abandoned me or that my parents tried to kill me?"

"Or maybe your parents are dead," said Jonathan.

"We can't be sure of anything," said the captain. "It has been thirty years. We do things differently now. I promise you, we'll find out."

"Ellie was a Jane Doe in the first file," Olivia noted. "She didn't even have a name."

Preston frowned. "I read the file yesterday but hadn't noticed the name. How could I miss that?"

Olivia gently placed her hand on Preston's. "When you read that file, you and Ellie were in distress. You had other things on your mind."

"I guess."

"There was no identification on you, Ellie," said Maria. "When we couldn't locate your parents, we selected another name for you."

Preston abruptly stood. "You named her?"

"What would you have us do, call her Jane Doe the rest of her life? We had no choice."

"Preston, relax," said Vincent.

When Maria explained, her voice was soothing. For Ellie, it was the one familiar voice among strangers. "When you were in the hospital, Liz and Rose never left your side. They were with you twenty-four hours a day. We named you Elizabeth Rose after the two women who saved your life. They cared for you until you went into foster care."

"What about my birth date?"

"It was impossible to know exactly how old you were. When you first came to us, you didn't speak. We thought you looked to be around three years old, but you could have been closer to four. We just didn't know. Since you were so withdrawn, we chose three because we thought being with younger children would be less pressure. You had already been through so much."

"Why did you pick the month and day?"

"It was Liz's idea," said Rose.

It was the first time Rose had spoken during the meeting. Ellie really looked at her for the first time. There was something about her. Some memory hidden away. Ellie wanted to hear what she had to say. Anything to help her understand what had happened so many years ago. To understand how they made the decisions that affected the rest of her life.

"When they removed the machines, and you breathed on your own for the first time, you were, in a real sense—reborn," said Rose. "Liz thought they should choose that moment as your date of birth."

Ellie now understood there was great thought in selecting her name and birthdate, much like a parent would have done. She nodded her approval. "What happened next?"

"I told Liz and Rose to step back. You needed time to bond with your foster family. That wouldn't happen if they kept seeing you."

Tears filled Rose's eyes. "It was one of the hardest things we've ever done."

Ellie looked at Maria. "And how did that work out?"

"Well, based on the number of foster homes, not so well."

"Ellie," said Rose. "When Liz found you, we were both college students. I was in nursing school. We were both single and too young to raise you on our own. She wanted to keep you, but the system wouldn't allow it. Not back then."

Olivia reached over and grabbed one of Ellie's files to review. Once she'd read it, she pushed it back into position and read the next. And the next. Until she read every one. "Tell me about these people." It was the home where Ellie lived when she was ten years old.

"Why that file?" asked Jonathan.

"Because they're different from the others. More affluent."

Ellie glanced at the woman in the photo. "I almost forgot about her. I don't recall much, but the pictures help trigger memories."

"You can thank Maria and Dominick for those," said Jonathan. "They pulled everything together."

"This was a nice family. They treated me like I was one of their own.

They took me to their church and tried to teach me about God." She smiled, then glanced at her father. "It didn't take then either. No one else ever tried. They even had me join a children's choir, where I sang in a concert for the first time. My performance shocked the people in the audience, but I was too young to understand why. I think I was surprisingly good for a kid."

She then realized who the older man was sitting across from her. The one person who hadn't spoken. "You're the choir director." Ellie's face lit up with a smile that reached her eyes. She walked over and gave Mr. Hubbard a warm hug.

"You weren't just good—you were spectacular, for any age."

"Soon after the concert, my foster father died. His death was sudden, though I was never told what happened."

"He had a heart attack," said Maria.

"After he died, my foster mother moved to her hometown to be with her family. She left me behind, and they placed me in a new home." Ellie lifted the photo and looked at the woman who deserted her. "She told me I was part of their family. Until I wasn't."

"Ellie, she was so grief-stricken she could barely take care of herself. She thought it was best for you to stay behind."

"Well, that's not something a ten-year-old would understand. It felt as though she abandoned me, like my birth parents. I never sang again after that. Not until I met you, Dad."

"And I never saw you again," said Mr. Hubbard. "I always wondered if you developed your talent."

"I'm a music professor at Georgetown University."

"Oh my." Mr. Hubbard wiped his eyes with a tissue. "I'm so happy to hear that. It does a heart good."

"The records show her behavior changed after that," said Olivia. "They moved her around more often. Is that true?"

"Yes," said Maria. "She became difficult to handle. More combative."

"You know I'm in the room, right? It's strange to hear people talk about me as if I'm not here."

Maria opened her mouth to say something and closed it.

"I figured out what I needed to do after they abandoned me."

"Which was what, exactly?" asked Vincent.

"She learned to take care of herself," said Preston. "We all came to that conclusion at some point."

Ellie agreed. "I became a thief, and a good one. That's when I learned to pick pockets. I saved enough money to move to New York."

Maria shook her head. "I'm so sorry I failed you."

"You didn't fail me. The system did. Besides, I was the best pickpocket in the city. I never got caught. And if they hadn't left me behind, I wouldn't have moved to New York and met my parents. Who knows if I would have ended up at Georgetown? Things are as they should be."

"Except someone tried to kill you," said Jonathan. "Twice."

"There is that," said Ellie, then grinned. "How does any of this help us find who's after me today?"

Olivia picked up the first file containing information about an abandoned child. "I would start here." Her announcement was obvious to everyone in the room. "Ellie, we need to find out what happened to your parents. Once we know that, I believe we'll find who's after you now."

"I agree," said Jonathan.

"Okay, that gave me a chill," said Ellie. "But why? Couldn't it be about a recent event? Why does it have to be about my past? Look at the photo. How could that little person be a threat?"

"The little one isn't," said Olivia. "Look in the mirror. You're not a child anymore."

"I agree," said Jonathan. "Something triggered all of this."

"How would I even find out about my parents? I didn't even have a proper name until you adopted me," she said to her father.

"There's always DNA, but that could take weeks, or even months," said Preston. "We don't have that kind of time."

"Truth is, we don't know what we don't know," said the captain. "This new investigation has just begun."

"This might be inappropriate, considering what we're talking about. I have something I'd like to share before I leave," said Mr. Hubbard. "It'll only take a few minutes." He handed a thumb drive to Dominick.

"When you joined the choir, you were so shy. You sat in the corner with headphones over your ears, listening to the records I made available to the students. You never spoke to anyone or practiced with the choir. When we were rehearsing for the Christmas concert, you came up to me and said you wanted to sing a solo. You were so convincing I couldn't say no, but I had a backup plan in case something went wrong. You wouldn't practice with the group or even alone in front of me. I never heard your voice until you walked on stage." He turned to Dominick. "Turn up your speakers."

Dominick pressed play and the sixty-inch screen hanging on the wall filled with the image of Elizabeth Rose. She was ten years old, wearing a white dress and a ring of baby's breath on her head. The moment she walked in front of the choir and sang *Ave Maria*, the entire congregation stood, as did the people in the conference room. Olivia and Preston gravitated toward the screen to see whether it was really Ellie. What they witnessed was pure magic. A young girl who barely spoke had the voice of an angel.

"If you close your eyes, you'd swear it was a grown woman singing," said Mr. Hubbard.

Ellie noticed they not only closed their eyes while they listened, they experienced every note. When the music ended, Mr. Hubbard's eyes once again filled with tears.

"I was pretty good."

"You think?" said Vincent.

"I'd hoped they placed you in a home that would encourage your music," said Mr. Hubbard.

Ellie glanced at her father. "My parents encouraged me."

"God works in mysterious ways, my dear. I prayed for you every single day."

Ellie, as usual, rolled her eyes at the mere mention of God.

"May I?" Preston asked Dominick and sat in front of his computer.

He brought up a more recent video of a concert at Gaston Hall at Georgetown. A camera panned the room to show the auditorium filled to capacity. Professor Elizabeth O'Brien graced the stage, and the crowd rose, as did Mr. Hubbard. He moved closer, as though to be part of the audience. Ellie stepped in front of the microphone wearing a sapphire-blue gown with a diamond necklace. With a nod to the conductor, she sang Puccini's *O Mio Babbino Caro*. Her performance captivated the audience in the auditorium and in the conference room.

Ellie noticed Mr. Hubbard had tears streaming down his face. She rushed to his side and wrapped her arms around him. "My adoptive parents helped me develop my music, but it was because of you I discovered I even had talent. Letting me sing in that concert years ago opened my eyes to the possibilities. I had to wait until I was in the right place to sing again, but you're the one who set me on that path. Thank you."

Jonathan appeared speechless. "You're an opera singer."

"No. I hate opera."

Mr. Hubbard's eyes widened.

Vincent laughed.

"I did that concert because the administration twisted my arm."

"What music do you prefer?" Mr. Hubbard asked.

"Pop," Vincent quickly replied. "Artists like Lady Gaga." He emphasized the word *Gaga*.

"And Alicia Keys. I'm a music teacher. Like you," Ellie said to Mr. Hubbard.

He placed his hand over his heart when he spoke. "You've made an old man's day."

Captain Crawford stood in front of the room. "This is the perfect ending to this meeting. Dominick will escort you out. Thanks so much for coming," she said to Charlotte, Maria, Rose, and Mr. Hubbard. "You've been a great help."

"Wait," said Ellie, then walked over to Rose. "I don't have many memories about that time. Not yet." She wrapped her arms around the woman who stayed with her day and night and nursed her back to health. "I wouldn't be here today if it weren't for you and Liz. Thanks for saving my life."

As the captain wiped her own tears, she turned to Jonathan. "Let's get to work."

CHAPTER 15

THEY RETURNED TO THE CONFERENCE TABLE TO BEGIN THE ARDU-ous task of combing through the files of Ellie's life, searching for any new piece of information. Even though Olivia had already read each of the files, she sat down and started again. Everyone except for Ellie, who rolled her chair to the farthest corner of the room. She'd behaved as though touching the files would send her down a rabbit hole of memories from which she'd never escape.

Vincent couldn't shake the feeling the ghost had been pulling the strings for months. From the day Ellie found her house, and Alex found his, to the letters *GA* written on the glass cabinet. Even to meeting these specific people. He suspected the ghost wanted Jonathan involved in this case, and, he wondered, what was so damn important about that bunny? His head spun with questions, but there were no answers.

Vincent stood by Jonathan as he observed his new team, assessing the skills they each brought to the table. Jonathan's eyes rested on one person, and then the next. And the next.

"Tell me what you see," said Vincent. "We'll compare notes."

"Okay." He considered for a moment. "Well, first, there's Preston. He sits, head down in front of his computer."

Vincent laughed. "If he's not in front of a computer, he'll have a book in his hands."

"Yes, but he's not only searching through the files. He's also searching online to make sure he doesn't miss anything. He's analytical and focused. Is he always this motivated?"

"Yes, always. His skills are like Dominick's."

"And then there's Olivia. She's kept an attentive eye on Ellie, without hovering. Even with all of Preston's technical ability, her skills as a psychiatrist might be the most important. At least for today."

"I agree. And Ellie?"

"Ah. She's the somewhat damaged, enormously talented, musician. Still, with all she's been through, she has a kind soul."

"That's true. Somehow, she never lost that part of herself. Even after living through such tragedy. But you're not seeing Ellie for who she really is. Not down here. I've never seen her like this."

"What do you mean?"

"I think her emotions are caught between fear and rage. Fear about what we're going to find out about her past, and rage toward the people responsible. She's all over the place."

"Well, that's understandable. She's probably concerned about her friends getting hurt or even killed. What do you think she'll do when we find the people responsible? I'd like to know what she's truly capable of."

Vincent shook his head. "I honestly don't know what she'll do. She's highly trained, Jonathan, and beyond angry. She's perfectly capable of taking these men out on her own. And believe me when I tell you, if these people try to hurt her family, she'll kill them where they stand."

"You honestly think she's capable of killing?"

"I have no doubt."

"That's not good. But my gut tells me she won't hurt anyone. Or at least, kill anyone. You asked me what I see in Ellie. I believe she's the heart of the trio. The balance. As an artist, she sees the world through a different lens than her two analytical friends. But I'm not sure how she can help with this investigation. She's also the victim, both as a child and a woman. I guess we'll find out soon enough. It's an impressive team. They come from different backgrounds but remain true to one another."

"Like you and Alex."

"Exactly."

"I agree. Now, what about me?" asked Vincent.

"You?" He laughed. "You're the one in charge. It can't be easy to control three independent thinkers."

"Lord. No truer words."

"What's the point of all of this?" Ellie interrupted their conversation. "It's all old news."

"It is, but technology has come a long way in thirty years." Jonathan walked over to the corner of the room to retrieve a box on the floor and placed it on the table. "You'll want to check this out. But I don't know if it will help us." The box was old and thick with dust and dirt, with a case number written in Sharpie across the side. "This is the only physical evidence from your case, but be careful, it's filthy," Jonathan told Olivia, who stood to get a peek inside. He lifted his grimy hands to warn her. "There's thirty years of dirt on this box. It doesn't look like anyone has laid a hand on it in decades."

"There's evidence?" asked Preston. "What kind of evidence?"

"Not much, I'm afraid."

Inside the box were multiple sealed evidence bags. Each contained one piece of clothing Ellie wore the day they found her. There was a white dress covered in lace. Another had a pink coat with the initials *J.O.* monogrammed on the lapel. A third bag contained white socks with lace along the rim, and a pair of pink shoes.

Ellie grinned. "Check out the lace. And the pink. They clearly didn't know me."

"You were three." Vincent smiled. "Your initials were *J.O.*—that's new. Does it ring a bell?"

Still sitting in the corner, she responded with a clear and concise, "No."

Olivia held the jacket up to give her a better view.

"It means nothing to me."

"There's technology available that can lift fingerprints from fabric," said Dominick. "With a piece of equipment called vacuum metal deposition, or VMD. It's in Washington State. It's worth a shot, but we'll need to send the coat out to get tested. They may also recover DNA."

Ellie frowned. "Someone's DNA being on my coat is a little creepy."

Olivia examined the clothes through the evidence bag with a fresh eye. "Look at the jacket and the shoes. These aren't your average child's clothing."

"She means a rich person bought them," said Ellie. "In case you needed a translation."

Olivia grinned. "She's right. They're of high quality. Check out the lace on the dress."

The men in the room shrugged, as did Ellie.

"So?" said Jonathan. "It's lace."

"No. It's imported French lace."

"How do you know it's French? It's in an evidence bag."

"Trust me, Jonathan," said Vincent. "You don't want to argue with Olivia about fashion. I imagine she knows every designer in the industry. And if she's not familiar with a person, she'll find others who can help."

"It's my superpower. I can give you a lesson on how to tell the difference between fine French lace and lace that is mass-produced, if you like."

"No!" Jonathan raised his hands. "I believe you."

"I can't see the label through the bag. I'm not even sure if they bought the clothes in the United States. But Uncle Vince gave me an idea."

"Uncle Vince?" Dominick asked.

"We became close when we were teenagers. Like family. We called each other's parents uncle or aunt. Uncle Dave is Preston's father."

"I thought you grew up in the system," Jonathan said to Preston.

"I did. Uncle Vince introduced me to my dad, David Bartlett. He became my foster parent. They adopted Ellie and me on the same day. Without them, I would probably be in prison."

Jonathan turned to Vincent. "You saved more than one person."

"Yes, I guess we did."

"How do you know all this?" Jonathan asked Olivia. "You're a shrink?"

"Because she comes from money. And she hoards clothes," said Ellie. "Expensive ones."

Olivia scoffed at the description. "I dress appropriately for my profession."

Ellie laughed. "You keep telling yourself that. How much did you pay for the clothes you have on right now?"

"Never mind. The clothes in evidence mean you may also come from money."

When Ellie muttered under her breath, Olivia snickered.

"I'd like to take photos of each of these items. They can stay in the packages. I'll email the photos to my friends to see if they can help pin down the name of the designer. It has been thirty years. I'm not confident we'll get what we need. It's a shot in the dark."

"What will that tell us?" asked Ellie.

"The name of the person who made them."

"Or what J.O. stands for," said Preston.

"That makes me even more nervous," said Ellie.

"Do it," said Jonathan. "Meanwhile, Dominick will send the clothes out to be checked for fingerprints and DNA. I also think we should step through what happened to you, Ellie. We'll go to the trail, to your foster homes, and then back to Alex's. You said you've blocked out much of your time living here. Driving around might trigger helpful memories."

"I agree," said Olivia. "But I think we should go to the trail at night. They found Ellie early in the morning, which means she was there in the dark. We want to recreate what Ellie saw."

"Alone. In the dark," said Preston, disturbed by the idea. "I'm not sure about this."

"I understand," said Olivia. "But what choice do we have?"

All the color left Ellie's face.

Vincent wondered how she would handle all of this. "Olivia," he whispered, then tilted his head toward Ellie.

"I think we should drive by Ellie's foster homes today, to see what she remembers. We can go to the trail tonight," said Olivia, then walked over to Ellie. "Why don't we go outside and get some air."

"Sounds great." They returned ten minutes later. Ellie announced her decision. "I'll go to the trail."

"You don't need to do this," insisted Preston. "We'll figure something else out."

"No. This is my decision. Believe me, I understand the stakes. What happens if I don't remember? What do we do next?"

"I'm more concerned about how you'll react if you do remember," said Preston.

"We'll take one step at a time," said Jonathan. "We can decide what to do next when we return from the trail."

Ellie agreed.

CHAPTER 16

WHILE PULLING THE FILES TOGETHER, DOMINICK AND MARIA had also created a spreadsheet with information about each of Ellie's foster homes. The document contained the names and addresses of twenty-two foster parents from eleven homes. They listed who was dead or alive, and why Social Services moved Ellie. It started with her first placement and ended with a tyrant who tried to rape a teenager.

After thirty years, a fair number of her foster parents remained in their original homes. A few moved to other areas in Georgia or in with their adult children. A handful of the foster fathers had gone to prison, and one foster mother. Two had died of cancer and one by a bullet. A few more retired to Florida, which seemed to confound Preston. He couldn't understand why anyone would move farther south. It was already hot enough to dissolve into a pool of his own sweat in Savannah.

Everyone agreed on a strategy—drive past the homes, take a photo, and stay in the car. The primary purpose of this exercise was to trigger enough of Ellie's memories to help in the investigation, not to relive the most dramatic moments in her life or to see any of the foster parents who still lived in the homes.

They took two vehicles. Vincent drove his own, with Dominick acting as his human GPS. He wasn't quite ready to believe the electronic voice in the car. The others were with Jonathan. They drove to the first foster home on the list and parked in front of the house.

Ellie immediately deviated from their plan and got out of the car. She stood on the sidewalk in front of a beautiful house and made a complete circle to view the entire neighborhood. Part of her wanted to remember something to get her life back to normal. The other part wanted that well-crafted wall to remain. She recalled nothing about the neighborhood or the house, then let out a breath of relief. *One down*, she thought. *Ten to go.*

When she walked toward the car to leave, a woman came out of the house and called her name. Not Ellie, but Elizabeth Rose. She considered whether to continue walking or to turn around and face this stranger. But the woman's voice wasn't angry—quite the opposite. Which left no compelling reason to leave. She reluctantly stopped and turned around.

"Oh, my goodness, it is you." The woman walked over and wrapped her arms around Ellie, who took one step back.

Vincent got out of the car. When the others opened their doors, he shook his head and mouthed the word, *No.*

"I'm Vincent O'Brien."

"I'm Maybelle Chambers." She reached out and shook both Vincent's and Ellie's hand.

"Do you know my daughter?"

"I do. She lived here years ago. Isn't that why you're here?"

"You remember me?" asked Ellie.

"Of course."

"How? I was three years old when I lived here."

"Well, it's a combination of things. When I saw you on the news, the color of your eyes caught my attention. There's something unforgettable about them, even now. And then it was your name—Professor Elizabeth Rose O'Brien. Elizabeth Rose was your name when you lived here. Are you married?"

Ellie shook her head.

"I Googled you and zoomed in on a photo on Georgetown's website. That's when I saw the birthmark on your neck. And I knew."

Ellie fingered the small mark but didn't know how to respond.

"Based on your expression, you don't remember me. That's understandable. You were so young. Please come in. You can tell me why you're here over a glass of sweet tea. Your friends are welcome."

"No, they're fine where they are." Vincent signaled for everyone to stay put while he and Ellie went inside.

"Please, have a seat."

Vincent sat in a chair while Ellie wandered around. She eyed the photos of Maybelle's husband and children on the walls and side tables, then moved into the kitchen to help with the tea.

A photo of a little girl sitting in a man's lap, clinging to a pink bunny, sat on the table. "Ellie, check this out."

She lifted the photo to get a closer look. "That's me."

"Yes," said Maybelle. "That's you and my late husband, Peter. Please keep it, if you like." Maybelle handed everyone their tea and sat down on the sofa next to Ellie.

"Do you remember him?" asked Vincent.

"No." She couldn't take her eyes off the large man in the photo. She pulled out her cell and took a picture. "Why would you have this displayed so many years later?"

"It wasn't. I stored it away in the attic. When I saw the report on the news, I pulled it out of storage."

"Why?"

She shook her head. "It's hard to explain. When I watched you fight for your life, it felt like déjà vu. I needed to see it again."

But Ellie didn't understand. Why would this stranger care about her? They hadn't seen each other in thirty years.

"Do you know what happened to my daughter?" asked Vincent. "Why she was in foster care?"

"No, not the details. Ask your social worker; she should know. I was told you almost died, and they didn't know what happened to your parents. But didn't you say Elizabeth was your daughter? You found her, right?"

"Sorry for the confusion. She's my adoptive daughter."

"Ah. Well, I'm glad you found a family. You were so little, Elizabeth, and petrified."

"Please, call me Ellie."

"Ellie. After watching you on YouTube with your students, that name fits perfectly. Elizabeth seems a bit stuffy."

"I agree."

"You cried nonstop the first three days you were here and refused to eat. Eventually you took to my husband and sat curled up in a ball on his lap, holding the bunny."

"Like in this photo?"

"Yes. I fed you while you were in Peter's lap. It was the only way you would eat. He even took off work for a couple weeks to help. You wouldn't play with any toys. All you did was curl up in the chair with the bunny. You needed so much more than we could give. You needed a doctor or a hospital. Someone to help you through the trauma. We tried for months, but we didn't know what else to do. I contacted your social worker and suggested she arrange for psychological help. She assured me that would happen."

When she grabbed a tissue and wiped a tear from her eyes, Ellie reached out and held her hand.

"It took us another month to recover after they took you. We never got over the guilt. You were our first, and last, foster child."

"I'm so sorry."

"And there you were, on the news. I couldn't believe it. Professor Elizabeth Rose O'Brien. Professor! There were photos on the Georgetown website of you smiling with your students. After you left here, we always wondered if we did the right thing. And look at you now. You grew up to be a beautiful, educated woman. That's all anyone wants for their children. Even fosters. I can't tell you how much it helps to see you."

Ellie didn't know how to respond—this woman was a stranger. Although, after hearing Maybelle's description of what had happened, she understood why she was glad to see her. Seeing the relief on Maybelle's face made the trip worthwhile.

"Why are you here now?" she asked.

"You watched the video," said Vincent. "The police in Washington, DC are investigating the attack. We're here to find out if the people who hurt Ellie here could be responsible for what happened at Georgetown."

"How is that even possible?"

"We're not sure. Ellie came to Savannah to regain memories she'd lost. To meet people like you."

She smiled, then placed her hand on Ellie's. "If you don't remember a single moment in this house, it's fine with me. Some traumas are best forgotten."

"I couldn't agree more, but I'm glad we met. At least I found out there were good people who helped me."

Ellie and Vincent thanked Maybelle for her hospitality and made their way to the cars.

Jonathan insisted they follow their plan for the rest of the afternoon.

They stopped at each house, took photos for future reference, and stayed in the car. As they drove, the neighborhoods had changed. In the beginning, they placed her with middle class, hard-working people.

When she was ten, they placed her with Amanda Jameson. Amanda's house was on the higher end of upper middle class and far better than any of the others. This was the home where everything had changed, and not for the better. Ellie believed she found a family with the Jamesons and then lost it. She found music and lost it. And she may have found God and lost Him as well. Sending her away from this home was the second event that changed her young life. Finding Vincent was the third.

After she left the Jamesons', through no fault of her own, Social Services placed her in a hellhole. Older children were harder to place, and with each new home, she had become more combative. Her life had shifted from upper middle class to lower.

An hour later, the car pulled up to the last straw that broke her. A place where she'd decided enough was enough. The home of Calvin Slocomb. The man who attacked her when she was not quite fifteen years old. When they pulled up, Calvin was sitting on the front porch.

"Uh-oh," said Preston. "Is that him?"

"Yeah, that's the bastard."

Ellie would never forget how he treated her. Seeing him now brought back memories of the fear. But the person who abused her was now a wrinkled, shriveled-up old man. This trip was worth it, she thought, if only to see him. Without hesitation, she opened the car door.

"Wait," Jonathan ordered. "We agreed to stay in the car. Don't let his looks fool you, Ellie. He can still be dangerous."

"Don't worry. I have my gun."

As the car door closed behind her, she heard Jonathan call out, "Gun! What gun?"

Ellie grinned but didn't turn around. She kept walking toward the old man on the porch.

"She's an armed woman about to meet the man who tried to rape her, face-to-face," said Jonathan. "What could possibly go wrong?"

"It's not a problem," said Preston. "She's not armed because of him. She's armed because someone is trying to kill her. What did you expect?"

"I expected to be told when someone in my car has a weapon."

"Sorry. I assumed you knew, or at least deduced."

"Deduce, my ass. Are you armed?"

"Yes." He pulled out a concealed carry permit from Virginia and waved it at him. "We all are."

"Does that include you?" he asked Olivia.

"Me?" Olivia gave an innocent look and didn't answer the question.

"You people are a pain in my ass! Stay here." He got out of the car and pulled his weapon, though he didn't raise his hand. He leaned against the car with the gun in full view as a warning to the old man on the porch.

Vincent joined him.

———

With the help of a cane, Calvin Slocomb stood the moment he saw her. "It's you."

"You recognize me?"

"Of course I recognize you. I may be old, but I'm not blind. You look the same, only a little older. Why are you here?"

"That's complicated."

"Huh," he grunted. "I watched you on the news. I see you're still handy with a bat. Though I guess I should consider myself lucky, since those men are dead."

"Yes, you should. One more to the head would have done it. I can try again if you like."

He laughed. "If you're here to find out if I was responsible for what happened, I assure you I am not. I would have good reason after ten years behind bars."

"You tried to rape me; you should still be behind bars."

"Huh," he grunted again. "You put me in the hospital."

"You're lucky I didn't put you in your grave. Where's Gunner?"

"Prison. Not a surprise. He didn't have a brain in his head."

Ellie let out a small laugh. "Can't argue about that."

"What do you want?" He was clearly getting impatient.

"I'm here to check you out. You've already answered my question."

"I see you still have nice tits. Especially now that they're a little larger." He sat down and laughed, then spread his legs. "You want some of this for old time's sake. I'm up for it."

"There's nothing there for me. Literally. Not then or now."

She turned to leave when the front door opened and a gigantic, powerful man, about six foot eight and three hundred pounds of muscle, walked onto the porch. "Nigel! Look at you; you're huge."

"Is that you, Elizabeth?"

She heard the other car doors open and turned to find everyone standing outside the cars. "Don't mind them. They're here to protect me from your father. How are you?"

"I'm good. Real good." He walked toward Ellie, then leaned in and gave her a warm hug.

He's still a gentle giant, she thought. She was thankful the years hadn't turned him into his father.

"Let's go over here," he said. They continued their conversation farther away from the house, out of earshot of the nasty old man.

"Why are you still in this horrible place? You're better than this family of yours."

He shrugged. "I came back when my brother went to prison. Dad needed my help to get around."

"I'd let him fall on the floor. What's Gunner in for?"

"Murder. He's in for life."

"I can't say I'm surprised. What about you?"

He glanced back at his father. "I'm a bartender in the historic district." He looked back again.

"What's going on?"

"I don't want him to hear. I got my GED and I'm taking business management classes at the community college. If he knows, he'll want me to stop going to classes and use my college money for whiskey. The man I work for wants to retire in a couple years, and I'll be the new owner."

Ellie's wide smile lit up her eyes. "He won't hear it from me. You're incredible. I'm so proud of you."

"I'm so sorry I wasn't home to protect you from him."

"None of that was your fault. Or mine. It was his." She nodded toward the porch. "Hopefully, he'll do the world a favor and drop dead."

He tapped his finger on his watch. "Nature will take care of him."

Ellie looked back at the old man. He was still staring at her. "Sooner than later, I hope." She hugged him again, though his size made it nearly impossible to reach around him.

Her trip down memory lane was nearly over. She realized there were some bright lights in her life. Maybelle and Nigel were among them. There was one more place to visit, but not until after dark. It was then she'd face her worst nightmare.

CHAPTER 17

THEY COMPLETED THEIR TOUR THROUGH THE WORST NEIGHBOR-hoods in Savannah and returned to Alex's. Jonathan and Dominick needed time alone to prepare for their visit to McQueen's Island Trail later that evening.

Preston wouldn't leave the car. "I'm going with you."

"No, you're not," said Jonathan. "This is a police investigation."

"You'll have to drag me out of this car."

"Don't tempt me."

"Jonathan, Ellie is my best friend. I am involved in this case. You need to trust that I can help."

"Fine, you can come with us if you don't get in our way. If you do, I swear, I'll handcuff you to the car."

"You can try." Preston smiled. "I'll just pick the lock."

"I have zip ties and I'm not afraid to use them. Don't push your luck."

Preston reluctantly agreed to his terms. Anything to be part of the investigation.

"Don't make me sorry I brought you," said Jonathan.

"You won't be."

At the precinct, they each re-read the original police reports, combing through every detail. It didn't take long. There was little information to go on. Jonathan reached out to Louis Thibodeaux, the detective who ran the original investigation. He called his home to arrange a meeting, without success. When no one answered, they made an impromptu visit.

Detective Thibodeaux's house had seen better days. The sidewalk crumbled under their feet and the lawn had turned to dirt. Anything that was alive had dried up in the Savannah heat years ago. Even the weeds withered under the hot Georgia sun. The house was run-down, with chipped paint on the doors and siding. The windows had so much grime, it was impossible to see inside.

"Do you know this guy?" asked Dominick. "Are you sure he lives here? Are you sure anyone lives here?"

"It's the correct address, but I don't know him. The name's familiar, though. I'll remember more once I see him."

Jonathan held Ellie's file in his hands, and as always, Preston brought a backpack filled with computer equipment. "What do you have in there?" asked Jonathan.

"My computer, and a little of this and that."

"This and that? Do I need to check for paraphernalia?" He shook his head, then rang the bell for the third time. He realized there was no sound, and knocked on the door, which sent a window shutter barely hanging on to the dilapidated house crashing to the ground.

Preston stood with his hands in his pockets and stared at the property and the trash in the yard while he waited. And waited. After what felt like an eternity, they turned to leave.

Louis answered the door with the help of a walker perched in front of him.

He was older than Preston expected, with a pronounced limp. It was no wonder it had taken so long to answer the door. Putting one foot in front of the other had taken great effort, and based on the grimace on his face, great pain. Preston glanced at Jonathan to gauge his reaction. He could see that Jonathan remembered this man.

"Mr. Thibodeaux, I'm Detective Jonathan Hadley. This is my partner, Detective Dominick Briggs."

He ignored Jonathan and stared straight at Preston with eyes as sharp as knives. "And who are you?"

"I'm Preston Bartlett."

"You're not a cop."

"No, sir. I'm not."

Treating Louis with enough respect to call him "sir" had done the trick. He invited them in. The decay continued inside the house, which smelled of whiskey and cigarette smoke. As did Louis. It was as though everything had melded together to become one stinking mess.

The tables and chairs held piles of junk mail and newspapers. Except for a recliner, which had been strategically placed across from the television. Ashtrays overflowed with cigarette butts, and a recycle container filled with empty bottles of Jack Daniel's whiskey sat next to the recliner.

Louis instructed Jonathan to clean off two spots on the sofa and take a seat. He ordered Preston to clear a chair while he shuffled to the recliner covered in duct tape. He held onto his walker until he was close enough to flop into the seat.

"Want a shot?" He lifted a bottle of whiskey to share.

"No! Thanks. I'm here to discuss one of your old cases," said Jonathan. "Are you up to it?"

"Of course I'm up to it." He sneered. "I may look old, but I remember everything."

"Good. Because we're working on a thirty-year-old cold case."

Louis frowned. "Which one? There aren't many. I closed most of my cases."

"Do you remember a case involving an abandoned three-year-old? She was a Jane Doe left on McQueen's Island Trail?"

He grabbed the whiskey and drank out of the bottle, as though to quell the pain before he spoke.

Preston wondered whether he was dulling the pain from his injury or from the memory.

"That's one of mine. Are you looking into it?"

"Yes, we are."

"Good. I'd like someone to catch the evil SOB who did that to her. You never forget the ones involving children." He drank again. "Why are you interested in this now? What's happened?"

"Jane Doe came to my office."

Referring to Ellie as Jane Doe made it all too real for Preston. This was the part of her life she'd not only hidden from her father, but from him. His heart sank.

Remembering this case had shaken Louis. When he picked up the bottle again, Jonathan grabbed it out of his hands.

"I need you sober to answer my questions."

Louis huffed.

When he agreed, Jonathan placed the bottle on the side table and opened the file. "There's not much to go on. I was wondering if something had gotten lost over the years. If not, can you at least give us some insight into what happened? More than what's in the file."

He shook his head. "I doubt it. It's thin because there wasn't much to go on. Other than a half-dead child." He closed his eyes and shook his head. "More than half, really. It was a miracle she survived. There were no parents, no missing person's report or witnesses, and no evidence at the scene."

He didn't need to review the file, Preston noted. He recalled every painful detail off the top of his head.

"I took those pictures. This was one of the cruelest things I've seen on the job. You never want to see a child intubated. Believe me, it's something you never forget."

Preston shook his head. He had a hard time believing that was Ellie in those photos. Even if he knew it was true.

"When I returned to the hospital, she was awake, with her knees curled up. That's when I took that shot." He pointed to the second photo. "She stared into space, barely blinking, then turned her attention to me. I swear to God, those eyes looked straight through me. It gave me chills. There was something about her. Something I couldn't put my finger on then or now." He turned to Jonathan. "This is one of those cases that stays with you."

"I know the feeling. We've all had cases like that."

"I have to admit, I wondered how she made out over the years."

"Her name is Elizabeth Rose O'Brien. I won't lie, the first half of her life was unimaginable. She lived in eleven foster homes. When she was fifteen, she ran away and was a homeless teenager in New York City. That's where she found a family. After that, she had a wonderful life. She's a professor at Georgetown University."

"A professor! Georgetown! You're kidding. Well, that's good news. You rarely hear good news today."

Preston saw pure joy on his face. As gruff as this man was, he cared about what happened to Ellie.

"They named her Elizabeth Rose when they couldn't find her parents. When I heard they placed her in foster care, I knew her life would suck. How did a child with dead eyes become a professor?"

"Dead eyes?" asked Preston.

Louis held the photo of Ellie in his hand. "Look at the way she stares into the camera. There's no light in those eyes. No life. I suspected some-thing terrible happened to her before being abandoned, but I couldn't find anything. What does she teach?"

"She's a music professor," said Preston. "She was a musical prodigy."

"Ah! Now, that makes sense to me."

"Why?"

"Look at her. There's an old soul behind those eyes. It's hard to explain. I don't believe the talent of eminent artists in history evaporate into noth-ing when they die. Somehow, the universe passes it on. How else would society keep moving forward? At least that's what I'd like to believe."

Preston understood. "You believe in reincarnation."

"I do. The thought of having a new body makes me feel better these days." For the first time since they arrived, he smiled. "I imagine she lis-tened to the music in her soul. That's what kept her spirit alive, even with all the crap going on around her."

"I like that," said Preston. Louis seemed to understand what it meant to be an artist. And he wondered why.

"Why is she here?" asked Louis.

"She wants to know who did this, and why," said Jonathan.

The thought of that brought more pain to his face. "Tell her to leave it alone. Nothing good will come of this."

"Well, I would agree, but she has no choice," said Jonathan.

"Why? What happened?"

"Do you watch the news?"

"No. My life is depressing enough. I watch sports."

"Someone attacked Elizabeth on campus. We're helping in the investigation."

"Helping? Down here? You want to see if the same person who at-tacked her thirty years ago also attacked her at Georgetown."

Jonathan nodded. "Yes."

Preston realized Louis may have a broken body, but his mind was as quick as ever.

"Can you help?" asked Jonathan.

"I have the case notes if you want them, but it's not much."

"That would be great."

"They're in the garage in a box labeled 'Open Cases.' Bring that box to me, and I'll show you what I have." Louis pointed to a hook that held the key to the garage. "Take that with you."

"Stay here," Jonathan told Preston. "Dominick, come with me."

Preston wandered around the house while he waited. The house was filthy and run-down, but Louis had filled the walls with art. There were oils and pastels and even sketches in charcoal. All expertly grouped together. The juxtaposition between the beauty of the art and the condition of the house was striking. Then Preston looked more closely. Each one held Louis Thibodeaux's signature. There was even an oil painting of his own house with crisp, white paint. The house had a yellow front door, with a garden in full bloom. This, Preston thought, was the man before his injury. An artist and a gardener, and the reason he understood what it meant to have an artist's soul.

"What are you doing?" he said, gruffly. "Sit down."

"I'd like to show you something." Preston displayed a photo of Ellie's home on his cell and showed it to Louis. The gardens were in full bloom.

"This is Ellie's house. I thought you'd appreciate it since you're both gardeners."

Louis's eyes softened when he looked at the photo. "I used to garden, before…"

Then he stopped talking. It seemed too painful for him to speak. Preston believed it wasn't his injury that caused the pain on his face, but the memory of what he'd lost—his art, his garden, all the color in his life. His spirit was dying, one bottle of whiskey at a time. He sat in the chair and held onto the phone, staring at the photo of a garden in bloom while his own garden had decayed into dust and dirt.

———

Jonathan unlocked the garage and opened the door. Stacks of boxes from floor to ceiling, front to back, filled the space, with enough room between each row to fit one person. "Look at this place. I hope you're not claustrophobic, Dominick."

"I guess we'll find out. This guy kept everything. How are we going to find one box in all of this? We'll be here all day."

Jonathan wondered the same thing, then walked down one aisle. Louis had marked each box, but there didn't appear to be any logical order to the piles. They'd have to check them all. "He labeled the boxes. That should help. He's an organized hoarder, I'll give him that."

"You're assuming what's marked is what's inside."

"Let's hope. Otherwise, you're right—this could take forever. There are case numbers on most of these. Look for the box marked 'Open Cases.'"

They separated to speed up the search, each taking an aisle.

"HELP!" Dominick shouted, then laughed. "I found it."

The box they were looking for was at the very bottom of a pile that reached the ceiling. Jonathan found a stepstool in the corner and handed it to Dominick. They worked as a team, moving one box at a time onto the driveway until they reached the one they were looking for. Once in hand, they reversed the process to return the boxes they didn't need. They shook off years of dust from their clothes and went back to the house.

"Place that on the floor next to me," Louis ordered. He pulled out a single file and handed it to Jonathan.

Inside were Louis's handwritten notes about the case, but it was no help. Louis was right. There was little to go on. But in the back of the file were four sheets of paper clipped together.

"What is this?" asked Jonathan.

"It's the crime scene," said Louis.

The sketches were a three-dimensional representation of McQueen's Island Trail drawn by a skilled artist. It started at the parking lot, then followed the trail. It ended on one page, and picked up on the next, and the next, until they reached the crime scene. Jonathan laid one page next to the other on top of the mail on the coffee table.

"Check that out," said Dominick. "There's a snake."

"There's a little face poking out of the bushes," said Preston. "I think it's a raccoon. Oh my God, I see vultures on top of the trees."

"They were waiting," said Louis.

"Waiting?" asked Preston. Then it came to him. "I don't want that image in my head."

They followed the road until it reached the waterfront, where a small, well camouflaged bench sat behind a row of overgrown bushes.

"A jogger found her lying on the bench," said Louis. He didn't draw Ellie in the sketch. "If Elizabeth had rolled off, she may have drowned."

"Check out the sky," said Dominick. "It's pitch black."

"There was a new moon," said Louis.

"Like it is now," said Jonathan. "The drawings show how terrifying it must have been. Would you mind if I take a photo of these? The area's changed since Hurricane Matthew. This will help us pinpoint where Liz McNeil found her."

"Keep them. I have no use for them anymore."

Preston took a photo of the pages and placed them back in Louis's folder. "We shouldn't take your art."

"Art! You drew these?" asked Jonathan.

"Yes. When I can't get a case out of my head, I draw what I see."

Preston knew exactly what that meant. "Once it's on paper, you can clear your mind and not think about it anymore."

"You understand," Louis said.

"I do. Ellie does the same thing with her music. I guess creative minds think alike."

"Wouldn't a photograph do the same thing?" Dominick asked.

"No. I went back to the scene multiple times. Each time it was different. There were no vultures when the police arrived. And the snakes and raccoons return after dark. What can I say—it helps me."

They could see what Ellie had experienced that night, and it moved each of them. Preston understood. That was the purpose of art. To touch people. To transport them to another place. But this place was terrifying.

"Louis, do me a favor," said Preston. "Hold your arm straight out in front of you."

"Why?"

"Just do it!"

When Louis lifted his arms, his hands were perfectly steady. No shakes, no weakness, and no physical reason not to paint. Preston grabbed the keys to the garage and stormed out of the house. Dominick and Jonathan followed.

"What are you doing?" asked Jonathan.

Preston didn't answer. He opened the door and searched the aisles, reading the labels on each box. He found what he was looking for in the far back corner. Louis had propped his easel against the wall, across from the only stack of unlabeled boxes in the entire garage. He removed three of them, along with the easel. Inside one box was an assortment of blank canvases with art supplies. The others had drawings he'd completed over many years. There was a lifetime of paintings and sketches hidden away in the stack of boxes.

"You carry these," Preston ordered Jonathan and Dominick. "I'll take the easel."

"What's going on?" Dominick asked.

Preston ignored the question and walked into the house. He leaned the easel against the dining room wall.

"What are you doing?" shouted Louis. "Put that back where you found it."

Preston shoved the dining room table against the wall and opened the easel, then placed the art supplies on the table.

Louis became apoplectic.

Then Preston handed him a photo.

"Who's this?"

"It's Elizabeth today." Preston had three photos of Ellie in his backpack. She was teaching a class in one photo and played violin in another. The third was a close-up of Ellie smiling into the camera. He handed him the third. "Paint this for your file."

"Why?"

"To finish the story. Look at her, Louis. Her eyes aren't dead, but yours are."

"What are you talking about?" Jonathan asked, now getting impatient.

"Jonathan, check the signatures of each of the paintings. They're Louis's."

"What's this got to do with the case?" Dominick asked.

Jonathan had taken a moment to discover what Preston had already figured out. Louis was the talented artist who not only drew the sketches but painted every piece of art in the house.

"Your talent helped you get through the toughest cases back then," said Preston. "It can help you get through this now." He pointed to the walker. "You have more to offer this world than police work." He grabbed a bottle of whiskey and slammed it on the table with such force it was a wonder it hadn't shattered into pieces. "It's time you stopped feeling sorry for your-self and get to work," he shouted angrily.

Louis frowned, but had no response.

"We have to go. I'm coming back to check on you, and those canvases better not be empty."

"Huh." Louis groaned as Jonathan closed the door.

———

"Sorry," said Preston. "I know that had nothing to do with the case. But I understand artists. He needs to paint to feel whole again."

"I agree." Jonathan slapped Preston on the back. "Good job."

CHAPTER 18

T O PREPARE FOR WHAT WAS TO COME, THEY LEFT LOUIS'S HOME
and drove to McQueen's Island Trail. The changes to the landscape
from the drawings were more consequential than Preston had imagined. The Category 5 hurricane in 2016 had changed the entire feel of the
area.

They used the drawings to guide them to the crime scene, to have
a greater understanding of what had happened to Ellie. Based on the report, her captor or captors drove to the midpoint entrance of McQueen's
Island Trail and carried her to the waterfront, then laid her on a bench to
die alone in the darkness.

The bushes that hid Ellie from view had washed away during the storm,
along with most of the bench. "I'm not sure if this will help Ellie," said
Jonathan. "There's not much left after Hurricane Matthew."

Dominick agreed. "The drawings will fill in the blanks."

"What did this guy do to her out here?" Preston asked as he examined
the scene. "Anything? Or did he just want to kill her?" After seeing the trail
firsthand, Preston understood why this case had haunted Louis all these
years. Someone left her to die, either by the poison or by something prowl-
ing in the wilderness, to be picked apart by vultures. "This location isn't far
from the entrance, but it's well hidden. It's a miracle they even found her."

Jonathan agreed. "No one would've seen him come or go. And he
would've had a quick getaway. No wonder the police report is so thin."

"'Him' come and go?" asked Dominick. "You're making assumptions."

"Most women would never allow animals to eat a child. That's horrific
under any circumstances. Someone had to be desperate or insane to do this."

"There are insane women," Dominick insisted.

"Could we not say *eaten*, please," said Preston. "I don't want that image in my head."

Jonathan nodded. "It was a man, I'm sure of it." There was pure anger in his voice now. "A gutless man who couldn't finish the job, so he left it up to the animals. The question is, was it her father or a stranger? And where is her mother?"

Preston shook his entire body in disgust. "The way you describe it makes my skin crawl."

"Maybe he thought she was already dead," said Dominick. "Or thought the poison would have killed her quickly. Or he didn't know about the vultures."

"Can we not say *vultures*, please?"

Jonathan looked at Preston. "Something triggered all of this. He could have run into Ellie somewhere and found out she was alive. That would've sent him over the edge. If the person who did this is responsible for what happened at Georgetown, he's desperate. We need to stay sharp with this one."

"He'll want to get Ellie before she gets him," said Preston. "He has to know she's coming after him. If he puts his hands on her, I guarantee you she will kill him."

"If he puts his hands on her, I wouldn't blame her," said Jonathan. "Let's get back to the group. We'll show Ellie what we have and see if she remembers anything."

———

They ordered pizza for dinner and talked about the university and Ellie's students while they ate. Anything but why they were in Savannah.

Olivia was the first to bring up the case. "Jonathan, have you spoken to the officer assigned to the original case? Are there additional details?"

"Yes. Louis Thibodeaux was the detective assigned to the case. We just came from his home. He kept information on some of his cases. Yours was one of them, Ellie. But his handwritten notes are identical to the official file. There wasn't anything new. What was helpful were the sketches he'd drawn of the scene. They're more detailed than his photos. We also visited the trail to see how much the area had changed in thirty years. Especially after the hurricane. It will be quite different from what you remember, Ellie."

"That night is a complete blank, anyway."

Dominick placed the printed pages on the table, linking one to the other. It appeared to be one continuous sketch, from the parking lot to the waterfront. They all stood behind Ellie and gave her time to examine the scene.

Preston watched over Ellie. As did Olivia, he noted.

Her eyes traveled from the parking lot and through the path, then widened when she saw the snakes and the vultures. She remained focused as she absorbed every detail of the trail.

Preston saw how much the images had upset her and handed her a beer, hoping the alcohol would help calm her nerves.

"Why do we have to go there at night? Look at it." She pointed to the page with the vultures. "It looks like death. My death."

"It might help trigger a memory if we go where it happened around the same time," said Olivia.

"I keep wondering why I want to put myself through any of this, or if it really has anything to do with what happened in Georgetown." She glared at Olivia, though her expression wasn't one of anger, but of fear. "And don't tell me it's better to remember. Look at those drawings. Why should I relive that?"

"Okay, we don't go," said Vincent.

His declaration surprised everyone in the room, especially Ellie.

"Isn't that why we're here?" asked Preston.

"Not if it's going to terrify my daughter. Tell me another way. I'm opened to suggestions."

Ellie shrugged, and the men had no helpful suggestions.

But Olivia did.

"Hypnosis. You can walk through the scene without physically being there and wake up the moment you identify the person responsible. But there are no guarantees it will work."

Unlike Jonathan, Preston noticed Olivia was careful not to imply it was a man or a woman who hurt her. "Wouldn't that be worse? Won't she experience the fear either way?"

"Yes. But it's more controlled with hypnosis."

Ellie raised her hand to get their attention. "Stop! For the record, I'll never agree to be hypnotized."

———

Ellie picked up her beer and left the house. She walked around the grounds, then sat in an Adirondack chair, facing the water.

A few minutes later, Vincent joined her. "May I?" He pointed to a chair.

"Sure."

Ellie and her father sat in silence for a few minutes, admiring the view, ignoring the obvious. "It's beautiful out here, and it calms my nerves, which have been all over the place since we arrived. The sound of the water relaxes me." She drank her beer and listened to the small waves lapping against the shore. "I've never been this jumpy in my entire life. Being haunted scared me, but nothing like this."

"That's understandable."

"The thing is, I'm not anxious because of the people coming after me. That's tangible. It seems black and white. In the end, I'll kill them, or they'll kill me. It's the unknown memories that have me so spooked. I've never felt this way before. This panicked. What do I do, Dad?"

"Sweetheart, I don't know. My opinion changed after Jonathan showed us the sketches. They're so realistic."

"I know, right? The drawings are dark, like it'll be tonight. I must admit, the skies in the drawings struck a chord. I guess I was lying down, looking up."

Those words, though not meant to cause pain, made Vincent close his eyes and shake his head.

Ellie placed her hand on her father's. "I'm sorry. I didn't mean to upset you."

"You're not the one who upsets me. It's the person who did this."

"What are you going to do when we find him?"

Vincent shook his head. "I honestly don't know. I could ask you the same question."

"I haven't thought about it in those terms yet. At the moment, I'm more concerned about remembering. I will say, I no longer have any hesitation about killing. If they get near me, they're dead." Ellie knew neither of them would feel free until these people, whoever they were, were behind bars or in a grave. "The detective's a talented artist, but I wonder why he drew them."

Vincent looked at her in disbelief. "Of all people, I'd think you'd understand why. What do you do when you're stressed?"

"I go to my music.

"And he draws, most likely for the same reason. To see a child in your condition couldn't have been easy. I suppose putting it on paper helped him move on with his life."

"Yes, and yet, here I am. So much for me moving on. When I was young, I blocked all this out of my mind for a reason."

"I understand. You did it to survive. I now have a greater appreciation for why your mind closed off those memories."

"I'm being forced to find the person who tried to kill me, even if he's not responsible for the attack at Georgetown. Because we're not sure if they're related. And I really don't want to relive my past."

"There's a difference between then and now." He nodded toward the house. "Look inside. You were alone in the dark then. Now there's a room filled with people who'll be by your side. We're all your family now."

"I won't be alone, but they're not the one reliving the worst day of my life."

"No, we're not. Don't forget, Ellie, this is your choice and yours alone. Don't allow anyone to force you to do something that goes against your instincts. Whatever you decide, we'll be with you." He patted Ellie on the knee and stood to leave. "Come inside when you're ready."

A few minutes later, Ellie heard footsteps behind her. It surprised her to find Charlotte walking toward her. "I expected Olivia to be standing there."

Charlotte handed Ellie her second beer of the evening. "I told Olivia I wanted to talk to you alone. She agreed."

"How did you manage that?"

"It's my Southern charm, darlin'," Charlotte said with the thickest Southern drawl Ellie had ever heard. "It's a gift."

Ellie let out a laugh. "You're a piece of work. I assume you have some great wisdom you want to impart. What is it?"

"Not wisdom, but an observation, if you're interested."

"Do I have a choice?"

Charlotte smiled. "Now, what do you think?"

Ellie laughed again, then opened the new beer and placed the cap in her pocket. "Fine. Get on with it."

"I watched you study the sketches. And I saw your face and your demeanor."

"And?"

"You reacted to the drawings as though you've been there. Not a memory, but something unexplainable. The same way you did when you walked into this house, and when you first saw Bun Bun."

"Well, I was there. That's not news."

"I also noticed the fear. A glimpse. What frightened you?"

"This entire thing frightens me."

"Now your father said you're not sure you want to visit the trail. It's not my place to share my opinion, but I'm going to, anyway."

Ellie was about to lose patience with this woman. "Why am I not surprised?"

"I'm a mother and, because of that, I sometimes notice what the men miss. I've helped my children work through many things."

"This is not something I fabricated," Ellie said with an edge to her voice. "It's not something you can fix by kissing my boo-boo."

"I know this is real. More importantly, it 'was' real. Now, it's a trail with grass and trees and water. And a memory."

"And snakes and vultures."

"Yes, but not the man. He left thirty years ago."

"You hope."

"Yes, I hope. The face of your monster is there. The image. You can choose to ignore it and keep a wall around that memory—and believe me, I wouldn't blame you if you did. Or you can face the monster under your bed. You'll remember his face, or you won't. If that monster returns in your actual life, Jonathan will find him and kick his fucking ass."

Ellie's eyes widened. She laughed out loud when this proper Southern woman swore. A real swear, not the *bless your heart* kind of swear.

"If nothing happens while you're there, you can leave knowing that you faced your fear, and it can never hurt you again."

Ellie let out a breath.

"Only you have the answer. We're all here to support you in

whatever decision you make." She patted Ellie on the hand and went back to the house.

By the time Ellie finished her drink, she'd decided. She was not now and had never been a coward. *Though,* she thought, *you wouldn't know that lately.*

If, as Charlotte suggested, the monster was in those woods, she'd be the one to kill it.

CHAPTER 19

After scouting McQueen's Island Trail during the day, they knew what to expect. The 2016 storm had damaged the road between the parking lot and the trail, washing away chunks of asphalt and leaving behind sizeable gaps filled with water. Construction workers, hired to repair the damage from the hurricane, had strategically placed large rocks in the gully to act as stepping-stones. There was no way to know whether the rocks would be visible after high tide. Even an inch of water over the stones in the pitch black could be problematic.

Once they crossed the small ravine, a locked aluminum utility gate blocked the entrance. Beyond the gate, the trail paralleled the South Channel of the Savannah River. A variety of plants and animals called this area home. While Ellie lay on the bench, she could've faced eastern box turtles, American alligators, as well as diamondback terrapins and vultures. All of which were part of Louis's drawing. The bench where Ellie laid sat a stone's throw from the water and was all but destroyed in the storm.

Everyone except Charlotte drove to the trail. As planned, it was dark when they arrived, but before high tide. There were no streetlights or even a moon to light their way. When Jonathan and Vincent turned off their headlights, it was pitch black. Even though they each had a high-powered flashlight, it was still daunting and hair-raising. The area matched the feel of the sketch exactly. With the help of the drawings, they were about to walk the same path as Ellie's captor.

"It seems different at night," said Preston.

Dominick agreed. "Yes, spookier. I keep wondering if something will jump out of the marsh."

"Oh, Lord. Let's hope that doesn't happen. Is everyone ready?" asked Jonathan.

There was a collective, wary *yes*.

"Watch your step," said Preston. "Ellie, let me know if this is too much for you. We'll leave."

Flashlights pointed in every direction. Some focused on the ground to watch their footing and check for animals, while others scanned the entire area to see what was beyond the gully.

"Okay, maybe this wasn't such a great idea," said Olivia. "It's eerie out here."

Ellie shook her head. "You think?"

Jonathan assured Olivia all would be fine, though he also appeared apprehensive. "Dominick, you take point. I'll follow in the rear. Everyone, stay alert."

As ordered, Dominick moved to the front of the line. He was the first to manage the stepping-stones. "Watch out for snakes," he shouted to the group.

"And alligators," Jonathan added, then smiled.

"Alligators!" Olivia shouted.

He laughed.

"Really, Jonathan? If I see any animals, I'm out of here."

When Preston also laughed, Olivia stopped talking long enough to punch him on the arm. "Now you'll have to carry me." She immediately climbed on his back.

Preston shifted Olivia into a more comfortable position while she carried both their flashlights. "You're such a girl."

"Keep walking," she ordered.

Dominick suggested he not carry her while crossing the water.

"It doesn't look that deep," said Preston. "But I wonder what's crawling around in there."

"Do you want a list?" Dominick shouted from the other side of the gully.

Olivia huffed, jumped off Preston's back, and walked the stepping-stones on her own.

Dominick scaled the steel gate. Ellie followed, with Vincent by her side, then Preston and Olivia. Jonathan and Alex stayed in the rear to keep an eye out. When they reached the trail, Ellie moved to the front of the line.

"Do you always take the lead?" Dominick asked.

Preston laughed. "Yes, she does!"

"I memorized the map. I know where I'm going."

Dominick demanded everyone stay behind him. As they walked the trail, a large snake crossed their path. "Snake," he shouted, then stopped and waited for it to slink away.

Olivia once again jumped on Preston, who protested. "Oh, for God's sake."

Vincent chuckled, then moved next to Ellie. "How are you?"

"I'm okay. Concentrating on where I'm walking and not why I'm here helps my nerves."

With each step they walked, and the closer they came to Ellie's nightmare, the more withdrawn she became. Preston realized that while Olivia never stopped directing him, Ellie seldom spoke. When he pointed his flashlight into the pitch black to find her, a gigantic bird swooped down past Ellie's head. Olivia jumped off his back, and he quickly pulled a knife.

"What are you doing?" asked Jonathan. "You need to relax, man. It's a bird."

"A *huge* bird."

"You are such a city boy."

"Damn right."

They snickered at Preston, then pointed their own flashlights into the trees to check for vultures. Preston monitored the ground for anything that wasn't human and held his knife so tightly his knuckles turned white.

During the commotion, Preston lost track of Ellie. It was hard to see in the dark, even with high-powered lights. He found her crouched down on the ground, with her arms cradled over her head. Vincent was kneeling beside her.

Olivia saw what was happening and ran to Ellie. She didn't scream or speak, though Olivia had done enough for two people. While the others stood back, Olivia took charge. "You're having a panic attack." She held Ellie's wrist to check her pulse. "Your heart's racing."

Ellie glared at Olivia. "Really? I hadn't noticed."

"Don't worry. Everything will be fine. I promise."

As the panic intensified, Ellie began to sweat. Her entire body trembled with fear.

This trip, Preston thought, *was a colossal mistake.* To bring her here in the dark to relive her worst nightmare was an error in judgment. His judgment. He should have refused to allow it.

Ellie placed her hand over her heart. "I can't breathe." She was in distress, in the dark, in the middle of nowhere.

"We have to get her out of here," Olivia ordered.

Ellie was still crouched down as she hyperventilated. "I can't move."

Olivia's voice remained calm, with no sign of alarm. Any concern she had about their surroundings seemed to disappear. She kneeled on the ground to soothe her friend and never took her eyes off her patient.

"Close your eyes and take slow, deep breaths. I know it's hard, but try to remember your meditation. Clear your mind and breathe in through your nose and out your mouth."

Ellie followed Olivia's instructions.

"Again, breathe through your nose and out your mouth. If something enters your mind, push it aside and concentrate on your breath."

Ellie changed into the lotus position, closed her eyes, and listened to Olivia's mesmerizing tone. Slowly she inhaled, then exhaled, and the panic diminished.

Olivia turned to Preston and whispered loud enough for him to hear, without disturbing Ellie's concentration. "If you see a snake or another vulture, use that knife and kill it."

While Olivia was busy helping Ellie, Preston saw a flicker of light from the trail. It looked as though the driver turned off the car's headlights. Someone was sitting on the side of the road. With their flashlights turned on, Preston knew whoever was out there could see them, but in complete darkness, the stranger's car was invisible.

Jonathan and Dominick also noticed. "Stay with them," Jonathan whispered to Dominick. He pulled his weapon and circled back to their cars, while Dominick moved closer to Ellie. Olivia never left her patient's side.

Preston looked at Ellie meditating. She was in her zone, working to control the panic, unconcerned about sitting on the damp ground or the possibility of animals nearby. He left her, pulled his own gun, and ran to catch up with Jonathan.

Neither man used their flashlights for fear of giving away their position. They scaled the gate, then managed each stepping-stone with ease and made their way to the parking lot. The car sitting on the highway sped away without turning on its headlights. Jonathan took a photo of the back of the car, but it was too dark to read the number on the license plate.

"Shit!" Jonathan shouted. "What are you doing here?" he asked Preston. "You're supposed to stay with the rest of them."

"The others are with Ellie. I was backing you up." He walked toward Jonathan until he stood inches in front of him. "Let's get something straight. I am here to protect Ellie. I'd prefer to do that *with* you, but I will never stay behind."

Jonathan pushed his finger into Preston's chest. "You are not a cop. And you are not my backup."

"You're welcome." Preston walked back toward the group. He stopped mid-stride and turned around. "I may not be your backup, but I am Ellie's. As you would be for Alex or Dominick."

Jonathan grunted. "We need to get everyone out of here. Go back to tell them we're leaving. I'll keep an eye out here."

"Will do."

———

By the time they made it back to the entrance, Preston had already explained what had happened.

"How can someone be following us?" asked Vincent. "Preston's father is the only one who knows we're here."

Preston considered. "No, he's not. Detective Ferris knows." He looked at Ellie to see how she was doing. He wasn't sure whether it was the meditation or getting her away from the area, but her panic was now under control. "Ellie, where's your phone?"

"In the car. Why?"

"Think, Ellie." He stared at her, giving her time to catch up, and waited for a response.

"Crap! I'm the leak."

"What are you talking about?" asked Jonathan.

"After the attack, Ellie couldn't find her phone. The cops couldn't find it either. A couple hours later, a student turned it in, and Ferris returned it to Ellie."

"Oh yeah, that's a problem," said Dominick.

Preston rummaged through Ellie's bag, pulled out her phone, and dissected it. It was in pieces within seconds, with the battery sitting on the ground.

"What's going on?" asked Vincent.

"There's a bug or some kind of tracking software on Ellie's phone," said Dominick. "There's no time to go through it now. They can't track us if we take out the battery, and they won't be able to turn the phone on remotely."

"It also means Ellie was right about the third man," said Jonathan. "The two people who attacked her are dead. If you're being tracked, someone else had to be there. Let's go back to Alex's house to discuss what to do next."

———

They climbed into their cars to drive back to Alex's, with one change. Dominick drove Vincent's SUV while Ellie sat in the back with her father. He wrapped his arm around her, and she laid her head on his shoulder.

"Dad, this seriously freaked me out."

"I know. I'm so sorry. We should have listened to Preston. He thought this was a bad idea."

"No. It was my decision. I wish I understood why I had the panic attack. Everything is still a complete blank."

"Things might be clearer after you've had time to calm down."

"Who is following us? Do you really think there's a connection between these two cases?"

"I don't know, but we're not leaving Savannah until we know one way or the other."

Ellie agreed.

CHAPTER 20

TEN MINUTES LATER, THEY ARRIVED AT ALEX'S HOME. THE DRIVE back wasn't long enough for Ellie to shake off the terror that crept into every pore of her body. Her distress wasn't because of the strange car, but from the darkness, and the panic that shook her in ways she'd never imagined possible.

Ellie believed confronting a ghost was the most frightening event in her life—she was wrong. Today, someone with no face or voice, other than the muffled sounds that resonated in the gloom, overwhelmed her. The memories she'd kept at bay for so many years had seeped through her well-crafted barrier. Now she had to strengthen the wall or knock it down altogether. That's what terrified her. Ellie hadn't decided whether she believed in ghosts, but her reaction in the darkness was all too real.

When they walked into the kitchen, Charlotte was sitting at the kitchen table with a glass of wine, flipping through Ellie's photo album. One bottle was open, while another sat on the counter surrounded by glasses, waiting for their return.

"Why are you still here?" Alex asked his mother. "You should have gone home by now."

"Not on your life. What happened?"

"Nothing happened," said Ellie with frustration. "I had a panic attack and couldn't remember a damn thing."

"A panic attack." Charlotte walked over and hugged Ellie. "I'm so sorry, sweetheart."

Ellie wanted to resist when Charlotte placed her arms around her. This woman was a stranger, and yet she couldn't bring herself to back away. Instead, she closed her eyes and ached for her own mother.

Charlotte sat Ellie down and poured her a glass of wine. "This might help."

"Thanks." Ellie picked up the glass and the opened bottle, and moved to the music room.

———

A few minutes later, Alex found her sitting in front of the piano. He apologized for invading her privacy, then pushed a button, which closed all the window shades simultaneously.

"Nice. Preston would love that."

"It's like a fishbowl in here at night. We don't want anyone to see you from the street."

"Good idea."

Alex turned to leave, but stopped when Ellie played the piano. "I see you retreat to music when you're stressed."

"That's an interesting way to put it. Yes, I do."

"What did you do before you met your father? I thought you stayed away from music after the concert."

Ellie looked at his thoughtful eyes. He listened to everything she'd said these last few days and paid attention to the details. "My father asked me that exact question years ago. It's hard to explain, but I'll try."

He sat down, and with those thoughtful eyes transfixed on her, she answered his question.

"Thanks to Mr. Hubbard, I discovered that music was a large part of who I am. If you believe in God, you might say, it's part of my soul. At least that's how my dad described it."

"That I can understand. How would you describe it?"

She smiled. "Another interesting question. I can't. At least not in those terms. I guess it's a gift I was born with. Good genes, nothing more. When you live in foster care, nothing is truly your own. They take so much away. After the concert, I realized, even at such a young age, no one could take my gift. But I was afraid someone would figure out a way to destroy it. So, I kept my talent to myself."

"To protect it," said Alex. "I don't blame you. Didn't you ever feel the need to play music or sing?"

"As I got older, I questioned my memory. I wondered whether my talent was real or imagined. When I was thirteen, I hitchhiked into the country. After the car drove away, I went into an empty field and sang as loud as my lungs would allow. But not before I made sure I was alone."

"I bet that felt great."

"It did. But I only did it once, to prove to myself I had talent. When I was homeless in New York, at night I picked the locks of a music store and slept in the storeroom. To be around the music. I always left before the owner returned in the morning."

"Wasn't there a security system installed?"

"Yes, but homeless kids are invisible. I stood outside for a week and watched him turn off the alarm. The numbers never changed."

Alex seemed unsure about how to respond.

Ellie could see this was beyond his comprehension. "I was safe and warm in the storeroom and surrounded by music. I loved it in there. But I didn't play any of the instruments for fear of making too much noise. So, I closed my eyes and composed music in my head. When I heard the music in my mind, I was never alone."

"I assume you sang again once you were safe with Vincent and your mother."

"Yes, they saved me in more ways than I can count."

"I'm so sorry about all of this, Ellie."

"Why? I should be the one apologizing to you. We've taken over your life. You should enjoy your newly renovated house, without hosting a group of strangers. Why should you be sorry?"

"I'm sorry for what Savannah did to you. For the abuse you lived through, and now this."

He spread his arms with a gesture that encompassed the entire house. Ellie understood he was speaking of Savannah as a whole. Of the time she spent, not only in his home, but in all the others.

"From what I can tell, you've had a good life away from here."

"I did. Yet, for some reason, I'm at peace in this house."

"Me too. There's something about this place." He pointed to the piano. "Play something."

"Any preferences?"

"Whatever you like. The last person who sat in front of that piano was the woman who tuned it."

She considered for a second, then played "Moonlight Sonata."

"Now that's what I expected." He smiled when the tune changed to Billy Joel's "The Piano Man."

She stopped mid-song and watched this generous man. "Why are you helping us? You're literally putting your life in danger for a stranger."

"If a person in need came to your door, you'd help them. I'm sure of it."

"My father would, but me? I'm not so sure. I'm not the person you think I am. At least not when I'm in this town."

"One of my strengths is being able to read people. I have a sense of the person you are, Ellie. How brave you are. I bet your students love you."

"Brave? I was cowering on the ground thirty minutes ago."

"You were having a flashback. There's a difference."

Ellie shook her head. "We shouldn't bother your family any longer. After they finish their wine, we'll go back to the hotel and meet Jonathan at the precinct. It doesn't seem fair to get you further involved in my drama."

Alex disagreed. "This house is more comfortable than a conference room. Besides, my mother wouldn't accept your leaving without knowing what happened to you."

"We're not leaving Savannah, but we shouldn't use your house as our home base. It's not right."

"Well, I'm not the one who's going to tell her."

"Coward."

They both laughed.

Alex stood. "I'll leave you alone."

"Thanks. I need a little time to digest what happened." This was, Ellie thought, the worst-case scenario. Her two worlds had collided. One she ran away from, with good reason. And the other, she would kill to protect. Two glasses of wine later, she returned to the kitchen with a question and a decision.

"How do we know if the attack at Georgetown had anything to do with what happened when I was young? I'm having a hard time connecting the dots."

"We don't," said Vincent. "We can't be sure until we have more information."

Jonathan disagreed. "We know there's a connection now. Someone followed you down here."

"You don't know if that car was waiting for me."

"Of course we do. They sat on the side of the road in the dark and sped off the moment we saw them. This is my job, Ellie. I know what I'm doing."

Dominick placed Ellie's disassembled cell phone on the kitchen counter. Both he and Preston examined all the pieces looking for a tracking device. There was none. He then reassembled the phone and checked for hidden spyware. "Here it is," said Dominick. "They've been tracking you. Don't worry, we'll disable it."

"I told you," said Jonathan. "They're here. *Now.*"

"Well then, let's get more information. Olivia, I want you to hypnotize me."

"Wait," said Vincent. "Why the sudden change?"

"Why? Listen to Jonathan. They are here. Besides, it's not fair to these people. Their lives could be in danger because of me."

Olivia's phone dinged while they were talking. "It's an email about the coat. No luck. Too many years have passed. It's not possible to track down which designer created a child's coat after thirty years. Especially without a label. I'm sorry."

"See? We're running out of options. Olivia, do it now."

"Hypnosis! Haven't you been through enough?" Preston argued. "There has to be another way."

"I would suggest therapy," said Olivia. "But it could take months to get results."

"NO! I've made my decision."

Now it was Preston's turn to pace. "You're making awfully quick decisions lately. And for the record, I didn't like the idea of going to the trail, and I don't like this," he shouted.

Preston seldom raised his voice, especially to Ellie. She understood his concern. But she had to put his feelings aside and do what she thought was best for everyone.

"It's risky," said Vincent. "There will be things you'd rather not remember. Are you prepared for the outcome?"

"No, but I have to do this. Especially if Jonathan's convinced the car was following us. Too many people I care about are at risk." She turned to Olivia for clarification. "Will I remember what happened during hypnosis?"

"Yes, everything."

As Ellie considered what to do, she thought about Preston's concerns, and her father's. And she wondered how she would feel when she remembered her past. But she had no choice. The monster was nearly knocking at the door.

"We should take some time to think about this," said Olivia.

"No! I need to get this over with. What's involved?"

Olivia frowned. "I'll do it, but you're making decisions without considering the consequences."

"I see the bigger picture."

She hesitated for a moment. "Okay then. Let's go to where you're most comfortable and you can lie down."

———

Ellie retrieved Bun Bun from Preston's backpack and moved into the music room with Olivia. Everyone else trailed behind.

"Do you all need to be in here?" asked Olivia.

"I'd like them with me." Ellie got comfortable on the sofa while Vincent and Preston stayed close. Alex and Charlotte stood by the door and Jonathan paced in the hall while Dominick kept watch by the windows.

"We'll use clinical hypnosis to focus your attention. It will help you recall events you've lost." Her response was serious. To Olivia, this was not a game. "I've helped patients recover lost memories with hypnosis and therapy. It's called dissociative amnesia. Sometimes a person loses part of their past after a traumatic event. I must tell you, Ellie, not every psychiatrist believes we should recover them."

"Why?"

"Because memories may be mixed up with something else that happened in your life. And hypnosis is the first step. Therapy should be part of the solution. We can decide what happens next, after this session."

"What do I do?"

"First, I want you to relax. Everything will be fine."

"Yeah, right! That's easier said than done." She grabbed at her jeans to wipe the sweat off her hands, then held onto Bun Bun for dear life.

"Let's do this before I change my mind. Promise you'll stop if something strange happens."

"I promise. You don't have to worry."

"Don't worry, says the woman who's not reliving the single day that changed the rest of her life."

"Hypnosis is a form of extreme relaxation. You're not asleep or under my control. Once you're hypnotized, I'll ask you to recall the day someone left you on the bench. You'll be an observer and should remain calm. Our goal is to see if you recognize anyone or have any information we can use in the investigation. Remember, I won't let anything happen to you."

The room fell silent and Olivia turned on a metronome. Her voice remained calm. Spellbinding. "Focus your eyes on the metronome's pendulum."

"Okay, now what?"

"Stop talking and take slow, deep breaths."

"More breaths. Wasn't I doing this on the trail?"

Olivia ignored her. "I want you to close your eyes when they get heavy." She walked Ellie through the steps to help relax each part of her body. First the toes, then the calves. The fingers and arms were next.

As her breathing slowed, Ellie's eyes closed.

"No one can hurt you. You're not afraid."

Ellie opened her eyes and laughed. "Really, I'm not afraid? Did you say that with a straight face?"

Olivia shook her head. "Let's start from the beginning." This time she eliminated that phrase.

Soon, Ellie's arms fell by her side, and she was in a deep trance. Olivia took her time and carefully helped Ellie relive the day she was abandoned.

"Try to recall when you were a small child. Around three years old. It was a time when someone left you on a bench all alone in the dark. Can you do that for me?"

Ellie nodded.

"Take slow, deep breaths."

She complied.

"What's your name?"

Vincent appeared stunned by what was a reasonable, yet unexpected, question.

"Jacqueline."

When Ellie spoke with the voice of a small child, there was a collective gasp in the room. Olivia turned and placed her index finger on her lips, asking for the room to be quiet. Even she hadn't expected this to happen. The young Ellie could barely pronounce her name.

"That's a big name for a little girl. I bet it's hard to say."

Ellie, who was now Jacqueline, nodded with a gleaming smile, proud of her accomplishment.

"Great job," said Olivia. "Can you tell me your last name?"

She shook her head.

Olivia didn't press. The goal for this first session was to find out as much as possible without upsetting Ellie.

"Jacqueline," she said quietly. "How old are you?"

She lifted her hand and counted one finger at a time. "I'm four."

Olivia grinned.

Vincent placed his hand over his mouth and closed his eyes while Preston remained stone-faced, never taking his eyes off Ellie. They were all waiting for the big shoe to drop. *What was coming next?*

"You're four years old." Olivia paused for a few seconds. "Can you tell me what you're doing now?"

When she violently shook her head, tears spilled down Olivia's face. She worried about what she was doing to her best friend. And she wondered whether this was a wise decision. "No one can hurt you." She paused. "Where are you?"

"In a car."

When Ellie rubbed her thumb and fingers together, Olivia looked up at Vincent. They both realized this nervous habit may have started at this exact moment.

"I'm scared," said Jacqueline. The corners of her lips quivered, and tears filled her eyes.

"I'm here with you. What are you afraid of?"

She pointed to what was most likely the front of the car.

"Who's there?"

She shook her head, refusing to speak.

Olivia asked again, "Can you tell me who you're pointing to? Is it a man or a woman?"

"A man."

The room let out another uncontrollable gasp, but Olivia understood. They were all worried about the same thing. *What had this man done to Jacqueline?* She questioned how the room full of people would react when they heard the blow-by-blow recall in the voice of a small child.

Vincent moved closer to his daughter, while Preston sat on the floor beside her.

"Jacqueline, do you know the man?"

"Dark. Bumpy road." Her eyes were wide with fear.

She didn't answer the question. At least not completely. Was it too dark to see the man, or was Jacqueline merely stating it was nighttime? This, Olivia knew, was the problem with hypnosis, and why therapy was used to help clarify what the patient had seen.

"Do you know where you are?"

She shrugged.

"Can you see out the window?"

"NO!" she shouted and thrashed back and forth, trying to get away. Tears rolled down Jacqueline's cheeks, and she held Bun Bun so tightly her knuckles turned white.

The answers were sporadic, with a few words here and there. There wasn't enough information to help. *Had she terrified her friend for no good reason?*

"Remember, you're Ellie. You're an observer and no one can hurt you. I'm here with you. Take slow, deep breaths."

Olivia noticed Preston and Vincent were also taking slow, deep breaths. When Ellie regained her composure, she continued. "Are you feeling better?"

"Yes," she said, in her own adult voice.

After she closed her eyes, she went deeper into the trance.

"Jacqueline, can you see the man's face?"

She didn't answer but continued to thrash back and forth. "Ouch."

"What happened?"

She rubbed her arm and scrunched up her face. "That hurt."

"What hurt?"

"Needle," she said in a sweet little voice, with her eyes filled with tears. When she cried, there was no sound. The corners of her lips quivered as tears rolled down her cheeks.

"Who is he?"

Jacqueline refused to answer.

"What do you see?"

"Water," she said in-between sniffles.

"Is the man still there?"

"No." She sounded drugged. "Dark." She pouted her lips and squeezed Bun Bun.

"Don't worry, you're not alone. I'm here with you." Olivia placed her hand on Jacqueline's, and her entire body relaxed. The simple touch appeared to help her feel as though she wasn't alone in the wilderness. "What do you see?"

"It's raining. Can you hear the birds?"

"Yes." She understood what that meant; the vultures were waiting.

"Sleep now." Jacqueline closed her eyes.

Olivia was about to bring her out of hypnosis when something unexpected happened. Jacqueline opened her eyes and appeared to be listening to someone.

"What's happening, Jacqueline? Is someone else there?" Olivia was almost panicked. All her displaced fears had returned. *Had someone else come to finish the job?*

"A lady."

"Lady? Can you tell me the lady's name?"

Jacqueline tried to sit up, but the drugs had taken hold. She lay back down and curled into a fetal position.

"Can you ask the lady her name?"

"Mo mo." She giggled and screwed up her face as she tried to repeat the words. "Mo mo," she said, again. "That's a funny name." She swayed her head back and forth as though she were listening to music.

Music, Olivia thought. *Another common thread in Ellie's life.*

"What's the lady doing?"

"Singing. Can't you hear her?" she asked with a surprised expression.

Olivia smiled. "No, I can't. Can you sing along? It'll help me remember the song."

Jacqueline hummed, but with no words, then closed her eyes and fell sound asleep.

———

After Ellie came out of hypnosis, she stared at Olivia. It took a few moments for anyone to speak.

"Well, that felt real," said Ellie.

"How are you feeling?" asked Olivia.

"I'm good."

Ellie stood and walked from one room to the next, shaking out her hands, wiping them on her jeans.

Olivia kept a close watch as she recalled what had happened. When all the color left her face, Olivia ran toward her. "Sit down and try to relax." She took her pulse. A few minutes later, her vitals returned to normal.

Her eyes shifted from left to right as she tried to remember. "Well, at least the man didn't rape me. I know the medical records didn't mention rape, but it's a relief to know."

"Have you seen him before?"

"I'm not sure. It was so dark. It feels like I should know him, and I don't understand why. I wonder about the woman."

"You don't know her?" asked Olivia. "Can you describe her? Or at least repeat her name. We couldn't understand what you said."

Ellie sipped from a bottle of water, then repeated the woman's name. She pronounced it the same way Jacqueline had, with the same results. No one understood, not even Ellie.

"Could it be another language?" asked Vincent.

"I don't know. She wasn't the woman who found me. I'm sure of that. Her outfit was interesting, though. She dressed in layers of red and white clothing. With a red printed scarf wrapped around her neck. And she wore a red coat that resembled a cape. Like the one the girl wore in *Little Red Riding Hood*. It even had a hood. Loved the clothes. Also, she was barefoot. I imagine she was poor."

"I don't care about the clothes. What about her face?" asked Preston, clearly frustrated.

Ellie frowned, then squinted.

"What?" asked Preston.

She stood up to pace again, then raked her fingers through her hair as the woman's face came into focus. "Oh my God." It was a phrase she seldom used, considering she had no belief in God. Sometimes it fit the moment.

Preston stood beside her. "You're making me nervous. What's going on?"

"Her singing voice was beautiful. It seemed so familiar." She knew the woman. At least she knew her voice. Then she abruptly stopped pacing and stared at Preston. "She's the ghost!"

"Ghost!" Jonathan said unexpectedly.

Everyone else seemed too engrossed in what Ellie was saying to notice.

After a short while, she appeared to understand what linked her to this woman. She grabbed Preston's arm in disbelief. "She looked so much like me. Her hair was different. It was straight and dark brown. But the eyes— they were exactly like mine. The same shape and the exact same color." Ellie knew her eyes had always been memorable because of their blue-green color. Something she'd never seen in anyone else.

She picked up the bottle of water and drank it down, then flopped onto the sofa. "I think she's my mother." Her eyes met her father's, and she said aloud what they all had suspected. "My mother is dead. Which means Preston's right. The ghost was protecting me."

"Half right," said Vincent. "Your mother has been protecting you."

"Ghost!" said Alex, then looked at his own mother.

Charlotte grinned. "I told you—there are no coincidences."

CHAPTER 21

WITH THE DECLARATION ABOUT A GHOST, ALEX'S AND Jonathan's eyes widened, but not Charlotte's. Vincent realized talk of a ghost didn't surprise her at all, and he wondered why.

"Let's go in the kitchen and I'll make a pot of tea," said Charlotte. "I think we have a lot to talk about."

They all moved into the kitchen and Charlotte put the kettle on. Jonathan pulled three beers out of the fridge, gave one to Preston and Alex, and then sat down, ready to listen.

Vincent gave him a look. "Aren't you on duty?"

"Really? You're telling us Ellie has seen a ghost and you're worried about my beer. I'm only having one, and Dominick's keeping watch."

"Fair enough," said Vincent. "Ellie, we're telling them everything."

"Everything, everything?" asked Ellie.

"Yes." He directed the rest of his comments to everyone around the table. "In a spirit of cooperation, no pun intended, I'll start this conversation with what happened to me eighteen years ago."

Jonathan heard the word *spirit* and twisted in his seat, then took a pull of beer.

"Then I'll get you caught up on what happened before and after the attack in Georgetown." He told the story of the ghost visiting him, about the items being moved around and the words "Train her" being written on the mirror. No one scoffed at his tale. Not today. Much to his surprise, even Jonathan and Alex appeared amenable to the idea of a genuine ghost.

"'Train her'? Couldn't it have meant to teach her about something in school?" asked Charlotte.

"I guess. Although it didn't happen everywhere in the house. Only in my gym. I assumed she wanted me to train Ellie in my expertise. My wife was homeschooling her, and once I taught her martial arts, the ghost never showed herself again. Now, after what's happened, I suspect she's been watching over Ellie since the day she died. If it is Ellie's mother, it seems reasonable."

"Reasonable? Can anything sound reasonable when you're talking about ghosts?" asked Jonathan.

Vincent smiled. "Good point. I thought it was a ghost when she came the first time, although I have no proof. My wife had no problem believing and suggested I do what I was told."

"And you did," said Charlotte.

"Yes, ma'am. I always did what my wife told me."

"You're a wise man, Vincent O'Brien."

"After that, there were no signs she'd ever visited until a little over three months ago."

"Three months?" asked Alex. "I bought my house three months ago."

"That's when she was haunting me," said Ellie.

"Haunted. By the ghost," Jonathan said slowly, emphasizing each word, one at a time. Then he took a long drink, finishing the bottle.

"Don't worry, Jonathan. She's a friendly ghost." Vincent grinned and patted him on the shoulder.

"If you call it Casper, I'm walking out of here."

Vincent laughed.

"What did she do?" asked Charlotte.

"She kept repeating 'Find Bun' through the static of my television," said Ellie. "Only at night, after I'd gone to sleep. She even wrote 'Find Bun' on a foggy mirror in my bathroom. Eventually, I told my dad. That's when I found out about her first visit. Once I realized she was harmless, I told her I wouldn't do what she asked and to leave me alone."

"That's probably when she came here," said Charlotte. "After she left your house."

"Seriously? Now you're telling me a ghost was in this house," Alex said to his mother. "You told me old houses make noises and not to worry."

"I didn't want to alarm you. Besides, she wasn't here for long. Once we placed Bun Bun on the mantel, she didn't show herself again. I guess we did what she wanted."

"So, you lied to me." He also guzzled his beer, then went to the fridge for another.

"Yes, I lied to you about a ghost. I didn't know how you'd react, and I wanted you to enjoy your new house."

Alex rolled his eyes.

Jonathan let out a nervous laugh. "Jesus."

"What happened here?" asked Vincent.

"The day Alex settled on the house, she led us to the bunny," said Charlotte. "He was going to throw it away. After I convinced him to keep it in plain view, she never returned. I guess your mother wanted you to have it."

Ellie appeared disturbed that they considered throwing Bun Bun away. "Until I walked in this house, I didn't understand what 'Find Bun' meant. I had no memory of the stuffed rabbit until I saw her."

"My turn," said Preston. "I think we should tell our ghost stories around the firepit."

Jonathan and Alex shouted, "No!"

Vincent chuckled.

"Fine. The ghost woke me up, screaming through the radio to save Ellie. That's how I got to the university in time."

"To save her from the men who attacked her?" said Jonathan.

Preston nodded. "Yes."

"Any more ghost stories?"

"Only one," said Vincent. "I swear."

"I'm going to hold you to that."

Vincent grinned, then crossed his heart with his fingers. "We made reservations at the Marshall House and added the address to my car's GPS and to Preston's Google Maps. I was driving and, I must admit, I have a habit of assuming the GPS knows where it's going. When it said, 'You have reached your destination,' we were in front of this house instead of the hotel."

Alex paled.

"She brought you to Bun Bun," said Charlotte. "That's sweet."

"Sweet!" said Alex. "What does a stuffed animal have to do with any of this?"

"I don't know," said Vincent. "I suspect we'll find out when it's time."

"You realize this is crazy, right?" Alex insisted, then finished his second beer.

"Yes. All I know is she brought us all together for a reason," said Vincent. "You each have skills necessary to solve this case."

Jonathan stood. "Okay, I lied. I'm having another beer."

CHAPTER 22

THIS NEW REALITY SPOOKED BOTH ALEX AND JONATHAN, BUT EVeryone understood the men trying to kill Ellie were the immediate problem, not the ghost.

"Jonathan, what happens now?" Alex asked.

"Now we send all of you to a safe house."

Ellie refused. "We'll be fine at the hotel."

"This is not a figment of your imagination," said Jonathan.

"What, you mean like the ghost?" She smirked.

"Hey. That car was at the trail for you, not me." He pointed his finger directly at Ellie. "They followed you all the way down here. Why?"

It amazed Preston that he wasn't sprawled out on the floor, which meant she liked this man, or at least respected the fact that he was trying to help her.

"A safe house is important," Jonathan argued.

"I don't think so. I won't have a bunch of cops I don't know guarding me. How do I know I can trust them? I'd rather be on my own. Besides, we're already checked into the Marshall House. That's safe enough."

Vincent walked between Ellie and Jonathan. "Ellie! Stop!"

"Jonathan, let them stay here," said Alex. "We have plenty of room."

"Look at this place, Alex. There are windows everywhere. Besides, they already know you're here. And let's not forget a cop is trying to help you now. And it won't be a bunch of cops you don't know. It will be me and Dominick."

"I agree with Jonathan—this is not a safe house," said Preston. "But I can turn it into one by tomorrow morning."

"How?"

"You leave that up to me." He paused, then glanced toward the living room, where Dominick stood watch at the windows. "With Dominick's help, if he doesn't mind."

"I'm in," Dominick said from the shadows.

"I have to get permission from my captain first. Tomorrow morning, Dominick will take you back to the hotel to pack, then you can return here. Tonight, you need to stay put."

Preston knew full well that would never happen. Not because of Ellie, but Olivia. She was a woman of privilege, with the best of everything. The thought of Olivia sleeping in someone else's T-shirt or taking a shower without her bag of essentials would be impossible to imagine.

"I'll go back to the hotel now and check out. Ellie can stay here. I'll pack her things," said Olivia. Her tone implied she was not asking for permission.

"I'll go with her," said Preston. "I can pack Uncle Vince's clothes and check us both out."

"It shouldn't take long for Preston since his clothes fit in a single backpack," Olivia added.

Preston snorted. "That's true."

Olivia stepped closer to Jonathan. "We're not the target and we can take care of ourselves. Don't worry, we'll be careful."

Jonathan looked to Vincent for help, but he left it up to him. He stormed out of the room, mumbling. "You people are a pain in my ass."

Eventually, they all agreed on a plan, with one exception to satisfy Jonathan. He would go along. "Dominick will stay here. And you." He pointed a finger in Ellie's face. "You stay here. Remember, you are the target."

"You point that finger at me one more time, and I'll break the damn thing off."

Preston grinned. This reminded him of when they first met Olivia. They each had their own baggage, and their own individual skills. And each had to decide where they were in the pecking order. Over time, they meshed. Now Jonathan was thrown into the mix.

"You'll also need to spend the night," Jonathan told Charlotte.

Alex agreed. "We shouldn't take any unnecessary chances."

"Any more chances, you mean," said Jonathan. "They already know we're here."

"We don't know if that's true," said Vincent. "But, yes, that is probable."

"Probable?" asked Ellie. "You really think it's probable? If we're putting these people in danger, we should leave."

"You'll do no such thing," Charlotte ordered. "Jonathan and Dominick can take care of things here."

"Then *you* go to a safe house," Ellie said to Charlotte. "Away from here."

"I will not. Everything will be fine. You'll see."

Ellie let out a breath in frustration. "I don't know what to do anymore."

"Welcome to my world," said Alex.

Ellie grinned.

"When I get back, I'll order what I need from the local electronics store," said Preston. "If we're lucky, they'll have all the parts I need. We can set up the surveillance system tomorrow. When we're finished, no one will get close to the house without us knowing about it. Then we can deal with them."

While they checked out of the hotel, Ellie sat in the music room with the doors and shades closed. She felt caged. It brought back memories of being locked in a dark closet when she was in foster care, but it gave her time to think without distractions. There would be no one pointing a finger in her face or someone telling her what to do. She'd make her own decision. But Preston's words kept rattling around in her mind. The security system wouldn't be able to stop them. She knew they could deal with them easy enough; they were all armed. But what of Charlotte and Alex? And the house?

She thought about the way she'd treated Jonathan, whose one crime was helping a stranger in trouble. And about the fact that they'd sequestered everyone in the house and put them all in danger. That Alex had opened his home to them, no questions asked, astonished her.

Ellie knew she'd regressed since the attack. No longer was she the professor, but the fifteen-year-old homeless girl who trusted no one. Especially cops. She gave Jonathan a hard time for no reason, and she cowered on the trail. She didn't like this version of herself. It wasn't who she was, not anymore. If there was a decision to be made about what to do next, she was the one to make it.

It was almost eleven p.m. when everyone returned with luggage in hand.

Ellie announced her decision. "Don't unpack; we're leaving."

When Charlotte stood to protest, she held out a hand to stop her. "This is not your decision."

Charlotte quickly backed down.

"I won't put your life in danger, Alex. Or your mother's. And I won't have this home invaded by thugs."

Alex frowned, but didn't protest.

"I think Alex should move in with Charlotte until this is over. Or at least until we're sure there's no risk," said Ellie. "Jonathan's right. We should be in a real safe house."

"I'm sorry, can you say that again?" asked Jonathan.

"Jonathan's right." She glared at him. "Enjoy it while you can. Those words will never leave my lips again."

He smiled.

Charlotte opened her mouth to say something, then closed it and looked to Vincent for help.

"Don't look at me. I agree with Ellie."

Charlotte huffed. "The ghost brought you here for a reason."

"Yes, for me to find Bun Bun. And I have."

"But you don't know why."

"No, we don't," said Vincent. "I'm sure we'll understand when the time is right."

"What brought this on?" asked Jonathan.

"I had time alone to consider my options. These are generous people. They didn't think twice about helping us. I can't let anything happen to them. Jonathan, I'm not the person you've seen down here. Being in Savannah has brought back the worst in me. That ends now."

"How about we work together from now on?" he said.

"I'd like that."

Jonathan reached out a hand to shake, but Ellie gave him a hug.

"I think Olivia should stay with Alex and Charlotte," said Jonathan.

"No! I have the same level of training as Ellie and Preston. I can kick butt with the best of them."

Jonathan's smile widened. "That is so hot."

"What is?" asked Ellie.

"A blonde in stilettos with a gun." He tilted his head. "I assume you own stilettos?"

Olivia didn't answer his question. Not directly. She aimed her sultry eyes at him, then winked and walked away.

Jonathan's face momentarily reddened.

Vincent watched the dance between the two of them and wondered whether Olivia was genuinely interested in this man. On this trip, she'd allowed herself to have moments of playfulness, and she directed that playfulness toward Jonathan. *The poor guy*, he thought. *He has no idea what he's getting himself into.*

Jonathan suggested they stay at Alex's, then move to the safe house in the morning. They all agreed.

"Tomorrow I'll check in with my dad to see if the students uploaded any photos," said Preston.

"What are you talking about?" asked Jonathan. "Is there something you forgot to mention?"

"I took photos of the spectators at Georgetown. Before I left, I sent out a tweet to Ellie's students and asked them to upload any photos that were shared. My father's reviewing everything."

"Why is he involved in this case?"

"Preston's father is Admiral David Bartlett," said Vincent. "He stayed behind in case Detective Ferris needed any additional information. He has skills that could be helpful."

"What skills?"

"He has perfect recall. The day of the attack, he walked the crime scene with Preston and scanned the area. Between his memory, the detective's report, and any photos, he'll be able to pinpoint any anomalies."

"Like the third man," said Jonathan.

"Yes."

"Send Dominick a copy of anything your dad finds."

"Okay. I'd still like to set up my own security system at the safe house. Even if the police already have one installed. Consider it added protection."

CHAPTER 23

August 25, 2017

THE NEXT MORNING, THEY MOVED TO THEIR NEW LOCATION. THE house had four bedrooms, surrounded by woods, with an unobstructed view of the road. Dominick pulled into the garage to unload his car. He'd brought boxes and boxes of equipment.

"Holy crap," said Jonathan. "What did you buy?"

"You'll see," said Preston.

Both Preston's and Dominick's expressions were that of a kid in a candy store, excited to open their new toys. The boxes contained pieces of a security system equipped with recording capabilities. They installed cameras and motion detectors along the perimeter, on the porches, and in strategic areas in the backyard. They'd even placed cameras in trees pointing to the street to record the license plates of any cars that passed by. Once connected, they could monitor the road and the entire property, front and back, from one screen. When someone passed through a motion detector, an alarm would sound, and they'd be able to see where the intruder entered the property and stop them.

"We're ready for them now," said Preston. By afternoon, he was beyond restless. He sat at the computer and played the video of the front street and counted the cars that had driven past the house. Anything to feel as though he wasn't sitting on his hands while someone was plotting against them. "One, two, three…"

"Preston," said Jonathan. "Stop."

He stood and moved from one room to the next. First the kitchen, then the dining room and finally the living room, making a complete circle. Again, and again. "I'm going crazy. How can you do this all the time?"

"Do what?"

"Wait in this house all day with nothing to do. I never realized how much I moved around during the day until I was cooped up in this place."

Vincent smiled. "We had to stop every hour for bathroom breaks on the way down so he could stretch his legs. But Preston, I think this has more to do with not having your own toys to play with. You sit in front of your computers at home all night long. You have your own computer with you. Download a computer game or something."

"I don't think I'd be able to concentrate on a game. Not when someone is trying to kill us."

"What do you mean, cooped up?" asked Jonathan. "You're in a four-bedroom cabin in the woods. Try sitting in a car all night, watching a door."

"I'd die of boredom if I had to sit in a car all night."

"You have the internet," said Vincent. "Search for something."

"Search for what?"

"I don't know. Use that big brain of yours."

———

Each time a car passed the motion detector, a photo was taken and saved to a file on Dominick's computer. To keep his mind occupied, Preston created a spreadsheet with information about each car. He listed the make and model, the color, the number on the license plate, and the time it passed the house.

As he examined the photos, he noticed something odd. He zoomed in on the lower corner of the image and saw a piece of a headlight. A sliver. He examined the other photos. The sliver was in every shot, which meant it hadn't moved since they'd installed the security system. It was too small to get information about the car or its owner, or to see whether anyone was sitting inside, waiting.

"Jonathan, look at this."

After Jonathan reviewed the photos, he agreed with Preston. They needed to check it out.

"I'm coming with you," said Preston.

"You are not a cop, remember. I'm supposed to be protecting you."

"No, you're protecting Ellie. I'm coming. I need to breathe in some fresh air."

"Fine, if it'll shut you up. It's probably nothing, anyway." He opened a padded case and pulled out a camera with a telephoto lens strong enough to count the legs on a gnat.

"Wow. Look at that," said Preston. "You're not fooling around."

"We're getting close enough to take a photo and see if anyone's inside, then we're coming back. So, take those deep breaths while you can. Got it?"

Preston agreed. He tapped his fingers on the side of his legs while he waited for Jonathan, eager to get outside.

———

They left from the back door and hiked through the woods toward the street. Jonathan pulled out his camera and zoomed in close enough to see inside the car. "There's someone in the front seat." He took a photograph of the car, the license plate, and the driver.

Preston wanted to beat information out of this man, to find out why he was following them and stalking Ellie.

Jonathan disagreed. He emailed the photos to Dominick and turned to leave.

"Is that all you're going to do?"

"Yes, until we have more information." He grabbed Preston by the arm to drag him back to the house. "Come on. We're going back."

"Why don't we go after him now?"

"Because it's not illegal to sit in a car. We'll wait and see."

"Wait? You're killing me."

Jonathan grinned. "I can see that."

Once inside, Dominick ran the number on the license plate. It was a rental. Every thirty minutes, Jonathan or Dominick would trek through the woods and take another photo. And each time, Preston tagged along. The car and the person inside hadn't moved in three hours.

"Okay," said Jonathan. "It's time to find out who this guy is."

Preston stood, ready to help.

"You stay here," said Jonathan.

"I don't think so. Dominick can stay inside to protect Ellie, and I can be your backup."

"My backup! How many times do I have to say this? You're not a cop! I don't want to worry about that guy and you at the same time."

"Well, unless you arrest me, I'm going with you. I can handle myself, and you know it."

"If you get shot, it's on you. Stay behind me and don't do anything stupid."

———

They hiked through the woods for the last time and moved closer to the car. Preston noticed the door was locked and pulled a spring-loaded glass punch from his pocket. Before Jonathan could stop him, he moved next to the car, barely making a sound. He placed the punch on the lower corner of the window and pushed the button. The tempered glass exploded into tiny pieces. Most of them dropped to the ground outside the car, but the unexpected explosion shocked the driver.

"What the hell?" he shrieked.

Before he understood what had happened, Preston opened the door and dragged him out of the car. He fell to the ground and placed his arms over his head and face as though protecting himself from a madman. "Wait! Don't hurt me!"

Jonathan pulled Preston away. "What's the matter with you? I said not to do anything stupid."

"What? Were you going to ask him nicely to get out of the car?"

"Yes!"

"Why? Someone is trying to kill Ellie, and you want me to be nice? Not going to happen."

Jonathan informed the man he was a police officer, and he was under arrest, then turned him onto his stomach and searched for a weapon. He had none. He placed handcuffs on the stranger and removed a wallet from his back pocket.

"Stand over there," he ordered Preston, pointing to the driveway. "I don't need you causing any more trouble."

"Not going to happen."

"Don't make me cuff you, too. Go search the car while I take care of him."

The man on the ground screamed, "I can explain."

Preston half expected him to burst into tears.

Jonathan placed the handcuffed stranger in a seated position while Preston searched the car. He removed one piece of luggage, a backpack containing a computer, a tablet, and a hotspot, along with multiple chargers. There was also a camera case with a lens that rivaled Jonathan's.

"Who were you surveilling with this bad boy?" asked Preston.

"The cuffs are too tight," the man shouted.

"Why are you watching the house?" asked Jonathan.

"I'm not who you think I am. I wouldn't hurt her."

When he used the word "her," Jonathan turned to Preston and pointed a finger, as though to warn him. "Stay where you are. You wouldn't hurt who?"

"Elizabeth. She's my sister."

Jonathan and Preston were both speechless.

CHAPTER 24

O NCE INSIDE, JONATHAN PUSHED THE HANDCUFFED STRANGER
into a kitchen chair. He and Dominick sat down across from him,
while Olivia moved a chair to the corner of the room to observe.
Neither Jonathan nor Preston had repeated the man's claim.

Preston leaned against the counter with his arms crossed over his chest,
staring at the stranger. He understood this was Jonathan and Dominick's
case. The interrogation was their responsibility, and he needed to give them
space to do their job. Although he would have preferred to beat it out of him.

Vincent and Ellie remained in the living room. Close enough to hear
everything and remain out of the stranger's view.

Jonathan spread out the contents of his wallet on the table. "Timothy
Watts," he read from the license. "Let's start from the beginning, shall we?"

Timothy nodded, warily.

"The address on your license is in Kansas City. Is that where you live
now?"

"Yes."

"You want to tell me why you're a thousand miles from home?"

"The car's a rental. First, I want to know who's going to pay for that
window." Timothy appeared more fixated on the car than the fact that he
was under arrest.

Jonathan glared at Preston, who remained stone-faced.

"Why are you in Savannah?" asked Jonathan.

Timothy moved around in his seat, trying to get comfortable. His face
reddened from the heat, with beads of sweat about to roll down his face.
"Are these cuffs necessary?" He didn't answer the question.

"Yes. I'll repeat. Why are you in Savannah?"

"That's complicated."

Jonathan stood and moved toward Timothy. "This isn't working. Let's go to the precinct."

He shifted away before Jonathan could grab him. "No. I'm telling the truth. It's complicated."

"Then uncomplicate it." He returned to the other side of the table and sat. "You have five seconds."

"I have to start from the beginning. My beginning. Not the one you choose for me. It's the only way it will make sense. You'll have the answers you want; I swear."

"If I don't like where this is going, Preston will finish the interrogation."

"I understand, but you have to be patient." He looked at Preston. "Both of you."

Jonathan agreed, though Preston had not.

Vincent moved into the kitchen and stood next to Preston, who continually glared at Timothy.

He sunk deeper into his chair. "I wasn't following Elizabeth. Not at first. I was following someone else, who led me to her."

When Timothy referred to Ellie by her given name, Preston realized he didn't know her. He'd probably never even met her. Everyone, including the students at Georgetown, referred to her as Ellie.

Timothy's eyes moved around the room, checking each person as though he were looking for someone, then stopped at Vincent, the elder in the group. His brown eyes looked at him, begging to be rescued from these people.

"Son, Ellie is my daughter. I suggest you tell us everything—and be quick about it."

He stammered, but the next time he spoke, he directed his comments to Vincent and dismissed Jonathan altogether. "It's not what you think. I told them outside, I wouldn't hurt Elizabeth. I was here to protect her. You need to trust me."

"Why should we believe you?" asked Vincent.

"Like I told them, Elizabeth is my sister."

That revelation sucked all the oxygen out of the room. They each stared, with their mouths open. Preston glanced toward Ellie to gauge her reaction. She appeared stunned. After he blurted those words, she moved into the kitchen and faced the man who claimed to be her brother.

"Sister? Did you say sister?" She could barely speak in more than a whisper.

Her reaction appeared tepid, as though what he'd said was unimportant. Preston knew otherwise. This had shaken her to the core.

"Well, kind of," said Timothy.

"Kind of?" Her voice was nearly gone. "What does that mean?"

"That's why I want to start from the beginning. To help you understand."

"Take as much time as you need."

"Ellie, I realize this is important," said Jonathan. "But we need to find out how he got here and who wants you dead. The family reunion may have to wait."

"They're both related," insisted Timothy. "Other people are after Elizabeth, not me."

"Please, call me Ellie. Jonathan, take those cuffs off." Her voice was no longer a whisper. She used a tone reserved for her students when she expected them to do as they were told.

Jonathan complied.

"Thanks." Timothy sat up a little straighter and rubbed his wrists, then wiped the sweat from his face.

"Other people?" asked Jonathan. "Are these other people responsible for what happened in Georgetown?"

"Yes. I assume so. But I wasn't at the university. I've never been to Georgetown or DC."

"Do you know who they are?"

"No!" he insisted. "Well, maybe." He shrugged. "I'm not sure. But it wasn't me. I swear." With his palms out and his hands raised in surrender, his eyes met Preston's. "I know you're angry and want answers. If I knew what was going to happen, I would have called the police. But I wasn't at Georgetown."

"We all need to relax," said Vincent. "Give the man a chance to explain. That means you, Preston."

Preston raised his own hands. "I'm good. At least for the moment."

Timothy sunk even lower in his chair. Any lower and he'd be on the floor in a pool of his own sweat. He'd already soaked through his shirt.

Ellie pulled a chair up to the table and sat across from Timothy. "Okay. We're ready to listen."

When he started with *"When I was four months old,"* Preston rolled his eyes. "Oh, good Lord."

He stopped speaking, as though to gather his thoughts. No one in the room spoke. There wasn't a grunt or a cough. As they waited, the kitchen fell so still, the tick of a clock resonated through the room. They could even hear the birds singing in the trees. Preston wondered how long it would be before Jonathan nudged him along. But there was no need. He started again.

"On my birthday, my girlfriend gave me a DNA test kit as a gift. For the last couple of years, she'd been tracing her roots, and she wanted me to do the same. It would be something we could do together."

"Okay," said Jonathan.

"When mine came back, none of the matches were familiar. Not one. A few were from America. Most were from Ireland or England. A handful of my cousins had taken the same test, and we had no common ancestors. That's impossible. The thing is, it showed me as being eighty-three percent Irish and the rest was England and Wales. But my mother's first-generation Italian American. What's the probability of that?"

"What did you do?" asked Jonathan.

"I showed the results to my mother. I never told her I was getting tested. She said they adopted me when I was a baby." He shook his head, shocked by his new reality. "Can you imagine finding out you're adopted when you're thirty years old?"

"In Kansas?"

"Yes. Someone left me on the steps of my mother's church when I was around four months old. She was the church secretary. My parents had been trying to adopt when they found me. I never knew about that either." There was more than a little irritation in his voice. "The priest called the authorities. They agreed to allow my parents to foster me because of their connections to the church."

"What did you do?" The pace of Timothy's answers clearly taxed Jonathan's patience.

"I felt disconnected. At first, I thought my head would explode. I wanted to know why she didn't tell me the truth years ago. She said they kept putting it off. After a while, they were afraid of how I'd react, so they said nothing. I thought about it for a while, then decided to find my origins."

"How did your mother feel about that?" asked Vincent.

"Vincent," said Jonathan. "I don't care how his mother felt. Please don't interrupt."

"Sorry. It won't happen again."

Preston understood. Jonathan needed to be the single person interrogating Timothy. One answer would lead to another question, and another. If someone interrupted, he might lose track of the questions. And any interruptions would disrupt the flow and confuse the situation.

"To answer your question, she was relieved. She didn't want to take this secret to her grave. Can I have my phone? I want to show you something." When Jonathan handed him the phone, he pulled up a photo. "This is what I was wrapped in when they found me. My mother believed the monogram might be important, so she kept it hidden in the attic. The police referenced the initials during their search but found nothing."

The letters *W.O.* were monogrammed on a blue blanket. Considering Ellie's coat held the initials *J.O.*, his story became more believable. Preston wondered why someone would abandon a baby in a monogrammed blanket. That could help connect the child to a family. Unless they hadn't noticed the monogram, or they weren't supposed to be found at all.

"She always wanted to give my birth mother a message."

"Which was?" asked Jonathan.

"That I was alive and well. That I had a good life. She gave me the blanket as proof. After that, I did what anyone would have done. I researched."

"What research?" asked Jonathan.

"The logical first step was to contact the people who matched my DNA. But most were second or third or even fourth cousins. Nearly all were in Ireland, not America, and they knew nothing about a missing baby. I assumed anyone who was a close relation hadn't taken a DNA test with that company."

"What did you do next?"

"When that was no help, I submitted a freedom of information request to receive a copy of the original police report. The local police did a thorough investigation and found nothing. They combed the area, but never found my birth mother. There was one witness named Dan Garrett.

Mr. Garrett saw a well-dressed white man on the church steps the night before they found me. The man was tall and thin. Nothing else was listed. According to the report, he walked up the church stairs, then turned around and left. At least Mr. Garrett thought he left. They didn't consider his account credible because he was a homeless drunk."

"Drunks are never reliable," said Jonathan. "And yet, you believed him. Why?"

"Because the car Mr. Garrett saw in front of the church was a Mercedes with out-of-state plates. He couldn't remember which state, but it wasn't Kansas. The church was closed. No one should have been parked in that location. Trust me, if you saw a Mercedes parked in that neighborhood at night, you'd notice."

"Okay, go on."

"According to the report, Mr. Garrett heard the man pounding his fist on the church door, then left. He could have walked around the building to the rectory, but he couldn't be sure because he'd passed out by then. He didn't know if the man left a baby on the steps."

"And the police?"

"They couldn't get anything else out of Mr. Garrett because he was too drunk. And the priest in the rectory said no one knocked on his door. After that, I started searching for missing children."

"Why missing?" asked Jonathan.

"Because a grown man was seen on the steps of the church, the exact night I was abandoned. Not a desperate young mother. It was a wealthy white man. I mean, what's the probability of that? It seemed suspicious to me."

"No one saw him with the baby, and you assumed this man was responsible?"

"Yes. I had to start somewhere. Since Mr. Garrett knew the plates weren't from Kansas, I expanded the search for missing and abandoned children across the country. It's easier to search across state lines these days than it was thirty years ago. It was a wild guess, I admit."

"You found something?"

"I thought so."

"Twice now you used the word probability. What do you do for a living?"

"I'm a research analyst. My specialty is finding anomalies in databases. It's the way my mind works."

There was a collective "*AHHH*" in the room.

"Research comes naturally," said Jonathan.

"Yes. Do you mind if I use my computer?"

Dominick watched every keystroke and made a note of each password phrase and file name.

He opened a directory named *fuckedup*, with the password phrase, *leftonthefuckingsteps*.

Dominick chuckled. "Love the passwords."

Timothy shrugged. "It seemed appropriate."

Inside were lists of sub-directories. He opened the directory titled *newspapers*, which included hundreds of articles from all over the country. Each contained information about a missing or abandoned child.

"I was horrified when I saw how many children went missing each year, but I had to put my emotions aside and continue my search. Most of the articles were about missing girls or people of color, or someone older, or younger."

"How long did this take?" asked Jonathan.

"About a year."

"A year! Wow. Sounds like you were a man on a mission."

"True. I work full-time, and I have a girlfriend. I searched when I had free time."

"When did you find what you were looking for?" asked Jonathan.

"Three months ago."

"Three months!" said Ellie.

Another collective "*AHHH*" filled the room as they grasped what Timothy had revealed.

"Does that mean something?" he asked.

"Yes," said Ellie. "It means you are the trigger."

CHAPTER 25

TIMOTHY APPEARED PERPLEXED, NOT SURE WHAT THEY MEANT BY "trigger." Jonathan insisted he continue.

"What did you find out?"

He clicked on an article from Kennebunk, Maine. The screen filled with the image of a mangled car and tractor-trailer. It was impossible to tell where the front of the car began and the truck ended. The vehicles fused together.

"Good God," said Jonathan. "How could anyone survive?"

"The front of the car had most of the damage. Three people in the back seat lived. The man and woman in the front did not."

Jonathan and Dominick scanned the article. The story ran in a local paper about a serious car accident dating back thirty years. Anderson and Gabrielle O'Rourke, visiting from Boston, died in the accident. The article didn't list the names and ages or any additional information about the three survivors.

"I think we're the survivors." He then turned toward Ellie. "In fact, I know we are. The accident was two days before my mother found me and we were both dropped off on the same day. I assume they, whoever they are, had to transport us to our locations. That took a fair amount of time."

"Dropped off," Ellie said with a snort. "That's exactly what they did." Her tone was sarcastic, but her statement and the sentiment appeared to go over Timothy's head.

"They?" asked Jonathan.

"There had to be more than one person involved. They dropped us off." He paused. "Sorry. They abandoned us on the same day. That's impossible. There had to be two or more people involved."

"Or maybe you're wrong," said Jonathan.

"No. Not in this case."

"How did you know they abandoned you and Ellie on the same day?" asked Jonathan.

Timothy clicked on an article about an abandoned little girl around three or four years old in critical condition in Savannah, Georgia. It didn't explain why she was critical, and her name was not listed. It was an article in a local paper asking the public if they'd ever seen this child or her parents. "Look at the photo. This is about you. Plus, the dates are the same." The photo was of Ellie sitting up in the hospital bed, staring at the camera.

"Why did you jump to this conclusion?" asked Jonathan. "The accident was in Maine and the O'Rourkes lived in Boston. Plus, the article didn't mention children. It seems like an enormous leap. And where did you find a connection between the O'Rourkes and the two of you?"

The barrage of questions didn't appear to rattle Timothy. He provided clear and concise answers as his clothes became more drenched in sweat. "Is it hot in here? I mean, is the air conditioning broken?"

Preston laughed. "No, it's not broken. It can't keep up. I've been told you get used to it. Who knows how long that will take?"

"How can people live here?" Timothy asked, as beads of sweat ran down his face.

"Timothy." Jonathan drew out his name, begging him to continue.

"Sorry. I didn't stop at this article. In fact, it was the last one I read. It doesn't even fit the criteria."

"The criteria being an abandoned or missing four-month-old boy on a particular date," said Jonathan.

"Yes. In all my searches, this one article kept showing up at the top of the list, no matter how I changed my search. The headline was about a car accident, not missing children, so I ignored it."

Preston and Ellie exchanged a glance. They each appeared to understand why this article rose above the others. Because of that, Timothy's theory became even more plausible, which gave them a reason to take him seriously.

"Until?" asked Jonathan.

"Until I had no other choice. Until there were no other articles to read. There had to be something in there, but I found nothing. I read it because after seeing the headline so many times, I needed to find out what had happened."

"You were curious. It was as simple as that," said Jonathan.

He nodded.

"What made you conclude children were in the car, considering there were none mentioned?"

"Nothing I can explain. It was something I had to explore. I submitted another freedom of information request to get the police report. It took awhile to receive, and it didn't help. Then I contacted the reporter who wrote the story to see if there were any unpublished details. I wondered if they removed pieces of the article before they uploaded it to their archive. There had to be a reason it kept showing up at the top of my search."

Now Preston shared a glance with Vincent. He, too, appeared to understand what that meant.

Dominick zoomed in on the author of the article. "That would be Cyrus Willingham." He pulled up a photo of Cyrus for Ellie to see. "Look familiar?"

"No."

"I called multiple times. He wouldn't talk on the phone."

"That's odd," said Jonathan. "Why not discuss a simple, but tragic, accident that happened decades ago?"

"I agree. That's why I went to his office in person."

Jonathan's eyes widened. "You flew to Maine to talk to this man? Why?"

"I needed to find out what happened. It niggled at me. I hate that."

Jonathan laughed. "Man, you're crazier than I am."

He shrugged. "Once a puzzle is in my head, I have to figure it out."

"And this accident had become a puzzle to solve," said Jonathan.

"Yes, that's right, at the beginning. When I arrived, Mr. Willingham explained he was a new reporter then, and this was the first time he'd covered a fatal accident. He showed me one of his photos. It was a bloody mess. He refused to give me any unpublished information for fear of upsetting the family."

"Did you find anything suspicious about the accident?"

"No. Anderson O'Rourke lost control of his car and drove head-on into the front of a truck."

"Whoa," said Preston.

"It was bad. Mr. Willingham asked why I was investigating the accident."

"What did you tell him?" asked Jonathan.

"The truth. I was searching for my birth family."

"That was your first mistake," said Preston.

"True. I figured that out a bit too late. That's when he hardened his position. He insinuated I was after their money."

"They're wealthy?" asked Jonathan.

"They're billionaires, although I wasn't aware of that. I thought he was being melodramatic. I wondered if there could be another reason not to help me. He had only one."

"Which was?"

"Ethics. He didn't think it was his place to help in my search. He thought the family had been through enough, and he wouldn't divulge any private information."

"It's understandable," said Jonathan.

"Well, that depends," said Olivia. "If there were children, what happened to them? They're adults now."

"I went to the police precinct and asked to speak to the officer at the scene. His name was Joseph Bushman." Timothy brought up the police report for Dominick to review.

"The woman at the desk was in her fifties. There were photos of children and grandchildren on the shelves. I figured she would help me. Older women feel the need to mother me, and they always want to give me food." That seemed to confound him. "What's with that, anyway? I don't understand it, but in this case it was useful. Most of the time it's a pain in my butt."

Vincent grinned. He, more than the others, seemed to understand why older women reacted that way. Timothy had a boyish quality about him, a gentleness in his demeanor and his expressions.

"The officer died three years ago, but she gave me the name and address of his widow."

"You called her?" Jonathan shouted in outrage. "To solve your fucking puzzle?"

"Well, if you put it like that, it sounds awful."

"Because it is awful."

"She had no problem with it. There were boxes with his notebooks in their garage. She let me look through them. She even brought me cookies and lemonade while I searched."

Jonathan shook his head. "Seriously?"

"I told you, older women like me."

"Do all detectives save their notes?" asked Preston. "Louis Thibodeaux did the same thing."

"They all keep some," said Jonathan. "Did you find out who was in the car?"

"We were. And a nanny named Felicia Romero. The children's names were Jacqueline and William O'Rourke. That's all I got from his notes. There were no photos of the children. Or at least I didn't find any."

Timothy couldn't have known about the monogrammed coat in evidence or that Ellie called herself Jacqueline when hypnotized. Preston remained silent to allow Jonathan to continue his interrogation. Now they all understood what that meant. Jacqueline O'Rourke fit Ellie's criteria.

"I don't remember any of this," said Ellie. "Would a three- or four-year-old remember being in this kind of accident?"

"Not necessarily," said Olivia. "Some things are best forgotten."

"I needed to find out what happened to the children," said Timothy. "I wanted to know where they were today to prove if I was on the right track."

"To find out if you were, in fact, William O'Rourke?" asked Jonathan.

"Yes. I investigated Jacqueline and William O'Rourke. There was nothing. I mean nothing. Not on Instagram or Facebook. Not even Snapchat or Twitter or any other dating or social media site a thirty-year-old would use today. Do you know how many millennials Google themselves to check their electronic footprint?"

"No," said Vincent. "How many of you Google your own name?"

Everyone raised their hand.

"Really?" said Vincent.

"It's impossible for them not to have an electronic footprint," insisted Timothy. "Especially if they're from a wealthy family."

Jonathan agreed. "You think they disappeared after the accident. What did you do?"

"First, I searched for the parents online, beyond the article in Maine. I found nothing about the accident. There should have been an article written about a wealthy family who died tragically. Or at least the dates of the funerals or condolences from the business community in Boston. Again, nothing."

"Did the money play a role in your criteria? It's my job to ask."

"I don't blame you for asking, but no. I found out that Bradford O'Rourke is the patriarch of the family. He had two sons, named Randolph and Anderson. I believe they came from old money. Their business is in finance."

"Or money laundering," said Preston.

He shrugged. "That's for someone else to find out. I didn't check into their business practices."

"What happened to the children?" asked Olivia, clearly frustrated. "I'm going to keep asking until I get an answer."

"Powerful people wanted them dead," said Preston. "That's what happened."

"Dead?" Timothy appeared surprised by Preston's comment. "Why?"

"Good question. We intend to find out," Jonathan insisted.

"We can assume the family mourned their loss in private without the press or the police on their doorstep," said Dominick. "It was an accident."

"Yes," said Olivia. "But where are the children?"

"They're right in front of you," argued Timothy. "Believe me."

"It means one of these people could be Ellie's killer," said Jonathan.

"A faceless monster," said Ellie. "They got rid of their problem."

"Out of sight, out of mind," said Jonathan. "If any of this is true, these people are at the very least guilty of child abandonment and attempted murder—twice. They're not monsters, Ellie. They're criminals."

"Both, if you ask me," said Ellie.

"I'm sorry," said Timothy. "Did you say twice? I'm not following."

"They abandoned you at a church, but they tried to kill Ellie when they dropped her off," said Preston.

All the color left Timothy's face as he added one plus one and came up with him being the "trigger." "Correct me if I'm wrong. You're suggesting the people who came after you in Georgetown are here now because of me. Because I discovered something I shouldn't have? Is that what you meant by 'trigger'?"

Preston could almost see his mind working, going through whatever evidence he had and coming to the same conclusion.

"Oh, my God. This is all my fault."

"No!" insisted Jonathan. "None of this is your fault. It's important that you believe that. It's the fault of the people who abandoned you and tried to kill Ellie."

"Kill! These people are killers." Now, even more sweat ran down his face.

Ellie handed him a tissue.

"It's okay. We'll take care of these people, one way or the other," said Ellie, with a tone that made a chill run down Preston's spine.

It was "the other" remark that concerned him.

"It's time to concentrate on the facts. The rest will fall into place," said Jonathan.

Preston agreed. He could only imagine what was going through Ellie's mind. *What happened to the children after the accident? Was she one of them?* He suspected they were about to find out whether Timothy was telling the unvarnished truth.

CHAPTER 26

"WHAT DID YOU DO NEXT?" ASKED JONATHAN.

Questions like this seemed to be part of the mantra for cops. As well as others, like: What did you do, or Who did you speak to? What do you know and when did you find out? These questions, asked multiple times in a single interview, were a cop's way of getting to the root of any investigation.

"You're an analyst," said Jonathan. "Cut through all the data. Just give us the important facts."

"In other words, spit it out already," Preston ordered.

Timothy let out a slight, nervous laugh. "Sorry about that. I tend to go on. It's a nasty habit."

"No kidding," said Preston.

"I tracked down Felicia Romero. It wasn't hard. I did a quick Google search. I pulled up the address, went on over and knocked on her door."

"You did what?" asked Jonathan.

Preston shook his head. "That worked out so well with Willingham."

"It seemed reasonable to me. I wanted to find out about the accident. She could tell me. At first, I was going to tell her I was a journalism student working on a class project. I decided to tell her the truth. It's easier to tell the truth. I don't have to keep track of the lies."

Jonathan placed his hand on his head while Preston raised a finger in the air and made a circle to urge him to speed this up.

Timothy either ignored Preston or couldn't change the way his mind worked. He pressed on. "She wasn't sure what to make of me at first."

Jonathan laughed. "Now that's a surprise."

"When I showed her the photo of the blanket, she realized I was telling the truth and let me in. She told me everything." He stopped talking long enough to wipe the sweat from his face. "May I have another bottle of water?"

Preston went to the fridge and threw the bottle across the room. It flew straight through the air and into Timothy's hands.

"Nice catch," said Jonathan.

"I played football in high school." After a few sips of water, he continued. "First, I need to give you some context that might be meaningful, or not."

"Oh, God," Jonathan muttered.

"Quickly," said Preston. "Or I'm going to throw you across the room instead of a water bottle."

"Gabrielle O'Rourke was born in Ireland. She wanted to deliver her children there, though Felicia did not understand why. Once they announced the pregnancy, they took a hiatus and returned to Ireland."

"It's a personal choice," said Olivia. "Especially if she still has family there. She might want to be with her mother after delivery."

"Olivia," said Jonathan. "For God's sake, don't interrupt him."

She grinned. "My apologies."

"When they came home with William, something happened." He appeared perplexed, as though he wasn't sure how to continue. "What name should I use when I'm telling this, William or Timothy?"

"Use William. It's easier to follow," said Jonathan.

"There was a tremendous fight between Anderson and his father. His father stormed out of the house and didn't return until the night of the accident. All Felicia remembered was Gabrielle crying all the time. There was one thing she wanted us to know, though." He met Ellie's eyes. "Anderson and Gabrielle loved those babies. They loved us."

Ellie frowned. "I'm not sure how I feel about any of this."

"She gave me photos of the family. They're under *fuckedupfamilyphotos*."

Dominic grinned, then brought up the file.

"Bring up that photo."

He pulled up a portrait of Jacqueline holding her baby brother. It drew everyone to the computer screen. They got up off their chairs and gathered around to see a three-year-old Ellie holding a baby in her lap.

"Jesus," Preston whispered.

Ellie closed her eyes, then shook her head.

"Are you all right?" Vincent asked Ellie.

"I think so."

Preston knew otherwise. He could only imagine what she was thinking. Both of her birth parents were dead, and someone tried to kill her. Twice.

"Felicia said Bradford O'Rourke seemed obsessed with William's birth. She thought that's what started the argument."

"Why?" asked Jonathan.

"She didn't know. The two men had a violent argument the day of the accident. She heard something about being cut off, but their voices were too muffled to understand what they were saying. An hour later, Anderson told everyone to pack their bags. They got in the car, and he flew down the driveway. She'd never seen him so angry."

"That's when the accident happened?" asked Jonathan.

"Yes. It was a long ride from Boston to Kennebunk, but his anger never waned. He lost control of the car."

"She confirmed it was a horrible accident, not murder."

"Yes. It was a miracle anyone survived. Anderson and Gabrielle died, but the three passengers were unharmed. Bradford told Felicia to take the kids back to Boston. Jacqueline was in shock and they all should have gone to the hospital. The O'Rourkes wouldn't allow it. Once Bradford returned home, he fired her on the spot. No one ever saw the kids again."

"Never?" Jonathan asked, stunned by this revelation. "How did she know they were gone once they fired her?"

"It's a close-knit community. Felicia and the staff have been friends for decades. They still are. Felicia called a woman who lived down the street to come over and meet me. She still works for the O'Rourkes and verified they never saw the children again. They were afraid to report their absence to the police. The O'Rourkes are powerful people. She described Bradford O'Rourke as a lunatic they all stayed away from."

"Or a monster," said Vincent. "Can you create a slideshow of all the photos? It would be easier for everyone to see."

After Dominick clicked a few keys, the slideshow began, but Ellie stood in the back, as far away from this new reality as possible.

"Ellie, that really is you," said Preston.

Vincent agreed. "Which means you are Jacqueline O'Rourke."

Dominick zoomed in on the baby's face. "I have to admit, he resembles Timothy."

Preston grunted. "How can you tell? All babies look alike."

When the screen changed to a portrait of Jacqueline, there was another collective gasp in the room. A little girl, with a gleaming smile, wearing a monogrammed coat and carrying a pink bunny, filled the screen. The same coat in the evidence bag. And the same bunny that sat on the kitchen table.

Ellie picked up Bun Bun and held her close to her heart but said nothing.

"Stop," said Vincent to Dominick. "Zoom in there." He pointed to a cutout in the matting.

As Dominick zoomed in, a lock of curly red hair came into focus.

"That's sweet," said Vincent. "They didn't want to forget how red your hair was as a child."

"What I see is DNA," said Dominick.

Preston agreed. "And what I see is a reason for murder."

"Murder?" Timothy asked.

"Yes, it's a way to tie Ellie to their fortune."

When the next photo came into view, Ellie hyperventilated. Her entire body vibrated as fear once again had taken hold. The same way she reacted when she walked McQueen's Island Trail.

"What's wrong?" asked Olivia.

She couldn't catch her breath enough to speak.

"You look like you're going to pass out." Olivia opened cabinet doors in the kitchen until she found a small paper bag. "Here, breathe into this. It will help."

As Ellie breathed into the bag, she glared at the screen, then her eyes shifted to her father.

"It's him," Vincent growled. "Isn't it?" His voice sounded primal, more animal than human.

Ellie didn't move. She kept her eyes fixed on the screen.

"Who? Where?" Jonathan asked, then realized she was staring at the computer. "What aren't you saying? Is that the man who hurt you?"

"No!" said Vincent. "That's the monster who tried to kill her."

CHAPTER 27

A DECADES-OLD PHOTO OF A TALL, THIN MAN IN HIS LATE TWEN-
ties filled the computer screen. Preston now knew this was the man
who abducted Ellie when she was a child. He suspected he'd returned to finish the job. He knew Vincent wouldn't allow that to happen.
If O'Rourke was responsible for the attack in Georgetown, he'd like to get
his hands on him. Without him, he wouldn't have killed a man.

After Ellie's reaction, everyone had instinctively taken a step back to
allow Jonathan to finish his interview with Timothy. They had to follow
his unusual thought process to get there.

"Timothy, who is that?" Jonathan pointed to the man on the screen.

For the first time, Timothy appeared speechless. He, too, stared at
the monster.

"Hey." Jonathan snapped his fingers in Timothy's face and pointed to
the photo. "Don't lose your focus now. WHO…IS…HE?"

"That's Randolph O'Rourke. That's what Felicia Romero told me, but
I don't know what he looks like today. Did he hurt my sister?"

"Dominick, run a background check."

"Already doing it."

"How did you find out Ellie was in Savannah? Be quick about it."

Timothy appeared to understand the gravity of the situation and
stopped his propensity to dawdle. "After they broadcast the attack on the
news, I received a frantic call from Felicia. I hadn't spoken to her since the
day we met three months ago. She swore the woman being attacked was
Jacqueline."

"Why?" asked Ellie.

"When she saw your photo on the news, the red curls reminded her of you."

"Why? I can't be the only person she'd met with red curly hair. It's been thirty years."

"I asked her the same question. She couldn't explain it. You looked so familiar. She figured it must have been because of my visit. You know, jogging her memory. Then she looked closer and saw the color of your eyes and ran to the computer and brought up the photo from the news. When she zoomed in on the image and saw the birthmark on your neck, she knew. Felicia said she'd never seen anyone with eyes that color before or since. No one else would have those eyes and the birthmark."

"Sounds reasonable," said Jonathan.

"Then she told me the O'Rourkes had to be responsible."

"Responsible for what?"

"For the attack in Georgetown."

Jonathan frowned. "Why did she jump to that conclusion?"

"I don't know. She was so hysterical she wouldn't answer many questions. She kept screaming for me to stop what I was doing and save my sister. Period."

"Which you set out to do."

"Yes."

"Did she talk to anyone else?"

"No. Only me. She didn't want to put Elizabeth in any more danger."

Dominick displayed a recent motor vehicle photo of Randolph O'Rourke. He was six feet tall, one hundred eighty-five pounds, with gray hair. "Check this out."

"Have you seen this man?" Jonathan asked Timothy.

Preston understood Jonathan was trying to tie the two cases together, especially considering Randolph O'Rourke matched the description given to Detective Ferris. Jonathan ordered Dominick to email the photo to Ferris.

"I've never seen him before," said Timothy. "Who is that?"

"Randolph O'Rourke."

"I told you, Jonathan. I've only seen the O'Rourkes in the old photos."

In an instant, Jonathan's lead had crumbled into pieces.

"Why are you here?" asked Vincent. "I mean, how did you end up in Savannah?"

"I followed Cyrus Willingham."

"What!" Jonathan stood up so fast his chair fell to the floor. "Why?"

"Because it made sense to me. I wasn't a hundred percent sure if Ellie was my sister. I couldn't walk up to her at Georgetown and introduce myself. Especially after the attack. She'd think I was crazy. Mr. Willingham would know. When they plastered her face all over the news, I thought I could convince him to help."

"Why would he help you?"

"Because he was a reputable investigative reporter before he became the owner and editor. This could be a big story. Think about it. A child was in a crash that killed her parents, and she ends up in foster care in Savannah, then becomes a professor at Georgetown. How did that happen? That could be huge. Since this was his first story above the fold, I thought he'd want to follow up. Wouldn't you? At the very least, he'd want to put the pieces together. I didn't suspect him of anything. Why would I?"

"But you did," said Jonathan. "At least you suspected something."

"No, I analyzed what I knew. I figured Mr. Willingham could help. That's all."

"Did you call him to ask about the attack?"

"No. I flew to Maine to speak to him in person."

"You flew to Maine! A second time! Why wouldn't you just pick up the phone? You're killing me here." The way this man's mind worked clearly flabbergasted him.

"Because I found out a long time ago, I get more information when I look someone in the eye when I speak to them. And because this was too damn important to chance being hung up on."

"Who did you speak to?" asked Jonathan.

"His assistant. She told me he was out of the office, then ordered me to leave. I couldn't get anything out of her." He seemed perplexed by the notion of a woman not responding to his charm.

It was clear he understood women responded to him, and he used those skills to get whatever he wanted. It was his superpower, Preston thought, and suspected he wasn't used to being rejected.

"You spoke to another woman, perhaps?" asked Jonathan. "Someone you could *convince* to help you?"

"I did." He blushed. "I'm not telling you her name. What she told me was confidential and she could lose her job."

"I don't need her name," said Jonathan. "What did you find out?"

"She walked into Willingham's office after his assistant left for lunch and checked the calendar on his desk. Nothing more."

"A paper calendar?" asked Preston. "Unbelievable. People still use them?"

"I know, right? Remember, he's old."

Vincent let out a breath. "Really?"

Jonathan turned around and glared at Vincent and Preston, then back to Timothy. "Why would this woman put herself at risk?"

"What risk? I told her Mr. Willingham was following up on his first above the fold story. I believed that was true." He looked worried. "Is she at risk? Other than losing her job?"

"Probably not. Besides, there's nothing we can do about it now."

"She said Mr. Willingham was an arrogant ass, and she'd be happy to help me steal his story." His eyes widened. "But I never told her I would steal anything. I swear. She gave me his business card with his cell phone number. It's in my backpack."

Dominick pulled the card out of a small pocket and handed it to Jonathan.

"He wrote one word on his calendar on the date he left. 'Savannah.' Nothing else. No flight information or hotel name, no mention of who he was meeting, or when he'd return. Savannah could have been a person's name for all I knew."

"Why did you decide the note on the calendar meant Georgia?" asked Jonathan.

"Why would he write Savannah in his calendar just after Ellie was all over the news? Ellie was raised in Savannah. It was too much of a coincidence."

"You thought he was following up on his story."

"Yes. I figured he could lead me to her, so I hopped a plane and came down here."

"You flew here to find Willingham. On a whim?"

"I guess. Why else would he come here? It seemed logical to me. You'll have to ask him why. I would have gone to Georgetown, but he came here, which was curious. Not criminal."

Jonathan shook his head. "I don't understand the way you think."

He grinned. "You're not alone."

"Why not call him? You have his cell number."

"I thought about it. I didn't trust that he would help me over the phone. When I arrived, I called numerous hotels in Savannah and asked to leave a message for Mr. Willingham. It took awhile, but I found where he was staying. If he came to Savannah to do something illegal, why would he use his own name? He may be arrogant, but he's not stupid."

"Hubris has brought down the smartest people," said Vincent.

"Maybe he wasn't the one doing something illegal," said Jonathan. "Or maybe he thought no one would connect him to Ellie, except you. Which puts you in danger."

Timothy frowned as he analyzed the possibilities.

It was then Preston recognized him for what he was—a decent man. He'd put Ellie's safety above his own without considering the danger. If Ellie were to have a brother, he'd be a good one.

"You were on a mission to save your sister," said Jonathan. "We all would have followed a similar path."

"Thanks. But my ancestry research started this whole thing. You might have considered it to be dangerous. I did not."

"Timothy, there's nothing dangerous about finding your ancestors," said Jonathan. "This is the exception. It's not your fault."

"It took a half a day, but I found him. Then I waited outside his hotel until he returned."

"And?"

"And then I followed him."

"Why not go up and talk to him?"

"Because he didn't tell me anything before. I doubted he would now, and I figured he'd protect his story."

"You hoped he'd lead you to Ellie. I understand. Where did he go?"

"Look on my computer for a directory called surveillance."

Dominick appeared disappointed by the file name.

"Sorry, I was too tired to come up with something catchy. There are photos and a spreadsheet listing locations and times of Mr. Willingham's movements. Dominick, bring those photos up."

He opened each photo until they all filled the screen, one next to the other.

"He moved around town to meet these men. I must admit, the neighborhoods were dicey. First, he met that guy." Timothy pointed to a tall, heavy man filled with tattoos. This man had every piece of exposed skin covered with art, from skulls and daggers to dragons. And what wasn't tattooed, was pierced, and each finger carried a large ring.

"That big guy introduced Mr. Willingham to the other two men. He handed each of them an envelope. They glanced inside, then slipped it into their pockets. I assume he was giving them money."

"Yeah, me too," said Jonathan.

"A payoff," said Vincent.

Preston agreed, but he didn't say what they all knew. Willingham most likely paid these men to kill Ellie. To finish the job. As Dominick clicked through the photos, Preston noticed each of the men had a weapon. It was hard to tell which had the most tattoos, but one thing was clear: this situation had just become more dangerous.

"Dominick, see if you can find out who they are," said Jonathan.

"Already on it."

"What happened next?"

"Mr. Willingham and the big guy drove to McQueen's Island Trail. I was too far away to see who they were following, so I got out of my car to get a closer look. I parked way back on the side of the road. See that photo?"

Dominick brought up a photo of the car. He moved closer to the screen and squinted to read the license plate. His camera listed the time and date on the photo.

"I hid in the brush to take the picture. It was so dark I had to use a thirty-second exposure on my camera to pick up the license plate. Even then I could barely read the numbers."

Dominick ran the number. "It belongs to Rufus Baxter." He pulled up his motor vehicle photo.

"Yes," said Timothy. "That's the big guy with the tattoos."

"Why didn't they see you?" Olivia asked.

"New moon, no streetlights for one. Plus, they weren't looking for him," said Jonathan. "Willingham didn't think anyone knew he was in Savannah."

"Except for the woman who helped Timothy in Kennebunk," said Preston.

"Yeah, but Willingham isn't aware of that."

"You didn't see me either. And you didn't notice when I drove past you." Timothy pointed to another photo of Jonathan chasing the car as it sped away. "I followed them to the big house on the water. There was a woman inside, but no one got close enough to disturb her. They parked outside the house for a minute, then drove off." Timothy took another drink of water before continuing. "God, it's hot down here."

"And?" asked Jonathan.

"I followed them back to Mr. Willingham's hotel. They split up at that point, and I went back to the house on the water."

"Willingham showed them where Ellie was staying. He must have tracked her to Alex's before Timothy found him."

"And then cased the house to find the best way in. That's what I would have done. Especially now, with it being so dark," said Preston. "It's a good thing we moved locations. Now they don't know where we are."

"Why did you go back to the house?" asked Jonathan.

"Because I figured Ellie would be in there. Why else would Willingham go to that house? Look, I didn't want trouble. I also didn't want anything to happen to my sister. I stayed in my car and watched."

"In case she was in the house?" asked Jonathan.

"Yes, it seemed logical. I saw her when you left to come here, then I followed you to this safe house. I assume that's what this is."

Preston realized something else about Timothy. He was a deep thinker who analyzed everything before making a move. But he wondered what would happen if he'd faced real danger. Would he have acted quickly enough, or would they have eaten him alive?

"Did they see you?" asked Jonathan.

"No."

"That's good. You should have called the police. Especially after seeing the thugs Willingham hired. You had to know we were protecting her."

"If I walked into your office with this story, would you have believed me? I have no evidence of wrongdoing. What would you have done if you were in my shoes?"

Jonathan shook his head. "The same thing."

"Besides, I didn't know you were cops at first. Why would Savannah police be protecting Ellie? From what? A mugger from Georgetown? They were already dead."

"You thought the case was closed and Willingham could help you find Elizabeth? That's it?"

"Yes, until he met those men. And I wasn't sure who to trust down here."

Preston snickered at his last statement. This time it was Jonathan who picked up the now half-finished bottle of water and threw it at Preston.

"I kept my head down. I wanted to see if Mr. Willingham would interview Ellie the next morning. Then I would introduce myself."

"And now?" asked Jonathan.

"When they followed you to McQueen's Island Trail, something was off. If my instincts were correct, I needed to protect her from them. Now, after seeing Ellie's reaction to the photo, I question all of my original conclusions."

"That's because you didn't have all the information," said Vincent. "Because they're human beings, not data."

"And because you're not a cop," Jonathan insisted.

"I'm so sorry."

"Don't be. Without you, we'd still be in the dark," said Vincent.

"Without me, he wouldn't be after Ellie." Then Timothy's expression changed as another important question entered his mind. "Since Mr. Willingham knows who I am, am I next?"

Vincent glanced at his daughter, now in the comfort of Preston's arms. "Only if you can link him to this murder. He hasn't seen you here, but Ellie can identify the boogeyman."

"Which boogeyman?" asked Jonathan. "There seems to be more than one."

CHAPTER 28

IT WAS TIME FOR VINCENT TO UPDATE FERRIS ABOUT THE INVESTIGA-tion. He hoped Ferris would help link the two cases together. He also wanted to check in with David, to give him their new location.

"Dominick, can you send me an email with the O'Rourkes' and Willingham's photos, along with any information you have? I'll forward them to Detective Ferris in DC. I'll also give him your email address and phone number for his records."

When Vincent's cell dinged with the new message, he went upstairs, away from the others. He called Ferris with an update before he forwarded Dominick's email. After their conversation, he closed the door, then called David Bartlett.

David and Vincent had shared many firsts. They became friends at the Naval Academy. They faced war together, both adopted teenage foster children, and lost their wives to cancer. After a lifetime of friendship, they would do whatever was necessary to protect each other, and their families.

Vincent paced around the room as he spoke to his friend. Hoping for some wisdom, or an inspired idea, to come through the line. Mostly, he needed to rehash the details and speak to someone over thirty-three years old. Someone who understood Ellie, and who understood him.

"We've found out a fair amount since we've been here, but not enough to connect the dots," said Vincent. "We know Ellie's birth name and the name of a few relatives."

"Relatives? That's good, isn't it?"

"It's complicated. Ellie's parents died in a car crash days before she was abandoned. Their names were Anderson and Gabrielle O'Rourke. Nothing suspicious there. It was tragic, but an accident."

The phone fell silent for a moment as they both absorbed this new piece of information. *Ellie was an abandoned orphan.* The weight of that lingered. As did the one thought both Vincent and David shared: *Who was responsible?* But Vincent already knew. Or at least suspected.

"I'm so sorry."

"Yeah, me too. Ellie's name was Jacqueline O'Rourke. Of that, there is no doubt. There are photos of Ellie when she was three or four years old. We don't really know how old she was when she was abandoned. Social Services made an educated guess. We believe Bradford and Randolph O'Rourke are her grandfather and uncle. Preston attached their photos."

"Yes, I see them. The old guy looks a little scary. I can't imagine having him as a grandfather."

"I agree. Randolph might be the one who tried to kill Ellie when she was young. The problem is, we have no proof. She had a panic attack the moment she saw his photo. Deep down, she remembered him, but not the details. So, we can't be sure."

"But you are," said David. "You think he's involved in what's happening now?"

"I do. It's a gut feeling. He hasn't been seen down here. At least not yet. We did have one unexpected piece of good news. Ellie has a brother."

"A brother! That's great."

"His name is Timothy Watts. His parents told him about being adopted a year ago. He's been searching for his birth parents ever since. We think he stumbled onto something he shouldn't have three months ago. It turns out, they were both abandoned on the same day, but in different states."

Vincent grinned when he thought of Timothy. He wondered what Ellie would be like today if they were raised together. Would she have developed the survival instincts that kept her alive when she was homeless? Or would she have that edge to her personality?

"Ah," said David. "He's the one who poked the bear."

"That's what it looks like. The most pressing matter is Cyrus Willingham. He's in the third photo. He's already here and has hired three thugs. We believe he's here to kill Ellie, although we don't know why. We'll look into the O'Rourkes after Ellie's out of danger."

"Well, now you know there's definitely a third man. How did they track you down there?"

"They bugged Ellie's cell."

"So, that's why it went missing. Ellie's instincts were spot-on."

"They were. The problem is, I don't know if Willingham was responsible for what happened at Georgetown."

"Two men?"

"Yes," said Vincent. "At least."

"It is getting complicated. How is Ellie?"

"As good as expected. She's different down here. I've never seen her like this. I expected an angry woman ready to fight. She's not that—at least not yet. She's afraid, and she's had two panic attacks since we've been here. I don't know if she's trying to remember her past or working hard not to. Especially when the panic comes. None of this was her idea."

"Or yours," said David. "And now she finds out her parents are dead. That is a lot. I'll check Timothy out, too."

"I doubt you'll find anything out of the ordinary with Timothy. Willingham's the one I'm worried about. Between the three men he hired, the police, and us, there're too many people with weapons involved in this case. And we need to keep Willingham alive to tie him to O'Rourke."

"Make sure the kids are aware of that."

"I will."

"I checked out the photos the students uploaded," said David. "There was one that might be helpful. It's a man, but you can't see his face. He's tall and thin with gray hair. He matches the description given to Ferris."

"Good. That will tie him to Georgetown. Email the photo to Preston and Dominick."

Vincent could hear the tapping of a keyboard as David forwarded the photo.

"It's sent. Vincent, try not to worry. We'll get these guys. Let me know if there's anything else I can do."

"There is one more thing…"

———

Jonathan paced at the bottom of the stairs, waiting for Vincent's return. Preston was in the kitchen, assembling a variety of sandwiches. Some were your standard lunch meat, but also fried eggs with bacon and the classic peanut butter and jelly.

"If we stay here much longer, I'm going to give Dominick a shopping list," said Preston. "I'd like to eat something other than sandwiches or pizza."

"What's he doing up there?" Jonathan continued to pace.

"He's calling Detective Ferris, and I presume my dad. He tells him everything."

"Why?"

"Because he trusts him. They've been friends forever. My father is like your Alex. I assume he'll forward the email to both Ferris and my dad."

Preston filled a plate with sandwiches to share.

A few minutes later, Vincent came downstairs and confirmed his assumptions.

"Your father had a message for you."

"I'm listening," said Preston. Though when his stomach growled, it was obvious he was half listening.

"Watch yourself."

"That's it? Really? I expected a diatribe of what I should or shouldn't do."

"I boiled it down."

Preston laughed.

"Your father is sending you and Dominick a photo a student uploaded. It might be helpful."

Preston nodded, then moved into the living room to hand out the sandwiches. But not before taking one for himself.

———

Jonathan and Vincent watched the three men eat while captivated by the computer screen. They drank between bites with an occasional grunt when the screen refreshed. Though, at this point, with nothing more to research, they were playing games.

"It's like a mind meld." Jonathan shook his head as he watched them. "I've never understood the appeal of computer games. Not the way they do. Preston's worse than Dominick."

Vincent agreed. "We're surrounded by geniuses. I don't know about Timothy or Dominick, but that's how I'd describe the other three. They're all geniuses in their fields. Consider them as the moth, and the computer the flame."

Jonathan shook his head. "There's a fine line between genius and idiot."

When Vincent looked at the three men staring at the screens, he let out a small laugh. "I can't argue with that."

"Tell me about Preston."

"There's not much to tell that you don't already know. He was in foster care, like Ellie. Besides his addiction to all things related to computers, he's a talented chef. He even has an organic garden. That pretty much sums him up."

"Chef? A real chef? Why didn't you tell me that before we ordered lunch meat? Tell me more about him."

"He spends most of his time in the basement of a building. If he doesn't have a laptop sitting in front of him, he has a book or chef's knife in his hand. Or he's digging in the dirt. He is brilliant, and a voracious reader, but the boy needs to get out more."

"A chef," he said again, then raised a brow as though he was reconsidering this man. "Now that's surprising. I've known one foster kid who hoarded food, but none who became a chef. I guess that was his way of dealing with food insecurity."

"That's very perceptive. I've wondered the same thing. That, or his foster parents were terrible cooks. It might have been the only way to get a decent meal. He even puts food up for the winter. If there's ever a power outage, his house is where you want to be. You'd never starve."

"Was he ever arrested?"

"No, never."

"Does that mean he's done nothing illegal, or they never caught him? I assume he was a hacker when he was young."

"He's a hacker now, but for the government." What Vincent wasn't telling Jonathan was that he and David knew little about their troubled youth. Preston and Ellie had both refused to talk about the past. "They put the past behind them to start a new life. They were two lost souls in need of a family. Ellie had stolen food to survive. Preston protected her. Knowing anything beyond that seemed unnecessary." Though, truth be told, both he and David had checked for a criminal record. Neither had one. A nugget of information Vincent kept to himself.

"He has a job at the FBI," said Jonathan. "How did that happen?"

"Preston found a family before he traveled down the wrong path. There was no reason not to hire him. He's a highly educated man of integrity with no criminal record, not an evil genius. Besides, he has skills the government needs."

Jonathan looked across the room at the three men who were still fixated on their computer screens.

When he frowned, Vincent saw apprehension on his face. He recognized they both had the same concern. "You don't have to worry about him."

"The woman he loves is in trouble. What's with that, anyway? Are they a couple or friends?"

Vincent smiled. He'd been wondering the same thing. "I imagine they'll figure that out by the end of this trip."

"I'm not sure about them."

"What do you mean?"

"If you had their skills, would you wait for someone to attack? I wouldn't. I don't assume you would either. If I loved her, and we both know he does, I'd be out for blood."

Vincent considered.

"What does 'being out for blood' mean to Preston?"

"I'm not sure. They're not alone, Jonathan. They have all of us. We'll be able to stop them before anything happens." As Vincent spoke, he wondered whether he'd lied to Jonathan.

"I don't want them to do something stupid." He took a deep breath and placed his hands in his pants pockets. "I'll be on the porch. I need to think." Before he closed the door, he turned to Vincent. "Just don't expect me to call you Uncle Vince."

"Admiral or Sir will do."

"Yeah, right. When pigs fly."

As the door shut, Vincent let out a full belly laugh.

While Jonathan was outside, Dominick printed and sorted all the documents related to this case. When he returned, Dominick removed a large painting hung in the living room and they placed photos of each person involved in the case on the wall.

"Ah. You're building a murder board," said Olivia.

"Yes. It's a visual way to see who's connected to whom," said Dominick. "Plus, it helps keep information straight."

"What about all the documents you just printed?"

"They'll go up on the board after we've reviewed them."

Olivia nodded.

Everyone, except Ellie, who was meditating in the corner of the room, gathered around to see what they'd done. It started at the top with the patriarch of the family, Bradford O'Rourke, then worked its way down to include Randolph and his brother Anderson with his wife Gabrielle. It resembled a family tree, but when they added Jacqueline and William to the wall, the tree had broken. They weren't placed below their parents. Ellie, who had a complicated history, was on the far left of the board, with Timothy on the far right.

"That's curious," said Vincent.

"What is?" asked Jonathan.

"See where he placed Jacqueline and William? Or is it Ellie and Timothy?" He paused. "I agree with Timothy. It is confusing. They're separate from the family and from each other, with nothing linking them together. It's an accurate representation, don't you think? This family tree is how they lived. Thousands of miles away from each other, with nothing connecting them. Which is what the O'Rourkes wanted."

"Then Timothy found the link. Which is why they're in trouble now," said Jonathan.

Olivia stood in front of the wall, examining each of the photos. She appeared to be inside their heads.

"What do you see?" asked Jonathan. "Did something catch your eye?"

"I'd like more information about Randolph. Look at Bradford. His face is hard. Unyielding. I suspect he was an abusive father who ruled with an iron fist."

"What else?"

"I believe Bradford is at the heart of all of this. Then and now. How did the staff describe him? A lunatic. Imagine having a lunatic for a father."

"Sounds like we were lucky to get away from them," said Timothy.

Olivia agreed. "But why get rid of the children? Did Bradford hate Anderson and Gabrielle that much? Or did he love them so much that seeing the children would be a constant reminder of his loss?" She tapped her finger against Bradford's photo. "I don't believe this man is capable of love. He fired the nanny the moment she stepped through the door. That's when the children disappeared. There's a piece missing. Without it, this board is incomplete."

"What else?" asked Jonathan.

She pointed to Randolph. "Well, he's the same age as Willingham, or at least close. I'm curious about their relationship. Where did they meet? How close were they? Why would Willingham do this kind of work for an O'Rourke?"

"We have no evidence he is working with the O'Rourkes," said Jonathan.

"Not yet. But there's something there. Don't forget, they abandoned Ellie and Timothy around the same time. There had to be two people."

"You believe Willingham was the second person. Why?"

"It's a possibility. Otherwise, why would he be coming after Ellie now? Randolph was the one who tried to kill Ellie when she was little, not Willingham. Based on Ferris's description and the photo Uncle Dave sent, Randolph was at Georgetown. There has to be a connection between the two men."

"Are you a profiler?" asked Timothy.

"I dabble."

Vincent laughed at the description. "You dabble? Is that how you'd describe it?"

"Spill," Jonathan insisted.

"I worked as a profiler for Homeland Security for a while. I've seen my share of lunatics." She walked to Bradford's photo. "Check out those eyes. He's the one in charge."

"Impressive. Hot *and* brilliant. All you need now is a gun."

She took one step closer into Jonathan's personal space. They stood face-to-face, close enough for him to breathe in her scent.

"You smell great."

"Do I have to educate every man in this room about how to speak to a woman?" Olivia stared at Jonathan, who cleared his throat. She backed away and walked to a large purse on the floor and pulled out a Glock pistol. She looked him in the eyes with a grin that filled her face, then winked.

Jonathan blushed. "Oh, man. I think I'm in love."

Olivia let out a laugh.

———

The painting Dominick had taken down caught Preston's eye. It seemed familiar. Then he noticed the signature. "Check this out. Detective Thibodeaux painted this years ago."

Olivia joined him to inspect the piece of art through the eyes of someone who knew talent. "A cop did this?"

Dominick stopped what he was doing and stared. "Really! Cops have other skills, you know."

"I didn't mean it that way." She brought it closer to Dominick. "Look at this. A skilled artist did this. He should do this for a living."

"It's the detective who worked Ellie's case," said Preston. "I agree. You may need to help him after this is over."

"I'd be happy to. I have friends in the art world who would love this."

———

Ellie came into the room and joined the others. She examined each photo on the wall in depth, hoping it would trigger something. It hadn't. When she saw the photo of Randolph, she removed it, turned it over, and placed it back on the wall. "I don't want to see his face."

Then Ellie noticed the photo of Gabrielle. She was stunning, with blonde hair and deep-brown eyes. Her complexion was flawless, and her makeup was perfect. "Who is that?" She pointed to Gabrielle O'Rourke.

"That's our mother," said Timothy.

"That's Gabrielle?"

"What's going on, Ellie?" asked Olivia.

"That's not the…" She stopped herself before saying the word *ghost*. Timothy wasn't aware of the ghost, and she didn't know how he'd react. "It's not the woman from my dream."

Olivia understood her meaning, as did Jonathan, who closed his eyes and shook his head.

"Your dream may not be correct," said Olivia.

"No! I've never seen this woman before. Or at least I don't remember ever seeing her." Then she examined the photo of Anderson. "Who's he?"

"He's our father."

Ellie frowned and moved closer. "I've seen his face, but it's a faint memory. That woman is not my mother. I'm sure of it. Why can I remember his face but not hers?"

"Because the brain's complicated," said Olivia.

When Ellie saw Bradford O'Rourke, she removed the photo from the wall and held it in her hand. "He seems familiar. It's a feeling more than a memory."

"What feeling?" asked Olivia.

"I don't know exactly. I think this man is pure evil."

"That man is our grandfather."

She glared at Timothy, then shook her head. "So, the blood of evil flows through our veins. That's just great."

CHAPTER 29

Dominick handed Jonathan the stack of printouts containing the backgrounds of Cyrus Willingham and the three men he'd hired: Kraig Gunter, Rufus Baxter, and Emmet Hendricks. He'd flipped through the pages with the speed of a skilled investigator searching for specific information.

First, Jonathan read Cyrus Willingham's file. "Willingham's background is unremarkable. Why he would get involved in something like this is beyond me."

After he reviewed Willingham's file, Dominick placed it on the wall under his photo.

"Money. It's always about money," said Preston. "Or the O'Rourkes have something on him. Remember, he may have been the person who abandoned Timothy. That could've been the stupid thing he'd done thirty years ago."

Olivia agreed with Preston, with some reservations. "Why was he roped into killing Ellie now, after all these years?"

"Because of me." Timothy lowered his eyes and shook his head in regret.

Ellie punched him hard on the arm.

"Damn," Timothy shouted. "What is wrong with you?" It was the first time they'd heard his voice raised in anger.

"Stop blaming yourself. None of this is your fault."

While mumbling something under his breath, he moved to the other side of Jonathan, away from Ellie.

Preston laughed. "Welcome to my world."

"Seriously?" Timothy grumbled.

"When you met with Willingham to discuss the article, he probably contacted O'Rourke," said Jonathan. "If they used their resources to confirm Ellie's death, they would have found out she was still alive."

"Why kill her now?" asked Timothy.

"Because Willingham knew you wouldn't stop looking for your sister. It would've exposed O'Rourke as the murderer, or in this case an attempted murderer. Which makes you a liability."

Olivia agreed. "You're on a mission. If they kill Ellie now, you'd investigate until you found them."

"We can't prove any of this yet," said Jonathan. "We're speculating. Let's move on." He read the next document. "Rufus Baxter. With a name like that, you'd either learn how to defend yourself or be harassed the rest of your life. No wonder he's a criminal. Why do parents do that to their children?"

"Actually, Rufus is the name of free open-source software. It's used to make bootable USBs." Preston smiled and glanced at Jonathan. "In case you're interested."

Dominick laughed. "That's actually true."

Jonathan looked at Vincent. "Remember...genius and idiot?"

Vincent chuckled.

"His appearance matches his rap sheet," said Jonathan. "He's been in and out of prison since adolescence for everything from assault and robbery to gun charges. No early release for him. What a surprise."

"What about the other two?" asked Vincent.

"They're younger, with fewer tattoos and piercings than Rufus. Thugs in training. Their rap sheets are filled with petty crimes, until they started stealing cars. Now they've graduated to murder for hire. Based on the dates of their incarceration, they likely met Rufus while in prison."

"We know how these three men met," said Vincent. "How did Willingham find them?"

"We need access to Willingham's cell and text messages to find out," said Dominick. "If O'Rourke's involved, we'll check his financials to see if money exchanged hands."

"I'd rather wait until he's in custody," said Jonathan, then walked closer to the murder board and stared at Willingham. "If he paid the three men, we'll have cause to check his finances. First, we need to get them off the streets. We don't want them calling the O'Rourkes."

"How long is all this going to take?" asked Ellie.

"A week, or more," said Dominick. "It depends on how deeply we dive into the O'Rourkes."

"No way. I'm not staying here for weeks."

"What would you like us to do? I'm open to suggestions," said Jonathan.

"Why not go to the hotel where he's staying?" asked Timothy. "Arrest him there."

"For what? Don't forget, he already knows what we look like. He followed us to McQueen's Island Trail, and they've been to Alex's house. We'd be giving away the element of surprise."

"True. But Timothy has his cell phone number," said Ellie. "I'll call him. It's me he's after."

Both Jonathan and Preston shouted "NO!" in unison.

"Let me meet with him," said Vincent. "You can record our conversation and I'll try to guide him into confessing."

"I have a better idea," said Preston. "One that may be more believable."

"Lord, I'm almost afraid to ask," Jonathan said, then reconsidered. "What do you have in mind?"

"Louis Thibodeaux can meet with him."

"Are you crazy? He's an old man who uses a walker, for God's sake. He can't defend himself from those men."

Jonathan's reaction didn't surprise Vincent. It was his job to protect the ones who were unable to protect themselves. And he placed Louis in that category.

Preston disagreed. "He's a mean old man, and I'll bet he was a nasty cop. I'm sure he's got some moves left. And you know they wouldn't consider him a threat. He could use being forced to retire to shake them down."

"How would he explain knowing about Willingham, and why he's here?"

"He has friends in the department. Use that. He could be an angry cop who overheard information about his old case. You know, some buzz around the office. You must admit he's cantankerous enough to pull that off."

Jonathan frowned.

"I think this case haunts him. You haunt him, Ellie. At least the memory of the three-year-old girl on her deathbed does. He'd want to close his cold case."

"We could protect him," said Dominick.

"I need to think." Jonathan made another trip to the porch. When he returned, he agreed with their plan for one reason—there was no other solution that wouldn't put Ellie at risk.

Vincent knew if they didn't move fast, Ellie would disappear. She'd walk up to Willingham and ask him to his face why he wanted her dead. If he or his thugs put their hands on her, she'd kill them where they stood. Of that, he had no doubt. Both Vincent and Jonathan wouldn't allow that to happen, and he believed, if what Preston suggested was true, neither would Louis.

"I need to call my captain. If she approves, I'll call Louis."

Ellie stood with her hands on her hips and faced Jonathan. "If she approves, I need to meet Louis face-to-face before any of this happens. That is not a request."

There was no opposition from Jonathan. He seemed to appreciate why she wanted to meet with him in person. Louis would place his own life in danger for her. If Jonathan were in Ellie's shoes, Vincent believed he'd do the same thing.

"I'll ask him in person," said Jonathan. "If he agrees, I'll bring him back here."

Vincent disagreed. "I don't think that's a good idea. As you said, they've seen us. Who knows if they followed you to Louis's house? I doubt they care about him now. He's an old man. They might look for you to lead them to Ellie. A plain-clothes officer can pick him up and bring him here."

Jonathan called his captain and then called Louis.

"He's in," said Jonathan. "A plain-clothes officer will bring him here to meet you. One more thing. He wants to meet with Willingham at a bar called Prohibition."

"Why?" asked Dominick.

"He didn't say."

They gathered around Dominick's computer to see where Prohibition was located. Then they reviewed the photos from the inside of the restaurant. It was dark and moody, with a vintage feel reminiscent of a speakeasy when Prohibition was the law of the land.

There were a handful of tables in front of the restaurant. One sat by the windows. The others were against the wall, with a bench on one side and two chairs on the other. A long bar ran down the right side of the restaurant, with tables for guests on the left and separate rooms for private events in the back of the building.

"This place could work," said Jonathan. "Louis could sit by the windows, so we can monitor him. We'll talk about it when he gets here. I asked him to come tomorrow morning, around eight."

Jonathan called his captain and arranged for a surveillance van and additional men to be in place the next morning.

CHAPTER 30

August 26, 2017

VINCENT HAD HIS OWN PRECONCEIVED NOTION ABOUT LOUIS Thibodeaux. He wanted to see his physical condition firsthand. To determine whether it was advisable, or even sensible, to put this man's life in peril—to use him as bait.

Early the next morning, an unmarked car pulled into the driveway and a plain-clothes officer opened the passenger door. As the officer reached out to help Louis, a cane cracked him on the knuckles. The sound of the angry old man brought a smile to Vincent's face, though he felt bad for the young officer trying to assist.

"Leave me alone," shouted Louis. "I can take care of myself."

The officer appeared dumbfounded—unsure how to help.

The spectacle, though amusing, had proved too painful for Vincent to watch. He wandered outside. Not to help, not exactly, but to introduce himself, and to be at Louis's side should he stumble.

Louis was about six two and stood stick-straight when he wasn't using a cane. He was taller than Vincent had imagined, with thick, gray hair and a lean body. He had a weathered face, with deep wrinkles around his eyes and mouth. Walking appeared to be an issue. Each step brought pain and agony, which was most likely why he seemed so timeworn.

"I'm Vincent O'Brien, Elizabeth's father." He used Ellie's given name so as not to confuse the old man.

He tilted his head and glanced at Vincent, then frowned as they took the stairs. Vincent worried it was too much for him, but he was wrong. The frown wasn't from climbing the stairs; it was because he was thinking.

He stopped mid-stride. "Father?" he asked.

"Yes. I adopted Ellie when she was seventeen."

"Seventeen! Why bother?"

"I've often been asked that question. We thought it was important for Ellie to understand she was our daughter and a permanent member of our family. And that we loved her." A bullet might have broken his body, Vincent thought, but his mind was as sharp as his own.

Louis nodded his approval and continued up the stairs.

———

Once inside, Louis spent a few minutes taking in the surroundings. He either ignored or hadn't noticed anyone else in the house.

Vincent interrupted his train of thought. "Have you been here before?"

"Yes. I spent a lot of time here over the years." His attention turned toward the painting Dominick had taken down. "Look at that. I can't believe they kept this." He handed his cane to Vincent and lifted the painting to get a closer look. His eyes moved across the piece of art as though he were visiting an old friend. He then carefully, reverently, leaned it against the wall.

Once more, his attention shifted. He shuffled to the murder board. Without saying a single word, he studied each photo and read every document.

Vincent could only imagine what was going through his mind as he relived the day he found Ellie.

"Does anyone seem familiar?" asked Olivia.

Louis was so engrossed in the work he hadn't noticed her standing off to the side. He jumped.

"Sorry," said Olivia. "I didn't mean to startle you."

But he said nothing. Not even a grunt. He appeared awe-struck by this beautiful woman. First, he inspected her eyes and cheekbones, and then the lips. Then his eyes drifted down her pale, long neck.

There was nothing sinister or even disturbing about his actions. Olivia was, for all intents and purposes, a specimen. Someone to paint. When he examined her face, Vincent saw admiration.

"You are stunning," said Louis.

"Thank you." She extended a hand and treated him with the utmost respect. "I'm Olivia Lombardi. I'm an unofficial consultant on this case."

He frowned. "Consultant?"

"Yes, I've done some profiling in the past."

"Huh. You worked for the government." It wasn't a question. In the blink of an eye, Olivia had gone from a beautiful woman to paint, to a member of the team. Louis was no longer the artist, but a cop. Her beauty became irrelevant.

He turned to the photos and pointed to Rufus Baxter. "I recognize him. He's been in and out of prison his entire life. Watch out for this guy. He might be dangerous. I'm not familiar with the others. Who's the one who hurt Elizabeth?"

Olivia removed the photo Ellie had turned around and placed it back on the board, but a voice behind them answered the question.

"His name is Randolph O'Rourke."

When Louis turned around, he gasped. "Elizabeth? You look just like the photo Preston gave me to paint. I'll send it to you when it's finished."

Vincent signaled for Ellie to have a seat in the kitchen.

Louis followed her lead. After a few minutes, he gathered himself. "Do you remember him?" he asked, referring to Randolph O'Rourke.

"I remember the face. And I think I remember you. But please call me Ellie."

"I'll never forget you." He grimaced. "I've never seen a small child intubated before. It's a miracle you're alive."

When he spoke to Ellie, his voice had changed. The gruffness and anger had disappeared. What Vincent heard was compassion and concern for the child he'd remembered. The child in the hospital room connected to machines, with countless bags attached to her tiny body. It would have been impossible to forget. Vincent hoped seeing the face of the woman sitting across from him would erase the image of the child he'd held in his memory for three decades.

"How do you remember me?" asked Louis.

"I'm not sure if it's your face or your voice. But I think you were at the hospital."

"I took the photos in your file. I'm sorry I didn't find these people back then. This was one of those cases that stays with you. That's why I'm glad to help now. I want these people as much as you."

Ellie reached out and placed her hand on his. "You're the second person taking responsibility for something out of their control. First it was Timothy. O'Rourke is the one responsible, not you."

"Who is Timothy?"

"He's a second child abandoned that night," said Vincent. "They left him on the steps of a church in Kansas."

"I'm confused."

"Timothy is my brother."

"And they left him in Kansas?" said Louis, clearly puzzled. "On the same night?"

"Yes." Ellie introduced Louis to Timothy, and the two men shook hands.

"How old are you?"

"I'm thirty."

"You were an infant when this happened, and Ellie was around three or four. Which means she could identify them, but you couldn't. That's why they didn't kill you. It also means there had to be at least two people involved."

Vincent listened to this retired cop sum up the situation they'd been examining in a matter of seconds. And his conclusions were spot-on. He not only understood what had happened, he knew some players involved today.

"You couldn't find O'Rourke then because there was no evidence to go on," said Ellie. "But there is now."

He frowned. "What evidence?"

"Me."

"Oh Jesus," he whispered, and the pained expression returned.

Jonathan pulled up a chair to the kitchen table to discuss their next moves. "First, you need to know, you don't have to do this."

Louis looked at Ellie and then at Timothy. "The hell I don't. But I have one condition."

"Which is?"

"I don't want these two anywhere near those people." He pointed to Ellie and Timothy. "That's a deal breaker. I won't be responsible for anything happening to either of them. Not again."

Ellie disagreed. "It's not your decision to make."

Louis leaned in across the table. "It damn well is." His voice was guttural.

As the two stared at each other, Vincent wondered who would blink first. To his surprise, it was Ellie.

"Get him out of here." She pushed away from the table and stormed into the next room.

Vincent noticed her attitude had mimicked Louis's. She was playing him...or was trying. But Louis had been a detective longer than Ellie had been alive. He wondered whether she'd met her match or Louis had.

Louis stood, though it took a minute to stand straight, and hobbled into the other room. "It's too late, little girl. I'm in this whether or not you like it. I'm perfectly capable of finding these men on my own." He pointed his cane to the murder board. "And I'll be damn sure you won't be in their crosshairs when I do."

Ellie walked over and stood across from the creaky old man. "Don't call me little girl."

"Little girl," he snarled.

The room fell silent until Vincent put an end to the madness. "Enough," he shouted, startling everyone. "You don't have to worry about Ellie," he said to Louis, then faced Ellie. "You won't be in the crosshairs, understand? Remember, we need Willingham to implicate O'Rourke. Save your rage for him."

Ellie took a deep breath, then paced. She shook her hands to shake off the anger, then agreed with her father.

"How about we get down to business," said Jonathan. "Have a seat."

They gathered around the kitchen table and created a plan. Mapping out every detail, including where Louis would sit in the restaurant, and where each cop and listening device would be located. Ellie would be in the police van with Vincent and Preston, close enough to see and hear everything, but far enough away from the killers to satisfy Louis. Timothy and Olivia would stay at the safe house.

"Why Prohibition?" asked Jonathan. "And why would they go along with this?"

"I know the owner. His father was a friend. Leave it at that."

Jonathan grimaced, then nodded.

He didn't ask questions, though Vincent had an inkling of what Louis meant. Chances were the owner's father was a fellow cop and based on their reaction, was most likely injured, or killed, in the line of duty.

"I think we're ready," said Jonathan.

CHAPTER 31

Jonathan pulled out Willingham's business card and placed a burner phone on the table. With the phone on speaker, he dialed the number. After two rings, a man answered.

"Is this Cyrus Willingham?" asked Louis.

"Yes. Who is this?"

"My name is Louis Thibodeaux. We need to talk."

Without saying a word, Willingham hung up the phone, and Louis immediately pressed redial.

He picked up the phone but didn't speak.

"Hang up again and I'll go to the cops."

After a few seconds, Willingham broke the silence. "Don't threaten me. Mr. Thibodeaux, is it? Or you'll learn firsthand who you're dealing with."

Louis let out a menacing laugh. "I know who you are, Mr. Willingham, and where you live, and why you're in Savannah." His voice was direct and convincing. Louis had years of exposure to criminals while on duty and understood the language of thugs.

His threats didn't appear to move Willingham. He remained irate and defiant.

"How did you get this number?" he shouted.

"That's not important. All you need to understand is that I know everything."

Willingham didn't respond. His breath, now a seething pant, came through the speaker.

"I know you hired Rufus Baxter and two other men. In fact, I suspect Rufus is listening to this conversation. Isn't that right?" he sneered.

A mumbled "Shit" made its way through the phone, and Willingham grunted.

"What do you want?"

This voice was crusty, different from the other. He sounded nervous, which, Vincent knew, gave Louis the advantage.

"Ah, Rufus," said Louis.

"Yes."

"I have information the cops would be extremely interested in. I want your boss to give me a reason why I shouldn't give it to them."

Willingham broke his silence. "What information? You have five seconds."

"I know what happened thirty years ago and why you hired Rufus and his men. I'm not someone to fuck with, Mr. Willingham of Kennebunk, Maine. You're the one who's a long way from home."

Vincent shook his head. He realized this was the type of cop Ellie avoided when she lived in Savannah. He imagined Rufus felt the same.

"What do you want?" asked Willingham.

"What everyone wants—money. We should meet to discuss my terms."

"Why should I?"

"Because you have no choice. I told you, I'll go straight to the cops."

"Where?" asked Willingham, angrily.

Louis delayed answering, as though deciding on a location. "A bar called Prohibition, at ten thirty this morning."

"Why there?"

"Because they have a great whiskey selection. I'll be sure to give you the bill."

Both Willingham and Rufus considered, then reluctantly agreed to his terms.

Louis was as dangerous as these men. And after years of being out to pasture, he was back in the game. Vincent worried he seemed to enjoy it a bit too much. He questioned why Willingham kept answering the phone. A hardened criminal would have calculated the risks and planned for the unexpected. And a hardened criminal wouldn't have brought his business phone to Savannah, or answer an unknown number. This man was naïve or stupid, or maybe a little desperate. All of which, he knew, made him unpredictable.

Louis and the team of officers arrived at Prohibition at nine thirty. Each cop walked through the restaurant and checked all the exits to prepare for their arrival. Jonathan played the role of bartender while the officers concealed themselves in the shadows, both inside the bar and outside the property. Vincent, along with Preston and Ellie, would be in the surveillance van, which held enough equipment to hear a pin drop.

They planned for Louis to sit by the windows. But once inside, and without explanation, he'd insisted on a different location. He'd chosen a table with bench seating on one side, facing the windows, with two chairs directly opposite. In order to see the men through the window, he agreed to sit on the chairs and direct Willingham toward the bench. Once the team was in place, Louis sat down and ordered a bottle of Old Forester 1920, a Prohibition style bourbon whiskey, with two glasses.

Vincent walked in and sat on the bench across from him. "I thought I'd come in and check on you one last time before they get here. Remember, I'll be in the van with Ellie. Are you sure you're up to this?"

"Of course I'm up to it," he snapped. "I wouldn't be here if I weren't. And I wouldn't put those officers' lives at risk."

Vincent picked up the bottle and read the label. "Is this for your nerves?"

"Nerves?" He laughed. "No." He poured two fingers of the amber liquid into a glass and held it up to the light. "Now that's a beautiful thing." He swirled the whiskey and watched with admiration as the tears flowed down the inside of the glass. "Whiskey is my drug of choice. This one is fantastic."

Vincent read the label more closely. "Wow…115 proof. Is this wise?"

"Trust me, it's not a problem. Consider it a prop." He placed the glass on the table but didn't take a drink.

Vincent shook his head. "You're an artist with a drinking problem. Seems banal, don't you think?"

He frowned at that description. "No. I'm a washed-up cop with a drinking problem. The artist is secondary."

"I don't think Olivia or Preston would agree with you. Don't let whiskey take away your God-given talent. The painting at the safe house is exquisite. And Preston told me there are dozens more hung on your walls, each one better than the last."

"The boy's got a big mouth."

Vincent grinned. "That he does. Do me a favor," he whispered. "I'd like you to put this in your ear." He handed him a small device.

"What is it?"

"It's a communication device called an earwig. It fits in your ear like a hearing aid."

He spoke to Louis as a test. "Can you hear me?"

"I can. We could have used this back in the day."

"This will allow me to speak to you while I'm in the surveillance van. You and I are the only ones who have this device. Please, keep it between us."

"Between you and me." He glared at Vincent. "Without telling Jonathan or Dominick."

"Yes. Consider it our little secret."

"They already have their own equipment in here. What are you up to?"

"If all goes as planned, nothing," said Vincent.

"If Jonathan finds out, he'll be pissed."

"You leave him to me."

Louis grinned. "Now this should be interesting."

———

Vincent returned to the van, and as he'd hoped, the officer running the equipment was not yet in place. His conversation with Louis was private.

Ellie stepped outside. "Is this a good idea, Dad? I'm worried Louis is too old. He might get hurt."

"Everything will be fine, but you need to stay inside the van. You're the target, remember?" He, too, prayed this wasn't a terrible mistake.

CHAPTER 32

VINCENT, AS WELL AS ELLIE, PRESTON, AND ONE OF JONATHAN'S officers, watched what was happening through the monitors inside the van.

Just before ten fifteen, Louis hobbled to the bar. "I have to pee. It's hell getting old." When he returned, he sat on the bench, once again deviating from their meticulous plan.

"What are you doing?" Vincent asked through the earwig, though everyone else in the van thought he was speaking to the monitor.

Louis glanced at Jonathan, who stood behind the bar. "I'm changing seats. Do you care?"

Jonathan frowned, then shook his head.

"That's not the plan," Vincent argued through Louis's earwig.

Louis rubbed his ear, sending a high-pitched signal into the listening devices, then let out a devious laugh.

Vincent's eyes widened from the assault on his senses and hoped his reaction went unnoticed.

Louis sat comfortably on the bench, waiting.

At ten thirty sharp, Cyrus Willingham arrived with his men. Emmet Hendricks and Kraig Gunter walked into the restaurant, checked for customers, then sat on two of the twenty-five stools in the center of the bar. Emmet ordered two beers.

"We're closed," said Jonathan.

When he placed a hunting knife on the counter, Jonathan served their beers, no questions asked.

Willingham and Rufus stood, facing Louis. "Let's go," Rufus ordered, and pointed toward the dark corner where booths lined the walls, with no windows and no potential witnesses.

Louis laughed. "Do I look stupid to you? You'll leave me behind with a knife to the heart. I'm not moving."

"What's down there, anyway?" Rufus nodded toward the back of the restaurant. "I don't trust you."

"And I'm supposed to trust you? It's a restaurant, you idiot. Check for yourself for all I care."

Rufus wandered through the restaurant but returned after a quick glimpse into a large space filled with empty tables and chairs.

"Take a seat or leave me to my whiskey."

When Willingham moved toward the chairs across from Louis, Rufus stopped him. "I'm not sitting with my back to the windows. You sit on the chair," he ordered Louis.

As Louis used his cane and tottered off the bench, he appeared older and even more feeble. He became someone for them to pity. He'd convinced the two men to sit in the exact location they'd planned and assured them he was no threat without uttering a single word.

"Clever old fox," Vincent said into Louis's earwig.

The two men sat on the bench while Louis had a seat on one of the two chairs across from them.

"Put your weapons on the table," Louis ordered Rufus.

"Not going to happen."

"Fine. Then I'll go straight to the cops."

"No! You'll die here."

"Not going to happen." He jammed the head of his cane between Rufus's legs. The handle was custom made, with curves to fit his hand and a pointed end designed to inflict as much pain as possible.

Rufus let out an agonizing shriek. He tried to push away, but the owner of the restaurant mounted the benches to the wall, making it impossible to escape. The more he struggled, the harder Louis pushed the cane between his legs. The feeble old man wasn't as frail as he appeared. Rufus was unable to pull the cane out of his hand.

His anguished howl roused the curiosity of Emmet and Kraig. They picked up their knives and moved toward Rufus.

Jonathan moved one hand behind his back and held onto his weapon.

"Tell them to stay back," Louis ordered.

"Everything's fine," he told his men, but his voice was barely a whimper. He signaled with his hand, and they returned to their seats, and kept a closer eye on Louis.

And Jonathan kept a closer eye on them.

Rufus's body shook from the pain while his partner remained expressionless. Most men would have grimaced after hearing his cries. Willingham appeared unmoved, without a sliver of concern. His indifference showed there was no allegiance among them. One criminal was paying another.

"Put your weapon on the table," Louis ordered.

Once Rufus complied, Louis placed his gun on the chair beside him, released Rufus from his grip, and moved the bottle of whiskey toward him.

Rufus immediately gulped it down as though his life depended on it, then slammed the bottle on the table and let out a deep sigh of relief. "What the fuck is wrong with you? I should kill you with my bare hands."

Louis laughed, then shifted his eyes to Willingham. "So, the old saying is true. There is no honor among thieves. You don't care what happens to these men." He turned to Rufus. "He must pay well."

He shrugged, then poured more whiskey into the empty glass on the table.

"Tell me what you think you know," said Willingham.

Louis ignored him. "You don't remember me, do you?" he asked Rufus.

He wiped the sweat from his brow and stared at Louis. "You're a cop," he said, loud enough for his men to hear. Kraig and Emmet picked up their weapons and moved toward them, ready to fight. When Rufus shook his head, they returned to the bar.

"Cop!" shouted Willingham. "Kill him."

"Kill a cop?" said Rufus. "Are you crazy?"

"Relax. I'm not a cop anymore. I retired a long time ago."

"From what I remember, you were a vicious cop. But look at you now—you're old and washed-up. What happened to you?"

"That's not important."

"Why should we take you seriously?"

"Because I have your weapon. And in your condition, even I could beat you to the door. We both know he's not a problem." He nodded toward Willingham.

Rufus snorted. "No argument there."

"These days, I keep my ear to the ground. The cops know there are people in Savannah looking for the professor. They're still trying to figure out who. I investigated on my own and found you. It wasn't hard. You are really sloppy," he said to Willingham. "I can tell the cops who you are, or you can pay me not to. It's as simple as that."

"Why wouldn't we just kill you?" asked Willingham.

Louis slowly drank the shot he poured earlier. "You're a Yankee. If you kill a cop in this city, I guarantee you won't make it to trial. Even if I am an old, retired cop. Besides, they know better." He nodded to Rufus and his men. "And you don't have the guts."

"He's right," said Rufus. "On both accounts. What do you want?"

"From him, I want money for my silence. But from you, I want you to tell me when you started killing for money. Why would you work for the likes of him?"

He shrugged. "Money's scarce these days."

"You were always a thug, but killing a young woman for a Yankee? That's not you. Or at least it wasn't. Did prison change you that much?"

"Are you worried about me now?"

"No! I'm worried about the professor. Ask him what he did."

"Professor?" Rufus appeared surprised by the reference. He turned to Willingham. "Why does he keep calling her a professor?"

"Shut your mouth," Willingham shouted at Louis.

Louis pulled out a file he'd tucked behind his back and opened it. He placed a recent photo of Ellie on the table. One where she was smiling at the camera, enjoying life. "He wants you to kill this woman, right?"

Rufus remained silent.

"She's a music professor. Why kill a woman whose only crime is teaching music? Did you even ask? Or is this all about the money?"

"Kill him," Willingham ordered, almost panicked.

Louis laughed. "Don't fuck with me, Willingham. Remember, I'm the one with the gun. Ask Rufus what I'll do with it."

"Listen to him. He'll kill you without giving it a thought."

Louis focused his attention back on Rufus and placed a second photo on the table. This one was of Ellie as a child, lying in a hospital bed, connected to machines. It was clear she was dying. "Willingham did this. He tried to kill her when she was a child, but he screwed up. A jogger found her in time. Now, thirty years later, he discovered she's still alive and wants *you* to finish the job."

Rufus studied both photos. "I've never seen a kid this sick before. Is that a doctor? Why is he kneeling?"

"The doctor was praying for God to save her."

Rufus reacted as they all had. He couldn't take his eyes off the little girl.

Louis laid another photo on the table. The child was sitting up with her legs drawn to her chest, looking directly into the camera.

"That's what trauma looks like." Louis violently pointed his finger at Willingham. "He took her away from her family, filled her with drugs, and dumped her on McQueen's Island Trail for the animals to pick apart."

Rufus remained silent, but his eyes spoke volumes.

"Imagine a three-year-old abandoned on that trail in the middle of the night. She was dying. Alone. Are you really going to kill her now? To finish what *he* started?"

As Rufus stared at the photo, his finger traced over Ellie's face. With a low, throaty growl, he turned his wrath on Willingham. "How could you have done this? She was a little girl, for God's sake."

"He's got it all wrong. It wasn't me."

It was clear Rufus didn't believe him. "Then who?" he shouted.

Vincent sat up straight and watched through the monitors as Louis turned one criminal against the other. It seemed even thugs had their limits, but Vincent worried Louis had poked the bear a little too hard.

"O'Rourke did that. Not me."

"Who's O'Rourke?" asked Rufus.

"He's the person paying you," said Louis. "You didn't know you were being paid by a child killer?"

"You knew who did this?" Rufus shouted, shocked by this new revelation. "And you did nothing? You let a child killer go free?"

"He did. For money. How much was your silence worth, Mr. Willingham from Kennebunk, Maine? The cost of owning a newspaper, perhaps?"

Willingham appeared stunned by the accusation. "But how…"

"I told you, I know everything."

Willingham's hands shifted unexpectedly, pulling a gun he'd hidden.

Louis was unmoved. "You're going to use that here?" He laughed. "I dare you. You don't have the guts."

He raised his hand and pointed the weapon at Louis's head.

Louis didn't even blink.

Vincent shouted, "NOW," and the officer in the van yelled, "GO, GO, GO."

All hell broke loose.

CHAPTER 33

Officers came out of nowhere. Some ran in the back entrance of the building, while others came out of the dark shadows inside the restaurant. Each shouted *Police!* with a voice designed to instill panic.

Jonathan had already drawn his weapon before Emmet and Kraig could lift their knives off the counter. "Guns trump knives, gentlemen. Don't be a fool."

The two men raised their hands.

Willingham heard the commotion behind him and turned to see what was happening, shifting his weapon away from Louis.

At that moment, Louis slammed his cane onto Willingham's hand and knocked his weapon to the ground, then pointed Rufus's gun at him.

"I'd suggest you look down before you make another move," said Louis.

He glanced at his shirt and saw a red dot pointed at his chest. "What is that?"

"That's from a sniper's scope," said Rufus, who raised his own hands up in surrender. "I should have known there's no such thing as a retired cop. Put your hands up before they shoot you," he told Willingham.

It was over in a matter of seconds. While the police cuffed Emmet and Kraig, Jonathan moved to the front of the restaurant to help Louis, only to find him in his chair, drinking another glass of whiskey with one hand and pointing a gun with the other. Willingham and Rufus sat across from him with their hands over their heads as Jonathan moved in and cuffed them both.

"I didn't realize we had a sniper in place," an officer said to Jonathan.

"We don't. Why?"

"There was an infrared scope on Willingham when we arrived. I assumed it was one of our men."

"No, it wasn't." He stormed out of the restaurant and marched toward Vincent. The two men stood, toe-to-toe, on the sidewalk. "You want to tell me what just happened?"

"I can explain."

Ellie saw a familiar face walking across the street. "Well, look at that. Why am I not surprised?"

Walking toward them, carrying a sniper rifle over his shoulder, was Preston's father, Admiral David Bartlett.

Preston laughed. "Me either."

David glanced at his son and gave him a wink, then joined Vincent and Jonathan in the street now filled with police cars and flashing lights.

Jonathan saw the man carrying a sniper rifle and moved toward him. "WHO THE HELL ARE YOU? AND WHY SHOULDN'T I ARREST YOUR ASS RIGHT NOW?"

Before he could answer, Preston and Ellie joined them. "He's my father."

"FATHER! Are you fucking kidding me! Why are you here?"

"He's added insurance," said Vincent.

"INSURANCE!"

"May I interrupt whatever this is?" ask David. "I'm Admiral David Bartlett." He lifted a hand to shake Jonathan's but lowered it when he'd refused.

"How long have you been here, Admiral?" he said with disdain.

"Not long. I came as soon as you found Timothy."

"Where were you?"

"In the woods. During the day, I stayed in my car, out of sight. I made sure to stay away from your cameras."

"The woods," Jonathan repeated. "Why?"

"I was your sentinel. If Timothy found the safe house, someone else could have."

"Sentinel?" Jonathan paced, stopping long enough to ask another question, then paced again. "You've been lurking—and you reported to whom? Vincent?"

Both men eyed each other, then nodded.

"How did you communicate?"

Vincent lifted his phone. "Text, mostly. Until we were operational. Then we used these." He showed Jonathan his earwig. "Both David and I had one. And Louis, of course."

"Louis!"

"It was the only way for David to hear what was happening inside."

"So he would know when to shoot," said Jonathan.

"I wasn't there to kill anyone. I was your backup, in case."

"In case!" Jonathan vibrated with anger. Red-faced, blood-curdling, anger. As he spoke, a vein pulsed in his jaw. "This is my operation. These people are my responsibility. You had no right."

"I agree." Vincent moved into Jonathan's personal space. "Understand this! Someone is trying to kill my daughter. I'll do whatever it takes to protect her, even if it means having a sniper in place."

His voice remained calm, although it was an octave lower than usual. A signal to those who knew him, it was time to back off. Ellie and Preston instinctively, simultaneously, took one step away from the two men.

"Jesus," Jonathan muttered, then placed his hands in his pockets.

"We didn't plan on using David here until Louis got involved. He was monitoring the safe house, that's all."

"Monitoring? You mean he was there to kill anyone who tried to enter."

Vincent shrugged. "Not anyone."

Jonathan's eyes widened.

"David has a unique perspective, with different training than the police."

"What kind of training?"

"He can neutralize a threat without firing a shot."

"Neutralize." Jonathan shook his head. He understood exactly what that meant. David would kill anyone who tried to breach the safe house with his bare hands, without making a sound. When Jonathan looked at Vincent now, there was fear in his eyes.

His reaction, Vincent knew, wasn't because of the threat, but of knowing what he and David were truly capable of. And understanding what it meant for a Navy SEAL to protect their families at all costs.

"He knows what he's doing," said Vincent. "When Louis became part of this operation, I wanted an extra pair of eyes on him."

"You wanted! It wasn't your decision to make."

"She is my daughter. And Louis is old and frail. To be honest, he worried me a little."

"Well, he worried me too. I don't appreciate being left in the dark." Still angry, he walked up to David and pushed his index finger into his chest. "YOU'RE DAMN LUCKY YOU WEREN'T SHOT."

Vincent thought David's self-control was admirable. If their roles were reversed, Jonathan would have been flat on the ground.

"Why not tell me?"

"Would your commander have approved a sniper on-site?" asked Vincent.

"No."

"There's your answer," said David. "Have your commander call me. It'll be fine. Trust me."

Jonathan scoffed at this stranger. "Trust you! Yeah, right! I don't know who you are, and you don't know my commander."

David slapped Jonathan on the back as he would his own son. "Don't worry, son." He walked away with his rifle over his shoulder.

Jonathan was still seething with anger. "*Son*? I'm not your son!"

———

The police arrested the four men, read them their rights, and placed each man in separate rooms. Captain Crawford questioned David and Vincent in her office. Alone.

When they returned to the bullpen, Jonathan stood with his hands on his hips, demanding answers. "What happened in there?" he asked his captain.

"He's a two-star, Jonathan, from the Pentagon, no less. What would you have me do? He didn't fire a single shot. We're lucky everything turned out the way it did. Leave it at that."

Jonathan huffed. "This is about politics. He's a sniper, for God's sake!"

"It's always about politics. The governor would have my ass if I arrested a two-star."

David shook the captain's hand and followed her into the observation room.

Jonathan took a deep breath to calm himself and prepared to interrogate the men.

———

The observation room was full. Vincent and David stood with the captain. Olivia and Timothy had driven to the precinct the moment the police released them from the safe house. Even Alex had arrived in time, although Charlotte stayed home. Louis remained in the bullpen.

Ellie stood in front of the two-way mirror and waited, eager to get started. It wasn't Rufus or his men she studied; it was Cyrus Willingham. The man with all the answers, or at least the important ones.

Jonathan and Dominick sat across from him in the interrogation room. At first, they remained silent. Jonathan sat up straight with his hands folded on top of a file on the table. Neither man blinked, but beads of sweat appeared on Willingham's forehead.

He opened the file and placed the photos of Ellie on the table. "Remember these?"

"I didn't do that. I told Louis, and I'll tell you, it wasn't me. It was O'Rourke."

"You're the one who's here, not O'Rourke. You're the one who hired those men to kill Ellie. In fact, nothing links O'Rourke to this case. Tell me why I should believe you. Why would he want to kill a small child?"

"I DON'T KNOW!" He banged his fists on the table and glared at Jonathan. "Ask him!"

"He's not the one who hired those men—you are. You realize, they have nothing to lose. They'll tell us everything. With their testimony, you'll be in prison for a very long time. Maybe even decades."

"LAWYER! NOW!"

"What about Georgetown? After I get in touch with the DC police, they'll charge you in that case as well. Two men died."

"You're barking up the wrong tree. I was in Maine. Check it out. I want my lawyer."

"That's your right. And when he gets here, we'll charge you with attempted murder, murder for hire, and anything else I can think of. Give me something to link O'Rourke to my two cases or you'll be in prison alone."

"Then there's Timothy," said Dominick. "Were you supposed to kill him, or was that O'Rourke, too?"

When Dominick mentioned Timothy's name, he squirmed. "LAWYER! NOW!"

From then on, he sat back in his chair and said nothing.

———

Olivia viewed the interview with the experience of a profiler. "I think he's telling the truth."

"We're wasting time," said Ellie. "It's time to go to Boston to confront these people. I'm sick of hiding."

CHAPTER 34

Without saying a word to anyone, Preston grabbed his backpack and left the observation room. He walked to the farthest corner of the bullpen, inserted a pair of earbuds, and sunk into an armchair.

"What's he doing, meditating?" Captain Crawford asked.

"No," said David. "He's thinking."

Ellie followed and sat beside him, but Preston was too deep in thought to acknowledge her presence. She reached out and touched his hand. His eyes were still closed as their fingers intertwined.

Vincent thought the gesture of linking hands was sweet—dare he say, loving. He'd noticed with each passing day their relationship had grown—changing from friendship to something else entirely. He understood they both needed this time away from the others to decompress, even if it was only a few minutes.

"What will happen to him?" Vincent asked the captain, nodding toward the interrogation room.

"Cyrus Willingham and his men will stay where they are for now. I want them close to answer questions."

"Willingham asked for his lawyer?"

"Yes, but the other three haven't."

Everyone left the small room to fill their mugs or grab a bottle of water and to order lunch. Vincent ordered for Ellie and Preston, who still appeared to be meditating, though he knew what Preston was doing was so much more.

As always, they instinctively returned to the group the moment the food arrived. They served lunch in a conference room, but the room was eerily quiet. Each person seemed immersed in their own thoughts.

"What's going on in that head of yours, son? I can almost see the wheels turning," asked David.

"Not much, I'm afraid. At least, nothing that Jonathan or Dominick hadn't already considered. I haven't had time to do my research."

Vincent understood what Preston wasn't saying. He'd prefer to be in his basement with his own computers. He was a hacker and knew other hackers. There were ways to find out information unofficially, and without being detected. But not here. Here he would be exposed. Here, he'd need a warrant.

"Talk to us," said David. "We can help."

Preston leaned back in the chair to gather his thoughts. "Well, my mind keeps going back to Georgetown. Remember, Ellie's instincts told her there was a third man. We believed her."

"Yes, we did," said David.

"Willingham's confident his alibi will hold up, and he insisted Randolph O'Rourke was the person who hurt Ellie thirty years ago, not him." Preston got out of his chair and paced. "It makes sense that Randolph O'Rourke was the third man. I keep wondering if the men at Georgetown were hired to kill Ellie or to bring her to O'Rourke."

"For him to finish the job."

"Yes. Or watch while they did. Either way, he would need to be close enough to see proof of her death. If Ellie's here, then he has to be here."

Vincent and Ellie stopped eating and sat up a little straighter.

"To be certain they took care of her once and for all," said David.

"Yes. Which means he's out there somewhere, which makes him dangerous. And if he knows Willingham is in custody, he'd also be desperate."

"How would he know?" asked Jonathan. "Willingham never said O'Rourke was in Savannah. And Timothy never saw him."

"We're missing something," said Preston. "Did he have a burner phone?"

"Neither Willingham nor his men had burner phones on them when we arrested them. We requested a warrant for Willingham's credit cards and phone records. We can even check the airlines, but it will take some time."

Timothy raised his hand. "May I say something?"

"You don't need to ask permission," said Vincent. "What's on your mind?"

"I doubt someone like Randolph O'Rourke would be without his personal phone. He's a business executive who would need to be in contact with his office. His phone would be like an appendage."

Olivia agreed.

"Plus, it's been thirty years, and he's never been caught. Why would he think he'd get caught now? In this scenario, he's in the background, giving the orders. Out of reach."

"Until now," said Jonathan. "And we have his man."

With a few clicks of the keys, Preston connected to the FBI and had Randolph O'Rourke's unlisted business cell phone number. Another click showed a pin on the map at O'Rourke's home in Boston. He wasn't in Savannah. At least his phone wasn't.

Timothy pulled out his cell to send a text.

"What are you doing?" asked Jonathan.

"I'm texting our nanny, Felicia Romero. I have an idea." He keyed in the message but paused before he pressed Send.

"Don't get other people involved in this case without asking me first," said Jonathan.

"You can trust her."

"And you know this, how? You've met this woman one time in your entire life."

"I realize I add little to this investigation. But you need to understand…you know criminals, Jonathan. I know people."

"What are you thinking?" Captain Crawford asked.

"Let's say O'Rourke is here and left his phone in Boston."

"We'd have no simple way to trace him," said the captain.

"He would still have to stay in touch with his office. He has a second phone, I'm sure of it. With a number he'd only give to trusted members of his staff."

"There are no other cell phone numbers listed for Randolph O'Rourke," said Preston.

"Before I get anyone's hopes up, let me text Felicia. I could be wrong. You must guarantee you won't expose them. Remember, she has a neighbor who still works at Randolph O'Rourke's estate. She'll help us."

"If he goes to prison, they'll lose their jobs. Isn't that against their best interest?" Captain Crawford asked.

"Everything changed when they found out I was alive. They hated what the O'Rourkes did to us. After seeing the reports on the news, they believe O'Rourke is trying to kill Ellie. They'll do whatever they can to stop it."

"These people are killers. Why would they put their own lives at risk?" asked Jonathan.

"To save me," said Ellie. "I don't like this, but what choice do we have? Call them. But only if you can protect them," she said to Jonathan.

Jonathan hesitated, then gave an all clear to send the text. Twenty minutes later, Timothy received a response with two cell phone numbers, and a message: "Randolph O'Rourke was out of town."

"I knew it." Timothy wrote two numbers on a sheet of paper and handed it to Jonathan.

The first was the number they already ran and was sitting in Boston.

Preston ran the second, and frowned.

"What?" asked Jonathan.

"This cell phone number belongs to Ellie and Timothy's father, Anderson O'Rourke."

The entire team gawked.

"Did they even have cell phones that long ago?" asked Ellie.

"Yes," said Timothy. He Googled it. "The first mobile phones were on the market in 1983."

Preston checked Anderson's number. "He's kept the number in Anderson's name and upgraded the phone over the years."

"I don't know if Randolph is brilliant or an idiot," said Jonathan. "Why would this number still be in use? Anderson O'Rourke's been dead for thirty years."

"Many business owners have multiple phones, but I didn't expect that," said Timothy.

"Trace the number," Jonathan ordered Preston. "See what happens."

The team now felt an urgent need to find out where this number led, if anywhere. Preston connected to the FBI and searched Anderson O'Rourke's cell phone. Within seconds, the results came back. The screen filled with the local map and a single mark pointing to the phone's location. Anderson O'Rourke's cell phone was in Savannah.

Jonathan and Dominick leaned in to get a closer look at the screen. "Crap," said Jonathan. "That's Charlotte Mathews's neighborhood."

CHAPTER 35

THE RUSH WAS ON. JONATHAN AND DOMINICK PULLED THEIR WEAPons from the drawers and hurried toward the elevator. The others followed.

"I'm staying behind," said Olivia. "I think Timothy should stay here."

Timothy stopped mid-stride and protested. "Why me?"

"Because O'Rourke is a dangerous man. He doesn't even know you're here. You need to stay off his radar as long as possible. It's safer."

Vincent expected Olivia to insist on going along, to be by Ellie's side when she met the monster face-to-face. He knew what that meant. She had more pressing things on her mind—something that couldn't wait.

"Stay safe," Olivia shouted as the doors closed.

After they left the building, Olivia paced around the bullpen, then began rummaging through Jonathan's desk.

"What are you looking for?" asked Timothy.

Olivia said nothing. She grabbed her computer, then walked into the observation room. Cyrus Willingham sat beyond the glass, awaiting his fate, while Olivia opened her laptop to investigate him.

Jonathan had already studied his criminal record. He had none. Olivia was interested in the link between Cyrus Willingham and Randolph O'Rourke. She wanted to know when and where their lives intersected for the first time, where they went to school, and if they had a close relationship. She suspected they had. And she wanted to know when and how Willingham became the owner and editor of the local paper—something

Louis had already discovered. She was searching for secrets hidden away for decades.

She contacted an old friend from her profiling days. A woman whose job was to uncover a lifetime of transgressions. Over the years, Olivia had learned to keep her friend's name out of any investigation. Spooks fly under the radar. There would be no printed documents of what they found. While she waited, she scoured the internet for any public records.

She wrote O'Rourke's and Willingham's names on a spreadsheet, with a column for each of them. Below their names, she listed each piece of information she and her friend had found. Soon the document resembled a murder board, but with the suspect in plain sight.

Olivia's research found that Cyrus Willingham had grown up in Kennebunk, Maine, where the O'Rourkes spent their summers. Their long-standing friendship had likely begun there. After scanning the archives of Willingham's newspaper, she found items that connected the two men. They were on the same baseball and soccer teams throughout their teenage years, and in each team photo, they stood side by side, with their arms over the other's shoulders. This was a lifelong friendship.

Their bond held as they aged, though their interests had changed. One rode horses, the other preferred chess club, and their SAT scores were nearly identical. Because of the similarities in their SATs, her friend continued her search. They applied to the same university, although Willingham was a scholarship kid while Randolph grew up with a silver spoon in his mouth. One majored in journalism, and the other, finance.

During their time at the university, Willingham's GPA was high, though he struggled a little in math. Randolph struggled in all his classes. His grades hadn't matched his SAT scores. Quite the opposite. Olivia and her friend concluded that this was where the young Cyrus Willingham had gone amiss. Her friend discovered Willingham's scholarship was given to him by Bradford O'Rourke's company. They both questioned what he'd done for his education. She now suspected whatever it was came with exceptionally long strings attached.

She thought about saving or printing the spreadsheet, but decided against it. Her memory would have to suffice. She walked back to Jonathan's desk, printed the public records she'd found, and placed them in Ellie's case file.

Louis watched with interest as she studied each document. "What are you looking for?"

Olivia was so engrossed in her work she'd either ignored him or hadn't heard a word he'd said.

Captain Crawford came out of her office and walked over to Olivia. "God, I can't wait until this baby comes. What are you doing?" she asked Olivia. When she flashed a stare, Captain Crawford raised a brow. The mere glance between the two women sent a message they both understood—*don't ask questions.* "I'm going back to my office to put my feet up. Call me if you hear anything."

Once the captain closed her office door, Olivia picked up the file, along with Willingham's cell phone, from Jonathan's desk. Timothy and Louis stood to follow, and she pointed her perfectly manicured fingernail at them both. "Sit!" she ordered.

They obeyed without question.

She used her charm to convince an officer she was part of the investigation, and he opened the interrogation room door. "Thank you." She smiled. "You can leave us alone." The officer waited outside the door, just in case.

Olivia had a certain grace when she entered a room that turned the heads of both men and women alike. Once she made eye contact with her prey, she was all business. Some, to their detriment, had misread her beauty as weakness, but soon discovered there was nothing frail about this woman. She was brilliant, calculating, and never walked into a room without a strategy.

The closed interrogation room door locked behind her, and by her request, Willingham remained unrestrained. There was no physical threat. Not from him. She could easily handle Cyrus Willingham. She placed the file on the table and sat down across from him. When she looked him square in the eyes, he, like many men, withered. Nerves appeared to be getting the best of him. Olivia patiently waited for him to compose himself enough to speak.

"Who are you?" he asked.

"I'm Dr. Olivia Lombardi. I'm a profiler, helping with this investigation." Both were true. She was a profiler, years ago, and she was part of the investigation, although in an unofficial capacity. It was another one of those lies of omission Vincent had often spoken about.

Willingham grunted.

"First, let me tell you what I know. We both know why you're here, Mr. Willingham. And who's pulling the strings." She placed a photo of Bradford O'Rourke on the table and slid it toward him. "Look familiar?"

After a quick glance, he pushed it away.

"You should know, Mr. Willingham, the police have Randolph O'Rourke's location. They're picking him up as we speak."

His face had changed from an angry red to a pale white as the blood left his face. He squirmed in his seat but still said nothing.

"I'm here because there's one question that keeps rattling around in my mind. Niggling at me." She thought of Timothy's explanation of how his mind worked and realized this had become her own obsession.

"Question?" he asked.

"Yes. What's in it for you?"

"What are you talking about?"

"He's the one with the power." She pointed to the photo of Bradford O'Rourke. "He's the one who controls Randolph. Once Randolph's alone in an interrogation room, that control will end. He'll tell the police everything."

Willingham grimaced, then sat up a little straighter in his chair. He placed his elbows on the table with his fingers locked together so tightly his knuckles turned white. The vein in his jaw pulsed.

"Does he control you, Mr. Willingham?"

It didn't take long for a reaction. "No one controls me," he snapped, and slammed both hands on the table. His pale face had once again reddened.

Olivia hadn't reacted to his outburst. She remained cool and expressionless and didn't even jump when he slammed his hands on the table. She just stared. "At first, I thought this might be about money, but now I'm not sure. I mean, money's part of it. There's more, much more. Then it came to me. The explanation for all of this."

"Explanation about what?" he asked with an edge to his voice.

"About the death of a child, or even two. About why you got involved with the O'Rourkes. And why you're here now."

Willingham cleared his throat and sat back in his chair, with his arms crossed over his chest.

"You see, I believe the truth started in the past. In your past. Something Bradford O'Rourke had arranged. Now you're here to kill Professor O'Brien to pay off a debt. I'm sure of it. But why? What debt could be so great that you'd kill a woman you've never met?"

"I don't know what you're talking about."

"I think it boils down to your first big mistake. The one that gave him power over you. Something in your youth."

She placed the photo of Randolph on the table next to his father. "Look at him. He's your friend. There are plenty of photos of both of you. All I had to do was check your own newspaper's archives."

Willingham shifted in his seat again.

"I'm interested in his demeanor, and his expression. It's clear you're the strong one in this relationship. You and his father." She pointed to Bradford.

The sight of the two photos together made Willingham sneer.

"Are you okay, Mr. Willingham? You look a little nauseous."

He glared at Olivia and hardened his expression.

"Cyrus." She used his first name, hoping to ease the tension. "Are you willing to rot in prison for this man?" Again, she placed her finger on Bradford O'Rourke's photo. "Because you're going to prison. So far, he's not."

Willingham pushed the photos away. "Lawyer."

Olivia ignored him. "I checked you out."

"There's nothing to see."

"I wanted to find out when you moved from reporter to editor to owner of the paper."

Willingham sank in his chair, as though he knew Olivia was about to expose his secret. Or one of them.

"You purchased the newspaper two months after Randolph O'Rourke tried to kill his own niece. Two months after someone abandoned William O'Rourke on the steps of a church. The police will get a warrant, Mr. Willingham. They'll go through your financials and expose your secrets."

"What secrets, exactly?"

"Who gave you the money to buy the newspaper, for one. I suspect it was Bradford O'Rourke. Your newspaper was part of at least one quid pro quo. The cop in charge of this investigation will find out before the ink on the warrant is dry. What did you have to do to pay off such a debt? Kill a child, perhaps?"

Willingham wiped drips of sweat from his face, then wiped his hands on his pants.

"I believe Bradford O'Rourke bought you off. You wanted to own the paper so badly you took his money and got rid of his grandson."

He shook his head.

"Were you supposed to kill the baby?"

"NO!" He shouted so loudly the officer's head peeked inside.

"Everything's fine, Officer."

Once the door was closed, Willingham placed his elbows back on the table with his face in his hands. "For God's sake, I didn't kill a baby. I wouldn't."

"No, because you didn't have the heart to follow his orders. Because you're not like them. So, you abandoned him on a church step. I'm guessing Bradford wasn't happy about that." Then she considered. "Wait—you didn't tell him."

Willingham shook his head.

"I bet it was a surprise when Timothy walked into your office."

"You can't even imagine."

"That's when you called Bradford O'Rourke to break the news. Another mistake. Still paying off that debt, are you? But it got me thinking."

"You need to stop doing that," he warned.

"Doing what?"

"Thinking. It'll get you in trouble."

"Is that a threat?"

"No. A suggestion."

Olivia grinned, then continued. "Randolph's job was to kill Jacqueline. Yours was to kill William. You both screwed it up, though Randolph tried to do his part. Now you're both here to fix your mistake."

Willingham shrugged. "You don't know what you think you know. I'm done."

At that, Olivia stopped talking. She paced around the interrogation room, running through the scenario in her mind until she discovered the missing piece.

She placed his phone on the table. "I want the phone numbers of everyone involved in this case."

Willingham laughed. "Good luck with that." He leaned in closer to

Olivia. "Lawyer." Then he leaned back in his chair until it teetered on two legs.

She had no intention of leaving the room empty-handed. "I'll only ask one more time."

He leaned in again and spat on Olivia's face. In one swift move, she grabbed his wrist and twisted his arm nearly out of the socket and pulled him across the table. He lay in agony, halfway on the table and halfway on the floor, unable to move. She wiped the spit from her face and rubbed it in his, then pressed his cell phone against each of his fingers until it unlocked. Only then did she release him from her grip.

She knocked on the door to leave while Willingham screamed for his lawyer. "Everything's fine, Officer." She moved into the observation room and placed another call.

Thirty minutes later, Olivia walked directly into Captain Crawford's office and shut the door.

CHAPTER 36

THEY PARKED THEIR VEHICLES AT THE END OF THE ROAD, AWAY from Charlotte's house. The distance made it impossible to see anything. They didn't know whether Charlotte was dead or alive or whether O'Rourke was even inside the house. But the distance gave them time to come up with a plan and maintain the element of surprise.

They huddled together to discuss their next move. The thought of Charlotte being hurt, or worse, weighed heavily on all of them. Vincent worried about Jonathan and Ellie. As a commander, he understood more than most what would happen to them if things ended badly—guilt would ravage them for the rest of their lives. Vincent and David were determined to make sure that didn't happen.

Jonathan glanced down the street. "I need to get a closer look."

"Wait. I can help." Preston retrieved his backpack from the SUV and pulled out a box about the size of a cell phone.

When he removed the lid, Dominick looked inside. "Is that what I think it is?"

Jonathan peeked into Preston's backpack. "What else do you have in there?"

"If I tell you, I'll have to kill you."

He shook his head. "How long have you been waiting to say that?"

Preston grinned.

When Vincent listened to Preston, he couldn't help but smile. In stressful situations, he was the one to interject subtle bits of humor. Just enough to take the edge off a tense situation. He was never sure whether it was intentional, but it had always come at the perfect time.

Preston removed a device from the box and unfolded what appeared to be small propellers, then handed it to Dominick.

"Check that out." Dominick gently lifted the device.

"It's a drone," Preston told Jonathan.

"I know it's a drone."

"The control panel attaches to my cell phone." He reached in the backpack and brought out a second device with two joysticks.

"I've never seen one so small," said Dominick.

"It's a prototype." He turned it over. "This camera will transmit a video to my cell. Assuming the curtains are open, we'll be able to see inside the house. They'll never hear it. It's a spy drone."

"A spy drone." Jonathan laughed. "Why am I not surprised?"

Concern filled Alex's face when he stepped closer to the drone. "The curtains should be open. She never closes them. God, I can't believe this is happening. I never should have left."

"I'm so sorry," said Ellie. "This is all my fault."

Alex disagreed. "O'Rourke's the one who's responsible for all of this, not you."

Of all the people involved in this case, Vincent worried the most about Alex. He was the least prepared. He'd shown them nothing but kindness, even after Ellie stormed into the house. Now the same monster who hurt his daughter had invaded Alex's world, and his peace of mind.

"You both need to calm down," said Jonathan. "I won't let anything happen to her. Or you, Ellie. It's our job to get Charlotte out of there. Once we do that, everything else will fall into place. She'll be fine. Trust me. Concentrate on the mission and get the rest out of your mind."

Preston agreed. "You sound like my father." He grinned when Jonathan gave him a look. "It's a compliment. I swear. You don't need to worry about either of us, Jonathan. We were trained by the best."

"Let's go," Jonathan ordered. "It's time to test out this drone."

———

Once they were close enough to the house, Preston sent the drone into the air. It barely made a sound as it flew across the street. First, he positioned the drone by the front windows and pressed zoom on the camera. It gave them an unobstructed view of an empty living room.

"She's not in there," said Preston. "Let me check the back of the house." He guided the drone over the house and into the backyard, where it peered through the rear door. There was a perfect view of the kitchen. "There she is. Looks like she's making drinks and serving a plate of cookies. She's feeding him. Do you always feed strangers in the South?"

Jonathan smiled. "Charlotte does. I think she's keeping him distracted until we can rescue her."

"Thank God she's alive," said Alex. "Where is he?"

Preston moved the drone to another window away from the kitchen door and found O'Rourke pacing. The screen on the cell phone was small, but it was large enough to see that nerves were getting the best of him. He was waving around a gun as he spoke.

"I wonder if he's talking to himself or to Charlotte," said Preston. "He'll shoot something if he keeps waving that gun around."

Dominick agreed. "I wish we could hear what they're saying."

"We need to get in there," said Jonathan. "I'm not sure how long Charlotte's famous Southern charm will hold him off."

———

They moved back to the car. "How are things?" asked Vincent.

"Charlotte's okay, but we need to move. I should call Captain Crawford. She'll want an update. Once she knows O'Rourke's holding Charlotte, she'll want me to wait until a hostage negotiator arrives."

"How long will that take?" asked Alex.

"Too long," said Ellie. "We need to take care of this now. I'm going in."

Jonathan stepped in front of her. "No, you're not."

Ellie took an additional step toward Jonathan before Vincent stopped her.

"We need to think about what we're doing," said Jonathan. "And be smart about it."

"Make a trade. It's me he wants. Come up with whatever plan you want as long as it includes me going in there."

Vincent and David shared a glance. They both understood what was behind Ellie's unyielding expression. Those same steely eyes stared back at them when she was a teenager who'd survived on the streets. And when someone tried to kill Preston days earlier. Now she focused those eyes and those same instincts on one mission: to save Charlotte, even if it meant putting her own life in danger. Professor O'Brien had disappeared, replaced by the woman trained by a Navy SEAL, determined to make things right. He and David would do whatever necessary to keep her out of harm's way.

"Jonathan, you know I can take care of myself," said Ellie. "He's an old man."

"An armed, unstable old man. You are not going in that house."

"Watch me."

"*Stop!*" said Vincent. "You can't do anything with a head full of steam. We either decide what to do together, or Jonathan will follow his captain's lead."

Jonathan took a breath, checked his watch, then glared at Ellie.

"Ticktock, Jonathan," said Vincent. "Which is it?"

Jonathan grimaced. "What do you have in mind?"

David stepped in to lead the discussion. "How many earwigs do you have with you, Preston?"

"Five."

"Good. That's enough for everyone but Alex."

"Except me? Why?"

"Because it's your mother. You're too close to this. We need you to take Vincent's car and block the other end of the street. We don't want civilians or cars to come down here. You'll be close enough to see everything. Trust me, Alex, you're the first person your mother will want to see when she's released. She'll want to know you're safe."

"Jonathan, you knock on the front door, with Dominick backing you up," said Vincent. "Preston and I can guard the rear in case he runs out back."

"Okay."

"I'm guessing he'll have Charlotte answer the door. If it's possible, pull her out of there when she answers. Hopefully he'll be far enough away that you can close the door, leaving him inside. Then you can negotiate until he surrenders. That depends on how close he'll be to Charlotte."

"Hopefully," said Alex. "What if he shoots my mother or Jonathan? You want me to go along with a plan that includes the word *hopefully*. Are you crazy? I'll go. I can handle O'Rourke. It's my mother. He can take me and let her go. Then you can do whatever you want."

"You're not going in there," insisted Jonathan. "This is our job. We know what we're doing."

Alex frowned. "Maybe we should call your captain."

"I realize this is hard, but you need to trust us," said David. "We won't let anything happen to your mother. Believe me. I'll have him in my sights the entire time."

Alex's eyes widened. "You'll have him in your sights! Really? You'll kill him while my mother watches. While she gets splattered with his blood."

"Only if necessary," said David. "We know what we're doing."

There was a coldness to his voice. Vincent understood David. He considered this a mission and put his feelings aside to concentrate on the task at hand. But this was personal for Alex. Vincent frowned, and David reconsidered his comments.

"Alex," said David, "I promise you I won't take a shot unless your mother's life is in danger. I truly don't believe it'll come to that. Be comforted in knowing, I never miss. Your mother's life is in expert hands."

"I don't like this," said Alex.

"Do you have a better idea?" asked David.

"We could call Captain Crawford, but I'm concerned it will take too long." He considered his options. "No, I don't have a better idea."

"Let's get into position," said David. "The clock's ticking."

"What about me?" asked Ellie.

"You're the target, not Charlotte. He may shoot the moment he sees you, and that may put Charlotte's life at risk," said Jonathan. "You stay by the car."

"I can stop him before that happens."

"I cannot, and will not, exchange one dead body for another. Everyone needs to come out of this alive. You stay back."

Ellie grimaced, but agreed.

"David, where are you going to be?" asked Dominick.

"He'll be up high." Vincent pointed to the trees across from the house.

"In the trees," said Jonathan. "Unbelievable. How old are you?"

He grinned, then gave Jonathan a wink. "Still young enough to beat you."

"Jonathan will knock on the door, when everyone is in position," said Vincent. "It'll bring them to the front of the house. He'll get Charlotte out."

After they reviewed every aspect of their plan, David walked to the SUV and returned with his sniper rifle.

Alex saw the weapon and turned white. "Christ."

Preston opened his backpack and pulled out a set of lock picks. "I wish Olivia was here. She gave us such a hard time for packing these."

"Do you know how to use them?" asked Jonathan. "Never mind. That was a stupid question. Remember, you're only out back in case he runs. You won't be needing those."

"Hey, I'm always prepared."

"Clearly."

Preston pulled another box filled with earwigs and handed them out.

"Son," said David. "Be careful."

He watched his father load his weapon. "You, too."

Everyone turned on their earwigs and moved into position.

David climbed the tree across from Charlotte's home, raised his weapon, and looked through the scope. "I'm in position," he said into the earwig.

"We're in position," said Preston.

Jonathan and Dominick moved to the front of the house.

CHAPTER 37

"ON THREE." JONATHAN COUNTED, THEN WALKED ONTO THE porch and banged his fist on the door. The sound was unmistakable and loud enough to travel to every corner of the house. It was the distinctive knock of a cop, and one he'd hoped Charlotte would recognize as a signal that help was on the way. He stood on the porch, far enough away that she would have to peek outside to see him.

"Who is it?" she asked through the door.

He knocked again without answering her question and stepped away, forcing her to stick her head out a small opening.

"Can I help you?" she asked. When she saw Jonathan, her eyes showed no fear. Simply irritation. She was ordering him to get this man out of her house without saying a word.

"Ma'am, we have a gas leak in the area. We're asking all residents to leave their homes and walk down the street." He pointed down the road, and Charlotte placed one foot outside the door to look in the direction he'd indicated. Jonathan couldn't see her other arm. He suspected O'Rourke was there, either holding her back or threatening her. She saw Alex in her sights, then glared at Jonathan and pursed her lips. He prayed she understood what was about to happen.

Randolph O'Rourke pulled open the door.

Jonathan noticed his fingers digging into Charlotte's arm. She glanced down, using her eyes to point to his other hand. It was a subtle gesture, but one he understood. There was no weapon visible, although he sensed it was there. "Sir, as I told your wife, there's a gas leak in the area. We're asking everyone to move to the end of the street while we check it out."

Jonathan watched O'Rourke, waiting for him to make a move. Then there was a slight shift—a twitch. Enough to see the edge of a gun. Without delay, he grabbed Charlotte's free arm. With one hard yank, he pulled her out of the house and into Dominick's arms with such force they both fell to the ground. The move was so unexpected, O'Rourke released her without leaving gashes in her bare arms. Though Jonathan wasn't quick enough. O'Rourke now pointed the weapon at him.

"Get her out of here," Jonathan ordered, then raised his arms and walked inside the house, hoping to keep O'Rourke distracted long enough to get Charlotte to safety. He now depended on the rest of the team to rescue him. Or at the very least, kill O'Rourke where he stood. All he had to do was get him into position.

"I don't have a clear shot," David said into his earwig.

As Jonathan moved deeper into the living room, O'Rourke followed. "Got him."

He nodded slightly, then raised one index finger a touch higher than the others.

"Got it," said David. "I'll wait for your signal."

"There's no gas leak. Who are you?" O'Rourke demanded.

"I'm Detective Jonathan Hadley." He could have lied and said he was with the gas company, but he decided against it. A decision he might question later.

"Detective? You're a cop?"

"Why are you in this house?"

"Why are you?" asked O'Rourke. "Don't forget, I'm the one with the gun."

Jonathan hoped to give O'Rourke a way out without getting either of them killed. But this man was irrational. He was sweating. Agitated. And he wandered around the room, waving the gun as he spoke.

"Charlotte's a family friend. When did you meet Charlotte?" He intentionally repeated her name.

It took a minute for O'Rourke to answer. He appeared deep in his own thoughts. As though he was wondering how this could have happened. "I saw her with Jacqueline at the other house." He raised his weapon. "I didn't see you."

"Why were you there?"

"I was watching the house, but I had to leave for a little while. When I returned, Jacqueline was gone, and the woman was there alone."

"The woman? You mean, Charlotte?"

He frowned, then looked at Jonathan. "Of course I mean Charlotte."

"If you're going to hold someone hostage, you should at least know her name. Use it."

"She came here with her son. I presume it was her son. I followed them."

"Why did you end up here?"

"I thought Jacqueline would come here to save her. She's who I want. Not that woman." Then he looked at Jonathan and caught his mistake. "I mean, Charlotte."

"You wanted to exchange Charlotte for Jacqueline. Is that it?"

"Yes. Where is she?" O'Rourke shouted.

"Not here. What were you going to do with her?"

"I'm not going to tell you. You're a cop."

With Jonathan's hands still raised, he stepped closer to O'Rourke. "Randolph, you need to put the gun down before something bad happens."

O'Rourke continued to walk around the living room but lifted the gun when he noticed Jonathan making a move. "Get back or I will kill you."

Jonathan moved back, then glanced out the window into the trees.

"I still have him," said David.

With each passing moment, O'Rourke's fate became clearer. He acted more desperate. More frantic. "How did this happen?" He frowned as he spoke, but he wasn't speaking to Jonathan. He appeared confused, as though he were wondering how any of this could have happened to him. "How can she be alive? It's impossible. He must be mistaken." He shook his head.

"Who is mistaken? You might as well tell me."

"Why should I tell you anything? You're a cop."

"Help me understand the last missing piece."

"What piece?"

"How you found Jacqueline, and why you want her dead. Cyrus already told us about William."

"You know about William?" O'Rourke frowned and raked his fingers through his hair, then wiped the sweat from his face with the back of his hand. "A detective found her. It didn't take long. He found out she lived in

Savannah until she was a teenager, but I think he screwed up. Or he lied for the money. People always lie for money."

"You could be right. We can always check her DNA to be sure."

O'Rourke said nothing.

"Why don't you put down the gun, and we can talk?"

"You know nothing!" he shouted.

"Okay. Tell me what I'm missing."

"It's too late." O'Rourke pointed his gun at Jonathan. "He'll find out if I let her go. Where is she?"

"Wait!" Jonathan's plea wasn't meant for O'Rourke, but for David—ordering him not to shoot. O'Rourke lowered his weapon a little. "Who will find out?"

O'Rourke shook his head and refused to answer.

"What does Jacqueline have to do with Professor O'Brien?" asked Jonathan.

"Don't play with me. I'm not an idiot. You know as well as I do, they're the same. Or at least that's what we were told."

"By the detective?"

"Yes!"

"You think Jacqueline is Professor O'Brien?"

"Yes. Why do I have to keep repeating myself?"

Nerves were getting the best of him now, Jonathan knew. "It's hot in Savannah this time of year," Jonathan said, to change the subject.

"Too damn hot."

"Yeah, Yankees say that all the time."

"I'm not waiting anymore, Jonathan. I'm coming in the back," Vincent said into the earwig. "David, a distraction would be helpful."

"Got it."

"I'm on the porch, ready to go," said Dominick.

"Randolph, listen to me," said Jonathan. "You need to put the gun down before someone gets hurt."

Instead of lowering his weapon, he raised it even higher and pointed his shaky hand at Jonathan's head. "You don't understand."

Jonathan spotted Vincent on the edges of his vision. He was inside the house, ready to attack, waiting until the time was right to make a move.

"Do you want to die?" asked Jonathan. "Because I'm not alone, and if you don't lower your weapon, they will kill you where you stand."

O'Rourke's crazed eyes glared at Jonathan. "It would be better for everyone if I died." He aimed the weapon.

"Look at your shirt," shouted Jonathan.

He glanced down and saw a red target on his chest—the distraction.

Jonathan backed farther into the living room, closer to a chair to dive behind should Vincent fail.

"Now!" David shouted.

Jonathan took cover.

Dominick crashed through the front door.

Vincent moved in with lightning speed and absolutely no sound. He placed his hand on top of O'Rourke's, shifting the weapon away from Jonathan and himself. In one quick move, he twisted the gun out of O'Rourke's hand, breaking his finger, then flipped him onto the ground. It was over in a matter of seconds.

Dominick handcuffed O'Rourke as he laid on the floor, moaning, then placed him in a seated position.

"You good?" Vincent asked Jonathan.

"I'm okay, thanks. You have some stealthy moves for an old guy."

Vincent handed O'Rourke's gun to Jonathan while Dominick pulled O'Rourke to his feet.

"My finger," he whined. "You broke my finger. I'm going to sue."

David walked up to O'Rourke, holding his sniper rifle. "One more second and you would have been dead."

Everyone returned to the house.

———

Ellie stood in front of the broken man and barely moved a muscle as memories blocked for decades revealed themselves. Bits of information and abstract pieces of a horror film came together to fill in the missing pieces of her life. The entire nightmare was now visible.

At first, she recalled the road trip from Boston, singing in a car seat and smiling while she watched the traffic. She liked car trips, she thought. There was no fear, though she remembered it seemed the ride would never end.

They stopped for lunch, and then dinner, and she napped a time or two. When she woke, the day had turned into night. She occupied her time by counting the streetlights that passed by the window. She counted to four on her fingers, then started over. Ellie remembered four was her favorite number.

After a while, her mood had changed. She cried to get out of the seat, to go to the bathroom, and run around. To be unshackled.

A man's voice from the front of the car barked, "Shut up. You'll be out of my hair soon enough."

Ellie frowned. Even as a child, his voice felt threatening.

"Pull over," the man told the driver. "I've had enough of this. Get rid of her." They drove down a long, dark highway with no more streetlights to count. There was only the darkness of a new moon. They pulled onto a gravel road. Ellie now knew it wasn't a gravel road at all, but a parking lot. The one by McQueen's Island Trail.

A man got out of the car. He moved too quickly to see his face until the rear door opened. The overhead light revealed the face of pure evil.

She fought to get away, but she was buckled in the car seat and couldn't move. Then she felt the injection.

The man ordered the driver to remove her from the car. "Throw her into the water. Drown her."

Hearing those words was too much for Ellie. All the color left her face. Her head was spinning out of control.

"What's going on, Ellie?" asked Vincent, interrupting her thoughts. "Are you okay?"

"What's happening?" asked Preston.

She was too immersed in her own memories to acknowledge their questions. She walked closer to O'Rourke. "There were two of you in the car."

"What?" asked Jonathan.

"You laid me on the bench instead of drowning me. But you're not the one who drugged me."

O'Rourke's face appeared sullen. "It is you."

"Ellie," said Vincent. "What's going on?"

"Look at you," she said to O'Rourke, ignoring her father. "You're a coward. Then and now. Why did you want me dead? Why did he? I was a small child, for God's sake."

"It was him, not me. I couldn't."

"You tried to kill a small child!" She shoved him. He took a step back to steady himself. Her ears rang as rage filled every inch of her body. "WHY?" She shoved him again with such force he lost his balance. Jonathan and Dominick caught him before he hit the ground.

She turned to her father. "I know what happened and who's responsible. There's one more man to arrest."

"Who?" asked Jonathan.

"Bradford O'Rourke. My grandfather."

Those words hung in the room.

"Your grandfather did this?" asked Alex, clearly shaken by the news.

"Bradford O'Rourke was the monster. Randolph went along. My grandfather was the one who injected me with the drugs."

Charlotte turned to O'Rourke. "Why?"

"I'm not saying another word without my lawyer."

Ellie glared at him, then pulled her own weapon. She stood an arm's length away with her gun pointed directly at his head, then moved her finger to the trigger.

"Don't." He stood with his hands cuffed behind his back, crying like a baby. "I'm sorry. It was him."

"Ellie," said Vincent. "You're an O'Brien, not an O'Rourke. We don't murder people. Put down the gun."

Her entire body shook with anger and tears filled her eyes, but she kept the gun pointed at his head.

"Ellie!" said Vincent. "Do you really want Charlotte to see someone killed in her own home?"

She glanced at her father, then at Charlotte, and after a few minutes, handed her weapon to Vincent. She turned to O'Rourke and kicked him in the balls and watched him fall to the ground. "Do what you want with him." She walked out the door, hearing screams of pain as she strolled up the street.

Preston ran to catch up.

CHAPTER 38

ELLIE ARRIVED AT THE PRECINCT IN TIME TO SEE RANDOLPH O'Rourke walking into the interrogation room in handcuffs. He shouted for his lawyer, screamed about the pain between his legs and his bandaged finger. He threatened to sue. And Ellie took great pleasure in watching the spectacle.

The disruption brought Captain Crawford, Olivia, and an African American woman out of her office. The woman caught Jonathan's eye. His body language and his mood had changed. Their connection, Ellie noticed, was unmistakable. They had a history. An intimate one. And based on his reaction, it had not ended well.

"What is she doing here?" asked Jonathan.

"I called her. Is there a problem?" asked the captain.

But, Ellie noted, the tone didn't suggest she was asking his permission.

"No problem here." He backed down and glared at the woman. His stance softened when their eyes met.

"I assume Randolph O'Rourke will have a high-powered attorney," said Captain Crawford. "You're aware of her specialty. She can help and you know it."

It was clear Jonathan understood her reasoning, even if he didn't like it. He nodded, but when the woman moved toward him, he recoiled and sat down at his desk.

"I read the file, Jonathan. And I watched the Georgetown video," said the woman. "This is a big case and, after what I've read, it couldn't get much colder."

He agreed.

She lifted Ellie's file in anger. "These people are animals. I'm here to make sure the charges stick. That's all." She slammed the file on Jonathan's desk and leaned in closer to meet his eyes. "I want them as much as you. Maybe even more."

This woman was beautiful, intelligent, and a tad dangerous. Ellie now understood why Jonathan was so drawn to Olivia. He had a type.

"Who are you?" asked Ellie. "And why are you interested in my case?"

Captain Crawford stepped forward. "This is Jolene Reddington, the assistant district attorney assigned to this case. I neglected to introduce you. I apologize. This is Ellie O'Brien."

Jolene shook Ellie's hand, and the captain introduced everyone else. When she introduced Vincent and David, she neglected to mention their rank. They were Vincent O'Brien and David Bartlett.

"I'm so sorry this happened to you, Ellie," said Jolene. "To answer your question, I'm interested because I specialize in abuse cases involving children. I take each one to heart."

"Why that specialty?"

"Because there's nothing more contemptible than the abuse of a child. It's my job to make sure the victim gets their day in court, and their abuser spends as much time behind bars as possible. Part of my job is to give the victim peace of mind."

Ellie suspected there were deeper, more personal reasons Jolene was so driven. She'd learned over the years never to get on the wrong side of a woman on a mission. Particularly if that mission involved a child—anyone's child. The need to protect was primal. Ellie hadn't had many powerful women in her corner when she was young, but she was certain Jolene would be the perfect person to prosecute this case.

"What gives you peace?" asked Ellie.

Jolene appeared taken back by such a simple question. "What do you mean?"

"Your job can't be easy. I assume you've had lots of sleepless nights. And dreams. I don't want my case to become your nightmare. Put O'Rourke in prison and throw away the key, but don't worry about me. I've moved on. Or at least I had until this happened."

"You are the sweetest thing. In all my years in this business, no one has ever asked that question. Don't worry about me. An abuser behind bars gives me all the peace I need."

Jolene walked toward Jonathan and stepped into his personal space. *Clearly*, Ellie thought, *subtlety was not her style.*

"Can we work together?"

Jonathan scowled at his captain, begging for an escape. "That shouldn't be a problem."

Ellie realized he was surrounded by powerful women. He had no choice but to go along.

Olivia pulled Ellie aside. "How are you? I'm sorry I wasn't with you today, but I had my reasons."

"How am I?" Ellie tilted her head and considered Olivia's question. She'd faced her fears, or at least most of them, and had one man responsible in her sights. She could have put a bullet in his head and felt nothing, but she walked away. O'Rourke would be in prison for years and would no longer occupy the dark space in her memory. She'd finally put her past behind her. When Ellie answered Olivia's question, it was with conviction. "I'm good. In fact, I'm great. There is one more thing to take care of, then I'll be ready to go home."

Captain Crawford, who stood within earshot of Ellie, interrupted. "Excuse me. I couldn't help but overhear. We can help with that last item."

"We?" asked Ellie. "You and Jolene?"

"No, Olivia and me. We've been busy with our own investigation."

"What investigation?"

"Come with me." Captain Crawford looked at the others, who were also eavesdropping. "You, too. Follow me."

"Why is O'Rourke limping?" Jolene asked Jonathan.

Ellie stopped mid-stride and turned to answer her question, causing everyone else to stop and listen. "Because I kicked him in the balls."

"You did what?"

"Charge me with assault if you like."

She shook her head. "Nope. Nope. No need for that. I wanted to make sure there was no police brutality."

"More like victim payback. Be happy he's still breathing."

With that comment, she raised her brows but said nothing. "And what happened to his hand?"

"He had a weapon pointed at Detective Hadley," said Vincent. "I disarmed him."

"Just like that?" she asked.

"Just like that."

"And you broke him in the process."

"When you place your finger on the trigger, it'll get broken when you're disarmed. There's a lesson there."

"And the lesson?"

"Don't point a weapon if you're not willing to suffer the consequences. He should consider himself lucky."

"Lucky?"

"He's still breathing, isn't he?"

She frowned. "Are you a cop?"

"No, ma'am. I am not."

"Well, okay then." She turned to Captain Crawford, who let out a small chuckle.

"Welcome to my world."

"Lord have mercy. Listen up," Jolene said loud enough to get everyone's attention. "In a few minutes, Jonathan and Dominick will update me on the events of the day. After that, they will take your statements. I must understand everything that happened. So, please be precise." She emphasized the word *everything*, and looked in Jonathan's direction. "Jonathan and Dominick may be familiar with all the players in this case, but I am not."

Captain Crawford scanned the entire team. Her eyes landed on Vincent and David. When David nodded, she rolled her eyes. "Please tell me you didn't shoot at anyone."

"No, ma'am, I did not."

When she saw his expression, she shook her head. "Lord, I'm not even going to ask."

"Wait. Shoot what?" asked Jolene. "Do you have a weapon?"

"Yes, ma'am. I do."

"Who else is carrying a weapon?"

Everyone except Timothy and Charlotte raised their hands. Louis raised his cane.

"Why are all these people armed?" she asked the captain.

"We're legally armed, with our own weapons," said David. "We've shown Captain Crawford our permits. And I might add, no one fired a single shot."

Jolene frowned. "I've seen the way you fight in the video, Ellie. It is impressive. And today your father disarms a suspect, just like that." She snapped her fingers. "Who are you people?"

Jonathan laughed.

"You think this is funny?"

"As a matter of fact, I do. That's Admiral David Bartlett and retired Admiral Vincent O'Brien. And if you must know, they were both Navy SEALs. They have more combat-level training than anyone in this building. You don't need to worry about them. If they wanted O'Rourke dead, he'd be dead, and they wouldn't require a firearm to do it."

"Jolene, we'll talk later," said the captain. "I'll explain."

"You absolutely will explain. As will you," she said to Jonathan, then pushed her finger into his chest.

Jonathan grinned, unmoved by her aggression. "This should be so much fun," he said sarcastically to the captain.

Captain Crawford opened the door to a small room with enough space to fit each person involved in this investigation. It was a tight squeeze. Two of the walls had large windows, each looking into an interrogation room. Ellie peered through one window and saw Randolph O'Rourke sitting at a table.

Jonathan pushed a button on a speaker and then abruptly turned it off after Randolph's whining voice filled the small space. "The man never shuts up."

Ellie peeked through the window on the other side of the room and let out a gasp. She took one enormous step backward, falling into Preston's arms. The second interrogation room held the monster, Bradford O'Rourke. Not in her memory, or her nightmare, but right in front of her. She grimaced.

"Do you recognize him?" asked Jolene.

Ellie nodded but didn't speak. Couldn't speak. All she could hear was the ringing in her ears as more memories flooded back. Memories about him and his angry face. The man radiated bitterness and hate. Most of all, she recalled her fear of him. In the light of day, she discovered he was nothing more than an old man. She stepped closer to get a better look.

He was tall, with broad shoulders like Timothy's, though she couldn't be sure of his height until he stood. He appeared to be about seventy-five or eighty, and in great physical condition for someone his age. His face showed nothing but loathing.

Seeing Bradford O'Rourke in the flesh gave Ellie clarity. He was family, but not. He'd shattered his own son beyond repair. And although she had her own issues from years of foster care, she now understood how much finding a family had healed her. Not being raised by this evil was a blessing. Randolph never had that chance. A lifetime of living with a monster had not only made him weak, but afraid, and dependent on his father. Bradford O'Rourke had never raised her, for which she would be eternally grateful.

Ellie moved to the other side of the observation room and watched Randolph. Bradford had ordered him to help kill a child. An order he'd followed and lived with for thirty years. She imagined the toll that must have taken. He was a broken man. After seeing her grandfather's demeanor, she understood. She felt a pang of sorrow for Randolph—a smidgen. But there was no sorrow for the monster. That man, she thought, should burn in hell.

"It was all Olivia," said the captain.

"I'm sorry, what?" Ellie was still caught up in her own thoughts, unable to hear anyone. "What did you say?"

"Olivia. She convinced Willingham to help us find Bradford."

"You spoke to Cyrus Willingham?" she asked, then hid a small grin.

Ellie understood how Olivia worked. She knew where the lines were and how to cross them without getting caught. She knew what she could do with people in the room and what she could get away with in private. Which explained why she stayed behind. The man never stood a chance against a seasoned profiler trained by Homeland Security.

Ellie also knew never to ask questions.

"Bradford and Randolph had rooms in the same hotel," said Captain Crawford. "They checked in a day after you arrived, Ellie, and did nothing to disguise their identities. We picked Bradford up soon after you left."

"It's been my experience that hubris brings the privileged down every time," said Jolene. "They never believe they'll get caught. Bradford O'Rourke is only saying one word: lawyer."

"My dad thinks they had to see my dead body," said Ellie. "He couldn't take a chance that I would survive a second time."

"Or Bradford wanted to pull the trigger himself," said Olivia. "He was the one who injected you."

"How do you know that?" asked Jolene.

"I didn't know for sure. Not until I saw them both together," said Olivia. "Randolph wouldn't have the stomach to kill."

"Olivia hypnotized me to help me remember," said Ellie. "I recalled a prick but couldn't see any faces. When I met Randolph in person, everything came back, including who injected me."

"Their defense attorney will say Olivia placed a suggestion in your mind when she hypnotized you. I'm not saying that's true," said Jolene. "We'll need more to counter that argument. All the people involved thirty years ago are here in Savannah. How did they end up here?"

"Ellie lost her phone during the attack at Georgetown," said Preston. "They had tracking software installed and later left it at the crime scene for a student to find. Neither one of them has the expertise to pull that off. It would have been too technical."

"Don't worry," said Jolene. "We'll find out who's responsible when we subpoena their financials and their phones. It'll come together fast."

"Cyrus, Randolph, and Bradford were in it together, then and now," said Vincent. "That's why they're all here. To make them all complicit and too afraid to talk. Bradford O'Rourke's plan, I suppose."

"Look at him," said Ellie. "Randolph's a basket case. He'll talk. If I were you, I'd record everything. I don't think he'll survive in prison."

"We'll put him on suicide watch," said Captain Crawford.

"What brought you to Savannah?" asked Jolene.

"It was my idea," said Vincent. "There was nothing in Ellie's life that would have caused anyone to hurt her. When Detective Ferris found out about the cold case, I thought we should investigate. To see if there was a link between the two events."

"Which there was," said Jonathan.

"It started here," said David.

"And we ended it here," Vincent growled.

Jolene stared at both David and Vincent. "You two are a little scary."

Jonathan chuckled. "Not just those two."

Ellie moved to the other observation room window. She half-listened to what they were saying but she couldn't take her eyes off her grandfather. Creases from age filled his wicked face, though there were no laugh lines. "There sits pure evil."

"We know nothing about his background. Not until the search warrants come through," said the captain. "His lawyers will get him out as soon as they get here."

"What do you need?" asked Ellie.

"A confession would be nice. Something to tie him to our cold case. Better yet, something to tie him to what happened in Georgetown," said Captain Crawford. "I realize we sent the coat to get fingerprinted, but he's your grandfather and your parents had died. It wouldn't be unusual for his prints to be on the coat. That piece of evidence is useless."

"You have me. My memories have returned."

"You were a child," said Jolene. "We need more."

"I'll contact Detective Ferris in DC," said Jonathan. "He'll want an update. If all three men are here, they might have been in Georgetown. At least Bradford and Randolph might have been together."

"I didn't see Bradford in any of the students' random shots," said David.

"He probably stayed in the background. Far enough away not to get caught. He's a smart bastard," said Jonathan. "He didn't account for Timothy following Cyrus and his son going off script."

"True," said Captain Crawford. "I still don't understand why Randolph did that."

Charlotte stared at Randolph through the window, then shook her head. "You know, I never felt he would hurt me. He seemed to be in the middle of a nervous breakdown, and I think he came to my house because he wanted to get caught. To be free of all of this. He's not from Savannah and your house was empty," she said to Alex. "My house was the only place to go where he knew you'd find him away from his father."

"Hoping for someone to put him out of his misery," said Olivia. "That would be the ultimate end, wouldn't it? Suicide by cop."

"Forever broken," said Ellie.

CHAPTER 39

ELLIE STOOD BY THE OBSERVATION ROOM WINDOW AND STUDIED Randolph O'Rourke. She wanted to get a feel for this man, to see whether she had any memories about him. Other than the time in the car, he was a complete stranger. He shifted in his seat as though he were uncomfortable. The kick to the groin had done its job. Seeing him squirm gave her some satisfaction, she'd admit.

He wore white pants with a royal-blue three-button polo. His shirt had a Stefano Ricci logo over his heart, though it was the Patek Philippe watch that caught her attention. He resembled a man with a need to flaunt his wealth. Ellie knew being locked behind bars would change all of that. They would strip away all the trappings that made him who he was. They'd replace the Stefano Ricci clothing with an orange jumpsuit and the watch with handcuffs.

Once his lawyer arrived, her chances of getting information would be nonexistent. Having answers would be the only way back to a normal life. Time was not on her side. "I want to speak to Randolph alone," she said to Jolene.

She acted as though the idea was ridiculous. "That's out of the question."

"Shouldn't family be the exception? He is my uncle. I know he'll talk to me."

"You're also the victim. Let's not forget, you haven't seen them in thirty years."

As their voices grew louder, the others took a step back. They'd inadvertently created a circle with the women in the center, as though they were about to witness a battle.

"If anything happened in there, my boss would have my head, and my case would go up in smoke. You must have deduced by now I don't like to lose."

Jolene appeared more concerned about winning than what was important to the victim. A character flaw Ellie had not expected.

"THIS IS NOT ABOUT YOU!" Ellie's powerful voice wasn't merely deafening, but indignant. With each sentence, she stepped closer to Jolene. "You weren't the one drugged and dumped, to be eaten by animals. You weren't the one attached to machines. Or the one who woke up all alone. Or the one who spent half her life in foster care. I need to talk to that man face-to-face." Ellie violently pointed to the interrogation room that held Randolph O'Rourke. She crossed her heart and raised her hand. "I swear to God, I will not kill him. Is that what you want me to say?"

Vincent looked toward the heavens when Ellie swore to God.

"What are you expecting?" David whispered. "A lightning bolt?"

Vincent shrugged. "These days, nothing would surprise me."

Ellie, who had been hypersensitive to her surroundings since the attack, was the only one who overheard their comments. She glared at her father.

Jolene's eyes bulged. "You swear you won't kill him? Really! You say something like that and expect me to allow you in that room? This is not a game."

Once again, Ellie moved closer to Jolene while the others took yet another step backward, pushing them against the walls in the small room.

"Don't insult me. I know damn well this isn't a game. This is my *life*! Do you honestly think I'd kill him in the middle of a police station? Give me a little credit. I need answers that can only come from him." She violently pointed again. "When his lawyers show up, I'll get nothing. And you know it."

"I'm coming with you," said Timothy. It was not a request. "He's my uncle, too. You of all people should understand I need to do this."

Ellie understood. He still felt as though this was all his fault, even though she'd tried to convince him otherwise. And it was the first time he'd insisted on anything.

Ellie took a breath to calm herself. "Here's what I propose. Timothy and I will talk to Randolph, alone. You can watch from the observation room and record everything. I'll inform him he's being recorded, and we'll leave if he asks. If he wants his lawyer, we'll immediately stop the interview."

Jolene paced within the circle of Ellie's friends.

"Is there a problem?"

"I'm trying to decide if I want to destroy my career over this case, because of you."

"Because of them." Ellie pointed to both interrogation rooms. "I know what I'm doing."

"You're making my job harder."

"I understand that, but it changes nothing. I need to go in there."

"This is against my better judgment. I'll go along with it for now. If I don't like what I hear, I'll pull the plug."

Ellie agreed.

"Use the earwigs," said Jonathan. "In case we want you to ask a specific question."

"Earwigs?" asked Jolene. "Who has earwigs?"

Preston raised his hand.

"Of course you do. Why do you have earwigs?"

"I brought them with me in case we needed them. I work for the FBI."

"FBI? Why didn't you tell me that before?"

"You didn't ask."

Jonathan laughed. "It's complicated. I'll explain later."

She shook her head. "What am I getting myself into?"

Dominick handed his earwig to Timothy. "Do you want to use one?" he asked Jolene. "You'll be able to speak directly to Ellie."

"Was that in someone's ear?"

"Yes," said Jonathan, then smiled. Jolene was not amused.

"No, thank you. You can keep it. Before I allow this, I need to sit down with Jonathan to get a complete picture of what's happened while you've been in Savannah."

"I understand," said Ellie.

"Lock your weapons in Jonathan's desk," said Captain Crawford.

Ellie removed a gun from a holster by the small of her back, unloaded it, and handed it to Jonathan. She reached in her pocket and pulled out an extra clip, then removed a knife and its sheath from her belt. The lock picking tools were the last of her paraphernalia.

Jolene stood by her side while she disarmed. "What, no gun strapped to your ankle?"

"No, that's it. I swear. Besides, those ankle straps are annoying." She smiled. "I have a Virginia concealed carry permit, and I've taken firearms training. The reciprocity agreement between Virginia and Georgia states it is legal for me to carry a handgun. Isn't that right?"

"Yes. You've done your homework."

"I have. Would you like to make a copy of my permit?"

"I'd like to see it."

Ellie handed the permit to Jolene.

"You really were prepared to kill him."

"No. I was prepared to defend myself. There's a difference. And, yes, I could have killed him and felt nothing, but I walked away."

Jolene shook her head and looked at Captain Crawford, then left the room with Jonathan.

———

When Jolene and Jonathan returned, Ellie requested two ice packs, two ibuprofen, and a bottle of water.

"Why? What are you doing?" asked Jolene.

"I've been told you get more with honey. That's never been my experience with thugs, but we'll give it a try."

After Ellie hugged her father and Preston, she and Timothy turned on their earwigs and opened the door to the interrogation room.

"Take the cuffs off," said Ellie.

"No!" Jonathan said in her earwig.

She looked through the mirror and pointed at the cuffs. "Crap," Ellie heard in her earwig. Jonathan walked into the room, removed the cuffs, then walked out, leaving Ellie with the man who tried to have her killed, twice.

When he closed the door, he spoke into the earwig one last time. "Don't do anything stupid."

She grinned, then placed the items on the table, along with a closed folder. She and Timothy sat in the chairs across from Randolph.

"What's this?" he asked.

"Exactly what it looks like. Ibuprofen for the pain, ice packs for your finger and your balls."

He stared at her, then dragged the items across the table.

"Don't think for a minute I'm apologizing. You deserve more than a kick."

He placed the pills in his mouth and drank the entire bottle of water in one long gulp. He laid one ice pack on top of his swollen finger, then closed his eyes and moaned when he placed the second between his legs.

"There are things you need to understand before we begin."

Randolph met her eyes, then Timothy's, but remained silent.

"There are people behind that mirror recording everything you say. See the cameras?" She pointed to each corner of the room. "You don't have to answer any of my questions, and we'll leave the room the moment you ask."

"Sounds like you're reading me my rights."

"I guess I am, in a way. We aren't cops. There is an assistant district attorney behind that mirror. I don't want you to speak without knowing they will use everything you say against you. Do you understand?"

"I do."

"Do you want us to leave?"

He considered for a few seconds. "No."

"Good, because I deserve answers."

They spent the next few minutes studying each other. Randolph kept staring into Ellie's eyes. It was a little disconcerting, but she stayed focused on her mission.

Randolph had an amiable face, with smooth, tan skin and few wrinkles, although she'd suspected his youthful appearance wasn't natural. That, too, would change in prison, she thought. He was tall and thin with gray hair and an athletic build. His demeanor couldn't be more different from his father's. Randolph appeared skittish—afraid of his own shadow.

The room was impossibly warm, causing sweat to drip from his face onto the table. Ellie half wondered whether the excessive heat was intentional—a way to collect DNA without a warrant. Timothy's foot bounced on the floor, sending piston-like sounds through the small room. She reached over and touched his hand. The simple gesture calmed his nerves.

"Who are you?" Randolph asked Timothy.

The piston sounds returned.

"He's William," said Ellie.

"You're William! I'm in this godforsaken place because of you. This is all your fault."

"My fault." Timothy chuckled. His mood changed. He stopped tapping his foot on the floor and his nerves had subsided, but the anger bubbled up to the surface. Anger, Ellie imagined, that had been simmering from the day he found out about his adoption. "I admit, I played a role in finding out the truth, but you're the one who tried to kill my sister. You're in here because of the decisions you made, not me."

"Why are you even here?" asked Randolph. "Nothing happened to you." His voice was indignant, which added to Timothy's resentment.

"Why am I here?" Timothy repeated. "Now that's a good question." He placed his hand on his chin while he considered his answer. "The reasons have changed since this whole thing started. You'd have to define 'here.'"

Ellie heard multiple moans through the earwigs and hid a small grin.

"Timothy, I swear I'll come in there," Preston said through the device.

"I came to Savannah to find my sister. To protect her from you. I'm *here*, in this room, because I wanted to face the man responsible for what happened to both of us. To analyze you, if you must know."

"Analyze me?" He let out a desperate laugh. "You'd be one of many. What have you decided?"

Timothy tilted his head and scrutinized this man.

He was thorough, Ellie knew. But time was not on their side. She wondered how long they would have to wait before he completed his methodical analysis. And how long before Preston came into the room to move him along. He surprised her with a quick response.

"I think you're a coward who depends on Daddy's money. I mean, look at you. The clothes. The watch." He checked under the table. "Even your shoes cost a fortune. Who are you without the money?"

Randolph laughed. "You're correct, on all accounts. I'm nothing without my money."

"You tried to kill a child for a lifestyle," he said angrily. "Then moved on as though nothing had happened."

Ellie wasn't convinced that was entirely true. Not after seeing her grandfather. There had to be more to this story.

Randolph placed his elbows on the table with his head in his hands. The gravity of the situation appeared to be setting in. He was going to prison for the rest of his life. "Why didn't you shoot and put me out of my misery when you had a chance?"

"Your misery?" said Ellie. "Because that would've been too easy."

"If it's any consolation, which you don't deserve, I had a wonderful life," said Timothy. "Judging from the looks of you, placing me on those church steps was the best gift your father could have given me."

Randolph raised his brows. "Boy, you have no idea."

"You will pay for what you did to my sister. The pain and suffering. The terror you put her through. I'd suggest you speak to whatever God you believe in and ask for forgiveness."

Ellie was stunned by what she was hearing. She had a brother coming to her rescue. That role had always been Preston's. It was an odd feeling, she admitted. Something she couldn't quite process.

"Pay? Is that what this is all about?" shouted Randolph. "The money. You want money."

Enraged, Timothy got up so fast he knocked his chair over.

Ellie stood, not knowing what he might do. "Sit down," she ordered. After they all settled down, she opened the folder she'd placed on the table.

"This isn't about the money." She placed the two photos from the hospital in front of him. "It's about this. It's about what you did to me."

Randolph couldn't take his eyes off the photo with the machines and tubes attached to such a tiny body. He pulled it closer to get a better look, and tears appeared in his eyes. He wiped a tear that ran down his face.

"We need a confession," Jonathan said in her earwig.

"You need to tell me everything, Randolph. I deserve answers. And it's the only way you'll be free of him."

They both understood she was referring to his father. He looked up at her.

"You know I'm right."

Other than the single tear, Randolph's face showed no emotion. His expression had softened, as though he accepted his fate. And then he told Ellie everything.

"Cyrus called my father after William showed up at his office. He was furious that Cyrus hadn't killed you when you were a baby." He looked to William, then shifted his attention to Ellie. "Then he found out I didn't drown you. I assured him you were dead. I saw you take your last breath.

He hired an investigator, to be sure. I'm not giving you the investigator's name. He did nothing illegal."

"I don't need his name," said Ellie.

"The detective convinced us he found you and even showed us your photo. It was impossible, but I knew it was you." Again, he looked at Ellie. "It was the red curly hair. But mostly the eyes. God, I'll never forget them. They've haunted my dreams for thirty years. And then I saw the birthmark."

"If you tell me what happened, it may help the dreams go away." Ellie understood for Randolph to decide his own fate was one thing, but she was asking him to decide his father's. To put a nail in his coffin.

He thought for a moment before he spoke. "My father injected you with something. I swear he never told me what was in the needle. He ordered me to dump you in the marsh. He said to make sure you didn't come out of the water. But I couldn't do it. I laid you on a bench near the water's edge, hoping someone would find you. I even thought about calling the police anonymously to give them your location."

"Why didn't you?"

"Because you were already dead. At least I thought you were. When I placed you on the bench, you opened your eyes and looked at me. You tried to speak, but there were too many drugs in your system."

"Yes, I tried to say your name, but I couldn't."

"I swear, I saw you take your last breath. I thought my father had killed you and there was nothing I could do about it. So, I placed you on that bench, hoping someone would find you and give you a proper burial. Or find out we were responsible and arrest my father. For years, I kept waiting for the knock on our door. It never happened."

"Until now," said Ellie.

"Yes, until now. You were right, William. I am a coward. I have always been," he said as he reflected on his past.

"My name is Timothy."

"After that, I became a drunk and a drug addict. Still am, if you must know. Anything to help get those eyes out of my mind. Prison would have been a blessing. At least then I could have told someone what had happened."

"What about Georgetown?" asked Ellie. "Did you hire those men?"

"Be careful," said Jonathan into Ellie's ear. "Don't lead him too much."

"My father ordered me to hire them. I didn't want to, but I didn't know how to stop him. Their orders were to bring you to my father, that's all. He wanted to be the one to put a bullet between those eyes, to be sure you were dead. How did you learn to fight like that?"

Ellie ignored his question and took a deep breath to calm herself before continuing. "Tell me more, Randolph. Why would he want me dead? I'm not leaving this room until you tell me."

"He hated you from the beginning."

Frantic to get more information, Ellie pushed harder. "Why? I need to know everything." She slammed her hands on the table. "Now."

He resisted, but only for a moment. "When my brother came home with you, my father saw the red curly hair and those eerie eyes, and that was it. God, he was furious. He and my brother had barely spoken since."

"What does my hair color have to do with anything?"

"He assumed you were the product of an affair. When they came home with a second child, he ordered Anderson to divorce his wife or be cut off from the family."

"Came home?" Timothy asked.

"Yes. You were both born in Ireland. Gabrielle was Irish. She wanted their children to be born there, but they never told us why."

"Is that what they argued about the day of the accident?" asked Timothy.

"Yes. Anderson refused to get a divorce. My father went crazy after the accident. He made plans to kill you both."

"Why?" asked Ellie.

"He wanted you dead because you were Gabrielle's children, not Anderson's. You scared him, and I never understood why until now."

"I'm sorry, what?"

"You would stare at him without blinking. It's kind of funny, if you think about it."

"Funny?"

"Yes. The man who is pure evil was afraid of a child. There are no redheads in our family or Gabrielle's, and he'd never seen eyes that color. In my father's crazed mind, you were not an O'Rourke. I don't know what he saw in Timothy. Once Anderson was dead, he wanted both of you gone."

Ellie stared at Randolph, unable to speak.

"You don't understand. In his mind, you weren't blood."

"Blood!" shouted Ellie. She realized what this was about. "This is about the money, isn't it? He tried to kill a child to keep his money in the family."

"Yes, it was about money. After he thought we killed you, it became about much more."

"I don't understand."

"My father is a psychopath. Make no mistake, he was lucid when he drugged you. His intent was to kill you. And the reason was because of the money. The rest happened later."

"The rest?"

"He became more crazed, obsessed with what he called your devil eyes. Soon after we returned home, he created his own reality to justify what he'd done. When he heard you were still alive, he thought you'd returned from the dead for revenge. And evil had to die."

"And you went along with him?" asked Timothy.

"Yes. He scares me."

"Will you testify against him?" asked Ellie.

"Yes," he said without delay.

"I have one more question." Ellie placed his cell phone on the table. "The number on this phone belongs to Anderson O'Rourke. Why would you be using my father's phone number thirty years after his death?"

Randolph stared at the phone, considering, then smiled. "Your father was a good man, and we were extraordinarily close. His loss almost killed me. Maybe that's why I went along with everything my father asked."

He held up a hand before Ellie could protest. "I realize that's no excuse. I went through Anderson's car after the accident and I found the phone on the floor. At first, I kept it because I couldn't bring myself to throw it away. Then I used it to keep in touch with my office when I needed to get away and stay off the radar. Few people had this number. Then it was a number I used to contact my drug dealer." He shook his head. "When voice mail became available, I had a friend copy the message from his house answering machine onto the phone so I could hear your father's voice. Call the number."

Timothy dialed the number from his own phone. Four rings later, Anderson O'Rourke spoke. For the first time, Ellie and Timothy heard their father's voice. Ellie closed her eyes, overwhelmed. It seemed so familiar.

"Keep it," he said.

Ellie declined the offer. "I think this means more to you than me. I'll give it to Jonathan to keep in evidence."

A knock on the door startled all three of them. Randolph's lawyer entered, and the conversation broke off. Ellie and Timothy stood to leave, but before the door closed, Ellie turned and faced Randolph. Their eyes met one last time. "I forgive you."

Randolph nodded, then laid his head on the table and wept.

Preston stood next to the interrogation room door and embraced Ellie the moment she stepped out. "How are you?"

"I'm okay, but I have one more person I need to see."

"No, you don't," said Jonathan. "You heard him. Bradford O'Rourke is a psychopath. I can't let you in there. Besides, his lawyer is already with him."

"I don't want to go in there. In fact, I don't even need to speak to him. All I want is for him to look into my eyes. I'll be sure not to blink." She smiled. "I want to make sure I'm the last person he sees before being locked up."

"We can't let you go in there," said Jolene. "There's no law against you being in the hall when he's taken downstairs to be booked."

Ellie agreed.

"It may take awhile," said Jolene.

"I'll wait."

It took an hour before Bradford O'Rourke and his lawyer left the interrogation room. Ellie strolled toward him—close enough for him to recognize her. She looked him square in the eyes.

"YOU! IT'S YOU!"

His lawyer was apoplectic. "Get her out of here."

Ellie wouldn't move. She stood her ground, but remained silent, using those sea glass-colored eyes to speak for her.

Bradford tried to squirm loose from Jonathan's grip, though that was an impossible task. The closer he got to Ellie, the more his face reddened. With gritted teeth, he snarled. "Who are you?" he shouted. "You can't be my granddaughter. She's dead!"

His lawyer told him to shut up, but he wouldn't stop.

Ellie continued to stare straight at him. Without blinking.

"It can't be you. I killed you," he shouted, and struggled to get loose. "Stop looking at me!"

Ellie didn't move a single muscle.

He turned away. "She's the devil. Don't let her look at you. I killed her once, and she came back," he told his lawyer, then looked at Ellie. "Why can't you just die!" His voice sounded more animal than human.

"Now that sounds like a confession," Jolene said to his lawyer. "Don't expect any deals from me. I'll share all of this with the district attorney in DC."

Bradford cursed and screamed vulgar threats until the elevator doors closed.

———

They finally made it back to Alex's house. Everyone, including Timothy, had settled in. Alex spent the night at Charlotte's home. He didn't want her to be alone after such a harrowing day. She humored him. Jonathan dropped Louis off before going to his own home, hoping to sit in a quiet room with a beer, but planned to return for breakfast.

CHAPTER 40

August 27, 2017

ELLIE'S SLEEP WAS RESTLESS WITH THOUGHTS OF HER PARENTS. Eventually, she gave up trying and walked downstairs. The glow of nightlights and small lamps on the counters helped guests find their way to the kitchen. She took a bottle of water from the fridge and went outside, hoping to get some sleep.

She didn't sleep—at least, not immediately. She laid on the chaise and looked to the stars and thought of the good people who touched her young life—dismissing the bad. It was the first time she had any visual memory of her parents. Even of Gabrielle, the woman she swore was not her mother. She recalled squeals of laughter, reminiscent of the day she found her home in Virginia, and now wondered whether that could have been a memory coming to the surface. They were a happy family, and Bun Bun was with her in every recollection of her young life.

Then Ellie thought of Liz McNeil and her gardens. This woman saved her from certain death and helped her feel secure, if only for a little while. In that short time, she'd imprinted her love of gardening into Ellie's memory. So much so, their gardens were identical. *How does one repay such a debt,* she wondered, *even after Liz's death?* Then Ellie realized her own gardens were a memorial to the person who saved her.

There was no memory of music—the most important part of Ellie's life. Who imprinted music into her being? An ancestor, perhaps. She'd always imagined being part of a musical family, but there was no one. *How could this be?*

And what of the woman with the sea glass-colored eyes? Had she somehow created her in her youth? Imagining what her own mother would have looked like? That mystery remained.

Ellie was inches away from a terrible headache. She closed her eyes and listened to the sounds of small waves breaking against the dock. Each time questions came into her mind, she pushed them aside and focused on the water. The mesmerizing sounds lulled her back to sleep.

Hours later, the clang of plates and laughter moved into Ellie's subconscious. Regretfully, she sat up. She could have slept hours longer. When she entered the kitchen, the aroma of chocolate, coffee, and bacon stopped her in her tracks.

"Good morning, sunshine," said Charlotte. "Did you sleep outside?"

Ellie grinned. No one had ever in her life called her sunshine or would have even thought of her in that way. "Yes, for a little while."

"I hope the mosquitoes didn't get you."

Ellie had forgotten how many times mosquitoes had eaten her up when she was young. "Thankfully, they left me alone. What do I smell?"

"That's our version of a mocha. Would you like a cup?"

Ellie was still uncomfortable with the Southern charm, especially so early in the morning, although she knew it was genuine. "Yes, please. What else do I smell?" She walked to the oven and peeked through the glass. "May I?"

Charlotte nodded.

Ellie opened the door and inhaled the aroma of bacon with honey and something else. "That smells great! And spicy. What is it?"

"A touch of cayenne pepper."

"On bacon?"

Charlotte smiled. "It's my little secret, darlin'. Breakfast will be ready soon. Alex, please pour Ellie a cup of coffee."

Alex pulled out a quaint teacup and saucer.

Vincent scoffed. "Son, that will not do. Ellie's never been a teacup kind of woman." He brought out a regular-sized mug. Vincent shook his head. The third choice was a cup that resembled a soup bowl with a handle. When Vincent nodded, Alex chuckled.

He half-filled the enormous mug with coffee, then added the thick Italian hot chocolate made with cocoa, sugar, and melted bars of dark chocolate simmering on the stove. He topped the mocha with a dollop of home-made whipped cream and again glanced in Vincent's direction for approval.

"More."

He grinned. "I thought so." After adding the proper amount, he garnished the top with chocolate shavings and handed the mug to Ellie.

"Thank you." Ellie closed her eyes as she drank. She moaned. "This is amazing."

Alex smiled and raised both arms in success. "My work here is done."

"And splendid work it is," said Ellie.

After finishing her coffee, Ellie left to take a shower and hurried back for breakfast. "What are you people doing? This is insane."

They filled the table with a smorgasbord of choices, from Belgian waffles to scrambled eggs with bacon and sausage, and brioche French toast covered with pan-roasted apples. And of course, it wouldn't be a Southern table without grits and biscuits with gravy.

"I didn't know we had a chef in the house," said Charlotte. "Preston cooked the French toast and apples. I shared some of our Southern recipes with him."

She looked over to find Preston at home in the kitchen with a spatula in his hand, then took a bite of bacon. "Lord have mercy," she said with an exaggerated Southern accent, mimicking the stereotypical Southern belle. "This is the most divine bacon I have ever had in my life. Take this secret home with you, Preston."

"Already planning to."

Charlotte laughed, then instructed everyone to sit before she said grace. There were moans of delight up and down the table as everyone enjoyed their meal.

"Don't forget to take Bun Bun with you when you leave tomorrow," said Charlotte.

Ellie wasn't sure what brought this up. "Excuse me?"

"Bun Bun." She pointed across the room.

The bunny sat on top of the hutch, but Ellie hadn't placed the stuffed animal there. And she suspected no one else had either. "Did anyone bring Bun Bun downstairs?"

Those with full mouths shook their heads, and the others gave a resounding "No."

"Crap," said Ellie.

Jonathan walked over and lifted Bun Bun off the shelf. He'd inadvertently squeezed the middle of the rabbit and frowned.

"What's going on?" asked David.

"It feels funny."

Charlotte sounded exasperated. "Don't say 'it.'"

"Well, what would you call 'it'?"

"'She'! The bunny is a 'she.'"

Ellie laughed.

"For the record, I will never call this 'she.'" He squeezed the bunny again. "There's something inside." He turned her over, and found hand-stitching on the bottom, and pulled a knife out of his pocket.

Charlotte jumped out of her seat. "What do you think you're doing?"

"I'm cutting off its head to see what's inside."

Her eyes bulged. "Give me that." She grabbed Bun Bun out of Jonathan's hands and handed her to Ellie.

Ellie's wide smile filled her face as she giggled at Charlotte. "It does feel like something's inside. Why didn't I notice that before?"

"Because you weren't meant to," said Vincent. "Everything happens in its own time."

She glared at her father. "Really?"

"Apparently your quest is not complete."

"Quest?"

He smiled. "Exactly how would you describe it?"

"As a pain in the behind." Ellie decided not to use the word *ass* in front of her hostess.

Jonathan flipped open his knife. "Do you want to find out what's inside?"

"I'm not sure."

"Put the knife away," Charlotte ordered. "Or I'll come over there and take it from you."

The expression on Charlotte's face made Jonathan snicker, but Alex gave him a warning. "I wouldn't take her on if I were you, Jonathan. I've seen that expression before."

"You're probably right. She looks a little scarier than normal. Makes you wonder what she'll be like when you have kids." He closed the knife and placed it back in his pocket.

Alex gasped. "Don't even put that out there."

All the banter back and forth was fine with Ellie. It helped relieve the stress of the last few days. "I don't know if I can take any more surprises."

"I doubt you have a choice," said Vincent.

"Wouldn't it drive you crazy knowing something was in there and not look inside?" asked Preston. "It's like having a Christmas present in your hand and never opening it."

She considered, then pulled away from the table and walked to the door. When Preston stood to follow, she put out her hand. "I need to think. I'll be back in a few."

"Do you want Bun Bun?" asked Charlotte.

She scowled at the stuffed bunny sitting on the table, then turned around and walked out the door.

———

A few minutes later, Charlotte followed Ellie and sat in a chair beside her. Ellie wasn't surprised. She half expected the mother hen to see how she was doing.

Charlotte handed Ellie the bunny. "She'll help you decide what to do."

"You realize it's just a stuffed animal, right?"

She grinned. "Of course. I enjoy harassing Alex and Jonathan. I've seen how you've reacted to her. She brings you comfort, probably in ways you don't yet understand. You held that bunny in every photo we've seen. I think she gave you the security you needed."

"And you believe I need the same security now."

"Something like that. Call it a mother's intuition."

Ellie let out a breath in frustration. All she wanted was to go home and get on with her life. "I don't know what to do."

"Sure you do. You just don't want to do it. Do you want answers or not?"

"It's a rabbit from thirty years ago."

"True. So, what are you afraid of?"

Ellie frowned. Now her frustration was with Charlotte for calling her out for her own cowardice. Although she understood her conclusions were right on the money, she didn't like it one bit. "I'm not sure if I'm ready for any new revelations."

"The ghost thinks you are. Why else would she send you to us? She wanted you to find the bunny for a reason, and I doubt the reason has anything to do with the O'Rourkes. Bun Bun was around before your parents died."

Ellie raised her brows. What Charlotte said was true. She had the bunny while she was part of a happy family. "And you think one of my parents placed something inside."

Charlotte shrugged. "If they had, there had to be a reason. That's what my intuition is telling me."

"Your intuition."

"Hey, I wouldn't knock it. It's a powerful thing. Remember, the ghost waited until you were safe before pointing you to the next piece of the puzzle." Charlotte placed a tiny pair of scissors in her hands. Small enough to cut the hand-stitched threads from Bun Bun. "In case you'd like some privacy when you open her up. Don't worry, I'll be able to stitch her back up."

"Thanks." Once Ellie was alone, she held the stuffed animal close to her heart. "What secrets are you holding, Bun Bun? Do I really want to find out?"

The thought of her deceased parents sewing a message inside her beloved stuffed animal weighed heavily on Ellie. She knew it had to have been important, or at the very least sentimental and personal to her. Otherwise, why hide it in her toy? She lifted the scissors and cut each stitch, then opened the incision with care. Inside was a small package wrapped in fabric and tied with a ribbon. She opened it and found two folded pieces of paper. The page on top was a letter. There were no specific names.

"To my darling daughter,

Come to me when you find this. I have a story to tell you.

I hope you'll understand.

Love, Mom"

It was signed with a kiss made with red lipstick.

Ellie's hands trembled when she unfolded the second page. What she saw took her breath away. She read the words, then held it against her chest and wept.

Minutes later, she looked up to find Preston standing in front of her, blocking the sun. He didn't say a word but squeezed in beside her. He reached over to wipe her tears, then wrapped his arms around her to help quell her nerves. She laid her head on his chest. After a few minutes, she gathered herself, though not enough to speak.

———

Preston waited patiently for her to hand him the two documents. He read the pages and realized what he carried in his hands, then leaned in and kissed her. A deep kiss from one lover to another. They both knew what that meant. Something else in their lives had changed forever. They held each other awhile longer, then went inside.

CHAPTER 41

I N THE KITCHEN, ELLIE HANDED THE PAGES FROM INSIDE BUN BUN TO her father. He read them, then looked at Ellie, but said nothing. It took him a few minutes to find his voice.

"There's so much I want to say to you, Ellie. I'm afraid I don't have the words." He held the pages in his hands with reverence. The first document appeared to be a note from Ellie's mother. It was sweet and, when read thirty years later with no context, a little cryptic.

It was the second page that took his breath away. The document held the one thing Ellie had always dreamed of—a link to her past. A musical one. The second page, handwritten in calligraphy, was a sheet of music. It was a beautiful piece of art, written in black ink, with a random splattering of letters in red and green that jumped off the page. Each letter was expertly drawn.

"These pages are so personal, Ellie. After a lifetime of nothing, you have a note from your mother. She's trying to tell you a story. Your story." He seemed overwhelmed by the enormity of it all and sat down at the kitchen table. "The sheet of music is beautiful—both the words and the art. These people are not figments of your imagination, sweetheart. They existed. And whoever wrote this music is speaking directly to you."

Charlotte came into the room. "What did you find?"

"It's a note and a sheet of music." She handed both documents to Charlotte.

She sat next to Ellie and held the pages in her hands. "Well, that's not something you see every day. This isn't just music, Ellie. A talented artist created this." After she read the lyrics, tears filled her eyes.

"But why?" asked Ellie. "And what does it mean?"

"Does it have to mean anything?" asked Timothy. "It's music. Unsigned."

Preston and Olivia gawked, as though what he'd said was sacrilege. Vincent understood. Timothy didn't know Ellie well enough to understand the significance. And he had yet to read the lyrics.

Jonathan reviewed both documents even more closely. "I think two different people wrote these. But it's a guess. I'd have a hard time believing the artist wrote the note. The calligraphy is so precise, while the note is a little sloppy."

Alex left the kitchen and returned with two plastic page protectors. He slid the pages inside for safekeeping, then passed them around the table.

Vincent thought for a moment, as he took a sip of coffee. "Timothy, read the note and tell me what you think."

"I wish my mother would have written something like this. It would have been an easy way to start a conversation about being adopted."

"You think that's what this is?" asked Vincent. "A note from Gabrielle to start a conversation?"

"I do. But I know my mother's handwriting. I don't know what I would think if I were in Ellie's shoes."

"Ellie, I think the O'Rourkes adopted you," said Vincent. "And this was your mother's way to tell you. But she died before that could happen."

"And to give me something written by my birth mother."

"Yes. To allow your birth mother to explain why she gave you up in her own words. It's a gift."

"It's all speculation," said Timothy. "Neither page was signed. You don't even know if they were meant for Ellie."

It was true, Vincent thought. There was nothing linking Ellie to the letter or the music. And yet...

"Do you remember what Randolph told me?" asked Ellie. "His father didn't think I was blood. And that's why I didn't resemble the rest of them. No redheads in the family."

"Stated by a psychopath who thought you came back from the dead. But go on," said Vincent.

"Bradford could be right. But not because of an affair. We could always take a DNA test and compare it to the lipstick on the note."

Timothy moaned. "A DNA test is what got us into this mess in the first place."

Ellie laughed, then picked up the music and read part of the lyrics aloud.

"Forgive us all, my darling child,
For sending you away.
It 'twas the hardest that e'er I've done.
I wished for you to stay.
But truth be told, too young I was,
Your precious soul was taken from me.
So, sit I am, with empty arms,
With memories of your sweet embrace."

"It does sound like an explanation for giving me up. Or for giving someone up."

"Yes, I agree," said Charlotte. "Now read the rest."

Ellie continued.

"A message from beyond, I heard.
'Twas a miracle from heaven above.
Our hearts are linked forever more.
In our music, and in our blood.
So, close your eyes and open your heart.
And let your music come to me.
Our Angel sent from heaven above,
Will send your music on her wing."

Once again, tears filled Charlotte's eyes.

"You're linked in music and in blood," said Preston. "If this is your mother, she's a musician. Which gives it more weight."

"The way it's written, she knew you would be musical," said Vincent. "Or would be when you were older. Otherwise, why use those words? That's curious. Maybe she was visited by someone. An angel, perhaps?"

Ellie appeared skeptical. "Okay, now you're going way past my belief system. I equate angels to God. You'll never convince me to believe in God."

Charlotte raised her brows in surprise, then frowned as though she'd considered Ellie's life experience. "I guess I would feel the same way if I were you. But you didn't believe in ghosts until recently."

"It's possible Gabrielle wanted to give me the music the day she told me I was adopted. It would have answered an important question. I've often wondered if I inherited my talent. And if so, from whom. Now, I'm convinced the woman I saw when you hypnotized me is my dead mother."

Charlotte disagreed. "You're assuming your birth mother is dead. She could still be alive."

Ellie held her head in both hands. "What am I supposed to do with this information? We don't know if any of this is true. It's a piece of music that could explain why she gave me away. She was too young. If she wanted me to find her, she would've signed it. End of story."

"What's the last part mean?" asked Preston. "Read that."

Ellie glared at him but conceded and read the last section of lyrics aloud for everyone to consider.

> "My last gift to you I give,
> Are written words upon this page.
> Look to the stars in heaven above,
> They'll send you home to me someday.
> So, close your eyes,
> and open your heart.
> And let your music come to me.
> Upon an Angel's wing."

No one had a clue. Alex left the kitchen and returned with a guitar and a bodhrán Irish drum. "I think you need to sing it to feel the true impact."

Ellie took the drum and handed the guitar to Preston. After they reviewed the music, they both decided it should be a duet. They sat around the kitchen table and put the heartbreaking words to music. When they finished, tears ran down Ellie's face.

"I agree. This is probably a note from Gabrielle. And the woman with the dark hair and sea glass-colored eyes was my birth mother. Which also means she's dead. This story ends here."

"I disagree," said Charlotte.

"You didn't see her. Our faces were nearly identical, except she had straight brown hair."

"I'm just saying, we don't know," she insisted.

Ellie left the kitchen to return the instruments to the music room.

When she came back, Timothy was holding the sheet of music. He wasn't reading it but examining it with an odd expression on his face.

"What's going on?"

He frowned. "It makes sense we're adopted. We're nothing alike. I mean, nothing alike," he emphasized. "We each have different talents."

"That could be true in any family," said Vincent.

"I understand, but bear with me. I won't take long, I swear."

Everyone laughed.

"Okay. Take as much time as you need."

"Vincent! Don't tell him that," said Jonathan. "Are you crazy?"

"I'll be quick." He crossed his heart. "I'm not a musician, but I have unique skills. My mind sees patterns others miss."

"Go on," said Vincent.

"Check out the music. It's beautiful. And we all agree, a talented artist created this. Did you notice how some letters are red and green? Everything written on this page was intentional. Now why would she do that?"

Ellie grinned. "I'm guessing you're about to tell us."

"Alex, do you have a blank piece of paper?"

Alex left the room and returned with paper and pen and handed them to Timothy. He wrote each red letter and each green letter in two groups on the same line. Under the red letters, he wrote the name *Alannah,* and under the green he wrote *Finnegan.*

"Holy shit," said Preston, then excused himself. "It's an anagram. Is that your name, Ellie? Or your mother's?"

"Now how am I supposed to know?"

Vincent grinned. "What else do you see, Timothy?"

He read the words at the end of the ballad.

"My last gift to you I give,
Are written words upon this page.
Look to the stars in heaven above,
They'll send you home to me someday."

"My last gift to you I give, are written words upon this page," he repeated. "That refers to your name. Or at least a name. Everything on this page has a purpose. So, what does it mean to *look to the stars in heaven above*?"

"Go on."

"See the star on the page? It's tiny, but it's there."

They moved in closer to see the minuscule dot over a letter *i* in the shape of a star.

"Oh, my goodness," said Charlotte.

Everyone else appeared shocked by the discovery, but Preston kept staring, repeating the words. "*'Look to the stars in heaven above. They'll send you home to me someday.'*" He tilted his head and frowned, then lifted the page and held it up to the kitchen light.

"Well, look at that," said Jonathan.

As the light passed through the page, a watermark of the United Kingdom and Ireland emerged.

"*X* marks the spot," said David.

"Star marks the spot," said Preston, then grinned.

Ellie just stared. "I have to think."

———

Almost frantic, she walked outside to clear her head and laid on a chaise under the live oak tree. The breeze and sound of the water helped her relax, and she unexpectedly fell into a deep sleep—something she needed after a restless night. This time Ellie didn't dream of Gabrielle or Anderson or a child's giggles. She dreamed of the woman with long dark hair and sea glass-colored eyes. The young woman wore the same clothes as she had when Olivia hypnotized her.

"Who are you?" asked Ellie.

"It's not important. I'm here to give you a message."

"Which is?"

"It's time to come home, darlin'," she said with a sweet Irish brogue.

"Home? Where's home?"

"You have all the information you need. It's time."

"I need more. Are you my mother? Time for what?"

When the woman disappeared, Ellie opened her eyes. She sat straight up and felt nothing but anger.

Preston was sitting at the bottom of the chaise. "Are you all right? You were moving all over the place."

"No, I am not!"

"What happened?"

CHAPTER 42

VINCENT AND DAVID PEERED THROUGH THE WINDOW AS ELLIE and Preston approached the house. They smiled when they spotted Preston kissing their joined hands.

"It took them long enough," said Vincent.

David agreed.

The closer they got to the house, the more they both understood something else had happened. Judging from the look on their faces, it was something important.

"There's news," said Preston.

Once more, they gathered around the kitchen table while Ellie told them about the dream.

"As the only psychiatrist here, I have to mention your dream may be your subconscious interpreting everything you've just been told. A lot has happened," said Olivia.

"I know it sounds impossible, but I have to believe it was the ghost," said Ellie. "At least for now. It was so vivid."

"What did you see?" asked Vincent.

"I got a closer look at her face. She wasn't a woman at all, but a teenage girl."

"Did she say anything?"

"Yes. She told me it's time to come home."

"I assume she's speaking of Ireland," said Vincent. "The star marks the spot."

"She did have an Irish brogue."

"Where, specifically?" he asked. "It's a small island with lots of people. Are you sure we can trust the accuracy of the map?"

"Whoever created this document knew what they were doing," said Timothy. "The artist was extremely precise with everything else. Why not this?"

Preston handed the music to his father. "Hold this up directly to the sun."

"Why?"

"She wrote to look to the stars from heaven above, not a light in the kitchen."

"Wouldn't that mean to do it at night?"

"It's a long shot."

David removed the document from its protective sleeve and held the page up to the window, allowing the bright sun to shine through the paper. The musical notes faded into the background, leaving behind a perfect image of the map and the tiny star. "Now, how did they manage that?"

Preston shook his head, then took a photo of the image with his cell. "I have no idea. Remember, this was created thirty-three years ago."

He forwarded the photo to his computer. After a few clicks of the mouse, the document appeared transparent, leaving a perfect image of the watermark and the star. He placed the now translucent document on top of a map of Ireland from Google Maps. Every curve and body of water was an exact match. Each time he clicked the mouse to enlarge the two images, the area around the star expanded, showing more detail on Google Maps. He now knew where to start their search, right down to a street name next to the tiny star.

"There it is," said Ellie. "The place where I was born. Or at least where Alannah Finnegan was born, or where Alannah Finnegan had a baby." She shook her head.

Timothy appeared unsure about the assumptions Preston was making. "That's only if our conclusions are correct. I'm concerned we're moving too fast. Let's not forget, it's been thirty-three years. They could've moved. Or we could be wrong."

"How do we find out if the O'Rourkes are my adoptive parents?"

"Legally, it could take years," said Vincent. "Ireland has had a history of questionable adoptions. They've since corrected their problems, but I don't know what it was like in the 1980s."

"Questionable?"

"Illegal. But you have a name. That's more than most. Sometimes, they would change names and birth dates on the official birth certificates to match the adoptive parents. It would prevent the children from finding their true origins. I don't know when, or if, that stopped. If this is from your mother, she was probably aware of what they were doing and created this to help with your search."

"Assuming I wanted to find them when I was older."

"It's a starting point," said Vincent. "That's something."

"More than that," said Preston. "It's a street name. How many people named Finnegan live in that exact location?"

"So, she did sign it," admitted Timothy. "Kind of."

Vincent watched as Ellie considered the possibilities.

She paled. "Dad, do you think I was born in one of those mother and baby homes I've read about?"

"It's probable. I don't believe they were as evil when you were born. Or at least I hope they weren't."

"And yet, they still performed illegal adoptions. Why?"

"For money. I've read stories about babies being sold to rich Americans. And the O'Rourkes were rich Americans."

"Do you think that happened to me? Could they have forced her to give me up? For money?" Ellie was clearly outraged by the thought of being sold.

"There's no way to know," said Vincent. "Not until you find your mother. Remember, you were born in the 1980s, not the 1930s."

"What happened to the birth mothers back then?"

Preston Googled "Irish adoption" and pulled up an article. "Some women were desperate to keep their children, but nuns and social workers coerced them to relinquish them."

"Coerced!" said Ellie.

"Not just coerced. They couldn't grieve. They were told to get on with their lives and forget about it. No counseling. No sympathy from the community. And many kept the birth secret."

"No wonder there was a reckoning in Ireland," said Charlotte. "I believe the younger generation is more open-minded. Can you imagine putting up with that today?"

"I need a drink. Do you mind?" Ellie asked Alex.

"No problem. After hearing that, we all could use one. How many glasses?" Four hands raised for wine; the rest wanted beer.

———

Charlotte directed everyone into the family room while Alex brought their drinks. She led Ellie to a chair that overlooked the river. "Sit here. It's the best seat in the house."

"Where's Olivia?" asked Ellie.

"She's in my office," said Alex. "She asked to use my computer to check her email."

"We should wait until she comes back," said Ellie. "She hates it when we start without her."

They all agreed. They spoke of the view and the weather and O'Rourke. But not the music from the bunny. Preston sat with his computer opened, researching. His face had changed from curious to angry.

Olivia had taken longer than expected. After twenty minutes, she finally appeared. She sat on an ottoman across from Ellie.

"What did you do?" Ellie pointed to the papers. "And what is that?"

Olivia hesitated. "I have contacts from my days working in the government. I asked them to do an unofficial check into Alannah Finnegan and Jacqueline O'Rourke."

"I don't like the look on your face. Do I really want to know what you found out?"

She reached out and placed her hand on Ellie's. "Alannah Finnegan is dead. At least on paper. My friend found her death certificate."

"What?" The group chimed in, in apparent disbelief.

"Now that's not what I expected to hear," said Ellie.

Olivia handed Ellie the death certificate. "This contains the date and place of death, name of deceased, sex, age, and cause of death. They listed the age as 0, and the cause of death is stillborn. It doesn't list the name of the informant. That's the person who was with Alannah when she died. Someone had to be there. A doctor, or a nurse, or even her mother. It's odd."

"We, at least, have the name of the hospital," said Preston. "It's somewhere to start."

"My contact also found a birth certificate with the same name. The date of birth and the date of death are identical, which confirms that Alannah died the day she was born. It also includes the father's name and the mother's maiden name. Their names were Paddy Finnegan and Bridget McHugh."

Ellie frowned.

"Alannah's birth parents are not dead, Ellie. Bridget McHugh married Paddy Finnegan when she was eighteen. Based on the year they got married, she was fifteen years old when Alannah was born. They had three sons. Liam Joseph Finnegan is twenty-nine years old. Then she had Ian Patrick Finnegan. He's twenty-seven. Sean Michael Finnegan is twenty-five."

She paused.

"What else?" said Ellie. "You might as well tell me everything."

"My friend did another search. She found the birth certificates for your brothers and Jacqueline O'Rourke." Olivia stood and placed the printouts of Jacqueline, Alannah, and her three brothers next to each other on the ottoman. "Jacqueline was born on the same day as Alannah. Look at the bottom. The registrar's name is the same on all five documents. Now, check out the registrar's signature on Alannah and Jacqueline's birth certificates. It's different from her brothers'. It is quite suspicious."

Ellie glared at Olivia. "Does this mean what I think it means?"

"Yes. My contact referenced other birth certificates with that registrar's name during that time frame and compared the signature. The only ones that were different are these." She pointed to Alannah and Jacqueline's birth certificates. "We believe these were forged. At least the registrar's name was."

Ellie sat, dumbfounded. "What about Timothy?"

"I'm sorry, we didn't check for yours," she said to Timothy. "More research would have to be done to determine when and where you were born. Ellie has a name. And this is all unofficial."

"It's okay," said Timothy. "I'd like to see how everything turns out for Ellie before I pursue anything."

"I have something," said Preston.

Ellie glared at him. "What?"

"There are no images online of Alannah's parents, but I found Sean." He turned the screen around for Ellie to see an image of Sean Finnegan standing on a stage, singing with a band. He zoomed in on his face. He had dark curly hair with eyes the color of sea glass. "It says he's a music professor."

Ellie's mouth nearly hit the floor. "Look at him. My God. There's no doubt that I'm Alannah Finnegan, but what does this mean?"

Olivia said nothing.

"Olivia! What does it mean?"

"It means, the woman you saw when I hypnotized you, or the woman from your dream, was not your mother. It also means someone probably sold you to the O'Rourkes."

"So, you're suggesting the O'Rourkes adopted me illegally, and my birth parents are still alive, but they think I'm dead."

"That sums it up," said Preston.

"Does that mean I was stolen? Couldn't she have put her baby up for adoption? And wouldn't she have seen the baby's body before she buried her?"

Vincent shook his head. He knew what had happened in Ireland, and even in some places in America, so many years ago. Some young women were sedated while in labor, then were told their babies had died in childbirth. But it wasn't true. The babies were sold to people willing to pay an enormous price. For Vincent, this was evil. The way the Catholic church treated women and their babies in those homes was cold and heartless. In his mind, those responsible should have been arrested for human trafficking. Now he suspected this may have happened to Ellie's own mother, and he wondered how she would react when the truth came out.

"There's no way to know until you find your birth mother. She wouldn't have seen the baby," said Vincent. "Not back then. When a baby died in childbirth, the nurses or nuns discouraged the parents from seeing or holding their child. The mother was told not to get attached and to move on with her life."

"You're kidding," said Charlotte.

"Unbaptized babies still carry the stain of original sin. As a result, funerals were denied, and in Ireland, babies were buried in mass unmarked graves in unconsecrated ground called a cillín. The Catholic church believed their babies would spend eternity in limbo. The in-between. And would never see God or their families again." The cruelty to these families was inconceivable to Vincent.

"If a mother never saw her baby, there would be no one to stop the thieves from selling them," said Preston. "All they would need is a few people in place."

"Let's pray that didn't happen in this situation," said Vincent.

"If it did, you should be praying for the people responsible," Ellie said angrily.

Charlotte looked more closely at the documents. "Check out the birth date."

Ellie read the date on the birth certificate. "Alannah's birthday is in October. That means I'm eight months older than I thought."

"Maybe the ghost wants you to go home for your birthday," said Charlotte.

David Bartlett was a man of few words, except with Vincent and Preston. Most of the time, he'd sit in a crowded room and listen. When he spoke, he was hysterically funny or dead serious, and everyone always stopped what they were doing to hear what he had to say. "I've been thinking."

Ellie turned to him. "About what?"

"All of this seems orchestrated, somehow."

"By whom?"

"The ghost, of course. Think about it. She led you to your house in Virginia, probably hoping you'd remember your past. When that didn't happen, she made sure Alex found the bunny. She woke Preston to protect you from the O'Rourkes, then guided you to this house."

"To find the bunny," said Ellie.

"Yes. She's been quiet since you got here until you were in the same room with Timothy and Preston. Then the bunny appeared in the kitchen."

"I don't understand."

"You're the musician who can play the notes. But you needed Timothy to notice the message inside the lyrics and Preston to discover the location." He smiled a little. "That's a crafty ghost."

"She waited until you were out of danger and the O'Rourkes were behind bars before she pointed you to the message inside. Everything in its time," said Vincent. "I guess the time is now."

Ellie handed over her empty glass for Alex to refill. "What am I supposed to do? I can't call her or knock on the door and say, 'Hello, I'm your dead daughter.' That wouldn't be fair. Not after all this time."

"Sweetheart," said Charlotte. "Believe me when I tell you, that woman has probably wondered if you were alive since the day you were born."

"Why?"

"She'd have to if she never saw the baby's body. And if she believed you were alive, how would a teenager fight the system? Do you think anyone would have believed her thirty-three years ago?"

"No," said Preston. "I'd think they'd want the problem to go away."

"I agree," said Vincent. "An unmarried fifteen-year-old with a baby in a Catholic country would be a problem in those days. At least for some people."

"In her heart, she knows," said Charlotte. "And I suspect she does a double take at every woman she sees, looking for those unique eyes."

"Really?" asked Ellie.

"Oh, my goodness. I'm certain of it."

"You think I should go to Ireland."

"You have no choice. Your mother needs to know you're alive, and it's high time you met her. She needs to see those eyes and hear your beautiful voice, and you need to hear hers."

EPILOGUE

October 2017

AFTER ALL THAT HAD HAPPENED, TIMOTHY PLACED HIS DESIRE to trace his roots on hold. Particularly after seeing what might have been. His wish now was to go home to Kansas and hug his adoptive parents.

Ellie took the semester off. She needed time to decompress, to work in her garden, talk to lawyers, and to go to Ireland in search of new beginnings. Their friends from Savannah insisted on seeing photos of Ellie with her birth mother. Especially Charlotte.

Preston hadn't left her side since their return from Savannah, and when the time came, Ellie's entire family flew with her to Ireland. Vincent, David, and Olivia dropped everything to support her and meet her Irish family. If things didn't go well, they would be there to console her.

It seemed fitting for Ellie to meet her mother on the day of her own birth, although she still had no idea what to expect. Would this woman recognize her the way Charlotte had suggested? Was that even possible? She wasn't even sure her mother had seen her own baby before the kidnappers whisked her away. Because that's exactly what they were, Ellie knew. They kidnapped a baby and sold her for money. Her blood boiled every time that thought entered her mind. She had every intention of finding out who was responsible.

What if they were wrong, and she wasn't sold, but given away? Many women in that situation had chosen to keep their life-changing blunder in the past, where it belonged. And having a death certificate would erase

Alannah's existence forever. Was that what this woman preferred? Did she want to forget her thirty-three-year-old mistake?

But how do you explain the music? Ellie thought. *If my birth mother didn't want to be found, why create a way to find her?* These thoughts and many others made sleep fleeting during the long flight. The closer they were to Ireland, the more nervous she became.

Vincent had reserved four rooms at a bed-and-breakfast in Cobh, Ireland. When they arrived, the owner of the B&B handed each person keys to their room. "This room is at the end of the hall," she said to Ellie and Preston. "It's far enough away to give young lovers some much-needed privacy."

Ellie's face reddened, and the woman smiled. Preston shared a glance with Ellie, but said nothing.

They each went to their room for a quick nap. When Preston heard Ellie singing in the shower, he dropped his clothes on the floor and joined her. Afterward, they met up with the others for lunch, but for Ellie, eating with a stomach filled with butterflies was impossible. Soon she would climb into the van and meet her fate. Crackers would have to suffice.

———

Preston brought a paper map as a backup, but Vincent used Google to start their journey. Things went awry after the very first turn.

"What's going on?" asked Preston. "We were supposed to turn right."

Vincent grinned. "Well, I guess someone else has her own idea about where we're going. At least we understand what's happening this time. We should enjoy the view while she directs us."

Cork Harbour was filled with brightly colored painted houses, with St. Colman's Cathedral perched on the hillside.

Olivia read from Google. "They started building the Cathedral in 1868 and it took over a half a century to complete."

"Have you been here before, Uncle Vince?" asked Preston.

"I came here with my father when I was young. He always wanted to retire here."

"It is beautiful," said Ellie.

"Wait until you see the rest of Ireland," said Vincent. "You may never want to go home."

"I thought this was home," said David. "At least, according to the ghost."

"Don't say ghost," said Olivia. "You're going to jinx us."

The idea of the ghost being with them wasn't unexpected and no longer frightening. Ellie had given up control of this adventure, knowing full well the ghost wouldn't leave until she completed her quest. She laid her head on Preston's shoulder and closed her eyes. She'd take a tour later.

"Any idea where we're going?" Vincent asked Preston, who followed along with his paper map.

"We're headed toward the Cliffs of Moher."

Ellie opened her eyes and chuckled. "I wonder if she's going to throw me over the edge?"

"Now that's not even funny," said Vincent.

Nearly three hours later, the GPS announced, "You have reached your destination." They pulled up to a quaint white cottage with a red front door. It wasn't the computer-generated voice. Ellie knew that voice—it was the woman from her dream.

"Stop," Ellie ordered.

Vincent pulled into the small parking lot in front of the cottage.

"It's her. I'm going to be sick." She looked at Preston, expecting him to toss out a sarcastic comment to ease the tension, but he didn't. Apparently, she wasn't the only person who was apprehensive.

"Who is it?" asked David.

"The ghost. It's the ghost speaking through the GPS. Park here."

"This is private property. I can't park here and the road's too narrow."

When Ellie got out of the car, the others followed. Vincent relented and put the car in park. They looked around to see whether there were other signs from the ghost. Something to point them in the right direction.

"There's a sign," said Preston. "Catherine's Cottage."

"That's not the kind of sign we're looking for," said Vincent.

Preston pulled up his phone to get the details on Airbnb. "This is a two-hundred-year-old renovated cottage."

"It's adorable," said Olivia.

Preston continued. "It's close enough to Hags Head trail and the Cliffs of Moher, without having to bother with all the tourists. What a great location. I wonder if it's being rented now."

"It is," said a woman who walked out of the house.

"I'm so sorry," said Vincent. "We'll leave now."

But the woman was friendly and wasn't pushing them away. "No, you don't have to leave. What would you like to know about the area?"

"I'm Vincent O'Brien." He introduced the others.

"I'm Deirdre. I own the cottage. It is being rented now, but I can check the calendar for openings if you like."

Vincent shook his head. "We don't know how long we'll be here."

"You're new to Ireland?"

"Just got off a flight a couple of hours ago."

"And how did you end up here?"

Ellie laughed. "That's complicated. Probably a wrong turn."

As Ellie spoke, the woman moved closer. She looked directly into Ellie's eyes. "And why are *you* in Ireland?"

Ellie thought that was an odd question. Why were most Americans in Ireland, and why did she single her out? "We're tourists."

"I don't think so." Deirdre moved a little closer to Ellie. "You seem to have something else on your mind besides the cliffs." She kept staring at her. Examining her. "You look worried. Can I help?"

"Who's renting the cottage?"

"That information is private. I can say they've been coming on the same date for over thirty years."

Ellie raised her brows in surprise, desperate to know where they were. "Where are they now?"

The woman hesitated for a moment. "You should take a walk to Hags Head, over there." She nodded to Ellie. "You might find what you're look-ing for." She nodded again. Each time she spoke, she implied it was Ellie, not the others, who needed to walk the trail.

Ellie took off. First jogging, then into a full-out run. No one could keep up. Even Preston and Olivia, who had trained with her, fell behind. Something pushed her along, almost lifting her off the ground. She stopped, or was stopped—she wasn't quite sure which—and waited for the others to reach her.

A woman and four men stood on the cliff's edge. Ellie couldn't be sure of their ages from where she stood, but they appeared to be a family on a picnic. There was a red plaid blanket on the ground, with a basket and bottles of wine on each corner to prevent it from being carried off in the wind. Long loaves of bread poked out of a basket. They looked out to sea with their instruments in hand.

Not wanting to disturb them, Ellie barely moved a muscle and waited. It didn't take long. They played traditional Irish music with the drum, fiddle, and tin whistle. Each one played beautifully.

Was this her family? Had she come from an entire line of musicians? And what of the woman? She had yet to show her talent. Ellie separated from the group and moved closer to the cliffs. Vincent and the others kept their distance, giving her the privacy she needed during the most important event in her life.

The whistle was replaced with a wooden flute, and the music changed to something Ellie recognized. The woman sang the music from the bunny. Her voice was powerful, and heartbreaking. She stood on the cliff's edge and told her story. In music. Ellie now understood why her mother came to Hags Head. She wanted the wind to carry the sound directly to Ellie, and after all these years, it finally reached her. Ellie placed her hands over her heart, feeling the woman's pain. She now knew this was her birth mother. Everything in her life had changed forever.

"Upon an Angel's Wing," Ellie whispered. The shock was so great her legs could no longer carry her weight. She fell to her knees, laid her head on the ground, and wept.

The music stopped unexpectedly, but Ellie was too wrapped up in her own grief to notice.

"Are you feeling okay, darlin'?"

Ellie looked up, straight into the eyes of her mother.

The woman frowned when she saw Ellie, then kneeled in front of her. She had brown curly hair and blue eyes, but not the special color that should have linked them. Ellie wondered whether all her assumptions were wrong. *How could this be?* This woman was singing the music from the bunny.

Neither spoke. They both appeared frozen, stunned by who was right in front of them. A sudden gust of wind startled them, catching Ellie's wild curls, exposing the mark on her neck.

It was then Ellie noticed the woman had the same birthmark. And in the same location. She immediately saw the resemblance. Their features were similar, as were their voices.

The woman also noticed. "Mary, Mother of God."

"Are you Bridget Finnegan?"

She nodded, unable to speak.

"I'm Ellie," she said in her American, Southern accent, then pulled the sheet of music from her pocket and handed it to Bridget.

Bridget gasped. She held her shaky hand over her mouth as tears spilled down her face.

"Are you my mother?"

It took her a moment to gather her thoughts. "Yes. How is this even possible?" She caressed Ellie's cheek, then stroked her long red curls. The two women cried together and, after thirty-three years, embraced for the very first time.

A few minutes later, Bridget wiped her tears and examined the music. "I haven't seen this since the day you were born. It just disappeared. I wondered what happened to it." She shook her head in disbelief. "How did you get this?"

"That's complicated. My adoptive mother hid it away. I believe she wanted to share it with me when I was older, but she passed away before that could happen. I found it a couple of months ago."

"How did you find me?"

"From your message hidden in the music."

Bridget's eyes widened. "You found my message. I can't believe it worked. Thank God. They told me you died, and to move on with my life. But I never believed them. I just couldn't."

A man with red hair and sea glass-colored eyes kneeled next to her mother. He looked into her eyes. His eyes. The resemblance was unmistakable.

"Alannah," he said the moment he saw her. He knew exactly who she was. They wrapped their arms around their daughter and wept. Any doubt Ellie might have had disappeared.

After the initial shock, Ellie and her parents stood. Bridget introduced her brothers. Liam, a pub owner, was the oldest. Ian, the middle brother, was a computer scientist. And Sean, the youngest, the music professor. He most resembled Ellie with dark-brown curly hair, like his mother, with eyes that matched their father's and Ellie's.

Ellie introduced her American family. She would tell them about the

O'Rourkes, explain how Vincent came into her life and how she found the music in the bunny, later.

———

A young, barefoot woman with long brown hair and sea glass-colored eyes appeared by the cliffs. She looked straight at Vincent, then disappeared. Based on Ellie's description, he knew who she was. The ghost had finally shown herself.

"Would you mind giving us a minute?" asked Vincent.

He and Ellie walked until they were out of earshot of the family.

The ghost appeared again. "It's time," she said.

She wore the same clothes as in Ellie's dream, but now she stood in front of her. And Vincent could see her. This was no figment of her imagination.

"I need more," Ellie insisted. "Who are you?"

"Mamó," she said, then disappeared into the mist.

Ellie and Vincent remembered the word. It was what she'd repeated when she was hypnotized. They believed she was too drugged or too young to say it clearly, but they were wrong. The ghost pronounced the word exactly as Ellie had, and they still didn't know what it meant.

"Well, that was useless," said Ellie.

"I disagree. Let's go back to your parents."

"You're my parent."

Vincent wrapped Ellie in a warm hug. "We all have a role in your life, Ellie. That will never change. There's room for everyone."

They returned to the family, and Vincent asked whether they'd ever heard the word Mamó.

"It's Irish for granny," said Paddy. "It's what I used to call my grandmother."

Ian displayed a photo on his cell of a girl wearing a red cape, with brown hair and sea glass-colored eyes. He handed the phone to his father.

"I haven't seen this photo in ages. She's so young," said Paddy. "Ellie, this is your great-grandmother when she was a teenager. Ah, you would have loved her. She opened her home to everyone with a warm pot of tea and a bottle of whiskey on the table." He smiled as he remembered. "She was a woman of few words, which was unusual for my family." He zoomed in on her face. "Look at her, Ellie. Our eyes came from Mamó's side of the family. I sure miss her. She died when I was thirteen."

Ellie laughed and shook her head. "A woman of few words."

"Why?" asked Bridget.

Ellie looked at Vincent, unsure of what to tell them.

"Everything."

Ellie nodded. "It may be hard to believe, but I've seen her."

"You've seen Mamó?" Bridget smiled. "It's not hard to believe. So have we. But only once."

"When?"

"The day you were born. She appeared when I was so distraught by your death. I told her to look after you. She nodded, then disappeared."

"Mamó," Ellie whispered, shocked by yet another piece of information about her past. Then she remembered the unexplainable events in her life. Surviving the accident when she was a child. Seeing Mamó when she was dying on the bench. The bat that rolled toward her when her foster father attacked. The branch that fell from the tree at Georgetown. And countless, countless others. It was all Mamó.

The ghost appeared once more and placed her hand on Ellie's cheek. She could feel her gentle touch. "Mamó," she whispered.

"It's time for me to go, darlin'." And in an instant, the ghost was gone.

Tears ran down Ellie's face, and her mother wrapped her arms around her. The simple touch of her mother and great-grandmother made the years of separation evaporate. Her great-grandmother watched over her from the day she left Ireland and kept her safe from harm. Now that the O'Rourkes were in prison, she brought Ellie home to her mother. The circle was complete. After all these years, it was time for Mamó to go home.

The End

ACKNOWLEDGEMENTS

Growing up, I was never a great reader, so the thought of writing a book had never crossed my mind. Then I discovered audio books, and everything changed. I took classes at the local community college and met other people from all different walks of life who also wanted to write. We created a critique group and gave each other the encouragement we needed to keep writing. In the end, we became friends. They brought great imagination and humor to the table every month. I would never have been able to write this book without each one of them.

Elsa Wolf and I drove to Georgetown University to walk through the crime scene. We visited Savannah, Georgia, to see where the characters lived. She helped me bring them to life. While in Savannah, I met Margie Novak on McQueen's Island Trail. She gave me the lay of the land. Without her, I wouldn't have known what Ellie faced while she laid on the bench. I appreciate her input. Close friends and family, like Elsa Wolf and Cheryl Holdefer, both published authors, Margie Bukowski, Gloria Summers and Libby Bowerman, took great pains proofreading the entire draft, some multiple times. I often texted Margie and Elsa, asking what they thought of this or that.

My husband, Lee, is the technical one with the patience of Job. He's the person I went to for clarification and ideas. He always inspired me to continue my writing.

The phrase it takes a village to raise a *child* keeps coming to mind. Here, it took these people to help make this book a reality. I want to take this opportunity to thank everyone.

ABOUT THE AUTHOR

Eileen Rodberg was born and raised in Baltimore, Maryland. She spent twenty-five years working in the computer industry before she discovered a love for writing. Now, she spends a significant amount of time writing or imagining.

During this process, Eileen discovered how much she's drawn to strong female characters who can take care of themselves, both physically and mentally. This is a characteristic you'll see in this debut novel and will continue in her future writing..

Made in the USA
Columbia, SC
09 July 2022

63164984R00174